Growing PAINS

BETTÉ PRATT

Copyright © 2020 by Betté Pratt.

ISBN   Softcover   978-1-953537-11-9

All Scripture Quoted is taken from the New International Version of the Bible.

All rights reserved. No part of this book may be reproduced or transmitted in any form or by any means, electronic or mechanical, including photocopying, recording, or by any information storage and retrieval system without express written permission from the author, except in the case of brief quotations embodied in critical reviews and certain other non-commercial uses permitted by copyright law.

Printed in the United States of America.

To order additional copies of this book, contact:
Bookwhip
1-855-339-3589
https://www.bookwhip.com

Epilogue

Vansville, Georgia was growing. For years it had been a comfortable little village, too small for a spot on a map, but there was a post office, one grocery store, one church and the Thomas Complex. That was a glorified name for the hardware store/four gas pumps/Laundromat that Brad Thomas owned and operated for years. There were several streets on either side of Main Street, which was the highway through town where the middle-aged and elderly residents of the tiny town lived. The World War Two veterans had built comfortable homes for their families and over the years their children had grown up. Some of them had left, others had stayed or returned, but there were few children in town now-a-days. The war veterans had mostly passed on and now their children were the older generation.

Over the years those few children scattered along the streets were bussed to the schools in Blairsville. That small city was about a half hour's drive away and Vansville's folks figured that was close enough. Vansville never had its own schools, not even an elementary school. However, they had grown and most of them had left, so that now it was rare to see a child in town. The other thing Vansville didn't have was a doctor or a medical facility, but Blairsville wasn't far. In years past, land hadn't been expensive, so everyone had his own parcel of ground where each couple had built a study house, making sure it sat squarely in the middle of the lot. Each home owner worked hard to keep his place looking good. Many of the ladies even had contests to see who could have the prettiest flower plots. Those contests had ended many years before, but the pretty flower strips in front of houses still remained. Many of the ladies had green thumbs and loved keeping their front yards looking beautiful.

Vansville had no apartment buildings and no developer had come to town with the idea to build any. The little town was just far enough from Blairsville that no one could consider it a 'suburb' of Blairsville. The residents planned to keep it that way, because they knew that apartments could bring an undesirable element to a town. People who rented an apartment didn't make a town where they lived a place where they stayed for decades and died when they were old. Many of them never darkened the door of a church, either.

The son of one of the town founders was Harvard Isaacson. He had purchased a large piece of property along Main Street and built a comfortable home for his wife, Isabel and his family. Back in the day families didn't need a mansion, but the house was comfortable and Isabel was happy to raise her three children there. She also had two flower plots under her front windows. On a sunny summer day people would call to her and wave as they went by her place. She still kept up the small flower beds in front of her porch. Now-a-days, she spent most of her time in her favorite leather recliner situated by the front window where she could watch her part of the world, her end of Vansville, going about its business.

Harvard's property sat next to the highway and at the edge of town. Because he was an enterprising man and had purchased such a large parcel, he built six large cabins – one of them, of course, had to be handicapped accessible. He put in a parking lot that would accommodate one car for each cabin and several more then hoisted a sign over the parking lot advertising them. He had built the cabins larger than many other overnight accommodations and put kitchenettes in each one because Vansville never had a restaurant, just a grocery store to buy food. They always told people making reservations to either bring their food or be prepared to buy it at the local grocery store and fix it themselves. However, the store was only open six days a week and closed at five o'clock, except on Friday.

For years the cabins were the first things someone saw as they came in town coming from Blairsville. There were always people who wanted to stop over night, or for a weekend. The tiny town was much quieter even than the small city of Blairsville which was a half hour's drive away. The renters always commented on the peaceful meadow they could see from the porch of their lovely cabin.

The Isaacsons' were always happy for renters who came during the summer for a week's vacation or even stayed a month to take advantage of the large rural area in the foothills of the Appalachians. It was a beautiful part of the country, with vistas of the mountains, sometimes shrouded in mist and that drew people. There were many trails with trailheads that originated in Vansville and went into those beautiful foothills. Some of those people claimed that the writer of the poem <u>America</u> had been visiting the Appalachians when he wrote about 'Purple Mountains Majesty' some years before.

Many of their renters were hunters and fishermen who came every year to hunt the acres of woods or fished in the sparkling streams. The cabins were Harvard and Isabel's source of income; they kept busy with caring and maintaining them. However, years after their children had grown up and moved away, Harvard became ill and died, leaving Isabel a widow, but she still had six cabins. Unfortunately, once people knew Harvard was gone, the long-termers started dropping off, perhaps they died, too. However, Isabel found it hard to keep up, not only keeping six cabins clean, but the cost of upkeep and utilities was escalating higher each year.

Many times since her husband died Isabel wished she didn't have to, but she had to fill her propane tank and that was a major expense. Her home used propane, but also her cabins and even if no one was renting, she had to keep minimal heat in them during the winter. If she didn't, she had astronomical plumbing and restoration bills otherwise.

She wouldn't admit it to anyone but herself, but keeping the cabins clean and ready for immediate occupancy was wearing her down. She had to do as much of her own care as she could and she was her own maid service. The only things she hired out were things she couldn't handle – plumbing problems, maintenance on the cabins, moving furniture; all things Harvard used to do and loved it.

For the first few years after Harvard died Isabel managed to scrape by on her social security and what she made from the cabins. However, the income from the cabins tapered off after deer season because the hunters and fishermen didn't come around much in the winter. Of course, that was when Isabel needed money to fill her large propane tank. However, she made up her mind she wouldn't sell or leave town except as a last resort.

She'd lived here for so many years and her beloved Harvard was buried in the town cemetery.

However, in the last decade younger people started moving to town. A rich man, Derek Casbah, who owned and was president of the largest bank in Blairsville, bought and renovated a large country estate outside of Vansville and moved there, then married his second wife, Millie. Millie had a young son, who didn't get along with his new step-dad, but of course, he must live with them until he finished high school. He had no intentions of going to college and had the idea of starting his own business once he finished his education. He planned to take advantage of the rural area around Vansville since it was in the foothills of the beautiful Appalachians and therefore there were lots of trails that spread out from the village. When he wasn't in school he was out walking the trails, anything to get away from his mom and her new husband.

Ramon DeLord, Millie's son, eagerly watched for any place in town to come on the market. Once he graduated he couldn't wait to move from living with his mom and step-dad into his own place. Finally the house on the west edge of town became available. He snatched it up and started immediately expanding the parking area and making it the starting point for all those trails. His mom wasn't happy about his move, but Ramon never regretted leaving the estate. His mom was never an easy person to get along with and his step-dad was busy with his bank.

Several years after Derek moved to his estate the old pastor of the one church in town had a massive heart attack and died suddenly. Bradford Sr.'s last request was that his children look after their mother. The pastor had been able to keep his wife's condition hidden, even from the church family, but with him gone, the children realized immediately that she couldn't live on her own. They moved her into an assisted living facility within a week of the funeral. She didn't do well without her husband and also died soon after him.

Bradford Thomas Jr. was their eldest son. He was the only one of the children who came back to live in Vansville. He saw a good thing in the empty lot in front of his parents' house and built the Thomas Complex. That consisted of a hardware store, four gas pumps and the town Laundromat. He managed it himself, but when he became sick with cancer he passed it on to his son. However, Bradford III was not interested in the church; he definitely wouldn't be the pastor. So when Bradford Sr. died, that forced the church members to either close the church or hire a new pastor. Brad had moved into his granddad's house, so the church had no parsonage to offer a new man. The church family debated for several months what to do.

After the church sat vacant for some time the town's people had a meeting and decided they needed to open the church again. However, middle aged and old people living on social security didn't have a lot to pay a pastor, so they inquired at several seminaries and hired a new graduate, Roger Clemens, but they told him right up front he would have to build his own place. When he came to see the town he fell in love with the little place, because he'd lived most of his life in Montana on a huge ranch, so he loved wide open spaces.

He bought a small spread outside of town and had a log house built. He also built a shed to keep livestock and immediately acquired a cow and some chickens. However, to keep body and soul together he had to supplement his meager income from the church. As he cleared his six acres, he sold some of the wood as well as keeping most of it for his own wood stove. He sold eggs and milk, but many times his church family hired him for odd jobs. He learned quickly how to handle the rudiments of carpentry.

After Ramon bought his house he worked hard revamping some of the trails he'd hiked so that the trailheads were in his parking area. As he had the money, he expanded his parking lot and subsequently his business expanded and became quite popular. Even so, he kept his business small, since he led all the hikes. Several years later, when people put pressure on him, he finally realized he couldn't do a one man show any more. He placed an ad in a hiking and camping magazine for a receptionist. He hadn't realized how far the circulation of that magazine reached until Sandy Bernard from Philadelphia answered the ad. He was amazed that the magazine had circulation so many miles away.

Sandy came for an interview, but she planned to move to the town even if she didn't get the job. After the interview, Ramon rented Isabel's handicapped cabin for her. She lived in that cabin for several months until she and Ramon were married. She quickly became the town's sweetheart, with her many talents and cheerful personality. She was an inspiration to most everyone in town. Now, if Sandy and Ramon were to move away, many town folks were sure the place would fold up and die.

Once Sandy moved to town many things changed in only a few years. Because Sandy was such a go-getter, Ramon had to hire more guides. His camping and hiking business was booming. His first hire was a foot-loose young single man, Duncan, with no place that he truly called home. Very willingly, Isabel rented him a cabin a month at a time. She was glad for the income that kept her propane tank filled.

About a year later, Isabel's cabins were no longer the first place people came to when they came in town. With more people moving into the rural area, some influential people felt a clinic needed to be built, so it was built on the east edge of town. A nurse that was hired to work there moved into one of Isabel's cabins and lived there for several months. After a somewhat rocky meeting, Nancy married Duncan. Duncan built their home on a parcel of ground behind Isabel's cabins that he bought from Brad Thomas. The first patient at the new clinic, who broke the ceremonial ribbon, was Sandy DeLord. Ramon brought her in sick and much to everyone's surprise, found out that she was pregnant.

There were others who moved to Vansville. Isabel's grand-daughter, Raylyn, brought her little daughter for a visit one Thanksgiving. Her husband had been killed in the Middle East several years before, but she and Roger fell rather hard and fast to Cupid's arrows over Thanksgiving dinner at Ramon and Sandy's house. Soon after New Year's they were married and little Heidi loved her new daddy.

Raylyn's mom, Isabel's daughter, Ruth, was a widow and lived in Detroit, but she finally stopped urging her mom to move to Michigan and moved to Vansville. Everyone knew she moved to be close to her grand-daughter and any more children her daughter had. She moved in with Isabel and they shared expenses and the care of the cabins. Isabel was glad her daughter came, but she wouldn't admit how very nice it was not to be totally responsible for taking care of those six cabins. Of course, Isabel would never admit she was getting older – heaven forbid!

A year ago on New Year's Day, Brad Thomas had a stroke and couldn't keep the complex running any more. His grandson, Natt, from Atlanta inherited the complex and lived in Isabel's cabin for some time until he married Sandy's sister, Marcy after she came to visit, then decided to stay and also work at the clinic as its phlebotomist. Natt's parents and grandparents built them a house next door to Duncan and Nancy on the new street that extended into the meadow behind Isabel's property.

That July, Brad's twin nephews came to visit. Eric, one of the twins, went on a hike and decided he loved the area so much he became a hiking guide and rented one of Isabel's cabins. Now that he was out of the military, Vansville called to him. Being a hiking guide in rural Vansville was far different from being in the military and doing tours in far off Afghanistan!

This past April, while it was still cold, the only violence that Vansville knew about happened in the meadow behind Isabel's cabins. Eric was at home on a rare evening and witnessed a car, with no lights on, backing into the meadow. It stayed momentarily then roared away. Thinking that was highly unusual, Eric left for the spot immediately and discovered an unconscious young woman. She had been brutally beaten, with several fractures and raped. Probably the criminal hoped she would die, since he tossed her out of the trunk, leaving her nearly naked on the cold ground. There was no ID with her. Fortunately Eric discovered her before she froze and called the sheriff. She was taken immediately to the Blairsville Hospital.

However, when she woke up four days later the hospital staff discovered that she had amnesia. She had no idea who she was or where she was from. At discharge, the hospital's resident doctor planned to send her to a nursing home. Only because Isabel visited her the night before and noticed how much she resembled Derek Casbah was she saved from being an unidentified missing person. While Derek made arrangements for his daughter, his wife, Millie ran off and tried to wipe out his bank accounts. Derek brought his daughter home and she lived with him until she saw her brother. He was the trigger to end her amnesia.

Just recently, Brad Thomas had another major stroke and was still in the rehab section of Blairsville Hospital trying to get back as much mobility and speech as he could. It wasn't going as well has his wife hoped. The stoke had been so severe that no one expected Brad to get well enough to even work at the store again. Because of that, Natt, his grandson and the store owner, contacted Brad's other nephew, Matt Thomas to move from Orlando to work as the second manager of the Thomas Complex. Matt, of course, would be living in one of Isabel's cabins. Right now, both Eric and Matt would be living there and Isabel was concerned that she would confuse the identical twins. They did look very much alike, but they were very different.

After all these years, besides those original public places there was a clinic that serviced the large rural area around Vansville and now the church held Sunday school after acquiring some portable classrooms. With the church growth, some of the members were talking about expanding the church, but so far it was only in the talking stage. Derek Casbah was a faithful member and contributor, but he couldn't foot the entire cost for a church expansion. His bank would be more than happy to negotiate a loan at a fair interest rate, however.

When Duncan had built his house on the edge of the meadow he'd made a long driveway, but when the Thomas's decided to build the house for Natt and Marcy they prevailed on the county to extend the street beyond Duncan's house so the new house could actually be on a street. What used to be a large meadow was now significantly smaller. If any more houses were built in town, those people must get along with the Roads and the young Thomas's.

All these new people that moved to town made it necessary to change the numbers on the population signs at the two ends of town. People traveling the highway now had to slow down when they reached Vansville, Georgia. No one could just blink and find themselves on the other side of town. In fact, the clinic was too big for anyone to ignore.

Yes, Vansville was growing and none of the originals were upset about it, just as long as no developer came along to buy up property and build an apartment complex. There were places in town that could accommodate such a complex, but the developer would have to go through the land owner first. The village council would make sure that wouldn't happen. Life was becoming quite interesting and it seemed something new happened nearly every week or two. The only thing that some people in town felt they still needed was some place besides home to eat. Natt had a 'coffee drinker's nook' in the hardware store and served very good coffee. The nook had a few chairs for those who had a few minutes to relax with a cup, but that was all there was in Vansville.

There were several single men in town who were tired of frozen dinners they bought from Alex's store or their own version of an egg and bacon muffin. Gas prices being what they were, a guy thought twice about going all the way to Blairsville for restaurant food or take-out. Some of those men weren't cut out to be hermits; they wanted some place in town to socialize. What better place than a restaurant? However, at this point in time a restaurant was still a dream in anyone's mind. People talked about it when they got together at 'the nook' or talked with Alex at the grocery store, but there wasn't any ground-breaking going on anywhere in town. So a restaurant was still just wishful thinking in people's minds.

One

Matt sat staring out the window of his second floor office. It wasn't yet opening time for the park, but he could see the heat waves shimmering off the asphalt parking lot. He dreaded that when the park opened for customers he'd have to leave this delightful AC for the highways and hedges of the amusement park where all those wonderful folks played. He knew they paid their salaries, but one of his men had called in sick, so he had to be out there. Today he'd be picking up trash – what was wrong with the trash barrels they kept in plain sight?

It would be a hot day, but then, it was the very last day of June and June had been a very hot month this year. Not to mention that this was Orlando, Florida where everyone expected it to be hot this time of year. It made him wonder what the rest of the summer would be like. Independence Day was Friday and his department would be swamped. He'd scheduled more men for the long weekend. Too bad he wouldn't be here to help out, but that was life. Uncle Brad didn't wait for the holiday to be over to have his stroke, the ornery cuss!

He remembered his phone conversation with his cousin Natt about Uncle Brad's stroke. If he hadn't had it there at the store it's anyone's guess when he'd have gotten to the hospital! Perhaps not at all, actually. With a half hour drive from the hospital to Vansville, Brad could have died before the medics even arrived. He knew his Aunt Joyce was quite the talker, but actions – she left those to her husband – or someone else. Natt had called the ambulance *then* called Aunt Joyce. Brad's stroke had been so severe that even before the ambulance arrived he'd been unresponsive. The doctors said only because of Natt's fast action had they been able to save him. Now he was slowly recuperating, but Natt didn't hold out any hope Brad would come back enough to stay in the store. Even before this stroke, Brad only could manage the cash box.

Matt had had a rare weekend off, so today was the first time he'd been in his office since he'd talked to Natt and could write his resignation. With the holiday weekend coming, he hoped he'd gotten enough of the crew on board that his department could handle things without him. He'd promised Natt he'd be there on Monday. Surely Jason would be agreeable. It was a bit ironic, he never gave any man on his crew a good recommendation if he gave less than two weeks' notice, but here he was, expecting his boss to let him go immediately. Well, he guessed he wouldn't need any kind of recommendation. He'd be working with family, in the tiny town of Vansville, Georgia, with a total career change.

Matt was an impressive young man. His job kept him in shape. Lately, he'd had to spend more time behind a desk, but now it was summer and more people came to the park, while more of his crew asked off for vacations, so he wasn't stuck in the office as much. Lately that had been a plus, he liked working outside. Disgusted, he shook his head, he hated the following he usually had while he worked in the park. His fair good looks never affected him all that much. His body? Well, he just lived in it. Swinging a hammer, pushing a broom, that's how he kept his muscles in working order, but, unfortunately, it also drew the women!

He sighed and finished typing the few words on the computer and felt a drop of sweat slip down his spine. For crying out loud, the air conditioning was on! He always kept it really cool in his office, since he was usually coming in from the hot park outside. What was the deal with the sweat? Remembering his phone conversation with his cousin, he shook his head and hit the print icon. This was something he had to do. Jason *would* understand.

He knew this was a bad time of year, summer and months with holidays that fell in or close to weekends could be really bad times in an amusement park and especially in the amusement capitol of Florida. However, his uncle Brad was barely recovering from a bad stroke. From what Natt had told him this was the worst one. If he hadn't been in the store where Natt had found him on the floor and called the ambulance, he'd probably be dead now. Blairsville hospital with the ambulance was a half hour's drive from Thomas's store.

Matt nodded. That was true, Aunt Joyce would have dithered around, called her pastor and when he'd come and told her she needed to call an ambulance immediately, she'd have finally called for one which, on a good day couldn't get to Vansville in less than twenty minutes. In matters like that, dithering, which Aunt Joyce did remarkably well, only made things worse and here he was, dithering! This had to be done, he had to resign today. Natt needed him in the store. He was sure uncle Brad would never go back to work. Even if he did go back to the store, he'd only sit there and drink coffee. Perhaps he'd be able to check out a customer a time or two. Or maybe not, it all depended on now much improvement Brad made in rehab.

Matt took a deep breath, stood up, resolutely walked to the printer and took his paper from the tray. He scratched his name at the bottom of the few words on the page and hurried down the hall to his friend – the boss's office. He stood outside the nearly closed door for just a moment and squared his shoulders. When he knocked, the voice behind the door growled, "Yeah, come on in."

Matt and Jason were friends they never did do pleasantries with each other, so as soon as Jason looked up Matt took the two steps up to Jason's desk and said, "So… I'm leaving…" He held a single sheet of paper at his side, but was disgusted to realize the paper crackled because his hand was shaking. He'd never been nervous talking with his boss before, but he felt another drop of sweat slide down his back. *What's the deal, Thomas? We're the same age I talk to him all the time! I consider him one of my friends! Thomas! Get over it! This is just another day in the amusement business.*

Looking shrewdly at the young man, Jason mimicked, "So… you're leaving…"

"Ah, yes, like here's my resignation…" Matt quickly whipped the sheet up and laid it on Jason's desk in front of the man. Again realizing his hand was shaking, making the single sheet flutter a little as he brought it up to lay it on the desk. He cleared his throat, trying to ground himself. Something that disgusted him even more, the perfect piece of paper he'd pulled from the printer only moments ago was wrinkled!

Matt didn't realize what a mess he'd made of the paper until Jason turned the paper around and straightened the sheet before he read the few words. After a few minutes, Jason looked up and Matt noticed his eyes seemed to look right through him. Jason slammed his hand down on the paper so hard that Matt jumped. Waving his hand at Matt, Jason blustered, "So you just walk in here, hand me this paper and think you'll walk out?"

"Well… well, yeah…" Matt said, uncomfortably. What was the matter with him? He cleared his throat, straightened his spine. He and Jason had been friends for several years; they were about the same age. "You know we talked before…"

Jason slapped his hand on the paper again and squinted at Matt Thomas. He shook his head slowly and said, "No, I don't think so, Matt. Maybe we did talk about it and maybe we did come to some conclusion, but a holiday was never thrown into the mix. Friday's the holiday and you know how hectic holidays are around here, especially for your department. At this point I don't have anyone as competent as you to replace you, so you won't walk outta here today. Friday'll be your last day. You take vacation hours – it'll be in the form of money, not time."

Jason leaned back in his desk chair, put his elbows on the arms and put his fingers under his chin. After looking at Matt for several seconds, he added, "So tell me again why it is you're leaving? Why couldn't you give more notice? You've been here long enough, you know summer is the worst time for anyone to leave and you're the boss of your department! You've had people quit on you! I mean, think a little. When was the last time you let a man go who came and said he was quitting immediately and didn't give him a hassle and a bad reference?"

Matt shuffled his feet, glanced down at the floor, then lifted his eyes and looked at his boss. The reason he was the boss, he'd been to college and had a business degree. Matt didn't. He was still standing; Jason hadn't invited him to have a seat, even though there was a chair only inches from where Matt stood. Matt took one step and collapsed into the chair before he said, "Well, see, you knew this would come, I told you before. My uncle in Vansville, Georgia had another bad stroke just the other day and my cousin needs another person in his store. He… um… well, anyway, I've worked in that store several times. I've told you about that, Man. It hasn't been that long."

Jason finally nodded, sat forward and rested his forearms on the desk. "Ah, yes, now I recall." Jason looked down at the sheet of paper in front of him. "So this stroke is quite serious? Didn't I hear you tell somebody the guy's had little stuff happen in the last few months, the docs gave him medicine, fixed him up so he's still workin'? He won't recoup well enough to get back in the grind? You know; modern science and all?"

Matt shook his head and also steepled his fingers under his chin. "No, my cousin said the doctors told his family that if he hadn't gotten to the hospital as soon after the stroke as he did he'd have died. They also said his age is a factor. He's still in the hospital, from what I've heard. I guess his speech was affected this time, too." Matt grabbed the armrests and added, "I guess all around it was pretty bad."

"I see. It's still after Friday, Matt. You know how busy a holiday can be around here." Jason shook his head. He pointed his finger at Matt's chest. "You, man, gotta be there!" Jason looked up at the big calendar on the wall. "Friday's only the first day of the long weekend, but we'll muddle through the rest if you're here on the Fourth."

Matt held in a sigh of relief and tried to loosen the death grip on the armrests. For a few minutes he wasn't sure if Jason would be reasonable enough to take his resignation. He could have taken it, but told him it had to be two weeks. He'd told Natt he'd be there on Monday... "Yes, um, thanks, Jason, for being so understanding, even so. Sorry I couldn't give any more notice, but that's the way illness is, I guess."

One side of Jason's mouth raised a little, as he relaxed back into his chair and became his usual friendly self and said, "Yeah, Matt, have a good life. You understand you'll be hard to replace, but hey, break a leg!"

Matt stood quickly, turned on his heel and took a step. "Yeah, I'll do that, Jase, thanks," he said over his shoulder, for once glad to get out of the boss's office. Before the day got too hectic, he rushed down to the accounting office. He knew he had vacation time saved up he hadn't taken a vacation since February. Still he'd been with this outfit long enough to have more vacation time coming. He'd put in today to get all his vacation time and maybe a personal day, he couldn't remember, hooked onto this paycheck. He was sure he'd need the extra money to tide him over until he and Natt could work things out.

Remembering how 'unbusy' he'd been at the store during February when he'd covered Natt's honeymoon, he wondered if he'd be taking a pay cut leaving here and going to the Thomas outfit in that little town. He shrugged, it really wasn't an option. Besides, he was getting a bit tired of being the boss of the maintenance department. Yeah, it paid well, but the headaches… he could do very well without them day after day. How hectic could life be in a hardware store in the little town of Vansville, even in the heat of summer?

It wasn't yet time to head out to the park when he reached his desk again. He sat down and thought about who he needed to tell he was moving. Of course, there were his parents; he'd call them this evening. He needed to leave a change of address form for the mailman and he must tell the building supervisor. He only had a cell phone and the utilities went with the apartment, since it was part of the amusement park package.

"Ah, I should send an Email to Emilyn. I tell her every time I move. Wonder if she cares I'll be moving back to Georgia?"

For some strange reason, Emilyn pulled into a parking space behind Barney's Diner nearly ten minutes before she had to clock in and get ready for her shift. That was most unusual, she knew exactly how long it took to get to work, since she'd been doing it for so many years. There were no streets closed, no detours she had to take today. It was a beautiful summer day, one that deserved a lazy afternoon at the beach, on an oversized beach towel, in a new bikini, a large, broad brimmed straw hat, with a huge iced tea and a good novel; not in uniform, waiting tables in a 24/7 diner, with a boss who, at best gave her a hard time every chance he could.

But then, life didn't always give you your druthers. For a working, single girl, it meant you were on the clock when your name appeared on the schedule. She had been doing that, at this diner, for more years than she cared to count. She looked out at the shimmering waves on the hot asphalt and sighed.

As she sat in her car, Emilyn made a lovely picture. She worked too hard to have extra pounds hanging on her body, but she had curves in all the right places. Because her mom was Swedish, she had lovely blond hair and deep blue eyes. The curls she was always trying to tame were compliments of her dad and his side of the family. At work, her boss, that curmudgeon, Barney, insisted that she keep those curls tamed somehow, either in a hairnet (ugh) or in a ponytail. Her dad was a tall man and her mom barely reached his shoulder, so she, of course, fell in the middle. The story of her life!

On the way to work, somewhere from the dark recesses of her purse, her phone chirped telling her she had an Email message. She had barely heard the chime, because the phone had probably slid through all the necessities she kept in her purse. After she parked at the diner, she looked at her large purse that sat on the passenger seat. She probably should buckle it in, it was big enough. She sighed; she really did need to clean out her purse soon, but not today.

Between gum wrappers, used tissues, a stray envelope or two, probably several of those were pay envelopes, and several other non-descript things that might or might not add significance to the life of a single young woman, she couldn't even zip the main pocket closed. Where else did a single, working girl keep such things?

She sighed and looked at the over-flowing black object. "Well, what else is new? It's the only place to keep important stuff."

When she'd been taking her purse in the diner, Barney was eager and more than willing to tell her that it was never a good thing not to keep her purse closed tightly. After all, someone could steal her blind and she'd never know. Actually, she knew that, but she rarely had much cash to carry in said purse. Usually, she had so many things more important to do around her apartment, like keeping clean uniforms on hand, because that same Barney was a stickler on clean and unwrinkled uniforms, and errands to run between the time she got up and headed off to work. Some little thing like cleaning out a huge purse didn't rank too high; especially when it was an ornery boss who told her that.

Still with a few minutes to spare, she dug into her large purse for the small devise that had just sounded. She scowled, who would be sending her an Email message? She rarely got Emails and usually those she got were spam. Her many friends always sent text messages – many – being a great exaggeration! She finally found her phone and pulled it from her purse pocket, but then she stared.

Am moving back to Georgia on Saturday. It's way north of you. I'll be a hardware store manager with my second cousin in Vansville, Georgia. Matt

After Emi read the short message for the second time, she shrugged and muttered, "I should care where my Ex is moving to? Who cares where you'll move to, Mr. Thomas! As long as it's not here, I don't care!" She decided she wasn't even interested enough to respond. She grinned, dramatically hit the delete button and said, "Just another spam!"

She pulled the keys from the ignition, pulled the ponytail tie from her purse and stuffed the purse under her seat. With the ignition off and the windows all up, because she'd leave it for eight hours, the car got hot in minutes, so she quickly stepped out of the car. She stuffed her phone in her left pocket and the keys in her right and put the ponytail elastic around her wrist. She'd fix her hair in front of the mirror in the break room. Maybe she didn't like her hair in a ponytail, but she didn't have to look bad with it in one. She smiled; she'd walk in with her hair down. Of course, that meant Barney would watch her with eagle eyes until it was up. He might even follow her into the break room to see that she put it up!

She trudged across the hot asphalt toward the back door of the diner. "It's hot!" she exclaimed and quickly yanked the back door open. With the grill going, the kitchen wasn't much cooler, but at least the sun wasn't blazing down and reflecting off the hot parking lot. Of course, she'd left her sunglasses on the dash, without her purse she had no place to keep them while she worked. Barney wouldn't tolerate bulging pockets. It was just good that her phone was one of those flat models. Of course, never even think he'd go for her oversized sunglasses hooked over her uniform neck!

Barney looked up at the clock over the kitchen sink and muttered, loud enough she easily heard him, "At least you're on time today. Been wondering if you'd make it."

Emi let out an exaggerated sigh, looked at the clock herself, then at her boss and said, "Barney, when was the last time I was late for work?"

He shrugged nonchalantly. "Oh, a bit ago, but one never knows…"

She knew he was goading her, but she said, "Right! Barney, you have us punch a clock, but you've told us it goes by six minute slots. Somehow, if a body isn't here before six minutes till, and clocked in before the time, that body gets docked for six minutes. I never have figured it out." She grinned at him. "Actually, I think it's just a bunch of malarkey!"

Barney, the ornery man that he was, only let his face do his best impersonation of a smile and shrugged one shoulder before he said, "Me to know…" He cleared his throat and added, "Oh, by the way – your hair's down."

Not gracing that with a comeback, Emi spun on her heel and made her way to the employee lounge shaking her head. The man was a curmudgeon, he always had been, but one of these days she'd be sure to thank Allison for getting her this job. Man, she'd been working here at Barney's for nearly ten years and the man still expected her to be late, incompetent, or a no-show! And to wear her hair down – in a restaurant, no less! She was none of those things and at work she never wore her hair down. The man knew it! What was the deal? She pushed the door to the brake room open. Thankfully she was alone for a few minutes. She needed the quietness, even if it was for only a minute or two.

She stood in front of the mirror, finger combed her hair and put it in a ponytail, but didn't have an answer to the question about her boss. Barney would be Barney, that was just a given. With her hair off her neck and out of her eyes, like the boss wanted, she headed back to the kitchen for an apron, an order pad and her timecard to run through the machine so she wouldn't get docked. It was time for another evening shift at the famous Barney's Diner.

Life was like that for a working, single girl. It was a job she got paid for, her tips kept her going. Most of the time she could pay the rent and feed herself. Even though she'd never wasted her money on a lottery ticket, maybe one day she'd win the lottery and wouldn't have to work at Barney's. She could only hope!

The alarm screeched. Today it wasn't soft music that started playing. The awful sound bounced off the bare walls of the tiny bedroom. Being a bachelor pad, there weren't any pictures on the walls or curtains at the window, besides if there had been the young man in the bed would have packed them away in the box he'd stuffed into his car at eleven thirty last night! Everything he owned had gone in his car last night, except for one suitcase. He'd left that for the morning essentials, intending to get an early start.

For several minutes nothing happened, the screech continued. Finally a hand came out from under the sheet and banged on top of the radio. After several smacks, more persistent each time one landed, the sound went off. After silence prevailed in the dark room for another few seconds a deep sigh came from the bed and the springs let out a protest as the body shifted. In the darkness a torso raised up and the arms became stiff.

Finally, a whisper said, "It can't be morning! It's still dark! I just went to bed, didn't I?" Some springs squeaked in the darkness and a louder voice said, "I can't believe it! I slept through four minutes of that awful screech! That noise is obnoxious! That's why I put it on buzzer so it'd wake me sooner and I never heard it!" He looked at the lighted digits again and shook his head. "It was a wicked day yesterday at the park. Jason was right, the holiday was bad and then I loaded everything I could last night, but still… sleep through four minutes of that racket? Unbelievable!" *These walls are so thin I wonder if that noise woke Garrison next door!* He would never know, he wasn't about to stop and ask him.

Matt bounded out of bed and rushed across the hall into his little bathroom. If he still wanted to be on the road at the same time he must move it! The floor was cold, but it helped wake him up. He took the quickest shower he'd ever attempted, pulled a razor across his cheeks, slapped a bit of paste on a toothbrush and vigorously scrubbed his teeth, then gathered up everything he could claim from the tiny room. In fifteen minutes he was back in the bedroom and dressed in the clothes he'd laid out the night before, glad that he'd taken that much time before he fell into bed. He loaded his last suitcase with the few things from the bathroom and zipped it closed, unplugged his clock radio, wrapped the cord around it, wrapped the whole thing in the quilt his grandma made – whoever cleaned the apartment for the next guy could figure out what to do with the sheets. He grabbed the suitcase handle and rushed from the room.

After putting the suitcase and the radio beside the door he made a quick walk-thru. The one bedroom apartment was furnished, but heaven forbid he'd overlooked something personal. He'd made sure he'd emptied out his refrigerator when he ate his supper last evening. Well, most of what he'd emptied out he'd thrown in the disposal. Green and black stuff on a block of American cheese didn't really hold too much temptation to guzzle it down, even though that was his favorite kind of cheese.

Within half an hour of waking up, he knocked on the apartment building manager's door. He'd notified him the same afternoon he'd handed in his resignation. While he waited, Matt moved from one foot to the other and tossed the keys he would return from one hand to the other, he was anxious to be on his way. He was about to ring the man's doorbell again, he was so anxious to be out of there, when the door cracked open.

When the man answered, hair sticking up at strange angles, sleepy eyed and still in his pajamas, Matt gave the man a smile, dropped two sets of keys into his hand and said, "Here you go, Hank, I know you can't give me back my deposit, but I left the apartment in as good shape as I found it. I'm out of here!"

Hank's hand closed around the keys Matt dropped; nodded and said, "Yeah, house rules, you know." He had to clear the frog out of his throat, before he said, "Have a good one…" But Matt was already several steps down the hall.

Without looking back, he called, "I'll sure do that! You the same!" Of course, those last few words were said to the closed door of the building manager's apartment. After all, it was the holiday weekend he planned to be a couch potato today.

When Matt had the handle of his rolling suitcase in his hand and the clock-radio under his arm, he reached into his pocket for the rest of the key ring. He juggled the keys for a second until he held the right one for the car door, then jauntily swaggered down the short hallway and fell into the door to the parking lot then raced for his car, unmindful that his suitcase bounced along behind him. He was glad that even though there was a tropical storm off shore a few hundred miles that the forecast was for good weather today. A long drive in bad weather wasn't something he liked to do. In Florida especially bad weather was terrible for driving.

The last time he'd had to travel in bad weather was the day he'd come back to Orlando from Vansville. He wouldn't forget that trip for a while! That had been March first, following an ice storm. He'd wondered how his cousin Natt had made the drive from Atlanta on that last day of February. He hadn't dared to leave Vansville, even though he was supposed to be working in his office in Orlando on the first, but couldn't even leave when he should because nothing had been done to the road. He guessed Vansville wasn't the top word on the priority list for the county road crew.

Even so, he remembered he'd nearly skated from his uncle's house to his car, only from the porch to the street, but he'd nearly fallen on his rear two times before he'd left! He and his car definitely didn't like that drive. He'd only encountered a few sand trucks along the way, but there were many, many more cars, trucks and semis decorating the median and the sides of the roads. It hadn't been until he'd reached Atlanta, some hundred miles south, that he'd felt safe enough going the speed limit. But this was July and close to hurricane season.

His car was so full he had to slide both the suitcase and the radio onto the back seat. He slammed the door, then remembered what time it was, but then slid behind the wheel. As he started the car his stomach growled. After he pulled the shifting stick into drive, he patted his belly and muttered, "Hold on, I'm stopping at the drive-thru in a second." As if really showing its impatience, his belly growled again, maybe even a bit louder. *Maybe I should have had a glass of water when I brushed my teeth!*

The sun was just peeking over the golden arches, promising a hot day in Orlando, as he turned into the fast food restaurant drive-thru close to his apartment complex. He ordered quickly, then put the large coffee in his cup holder and opened the wrappers of the breakfast biscuits he'd purchased on the passenger seat. He took a huge swallow of coffee and a big sniff of the food, hoping that would quiet his rumbling stomach for a few minutes, then pulled the shifting lever into drive. Only minutes later Matt turned on the street leading to the interstate north. He was out of here, on to another job, on to bigger and better things. He hoped.

As the light turned green, he turned the wheel and pushed his foot down, he muttered, "Well, this'll be different. All these ten years I've been on my own. Even though it's tiny, Vansville has family. Not just Uncle Brad and Aunt Joyce, I'll be working with a cousin and my brother's already living there." He shook his head. His twin, his over-achiever, ex-Marine, twin was a hiking guide! *Go figure!*

He took a large mouthful of the warm breakfast biscuit and headed under the sign for the interstate north. Very soon he cranked up his air conditioning and then only a few minutes later pushed a favorite CD into the machine on the dash for some diversion. Interstate driving in Florida could be rather boring. He had several hours of driving ahead of him and he planned to arrive in Vansville, Georgia with time enough to get his car unloaded and get settled in his new residence – one of Isabel Isaacson's cabins - hopefully before dark. He hadn't lived in one of her cabins before, but he'd spent quite a bit of time in his brother's in February. Aunt Joyce was a nice lady, but when you lived alone…, well, she could talk the hind leg off a mule! He'd always said if he wanted diversion it would be of his own making – TV, DVD's CD's – not his aunt talking his ear off!

"Wonder what Eric's doing today? Is he out on a hike or is he on that new job yet? I don't remember when he said that sheriff's job starts." He shrugged, the town was small enough and probably he'd be neighbors with his brother. He'd find out soon enough.

South of Atlanta he stopped for gas, but also got his lunch to go and wheeled on down the road, glad he was making such good time. So far, he hadn't seen any troopers on the road and no accidents to block traffic and slow him down. That was a good thing considering it was the Saturday after the Fourth of July. Of course, probably most people stayed where they were on the Saturday after a holiday. In fact, after he'd thought about it when he'd left Jason's office, he was surprised Jason had let him off after Friday. People often stayed in Orlando more than one day and took in several parks while they were there. In fact, as he'd gone around working in the park he'd heard several families talking about where they'd go tomorrow. Too bad he'd never visited any of the other parks in Orlando. Working at this amusement park was a job, other than that he didn't really care what went on in an amusement park.

It was the chime for a text message that woke Emilyn Saturday morning. She sighed and looked at her clock radio. She knew she hadn't set the thing, why get up early when she didn't work until four in the afternoon? The clock said it was after eight o'clock, but she'd worked her tail off at the diner the evening before until midnight then had to come home. Because the holiday she'd worked was the Fourth of July, people were still out when she left the diner. In fact, someone had come in the front door as she'd hit the swinging doors. She'd heard Naomi greet the people as she hustled into the kitchen and tossed her apron into the bin.

Fireworks were still brightening the sky, even at midnight. It was not the quiet drive home it usually was. Usually, Fridays, after midnight, were more quiet than this one had been. She couldn't believe it on the front parking lot of the diner was a group of people setting off fireworks and sparklers. On the streets between the diner and her apartment complex she'd had to dodge several groups of people still celebrating in the street! Her apartment complex usually was quiet, but when she'd pulled on the parking lot the whine of a large fireworks had startled her. By that time, it wasn't even the Fourth any more!

Shouting and more whines had kept her awake, even though her body was craving sleep. She'd pulled the pillow over her ears, but it hadn't helped at all. Most people had holidays off, but couldn't they be a little considerate of those who had to work? Still, how would anybody know? She hadn't told a soul where she lived that she had to work the holiday. She figured as a single woman the fewer people who knew when or where she worked the better. This wasn't a bad town to live in, but she was a single girl after all. She was friendly to her neighbors but she'd never made any true friendships.

With a great sigh and still under her light covers, she pulled the little devise down onto the bed and grumbled, "Nobody thinks us waitresses that work second shift in twenty-four-seven diners need to sleep sometimes. Besides, yesterday was the holiday and the diner was packed out all evening. I thought people had picnics on the beach on summer holidays. We've got a really nice beach on the lake out of town. The diner sure isn't a picnic or on the beach! People came in by the car load, it sure was one hectic place last night and we didn't have an advertised special! So what was the deal?"

With another sigh, still under the light cover, Emilyn rubbed her eyes to get the film and sand out so she could see and punch some keys, saw who the message was from and read, *So, Emi, come join us on an adventure! Alli*

Allison was a dear friend. Emilyn had known her and Jack for a long time, but she still replied, *An adventure? What are you talking about?*

Almost immediately a new message popped up on the screen. *Yeah, we're gonna open a new restaurant in a couple of months. We want you to be part of it.*

In this economy? You're gonna do what? Are you crazy?

No! That's the beauty of it! The guy's so anxious for this to happen he'll supply the land, build the place to Jack's specs, just so we'll do it! It'll be the only eatery in town, so it can't fail! We're gonna go there next weekend to look around. Come on, go with us. Besides, you need a break from that diner – and Barney.

Knowing she wouldn't get back to sleep, not this morning, she pushed the cover to her waist and sat up, before she wrote: *I gotta ask off, I can't just up and leave, you know.*

Well, ask, silly! Get Friday, Saturday and Sunday. We'll make a weekend of it!

I'll try. Where is this place?

A little place close to Blairsville, Georgia. Up north, you know. It's in the foothills of the Appalachians called Vansville. The man says it's a growing town.

Emi's covers made a huge arc, her feet hit the floor and she screeched involuntarily. Fortunately, smartphones don't send screeches, but what Emilyn wrote back was; *Do you know what's in Vansville? My ex sent me an Email the other day. He'll be a store manager in Vansville starting Monday!*

So? It's been ten years, Emi. You're over him, right?

Not about to tell Allison anything about her Ex-husband, Emi texted back; *Yeah, sure, yeah. I'll try to get off.*

Good, let me know!

Emilyn shut off her phone, dropped it on the pillow, let out a long sigh and headed for her bathroom. There was no sense trying to get another nap, learning that upsetting news took all the sleep away. "Woman, why did you tell her you'd go to Vansville?"

As she stood under the warm water, scrubbing her hair and washing her body, she thought about Allison's question. Was she really over Matt Thomas? Yes, it had been ten years, since he'd left her a devastated twenty year old with divorce papers and not much else. At least she hadn't been pregnant! But she wasn't much else either. She'd had to grow up fast. That was the hardest part! She couldn't go home to family, no she *wouldn't* go home to family! Before a month was up she'd had utility bills come in the mail and the apartment manager came for the rent she didn't have. Who knew an eviction notice could come so quickly! Didn't apartment managers give young, devastated girls a break? *Obviously not.*

That's when she'd turned to Allison and Jack they'd pulled her out of her funk. Allison had taken her to the employment office and helped her get her first job as a waitress. She'd been waitressing ever since and now they wanted her to go in with them in yet another eatery. *Is that all*

I'll ever do with my life? She sighed, letting the warm water ease the ache in her back.

As she shut off the shower, she muttered, "Wonder if it'll be just them and me or if they're gonna hire more people?" Who knew? At this point it really didn't matter. It sounded like all that had happened was some man had asked Jack to start a restaurant – in Vansville. Emilyn shuddered and turned the faucet off with much more force than she needed to. It wasn't that the water had turned cold, but just the thought of seeing her ex sent goose bumps up her spine and down her arms. The shower head was still dripping as she quickly grabbed her towel and wrapped up in it, she was shaking all over!

What would it be like to see her handsome ex after a decade? He'd been working maintenance in an amusement park for nearly that long. Was he still in shape, had he changed his hair style, did he shave? She let out a loud 'harrumph!' Who cared what Matt Thomas looked like! He could look like a hairy ape and she wouldn't care, right? *Right!*

After dressing in some ratty clothes, she wandered into the kitchen, poured a cup of coffee from her automatic coffee maker that started brewing a pot when the timer and the clock got together. It was her only indulgence, but she knew she'd always have a good cup of coffee when she got up in the morning. She figured a working girl needed *something* good in her life. When you worked at a diner full time what else did you get? Nothing much that cost a lot, that was sure! A coffee pot on a timer? Wow! Too bad it didn't measure out the coffee and fill the reservoir all by itself too and maybe sing her favorite wakeup song and…

As she sat eating her last stale donut and sipping her good cup of coffee her thoughts turned to the text conversation she'd had with her friend. For all Allison knew she was over Matt Thomas. She'd worked hard to tell the world she was a big girl and was getting on with her life just fine, thank you very much. However, her heart of hearts knew how very wrong that was. No, she didn't think of him all the time, but usually something in a day reminded her of her handsome ex-husband. She readily admitted, she'd really loved the guy.

She had to admit that Matt had left her devastated! They'd met their junior year of high school and been inseparable from that summer until the next year when they'd graduated together. As an eighteen year old she loved Matt Thomas, he was her everything. Only a few days after graduation, much against both their parents' advice, they'd had a tiny wedding in front of Matt's pastor in his office and gone on a weekend honeymoon. They'd only gone two towns away to a modest hotel; that was all Matt could afford for their honeymoon. Goodness knew, there wasn't any money coming from her home!

They'd come back to jobs they'd lined up, but they were jobs the employers would only hire high school graduates for. They didn't have the experience or the qualifications for something better. Their income barely put them in a one bedroom, furnished apartment, paid utilities and got them a phone – a land line - kept clothes on their backs and food on the table, but hardly put a penny in savings. Still, what eighteen year olds even thought about putting money in savings? Their major concern had been if the condom had a hole in it!

Not long after that the quarrels started. First it was about church Matt wanted her to go with him. Why had he waited until they were married to tell her how important that was to him? That was the major thing that Matt's parents griped about, but he hadn't made much of it until after the wedding. His parents said something about 'yoked'. What was that about? She'd heard about oxen being yoked together. Oxen – her and Matt?

She shook her head, she really couldn't see the point. She'd never been to church. Nobody in her family had ever been or taken her that she knew about. Why was it so important? Working her job through the week, she felt it was her right to sleep in on Sunday. However, Matt got up dutifully every Sunday and went to church. Had he done that before they were married? She didn't know, he'd never asked her to go with him until after they were married. Come to think of it, he probably had, when he'd drop her off at home Saturday night he'd tell her he'd see her Monday morning. But had he ever asked her to go with him to church on Sunday? She couldn't remember that he had.

After they were married, instead of coming home for her after church and then going to his mom's for Sunday dinner, he'd go right from church and spend the afternoon. She knew it wouldn't have been that much out of his way to come for her, but he'd never asked about taking her for dinner. Still, that wasn't so bad, she'd slept in then cleaned the apartment, but then he'd come home in the evening and complain about her cooking. When he walked in the door she could smell the kitchen smells on his clothes and usually her tummy would rumble. She knew she hadn't had meals like he'd had at his mom's table.

He didn't just complain about Sunday, though, he always compared her cooking to his mom's. Hers always came up short. She was a new bride, her mom hadn't let her in the kitchen much her dad was such a stickler, especially when he was drunk, but she tried. She remembered well the evening after their first paychecks. Actually, except that Matt never struck her, one could call that fight a 'knock-down-drag-out fight'. Well, soon it was about most everything.

They'd come home from work nearly every evening and soon the words started. Instead of cuddling on the couch to watch TV, Matt splurged and bought a second TV so he could watch what he wanted in the bedroom. Instead of working things out, as twenty year olds Matt had thrown his apartment keys at her and walked out. Adding insult to injury, he'd told her she wasn't welcome to go with him. Her feet glued to the floor, she'd gapped at two keys on the floor and the closing door. With the snick of the door latch huge tears streamed down her cheeks. As the door clicked, her knees gave out and she slumped to the floor into a heap, her face awash with tears. Two weeks later Allison had come for a visit, found her still puffy-eyed and nearly starved and taken her in hand.

Where he'd gotten money for a divorce she still didn't know, but it wasn't long before she had divorce papers in her hands and soon after that she saw Matt for the last time before the judge. She heard from him occasionally, like the other day when he Emailed her he was moving to Vansville, Georgia. So what did she care? At the time, she didn't give it a second thought. So she was fifty miles south of Atlanta, he said Vansville was more than a hundred miles north. She was confident she'd never enter a town a hundred and fifty miles away, not when she worked at her job five days a week.

Was it ironic that her dear friends were going to the same little town to start an eatery and wanted her to be partners? Wasn't it just the other day somebody talked about Murphy's Law? Yeah, as a single girl, she knew first-hand about Murphy's Law! It never seemed to fail, if something bad was going to happen, it would happen to her.

Disgusted she'd been thinking about a man she should have forgotten about a decade ago, she looked at the half full cup of coffee. There was no steam coming from it and when she put it to her lips the smell of the nearly cold liquid made the last mouthful of dry donut nearly exit. Making a rude noise, she stood up, dumped out the few mouthfuls of cold coffee and sighed. She had laundry to do and Barney's Diner waited for her this afternoon. In fact, she had that purse she needed to clean out. She wracked her brain didn't she have something else more exciting to do today than clean out her purse? Maybe not.

Matt walked out of Isabel's house with the key to his cabin. He had made good time, there were several hours of daylight before the security light would come on in the parking lot. This time of year he'd have a long evening to enjoy the little town of Vansville. July in Vansville was nearly worlds apart from February in Vansville.

Just as he bounced down her porch steps an SUV wheeled onto the parking lot. He recognized the car and changed directions to go speak to his brother. As Matt stopped on the walk, a very disheveled man stepped from the car. "So," Eric exclaimed, "I see you made it! You'll start at the store on Monday?"

"That's the plan! What's on for the rest of your day?"

Eric slammed the driver's door and hurried around to his passenger door, tried the handle, then made a disgusted noise, dug his key from his pocket, beeped the door unlocked and pulled the door open, then took hold of the straps to a massive, grungy backpack. Attached to the bottom was something else encased in a waterproof case, but looked like it had ten pounds of dirt on it. Pulling the huge pack out, but letting it fall to the ground, he said, "I'm under strict orders to be ready for pickup in half an hour to go to Derek's place for a picnic supper. Since Ramon and I weren't here over the holiday, we're doing it today. You just got here?"

Matt looked at his twin. There wasn't much to classify them as identical at this point. The man had on grungy clothes, dusty hiking boots and sported a five day beard. He couldn't see his hair Eric had a bill hat pulled down over it; even that was grimy. The only thing that classified Eric as a white man was his face, from his nose up. Eric almost looked like he'd laid down in a mud puddle and wallowed in it, then stood in the wind and dried out. Matt had never seen his brother so disheveled. It had only been months ago he'd mustered out of the Marines!

He looked at the huge object on the ground and exclaimed, "Man! How on earth do you carry such a thing?"

Eric shrugged. "On my back?"

Matt made a face. "Yeah, yeah. Well, I won't keep you. I got one carload to empty into my new palace. Say, isn't that Derek that rich guy lives out of town?"

"Yup, I understand even his estranged son's here with his wife and daughter, so that'll mean the whole family is here over this holiday weekend."

Matt scowled. "And you are crashing the party? What's with that?"

Eric grinned at his twin and started walking, the straps of his backpack over his forearm. "Nope, I was invited, so it can't be called 'crashing the party' now can it?" He wasn't about to tell his brother that Carolyn Casbah was the love of his life. In fact, Eric had only admitted that to himself on the short drive from DeLords to his cabin. However he was pretty sure he'd never told Matt about Carolyn. Now wasn't the time to do that, either.

"Guess not. Well, enjoy, see you later."

"Sure, I'll guarantee it, since we're neighbors now."

Matt made a face as Eric reached the walk to his cabin. *Eric always was a smart mouth*! At least that's what their mom always said.

The brothers parted company, Eric hurried as fast as he could with the heavy backpack banging his leg as he walked across the cement and up the steps to his cabin. He would not put the heavy thing back on his back even for that short distance. Besides, it was so grimy he didn't want to put it on his back for fear the dried mud would fall on him even more.

Two

However, Matt went to his car for an armload of things to take in his cabin. It would take a while to get everything in his cabin; after all, he had all his worldly possessions in that car! He hadn't had much time to think about it until now, but he was excited about this move. As he'd pulled away from the entertainment capital of Florida it felt like a weight fell from his shoulders. Could it be he was growing up? Well… maybe. Being employed at an amusement park and being a store manager weren't exactly in the same genre.

Matt made several trips, dropping each armload on something in the living room of his cabin, deciding to empty his car before he arranged anything inside. If he didn't do that it could be supper time before he was finished. After he'd taken a few loads inside the cabin, a light blue van wheeled onto the parking lot and the driver blew the horn. Matt was outside for another load and looked up as Eric rushed out of his cabin, a changed man. He waved absently at his brother then waited as the big passenger door moved back and a lift slowly moved to a standing position on the ground. All Matt could see was one bench seat with a baby seat on it.

As he stood there, the horn tooted again and a hand waved from the passenger seat, so Matt grinned and waved back. From inside he heard, "Hi, Matt!"

"Hi, back at ya!" he called and grinned. The person who waved had to be either Ramon or Sandy. "Well," Matt muttered to himself, "I guess DeLords are taking Bro out in the country." Matt scowled. The last time he'd been here Casbah hadn't seemed all that friendly, even with his step-son and now they and Eric were going out there for a picnic? Maybe he'd ask about that sometime soon.

He watched as his brother stepped on the lift then reached for the handle. Obviously there was a mechanism to move the lift there, because the lift started whining and moved off the ground. Matt always was amazed at the lady who needed the van with a wheelchair lift. How could she always be so cheerful and still have to be in a wheelchair every minute of every day because she was paralyzed from her waist down? He knew she was an amazing woman. Sandy was the only person he knew who was paralyzed, but he knew she was one of a kind. He'd had some very short term dealings with handicapped people at the park and none of them were like Sandy DeLord in any way.

Not only that, she now had a baby to take care of! Back in February, the baby hadn't even been a year old, but he'd been far advanced to Matt's way of thinking. If you're always in a wheelchair how do you potty train a child? Well, on second thought how do you teach a child to walk if you're in a wheelchair? He made a face he sure was showing he didn't know much about children! Children overran the amusement park, but nobody threw one in the trash can, he'd been spared. He pulled another box from his trunk and slammed the lid on the empty cavern. It was time to start putting things away inside.

Even before the door closed on the van Matt heard a little voice exclaim, "Ick!"

"Ick?" Matt said to himself. "Their little boy calls him 'Ick'? An ex-Marine? How funny is that!" Matt grinned as the trunk lid snapped shut after his last box. His bigger than life ex-Marine brother answered to a tiny child who called him 'Ick'! Matt juggled the big box so he could make the step and headed up the walk to his cabin three doors down. He guessed life would get another dimension now with family here. The light blue van threw gravel as it headed for the highway. "Ramon must be driving!"

Matt continued to unload his car, but every time he saw his twin for the first time after a long time his thoughts always turned to one time he could never personally recall, but was a major event in both their lives. They were babies, but being twins in their small hometown made them locally famous. Their parents didn't discuss the event much but even their aunts and uncles and especially their grandparents hashed it out when they saw the boys.

The first time Matt remembered hearing about it was when he was three years old. His grampa Thomas talked about when baby brother Eric was found after he'd been kidnapped. It was almost like Grampa bragged about 'finding' Eric. He wasn't really sure, but from the talk that went around, Eric had disappeared from their crib when they were only about a month and a half old. When their mom had come in to their room one morning only Matt was in their crib. She'd searched the house, every room, under beds, in closets. Their dad had stayed home from work to help her and be with her. Their mom had been frantic and had the neighbors and the police scouring the neighborhood and the woods around for hours.

From what he'd always heard, the police had convinced his mom to stay at home with the younger twin, who was Matt, and wait while everyone else formed teams to search for his brother, Eric. She had just come from their room, after changing Matt's diaper and putting him down for the night that same evening when Grampa Thomas barged into the house with a dirty, hungry Eric screaming in his arms, exclaiming, "Look who I found!"

Even at three years old he remembered asking, "Why just him, why not me? How come nobody wanted to take me, too?" He'd never forget the look on his mom's face when he'd asked that question. That was the first time Matt had felt the difference between himself and Eric. Until he'd married Emilyn and done something ahead of his brother he'd felt inferior. Back then and even now, Eric was the over-achiever and Matt was just along for the ride in life. Eric had been the scholar, Matt had just skinned by, Eric was the class valedictorian, Matt just pulled through. Eric got scholarships to college, Matt got a diploma. Matt married Emilyn, Eric went to college and joined the Marines. Eric was a hero in Afghanistan, Matt divorced his wife and worked as a maintenance man at a theme park in Florida. The list could go on.

Eric didn't know his brother's thoughts he decided that was just as well. He closed up the van, then turned with a smile and moved toward the bench seat where the little boy sat in his car seat with his hand out and a huge grin for one of his favorite people. Eric loved tiny Jon DeLord, he was a terrific child, but today he couldn't keep his thoughts from being down in the dumps. Would he ever have the blessing of a child of his own? After all, he was thirty years old. Eric moved beyond Jon's seat and sat down on the bench beside him, before he said, "Hi, there, buddy! You all ready to go see Japa?"

Jon nodded vigorously and kicked out his feet. "Japa! Got dogs!" Since Eric hadn't taken the little hand, Jon impatiently waved it in Eric's face. Eric took it, smiled at the little boy and patted his shoulder.

Eric looked toward the front and asked, "Derek has dogs? That's a new development, when did he get canines?"

"Man," Ramon said, "get with the program! Hot dogs, you know, on the grill."

"Was that Matt?" Sandy asked.

"Yup, he'll start with Natt on Monday."

"Ah, good, I'm sure the poor boy's overrun with coffee drinkers," Ramon surmised. "'Course he's got a better personality than the other guy who was there."

"Hey, don't knock it!" Eric exclaimed. "The guy makes a mean cuppa!"

"Yeah, I'll give him that, although I'm real partial to the stuff I get at my house every time I want a cup."

Eric shrugged. "Yeah, I guess you got that advantage."

"I sure do and I'm glad!"

The ride to Casbah's place was quiet. Even Jon was content now that Eric had taken his hand. When Eric had brought his hikers back earlier, Sandy had told him about the picnic and that Carolyn's brother and his family had come from Alabama. Just seeing her brother had brought back her memory – all except memory of her attack. He and everyone else, knew what that meant, it meant that Carolyn would be leaving Vansville soon to take up her life as she'd known it, before the horrendous attack back the middle of April. Of course, he couldn't know what she had gone through, he only had seen the results and they were horrendous! He'd been the first on the scene and reported to the sheriff.

As he buckled his seatbelt, Sandy told him Carolyn was planning on going back to Atlanta tomorrow when Lance, her brother, left to go back to Alabama. With her memory back, she knew she'd moved to Atlanta for a new job. However, Lance had told her she had no job to go back to, but she needed to see to her apartment and Eric knew she'd probably look for another job, since Atlanta was so much bigger than Blairsville or Vansville.

He had known she would, they had both known she would. Until she got her memory back they didn't know what she'd done for a living or where, but they both knew she wasn't from Vansville. She was only here because the criminal had tossed her out here and Isabel had brought father and daughter together soon after she'd been released from the hospital, but still suffering from amnesia. Nothing anyone in Vansville could do had penetrated her amnesia, but it had taken only the sight of her brother to do that. The brain was an amazing thing.

However, Eric was crushed by that news. He'd finally admitted, if only to himself, that Carolyn was the love of his life. He had tried so hard to not let his heart get involved in his times with Carolyn, because he was sure if she ever got her memory back she'd have to go back to wherever she had been to see about what was left of her life there. However, as anyone knows, hearts and minds don't always work together. When a heart finds its soulmate, the mind doesn't have too much to say about it. Sometimes Cupid has a special arrow that figures out how to work around armor and walls. Cupid had used a really strong arrow on him!

Eric didn't know it, but Carolyn had also tried not to let Eric passed her wall, after all, until just the other day she didn't know if she was married, engaged or had a special friend, but there again, Cupid's arrow had hit its mark. Another factor, Carolyn hadn't known where her dad was in a dozen years and she'd found him in Vansville. Now she must leave, so she was already feeling hollow inside. Even before she'd gotten her memory back she'd felt such a kinship with her dad. He'd told her how they had been when she was much younger. Now she was leaving him again and it made her very sad. However, she glad to finally see her brother and sister-in-law and of course, her little niece.

Eric and Carolyn sat together at the picnic table on the big deck and seemed to be in their own little world during the meal. Even after all the food was cleared away they sat together holding hands. Several times, anyone could see Eric's arm had slipped around Carolyn's shoulders and he was hugging her to his side. When conversation was going on around them they'd stolen several kisses. It was obvious they didn't care who saw them, they were happy to be together and nearly distraught that today was the last day they knew they could be together. They knew Carolyn must go and Eric must stay.

When it was dusk and conversation started to lag, Linda took Brenda inside to bed. About the same time, Jon sleepily climbed up on Sandy's footrest with his hands up to find his place on Mama's lap to nap. Of course, Sandy obliged him that was his favorite place to nap when he couldn't be in his own bed. When Linda came back to the deck Ramon looked at the lovers and sighed. They had been looking in each other's eyes for many long, silent minutes.

After an exceptionally long kiss, Ramon said, rather loudly, "Ahem, I believe it's time to take this little guy home to bed. Are you ready to go, Eric?" He knew he'd better say the man's name or he probably wouldn't get a response.

"Hmm, what was that?" he asked, as he reluctantly pulled away from Carolyn, but kept her inside the circle of his arm.

"Come on, man, it's time to get on back to town."

Almost like a little kid, he whined, "Do we have to?"

Winking at his wife and grinning at the backs of the couple, Ramon said, philosophically, "Well, it is dark now and when it's dark it is customary to sleep in one's own bed when one is this close to it." He continued, dryly. "Thought you'd spent the last several nights on the ground, in a tent, in a sleeping bag. Won't Isabel's full sized bed feel better than that?"

Eric sighed, "I know, give us a minute."

However, he brought Carolyn up with him and quickly pulled her into his arms. She went willingly, putting her arms around him. After several long kisses, Eric pulled away, but only to wipe the tears from Carolyn's cheeks with his thumb, then he kissed those places and her lips once more. Ramon lifted Jon from Sandy's lap and Sandy started her chair motor, but it seemed Eric and Carolyn were oblivious, even to the whine of Sandy's chair. Still, they walked slowly arm in arm behind the little family.

Tears slid silently down Carolyn's cheeks, as she walked inside Eric's arm to the van. Anyone could see that Eric was blinking furiously, but no tears came from his eyes. Several times before they reached the garage Carolyn swiped at her cheeks, but it seemed there were always more coming along behind. Several minutes later, after another long kiss, Eric watched as the DeLords boarded the lift. Of course, Ramon immediately sent the lift back down as soon as his family was off. Before it hit the ground, Eric deposited another kiss on Carolyn's lips then slowly peeled her arms from around his neck. He stepped on the lift, but obviously Ramon had his hands on the mechanism inside, the lift started up. Ramon raised his hand, but Carolyn couldn't see it, tears were completely fogging her eyes.

Reluctantly, Eric stepped off the lift and Ramon started the door closed. He slouched onto the bench seat of the van as Ramon finished closing the van door, but his eyes looked immediately out the large window to the beautiful young woman standing in the doorway of the garage, tears streaming down her cheeks. Her brother stood behind her, his hands on her shoulders. Two tears slid slowly down Eric's own cheeks as he looked back at her. He couldn't believe the moisture on his cheeks! He was ex-military! He'd watched many of his comrades brought down with enemy fire – but this was different… this was Carolyn.

Could a loving family like Ramon have be in his future? Eric let out a long sigh. How could it, his love was leaving at first light. Before he'd moved to Vansville he'd held onto hope that one day he could love a lady and have a family with her. But she was leaving… and he was staying. Today he was a hiking guide, but in less than a month he'd be a deputy sheriff, still here in Vansville. What was the hope in that? Surely Carolyn's future was in Atlanta. Vansville and Atlanta were both in Georgia, but not close enough one of them could commute. Besides, who ever heard of a deputy sheriff who commuted? There wasn't much off time in that profession. Even if he was scheduled off, at a moment's notice he could be needed.

Being the only deputy in the area, he was bound to be busy. When he'd been in the sheriff's office to officially take the job they'd looked at a county map together. He'd have jurisdiction over many acres of undeveloped land. In the foothills of the Appalachians it was anyone's guess where the hillbillies lived and what kind of livelihood they had. There could be thousands of stills and hundreds of acres of illegal crops!

When the door was closed, Ramon brought Jon over to the bench seat to fasten him in his car seat. The little boy woke up long enough to stretch out his hand toward Eric and exclaim, "Ick!" Eric took the little hand, but without acknowledging his friend, he looked back out the window in the door, because his love still stood in the entryway of the garage. While he felt the tiny hand in his, he felt a tear work its way from the corner of his eye and slide down beside his nose. He wondered if he'd ever have the honor of a son or daughter of his own

As Ramon started the van, after Sandy fastened her chair in place, Eric shook his head, but kept his eyes focused on the lovely lady standing in the doorway. He was glad they were in the garage and the door was up, that meant the light was on and he could easily see her. The love of his life, the lady he knew was his soulmate, was leaving for Atlanta at first light tomorrow. She remembered she'd had a car, but the family decided the criminal had used it to kidnap her and then had burned it up to destroy the evidence. Someone had reported a car fire soon after Eric had discovered Carolyn's unconscious body back in the woods behind Isabel's property back in April.

At this point in her life, she had to rely on someone else to transport her. Lance was the means of that transportation and that meant she had to leave with his family in the morning. Even though they knew she had been replaced at the job she'd started, surely she would find a job there in her field. There were several hospitals and even another medical center in Atlanta where she could apply. She knew she'd be one busy woman in the next few days, with putting in job applications around the city and replacing cards, licenses, her cell phone and buying a car. Perhaps she'd be so busy she wouldn't remember Eric – or not.

They also knew Eric must stay. Through July he was a hiking guide for DeLord's. In fact, tomorrow his replacement was going with him as a guide-in-training. August first he was to become that deputy stationed in Vansville. Except for Carolyn's near fatal experience, Vansville seemed like a peaceful enough place, but for some reason, the state law enforcement was convinced and had passed on their conviction to the county sheriff that the rural area that surrounded Vansville was big enough to warrant its own deputy. He would never disagree. He had mustered out of the Marines and didn't want to return to military life, so being a deputy sheriff was a good option.

His eyes never left Carolyn's dear face as the van moved from the garage down the long driveway toward the country road. Even as the van moved out of sight, two more tears slid down his cheeks. He wiped them away with his thumb and forefinger. Under his breath, he murmured, "Darling, how I love you. I love you so very much!" *God in heaven, if there's any way, bring back my darling Carolyn to me, I love her so much.*

Carolyn stood in the doorway watching the van pull away. Tears streamed down her cheeks, her brother stood silently behind her, his hands on her shoulders watching the van. Because of the anger he'd had against his dad for twelve years, he and Carolyn had been very close, for a while, until Lance married Linda it had just been the two of them and they had shared everything, including thoughts, but not about their dad. Lance had been too bitter. However now the bitterness was gone. Carolyn was glad God had taken Lance's bitterness away, now she would pray that he'd let his relationship with his Savior take care of the rest of his life.

When Lance had entered the house, she knew God had cured Lance's bitterness and she was glad. Something else God had added now she knew where her dad was, her beloved dad. She'd never lost that love, even though for her brother's sake, she'd buried it and hadn't talked about her dad in years. Now she could come visit. Because of Eric she knew she would every chance she had. Things must turn out right, somehow!

As she watched the van's taillights fade away, she whispered through her tears, "Lance, I love him! I love him so much! How can we...?" Lance squeezed her shoulders, but he kept silent, he had no answer. He had known Linda for a long time before he'd married her; he knew deep, abiding love. However, he couldn't give his sister any reassurances. He hadn't let God into his life in many years, so he didn't have that reassurance to give her. Finally, when the taillights were long gone, they turned back into Derek's house and closed the garage door. She must pack. First light came very early during July. Of course, packing wouldn't take too long, she hadn't been doing any major shopping since being in Vansville and her wardrobe consisted totally of things her dad had paid for since she'd been out of the hospital.

Sandy looked back at the desolate young man and said, "Cheer up, Eric. I have it on good authority that Carolyn has no job to go back to in Atlanta."

Sadly, Eric nodded and let out a long sigh before he said, "I know that, Sandy, but what is there here for her? She has a master's degree in physical therapy. There's no clinic or anything in Blairsville that would touch her or try to pay her what she's worth. The clinic here wouldn't employ her you and I both know that!" As the trees beside the road slipped by, he heaved a sigh and continued, "She's going back to Atlanta because that's the logical place for her to find work in her field."

"But Eric, God doesn't work according to man's logic," she countered immediately. "We must let Him do His work."

"I know that, but…"

Sandy waved her hand to keep him from making an excuse. "You know that verse that says, 'If you have faith as small as a grain of mustard…'?"

"Yeah, I know it."

Giving him a compassionate smile, Sandy said, "Perhaps, you need to work on your faith so it'll be at least as big as a grain of mustard?"

Letting out a long sigh, Eric whispered, "I'll try, Sandy, I'll try. But right now, this minute I'm fighting separation. Mustard seed doesn't hold much appeal."

"Oh, I know, but God has a plan!"

"Yes, He does. I could wish it was to keep her here for me."

Hardly letting him finish his thought, Sandy said, "Perhaps it's not to keep her here but to bring her back."

"It's a long shot," Eric sighed.

"That's true, but God can do anything but fail!"

"Say," Ramon said, "your brother's here now, he'll help you through this crisis."

Eric nearly snorted, but remembered just in time that he had a sleeping baby beside him. "My brother? Help me through losing the love of my life? Man, he bailed on his wife when he was twenty! How could he help me through this?"

"So bring him to church tomorrow."

"Yeah, I'll do that, but help through a crisis? I doubt it. From what I remember of my brother, even back in February, all he's done with his life is get older."

Sandy nodded. "Even that helps sometimes."

The little boy beside him let out a long sigh in his sleep. Eric turned tender eyes on the child and murmured, "Yes, even age helps sometimes."

Matt had finished putting his things away and shoved his suitcases and boxes into the back of his walk-in closet when he heard a vehicle on the parking lot. He looked around his place with satisfaction knowing he'd found a place for everything. By now it was dark and also Saturday. He'd determined when he took the key from Isabel he'd empty his car and settle in.

He'd followed that plan until his stomach growled. Putting his things away hadn't taken him to the kitchen area, but when his stomach growled, he turned until his eyes rested on an empty counter. Glaringly, the empty cupboards stared back at him. The only things in those cupboards were the things Isabel stocked for her renters; dishes, a few glasses and mugs and pots and pans and two drawers had silverware and dishtowels and rags. Without looking, he knew his refrigerator was running, but cooling nothing. The ice cube trays that came with the machine were full and frozen, but nothing of his was in the freezer! His empty stomach had growled this morning, asking for breakfast. Now a second time today? He was a dunce!

He sighed and shook his head, how had he forgotten that there was no restaurant in Vansville? He'd lived here for a month in February and eaten with his brother several times, but never at a restaurant, because there wasn't one in town. He went out on the porch to see the few colors left of the sunset. That was free, you didn't have to buy it a half hour's drive away, but it also didn't fill up an empty stomach. Lunch had been a long time ago. As if on cue his belly let out a noise and Matt sighed, glad that he was alone and no one had to hear his stomach growl.

Eric let himself down on the lift and Matt watched the slow moving object hit the ground. He saw his brother wave half-heartedly at the van as it left, then look at his own SUV, then turn, his head down, toward his cabin. "Hey, Bro, I'm here!" Matt called from his porch, not sure why his brother looked so dejected.

"Such a sad substitute," Eric muttered. On the next breath, he said, "Come on down to my place! It's not late, share some tea with me."

"Sure, I'll take you up on that."

Glad to take his mind off his empty stomach and to forget about his empty cupboards and refrigerator, Matt jogged down his steps and met his brother in front of his cabin. Falling in step beside him and going with him up the steps to his porch, he said, "I won't pass up your tea. You get it by the jug from Alex?"

"Yup, he keeps me stocked."

Matt slouched into a wicker chair on the porch, while Eric went in his place for mugs and his gallon jug of tea. As Eric disappeared inside, Matt hoped his empty stomach wouldn't give him away. He shook his head. How could he forget there wasn't a restaurant in town and the grocery closed at five o'clock? He'd been here for a month in February! Eric came back with the tea, but also a box of store-bought chocolate chip cookies.

"You'll need to get some, Bro, it's the best tea on the market and it's not that expensive. I know you're like me, tea is your beverage of choice," Eric said, as he sat down in the other wicker chair on the porch, his hands full. He set the mugs down on the little wicker table between the two chairs, then poured each one full.

Matt picked up one of the mugs and took a long swallow, before he said, "I know that and that's what I planned to do, but he's closed."

Eric nodded and raised his mug to his lips, before he said, "That he is. He's open six eights, late on Friday and not on holidays. In fact, I think he asked around and decided not to open today so he could take a long weekend to visit family. That's life in a little town you're not in Orlando anymore, Bro."

Matt sighed and snagged a cookie, glad that his belly hadn't given him away. "Yeah, I know. I'll have to go back to Blairsville tomorrow, early. I never thought about food when I came through earlier. I could have stopped at a supermarket if I'd thought about it. Actually, I never thought about it until I had my car unloaded and took a gander at my bare cupboards in the kitchen. I looked out the window and saw Alex's place was dark as a mausoleum." He looked at his watch. "If I went back now, I know there'd be a store open, but I wouldn't get back here till midnight and I've been on the road all day...."

"Hey, come on over here in the morning! I'll feed you breakfast, then we'll walk together to church. Be here at eight fifteen."

Matt made a face, but he said, "Sure, I'll never turn down breakfast food."

"So why the face?"

Wishing he hadn't been quite so free with his face muscles, Matt pulled his free hand down over his face and said, "Umm, haven't been in church since the last time I was here. Been sort of neglectful, I guess."

Eric nodded then looked at his brother over the top of his mug. "Figured as much. Why is that, Bro? What happened to your roots?"

Knowing he was making an excuse, Matt said, hesitantly, "Well, the park's open seven days a week for two shifts. I went along, never took Sunday's off. Me along with my staff, if the schedule came out with your name in the slot you did it. My roots? I know Mom and Dad sure taught us right, but well, I guess I sort of left them behind. You know Emilyn never had much to do with church things. Things like that didn't seem quite so important back in high school and when I was married to her, you know?" Matt shrugged and took another swallow of tea. "Life sorta got in the way, I guess."

"I kind of thought that. When I was overseas I couldn't do without my faith. I'd have been lost without it. In fact, several of us guys helped each other out more than once in some really hard times. Several of us had Bible studies together and prayed together a lot.

"Now you know as a hiking guide I can't come back to go to church when I'm leading a group, but a lot of them are church youth groups and often they'll have devotions on the trail. I have my devotions every day regardless if the group's Christian or not and I'm in church every chance I can. It can be done, Brother. Really, it can."

Matt let out a long sigh, nodded and said, "Yes, I know. I'll be here for breakfast, but I'll go with you."

"Good. Good to hear, Bro. It's kind of like falling off a bike – you need to get up and get back on soon as you can."

"I know. I will, starting tomorrow."

"Good, be sure to bring your Bible."

Matt sat and looked out at the darkening western sky across the meadow before he said, "So they have Sunday school for everybody? It's not just for the kids?"

"That's right. Ramon and Derek both have adult classes."

"So we go to Ramon's?"

"Yup, he's a good teacher, too."

"I'll be glad to listen. February was several months ago. I guess you couldn't be a teacher being a hiking guide?"

"No, not hardly. Even a deputy is pretty much on call twenty-four-seven, so I'll never volunteer, but Ramon's really good. We're working through the book of John right now."

"Good to know."

Saturday afternoon Emilyn came puffing into the diner through the back door with only five minutes to clock-in time, her loose blond hair swirling around her shoulders, stuffing her phone in one pocket and her keys in the other. Barney, her boss, made a production of looking at the large clock over the door into the eating area then scowled at Emilyn.

However, before he could say anything, she exclaimed, "Barney! Don't you dare say a word! You know I'm not late, I still have five minutes, but there was some street construction I didn't know about. The street was blocked off and they hadn't posted any signs. I didn't know I had to take a detour until I was almost in the hole."

"Should plan for that."

Finding her timecard, she ran it through the slot and exclaimed, "Oh, sure! Give me a break, will you? I mean, I guess I should call the street department just like I call the weatherline every day for updates!"

Barney nodded. "Yup, would be good." Emi threw her card back in the slot and glared at her boss, but didn't say anything.

Emi let out a long sigh she had other things to do before she started. What could she answer to that? The man was incorrigible he had to have the last word. She'd learned that several years ago. She left the time clock then went to the large drawer that held clean aprons. She tied one on and found an order pad to stick in the pocket. She sighed, like it or not, another shift had started. Before she went through the doors into the dining area she took a band from her pocket and made a ponytail. She knew, Barney made a point of making sure all his wait staff kept their hair away from the food they served.

Later, Barney took off his chef's apron and Emi said, "Oh, Barney, I need to ask for next Friday, Saturday and Sunday off." She smiled sweetly at him. "I wouldn't be too mad if you added on the Monday after that, too."

"What the h... um, dickens for?"

"A friend of mine wants me to go out of town with her for a long weekend." She wasn't about to tell him this was possibly a new job. Looking significantly at the board where he always posted the schedule, Emilyn said, "I noticed you haven't posted the next schedule yet. It wouldn't be too much trouble, you know."

Barney plucked his bill cap off a hook by the back door and with a flourish set it on his head. He put his hand on the doorknob and said, "I'll let you know tomorrow, Blondie." Looking up at the same announcement board, he said, "Then again, I got stuff to do. Maybe there's somebody else who needs that time worse than you do."

"But you could give me a clue today. That way I could tell my friend sooner."

Shaking his head, he opened the door and said, "Nope, tomorrow."

After Barney was gone, Emi sighed. "He can be such a royal pain," she muttered.

"He's the boss," her friend, Marge, shot back.

"Oh, sure, I know that! But don't you wish sometimes he'd give a little? I mean, after all, tomorrow the schedule's supposed to come out! If he'd post it for more than a pay period a body could do some planning."

"Yeah, that would be good."

Later, during the dinner time, she went through the swinging doors with a damp rag to wipe off one of her empty tables when the front door opened. Emi glanced over her shoulder and groaned. One of her least favorite customers walked in. The man had wayward hands and always seemed to sit at her table and use those hands to his best advantage. Of course he saw her, so he bypassed the menu stand and sauntered over to one of her clean tables. He sat so she'd be sure to see him or perhaps it was so he could better watch her. The man was a good ten years older than her, but he'd taken a shine to her. Why couldn't one of the younger men that came in on a regular basis have eyes for her?

Letting out a breath, she went to the work station, left her rag and picked up the carafe of decaf coffee that had just finished perking and went to his table. One thing she knew for sure, the man drank decaf coffee when he came to Barney's diner. "Ah, my favorite waitress is on!" he exclaimed. "You know I'll have some of that brew."

As the man turned his cup over, Emilyn filled it, then quickly stepped back, away from those roaming hands and said, "So what'll it be, Harry? I noticed you didn't stop for a menu."

Harry picked up his cup immediately and held it under his nose. "Oh, the house special, you know me, Emi."

"Yup! All you can eat for as little as possible. I know."

Harry grinned. "Sure! Gotta work every angle. Single man, you know. Besides, chicken and dumplings are one of my favorite meals."

Emilyn sighed again, "Yeah, I know." She whipped out her order pad and made a few lines on it. The cook would know what she meant. Quickly, she whirled away from him and as she headed for the kitchen, she ripped off the sheet from the pad. That particular dinner was one of the diner's best meals. Lots of people in the area knew that and came in when it was the house special. From evidence through the day that had been the case today. Cook never seemed to be much ahead on chicken and dumplings days.

When she came back with his order she had to get close enough to place the plate in front of him and Harry was ready. She noticed he'd put his cup down and his hand closest to where she must go was empty, hanging at his side. She placed the plate down, if Barney saw her do anything else, he'd have a fit! Harry immediately snagged her around the waist and kept his hand there, even though Emilyn tried to move away. Harry looked up at her and winked. He knew very well what he was doing and knew Emilyn's feelings about it, too.

That didn't matter to him Emilyn was a beautiful woman, blond, blue-eyed, curves just right… "So, sweetheart, go out with me your next night off."

Emilyn wouldn't fall for that! She knew Harry drank, they didn't serve alcohol at the diner, that's why she worked here at this particular restaurant, but she knew he went to places that served alcoholic drinks. He never came here on Fridays, because Friday he got paid and went to a bar for the evening. He'd told her he went to watch the big screen they had there, but he never said he didn't drink when he went there. She knew he didn't just sit at a table to watch some picture or some game. She never saw him except when he came here, but what single man ever went to a bar on a Friday and didn't drink?

She'd lived in a home where there was an alcoholic who put his family through hell when he was drunk and used his money for his habit. She didn't drink and she wouldn't go with a man who did. She made that vow as a teenager and she'd stuck to it, even after her husband left her. She often wondered why her mom had put up with it. There had to be men out there who didn't drink, but a single life was better than a beating every Friday! She'd watched her mom suffer through several of them and gotten a few herself until she'd married Matt and left that behind.

"Nope, Harry, I'm going out of town my next day off." *I hope it'll turn into something more.* She smiled sweetly at him. "Will you please take your hand away? I'm working; the other customers don't need to see me with your arm wrapped around me. Besides, somebody at that other table needs a refill and Marge is on her supper break, so let me go!"

Harry huffed, "You sure are a spoil sport!"

"Yup, I work at it!" She waited until the man's hand loosened slightly, then whirled away and hurried back to the coffee center for the carafe.

Harry watched her go and shook his head before he picked up his fork. *Why won't she go out with me? I'm a decent catch, my looks are decent, hey, I even have all my hair! I don't wear a beard, I don't smoke, don't do drugs, I only drink a little on Friday nights. She doesn't wear any rings, surely working here, she's not married...* He dug into his chicken and noodles, it was as good as usual, but he would rather go home to a wife who could cook for him. Maybe someday he'd convince a beautiful woman he was a good catch. He sighed and watched the beautiful woman serve somebody else.

When Emilyn went off at midnight she sank into her car and let out a long sigh. As always, she was glad another shift was over and she could go home to bed. It had been busy, but not like the holiday. Her tips were close to average, but she'd never be an instant millionaire as a waitress. She was glad not all her customers were like Harry. He gave her a bill for his meal and told her to keep the change. After she'd rung up both the meal and dessert and all the coffee he drank, that's all she could keep, the change! "He had the nerve to ask me out!" she grumbled and turned the key in the ignition. *Like I'd go out with such a skinflint!*

She left the employees parking lot and headed for her normal street to go home. At the last minute Emi remembered the road work and turned on the detour. It was midnight, after all and she'd just worked a busy eight hour shift. She'd looked down the street when she came to work. It looked pretty extensive, tomorrow was Sunday, the street department didn't work on Sunday, only emergencies. Why had they even started on something the day after a holiday that was also a Saturday? She shook her head. Only the street department knew for sure. It certainly wasn't something they divulged to the general population on any given day! As far as she knew the street department didn't have a customer hotline you could call to find out about detours.

Sunday morning, Isabel looked up from reading her Bible to glance out her front window in time to see her newest renter leave his cabin. She must admit, the boy was a good looking specimen, just like his brother. Ruth came in the living room to announce breakfast, but Isabel nodded out the window at Matt and said, "That boy is Eric's twin. How am I gonna tell them apart? I know they could pass for each other!"

Ruth looked out the window at the young man and said, "Don't know, Mom. He does look an awful lot like Eric, that's for sure."

Isabel kept watch as Matt turned on Eric's walk and said, "Of course, their hair style's different, Eric still keeps his short like when he was in the Marines."

"I guess that'll help some," Ruth agreed. "Their jobs are a bit different, too. Didn't you say that one's starting at the store?"

"Yes, he'll help Natt with his store starting tomorrow and Eric's still a hiking guide. Now that'll change the end of the month."

Matt didn't see Isabel and he didn't know that her favorite chair sat so she could see everything at her end of town. He walked up Eric's steps and pushed the door open. He knew his brother would have his door unlocked. His stomach growled appreciatively as the aroma from the bacon Eric lifted from his skillet reached him. "Mmm, do you do this often?"

"What, make breakfast?"

"Yeah, with bacon and eggs?"

"Usually when I'm home I try to fix good stuff. Those little dri-packs leave a lot to be desired when a body's on a trail. It's not too often we have a cook who knows how to do a good job over an open fire. Usually there's good coffee for breakfast and maybe some of them will bring those packets of stew you can reconstitute with brook water, but usually that's it."

Matt nodded. "Yeah, I can appreciate that! It has been a long time since the settlers took wagon trains through these parts."

"Oh, yeah and usually the youth leader's wife has to keep track of the girls. That in itself is a full time job."

After they'd enjoyed a good breakfast, Eric and Matt left his cabin just as Ruth and Isabel left their house to go to their church in Blairsville. On the walkway to her car, Ruth said to her mother, "That's Eric and his brother? They are twins! That's sure! Look at that! Both with white shirts and a blue tie and they don't even live together!"

"Yes, they are. How do you tell them apart?"

"Hey, that'll be a challenge!" Thinking for a moment, Ruth continued, "Of course, through the week it won't be hard. Eric won't be here and Matt'll be working at the store."

Isabel grinned. "Next month that boy'll be wearing some kind of sheriff's outfit!" She let out a loud huff. Quite loudly, so the young man would be sure to hear, she said, "He'll be parking a sheriff's car here on the lot! Can you imagine? Why, it'll give such a bad impression, nobody'll rent for those overnights!"

Even Ruth could appreciate a man who was in shape, as she said, "Oh, my!"

One of the twins waved and gave the two women a big smile, then gave them a two fingered salute. "Hi, Isabel, Ruth! It's a gorgeous Sunday morning." His smile turned impish, as he said, "What was that you said about my means of transportation?"

"Ah, that's Eric," Isabel muttered and Ruth nodded, agreeing. Isabel ignored his question and said, "It is that, Sonny. So I guess you're off today."

"Yes, that I am. I'm making sure my brother gets to church."

"Ah, yes, I'm glad to hear that, Sonny! Be sure you check out Roger's sermon for me. Make sure he keeps on track."

Eric chuckled. "I'll do that, Isabel. You know I'll keep you posted. I also heard that Derek has a good study going in his class for Sunday school." That was a running joke between them. They both knew Roger gave a fine sermon, one that came straight from the Word and blessed people's hearts. They also knew Derek was a fine teacher for the older crowd, but Isabel had gone to church in Blairsville for many years. She didn't feel the need to change. Ruth went with her even though Roger was her son-in-law.

"Say, after we get home from church come share the roast Ruth put in the oven. It's more than we can eat at one sitting."

Three

Eric grinned. His eyes twinkled, as he said, "Are you sure, Isabel? I mean, think about it, Matt's appetite isn't any smaller than mine. There may not be too much left for you two."

Acting disgusted, Isabel retorted, "Sonny, we bought this one on special at Alex's the other day. It's big enough! Besides, you know ladies always get first choice."

"Okay, you're on! See y'all later."

Giving another huff, Isabel pulled the passenger door open on Ruth's car and said, "Yes, of course! Now don't eat too many of Marcy's sweetrolls! You need to keep your figure even once you leave that hiking service. You know I can't abide a policeman or a sheriff who's got one of those pot-bellies!"

Eric threw his head back and laughed. "Isabel, I don't think you need to worry much."

"No, I don't think so, either," Ruth whispered.

"I know, but you can't let that boy know how good he looks," Isabel whispered back. "See you boys later!" she called and pulled the door closed.

Isabel and Ruth had a half hour drive to their church in Blairsville, so Ruth started up, but Eric knew that at the little church in Vansville, Natt made his delicious coffee for their Sunday school class and his wife, Marcy, had promised a batch of sweetrolls. Eric and Matt had eaten a hearty breakfast at Eric's table, but what two young men couldn't make room for some of the best sweetrolls in town, even if they didn't drink coffee? Life couldn't get much better than that! The twins left the parking lot as Ruth pulled the stick into drive.

Only a few minutes later, the twins walked up the steps to the little church and Roger met them at the top. "So, the brothers Thomas are with us today!"

Eric held out his hand and said, "That we are, Roger."

After shaking Eric's hand, Roger turned with his hand still out to Matt and said, "So, I guess you're here for the duration now?"

Matt took the pastor's hand and said, "Yes, I left Orlando yesterday morning, early. I'll start with Natt tomorrow."

"Good to see you! We're glad you're back." Roger turned back to Eric and said, "I guess Carolyn left for Atlanta?"

Eric's face immediately lost its smile. Anyone who knew Eric really well would know the smile he had on his face was only for show, it didn't really reach his eyes. He swallowed a sigh and said, "Yes, Lance had to leave for Alabama today to get back to his job tomorrow. She doesn't have a car and since it's a good ways for Lance, they had to leave at first light this morning to get her back and get the rest of the way to their place today."

Roger made a face. "I'm sure that was hard."

Eric nodded, then swallowed and whispered, "Yeah, it was. You probably have some clue about that yourself."

"You know it, man!"

Roger put his hand on Eric's shoulder and squeezed it. After a minute, he lifted his head and pulled in a deep breath, before he said, "I'd say Natt's got his coffee going already and I saw Marcy with a suspicious tin in her arms a bit ago."

"Yup. Her sister let me in on that yesterday when I brought my hikers back." He grinned at the young preacher. "That's why we got here before you rang the bell."

Roger chuckled and slapped Eric's back. "Well, don't let me keep you. Just bring 'em on back for the singing."

"Oh, we'll do that!"

"Singing?" Matt said, once they were inside the door. "You have singing for Sunday school? What gives?"

With a grin, Eric exclaimed, "Yep! Now that we've added Sunday school, Ramon and Sandy come here to church. The praise team doesn't do the worship for church anymore. Once they started coming regularly, people asked for her, so Sandy plays for church. So the praise team wouldn't feel left out, they have a short song service before classes break up. I guess that hadn't started when you were here last?"

Matt shook his head and fell in step with his brother. "I remember we had Sunday school classes, but there wasn't any singing before hand."

Eric grinned. "Well, we're right uptown now!" Eric also sniffed. "Come on, let's get back to our room and get some of that good smelling stuff! I swear Natt must order gourmet coffee, not just your run-of-the-mill house brand."

Matt nodded. "I'm right behind you, Bro! Tea might be my beverage of choice, but that sure smells good."

Eric was almost through the door into their classroom when Matt tugged on his arm and asked, "Umm, what'd I miss? Carolyn? Who's Carolyn?"

Trying for a cheerful, nonchalance he really didn't feel, he took another step into the classroom. He took another step toward the small table with the coffeemaker with a carafe full of brown liquid and the large tin with delicious looking sweetrolls. He reached for a sweetroll and said, "She's Derek's daughter. She was kidnapped by some criminal from Atlanta back the last part of April. For some reason the criminal drove her all the way up here, but after she woke up she had amnesia. She had no idea who she was or where she was from until the other day when she saw her brother again.

"Now she remembers everything but the actual assault, which is good. I mean, when I found her, she was in really bad shape! I called the sheriff and he called the ambulance immediately. Isabel saw her in the hospital just after she woke up and saw a family resemblance between Derek and Carolyn, that's how they got together. Otherwise, who knows? She might have gone through life not knowing who she was or where she was from!"

Much too astute, but his twin after all Matt, followed his brother closely to the refreshment table and asked, "And what was so hard for you?"

"Well," Eric said, "I was the one who found her in those woods behind the cabins just after the criminal threw her out of the trunk..."

"Yes?"

Realizing finally that his brother wasn't going to let this go until he admitted the truth; reluctantly, Eric finally said, "Well, we, umm, tried not to, but we fell pretty hard for each other once she left the hospital. She lived with Derek all that time."

"So you love her?"

"Yes," Eric murmured, "with all my heart."

"But she went back to Atlanta today."

Eric nodded. "And probably won't be back any time soon. I mean, she has an apartment there. She's well educated and well known in her field, what is there here?"

"You could propose…"

Eric jerked around to stare at his brother. When the hot brew finally hit his hand, Eric jerked the carafe up and asked, "And keep her from a good job? I mean, she's well known!"

"Just a thought, Bro."

"Umm, yeah." Eric cleared his throat and set the carafe back on the hot plate. "Yeah, I'll have to give that some thought, but umm …" with that, he ran out of steam.

Matt reached for a cup and the carafe. His eyes twinkling, he asked, "Bro, I always thought you were sorta smart. Didn't you ever think of that?"

Eric cleared his throat. "Bro…"

Just then Ramon cleared his throat. "Hey, guys, singing's gonna start real soon."

"Yeah, we're on our way."

His eyes twinkling, he knew what the brothers were saying, Ramon added, "Just sayin'."

Ramon's young adult class had started a series studying the book of John. This was the Sunday for part of the third chapter, but the lesson included the sixteenth verse. Matt read along as Ramon read the passage aloud. However, the words of verses sixteen and seventeen seemed to be written in neon for him. His eyes read the words over and over.

"For God so loved the world that he gave his one and only Son, that whoever believes in him shall not perish but have eternal life. For God did not send his Son into the world to condemn the world, but to save the world through him."

Matt didn't hear much of Ramon's lesson, even though it was good and others, including Eric, were helped and strengthened in their faith, but Matt sat with his Bible open, still reading those verses. Eric's question about his roots came to his mind. A time long ago in his childhood flashed through his mind. His mom had read from a children's Bible story book before bedtime, as she always did, but she had brought her Bible with her. As they sat on the side of Eric's bed, Eric on one side and he on her other snuggled next to his mom, she had closed the story book but she'd opened the Bible. Eric had watched her turned pages she had a certain place in mind.

Matt remembered as if it was last evening. "Boys," she'd said, "we've read our story and it was a good story, but there's something I think you're both old enough to understand and it's here on this page." She put her finger down and pointed. "Do you see this word, it's 'world' and, this one, it's 'whoever'?" They'd both nodded, but Mom had continued, "Well, that whoever means you, Eric and you, Matt." He remembered Mom hugged them both.

She'd looked at Eric, then him and said, "God loved both of you so much, so very much, that He sent His only Son to die on that awful cross to take away your sins. You know what I'm talking about, all those things, all that mischief you get yourselves into that Daddy and I get after you for. You both need to ask Jesus, God's Son, to take away all your sin and to make your hearts clean and new." His eyes closed, he could see the three of them, the Bible on Mom's lap and her arms around them. She'd pointed out the words then put her arm back around Eric.

Tears came to Matt's eyes as he sat on that hard wooden chair in that portable classroom, behind the little church in the tiny town of Vansville, Georgia. His index finger rested on that verse and a tear dripped onto his finger. He blinked and swallowed hard to keep any more tears from falling, but another leaked out. He pushed his thumb and index finger into the corners of his eyes to keep more from falling. As a young boy he had asked Jesus to come into his heart that evening, but between then and now, he'd turned his back. He knew it wasn't God who'd turned away from him, but he'd turned his back on God and left his roots behind. All these years he'd blamed it on Emilyn, but he'd been the one who turned away. Even while Ramon still talked Matt closed his eyes and pulled in a deep breath.

Before the church bell rang for the church service Matt spoke in his heart as another sinner had once said, *God, be merciful to me, a sinner.* As Jesus said in that scripture about that sinner, Matt left the class for the church service justified. Now he could sing the songs and truly his heart was happy as it hadn't been for a long time. As Ramon greeted him on the way out of the classroom, Matt gave him a genuine smile. His heart finally felt right.

"Glad you came, Matt," Ramon said. "Glad you're back in town. I'll look for you next week, even if Eric isn't here."

"Thanks, I'm glad I came, too." Matt knew Ramon was just being friendly and greeted him as the teacher, but Matt had a different reason for being glad. He was finally right with God. Maybe when he walked back outside there'd be a silver lining on the clouds.

Much to Matt's surprise, Eric sat beside Derek during church. Matt felt a bit strange, he didn't know the man except by sight. However, the older man was very friendly and shook Matt's hand before the service. "Howdy, there, Matt. Could tell you're Eric's brother, but he told us last night you're his twin. You're not here visiting, are you?"

Matt took his hand back and sat down in the chair beside Eric. "No, sir, I'll be starting at the hardware store with our cousin Natt tomorrow."

Derek looked over to the spot where Brad and Joyce usually sat and said, "Ah, that's right. Brad's had that really bad stroke. I see Joyce isn't here, even today."

As another person scooted in beside him, Matt said, "Yes, we don't expect he'll ever come back to the store."

"That's too bad. I guess it was his life for many years."

"Yes, it was."

Sunday morning it was a church bell ringing down the block that woke Emilyn. She looked at the digits on her clock, put her head back on the pillow and closed her eyes. "I'll get up in a few minutes," she whispered. "I promise I will. I know I got laundry to do."

Emilyn had never held much stock in going to church. Her parents never went to church, not even on Christmas or Easter, so she never thought it was important. Her dad wouldn't, not being an alcoholic and her mom only had work clothes, nothing fancy for some high-falutin church. She'd never known either set of grandparents, so she didn't know if they went to church or not. They'd lived far away and had died while she was still very young.

None of her aunts or uncles lived close by, so no one from her family or any neighbors had taken her to church as a child. She'd watched several on her street walk by or get into their cars all dressed up on Sunday and she'd heard church bells ring, but it never meant anything much to her. Besides, if your dad's an alcoholic and your mom has to work sun up to sun down just to keep food on the table, what's so important about church? It was just another day to sleep in and keep her and her brothers out of mischief.

The first time anyone mentioned that going to church was important was when Matt Thomas showed an interest in her when they were in high school. He'd talked about how important going to church was and tried several times to get her to go with him, but she always put him off. After all, Sunday wasn't a day they spent in classes together, so he'd have to make a special trip to collect her to go to his church. Since her mom worked so much, she relied on Emi to keep the house clean and what food they had for meals cooked. Mostly Sunday was the day to do those chores. Even after she was married that's how she occupied her time. After Matt left for church she'd clean the apartment.

Something he called 'salvation' he said was super important. She always wondered how you got 'salvation' in some building. Didn't a lifeguard 'save' somebody drowning in a lake? Or a fireman 'saved' somebody from a burning building. Maybe that wasn't it. However, she couldn't work up her own interest to match his. After they were married that was one thing they quarreled about. As their marriage went on, the list grew. Finally, he'd told her he had a new job in another state and she wasn't welcome to come with him. As he threw his set of keys for their apartment at her, she'd been devastated.

After the church bell stopped she fell back to sleep, another nap couldn't hurt. The chime on her phone, indicating a text, finally woke her. She looked at her clock and realized she'd slept another hour. She sighed, knowing she should be up anyway and swung her feet off the bed and sat up. Pushing the hair from her face and scrubbing her eyes to get them to focus, she finally felt awake enough to read the message.

She activated the screen and read; *So, did you get the time off?*

I asked for it, but old Barney, well, being the ornery man that he is, said he'd let me know today if I could have the weekend.

So take off!

Alli, I'm a working girl. I'm single. I need the job until I get something else.

Yeah, yeah, let me know!

I will soon as I know.

Good to know, see you!

Emilyn rushed into her bathroom, took a quick shower then started her washer. She needed a clean uniform today. She knew if Barney gave her a four day weekend, she'd be working every day through Thursday, so it was essential to get her uniforms all washed and dried today. That was one thing she had to give Barney. He ran a tight ship. You didn't stay on at the diner if you were late consistently and your uniforms couldn't show dirt or be wrinkled. The pay wasn't all that great, but it was a good job and her tips kept her going. She guessed she'd live with that a while longer until something better came along.

Would a job with Jack and Alli in Vansville be better? Those two thought so and maybe they were right. Usually, a waitress made minimum wage and her tips filled in most of what she needed. What could she think she'd make at a restaurant in some little Podunk? So it would be the only eating place in town! Her teeth smashed down on her bottom lip. It was the same town where her Ex now lived!

She dressed, combed out her hair, filled her washer and started the machine, then worked her way into the kitchen for that good cup of coffee. She'd remembered to stop for groceries, so she had some decent muffins and a bunch of bananas to have for a much more wholesome breakfast than that stale donut she'd had the other day. As the washer chugged in the bathroom, she ate and checked through her messages. She sighed, she had so many friends she didn't have any messages she hadn't read or responded to. How many friends could you have when you always worked the afternoon shift and worked five days a week?

Later, Emilyn walked in the door at the diner for her afternoon shift and as she pushed her keys into the right pocket of her slacks, she looked at the message board straight ahead where Barney posted the schedule. Yesterday, the schedule that was there was disgustingly grease stained, but Emilyn could see this was the new one. Still pulling her hand from her pocket, she took a closer look. She nearly ripped her pocket, pulling her hand out, but didn't, of course, but she had to wrap her arms around herself to keep from rushing over to the man at the grill to hug him. He'd given her the four days she'd asked for!

"Barney!" she exclaimed, "You gave me the four day weekend! Oh, man! Thanks so much! That is so cool!"

"Yeah, yeah," he said, nonchalantly, as he flipped a burger on the grill. "Nobody else asked for nothin' so what the…"

Before she started work she rushed into the break room and pulled out her phone. *Alli, Barney gave me the four day!* she texted.

Great! came back immediately. *How about we pick you up, real early, say eight o'clock Friday morning. It'll take a while to get there. After all, it's quite a ways north of Atlanta.*

OK, but can I sleep in the car?

Sure, if you must.

I don't get off until midnight and then I have to drive home. I don't fall into bed until one or so, but I'll be ready.

Super! See you, we'll take a tour.

Barney walked in the break room just then, so Emilyn typed quickly, *Great! I'll see you then. Gotta go!*

"So what's the four day for?" Barney slouched into a chair and asked, barely letting Emilyn shut off her phone.

Emi slid the phone back in her pocket and pulled out her ponytail elastic. She turned her back on Barney and looked in the mirror to get her ponytail right. Barney nearly always watched her until she put her hair up. You'd think she only started working here! As she put her hair up, she said, "Barney, I'm going out of town with some friends." She wouldn't tell him it was possibly another job. "We're going north to the mountains, so it'll take most of the day to get there. As if it's any of your business anyway!"

Squinting at her and putting his fingers together under his chin, he said, "You'd better come back, Woman!"

"I will, Barney, I promise." *Even if it's only to quit.*

The older man slid his feet out in front of him, like he planned to settle in and said, "I'm a bit leery, you're too happy about that four day."

Pulling in a long breath then letting it out, she exclaimed, "Barney, I haven't had a vacation in months. Here it is summer and I'm still stuck here. I go from my apartment here to work day after day. You rarely give two days off together. Why shouldn't I be excited about four days in a row off? Come on, give me a break! And going out of town… I do have some friends, you know."

"Yeah, okay, just be sure it's only four days! I 'spect you back on Tuesday at four. You're on the schedule, so no sloughing off!"

"Don't worry!"

"Yeah, yeah, get on out there and do your job."

Emi sighed and looked at the clock. "Barney, there's still five minutes before shift change. I'm on my way to get an apron then I'm on. You'd think I was the only one who worked here, you know."

Barney muttered, "Achally, I sometimes wonder even about you. That Harry critter got his hands all over you! Makes a guy wonder."

"Humph!" Emi grunted and left the break room. Barney was right behind her, obviously he'd only wanted to check up on her and torment her. The nerve of the man! Thinking just because Harry put his hands on her that she was leaving her job! "Barney, in case you don't know, I can't stand that Harry! He is no friend of mine. I try my best to keep away from him, but you gotta step close to put his plate down. He always makes sure he's at my table."

"Makes a body wonder." There was that last word thing again!

"Seriously? Give me a break!"

"Yep, seriously."

After the service, Eric and Matt greeted Ramon and Sandy. "So, you bachelors have a place to go for dinner?" Ramon asked.

Eric chuckled. "As a matter of fact, Isabel invited us to help her out of some of her roast. I warned her, but she said she had enough to feed both of us and them."

Sandy grinned at the twins. "I pity the poor ladies! You, I know how much you eat, him, he's a loose cannon."

Matt looked at Sandy and scowled. "Now wait a minute! I can curb myself!"

Skeptically, Sandy said, with a smile, "Well, I hope so, for their sakes. They're nice ladies and all, but they still must stay on a budget."

"Besides, I'll have to eat and run, I didn't buy groceries in Blairsville on my way here, so I must go back this afternoon. With Alex's store closed and all...."

"Didn't buy groceries!" Sandy looked at the young man, horrified. "You were here in February, how could you forget that soon?"

"Hey, Bro never told me Alex closed down the day *after* a holiday! Besides, while I was here that month I stayed with Aunt Joyce, so I didn't have to feed myself. Even if she wasn't there, she always had stuff in the fridge."

"Well, we don't keep up with that entertainment capital of Florida. We're a little town." Ramon nodded. "Yeah, I guess I did forget you stayed with Joyce." He grinned at the young man. "So why not live there now? With Brad in the hospital surely she could use the company."

Matt rolled his eyes, shivered and grumbled, "That woman can be tolerated for short periods, maybe five minutes long. I was about to climb the walls in just a week back then. I wasn't sure if I was sane or loony and I could only get away when I went to the store. Now I'm gonna live here, please, spare me from her constant chatter."

Ramon shrugged. "Just a thought."

As the twins left the church, with Ramon's family behind them, he said to Eric, "Have a good day off. See you tomorrow."

"Yep, bright and early, man! Need some of Sandy's coffee to get going. Didn't you say this group doesn't have one of those built in 'lady that cooks over an open fire'?"

Ramon nodded. "Unless things have changed from last year, that's the way it is. You remember you have a guide-in-training tomorrow?"

"Yep! I'll get him broke in good," Eric said, chuckling. "I had a lot of practice overseas bringing those greenies up to par."

Ramon nodded, chuckling. "Yup, you do that!" He patted him on the shoulder. "I'd expect nothing less from an ex-Marine."

The little boy sitting on his mama's legs grinned and waved, "Bye, Ick!" Clapping his hands together, he said, "Daddy got dogs!"

Eric chuckled. "Oh, good! See you, little guy!"

"Uh, huh!"

As the twins sauntered down the walk toward their cabins, Eric said, "Say, Bro, you'll have plenty of time to change clothes before Isabel and Ruth get home. When you're changed come on over to my place, I got another jug of tea we can start on. Surely all that chatter you did there at the end, you're dried out."

"Will do, sounds good." Watching the little family going to the blue van, Matt said, "That little guy is precious! He calls you 'Ick'?"

His eyes twinkling, Eric quickly agreed, "Yup! I remember the first time he did that. Sandy said my name and before I could answer Jon piped up with 'Ick'. Sandy tried to correct him, but 'Ick' has stuck. I figure one day he'll get it, but for now I don't mind."

Matt chuckled. "I think it's precious! How old is he?"

"About sixteen months. He's sharp as a tack! He's nearly potty trained and he's been walking since before his birthday." He shook his head. "How Sandy can do that I don't know and Ramon is gone most all week every week. It's amazing!"

Matt nodded. "I agree. I wondered about that last night."

"Neither of his parents went to college, but they are both very intelligent, so I'm sure Jon's come by it naturally."

Around the dinner table, Isabel looked at Matt and said, "So, you're his twin. Did you go in the Marines, too?"

"No, ma'am, I never was in the service. I took a job right out of high school for a couple of years and then moved to Orlando to an amusement park. I worked up a bit over the years there, so I could leave on pretty short notice." Matt felt inferior enough just being the younger twin without telling anyone he hadn't gone to college or that he'd married a girl when he was too young to act like a responsible adult then divorced her when the going got a little rough for his liking. Some older people really frowned on divorce. He was glad his brother didn't inform her.

Isabel smiled and said, "Well, Sonny, I guess Natt needs your help there at his store. I guess old Brad's not up to it. I'm sure you'll give him a good job."

"I hope to, Mrs. Isaacson."

"Sonny, I'm Isabel to all my friends and I haven't met a soul who isn't a friend." She shook her finger at him. "Now don't you forget that!"

"Yes, Ma'am!"

As Ruth cleared the table, Isabel said, "Now, Sonny, if you must go to Blairsville get on down the road."

"I will, Isabel. In fact, Eric's going with me so I can find where I'm going faster. He informed me that if he goes we must be back in time for church tonight."

"Of course! That's a given, Sonny."

Going out the door behind his brother, Eric said, "Thanks for dinner, Isabel!" He chuckled. "Hope you ladies had enough of that roast. It was really good. Oh, and by the way, in case you forgot, we have an evening service here you wouldn't have to go back to Blairsville."

"Yes, I'm sure glad you saved a little for me and Ruth." She gave Eric one of her glares, but didn't answer the last half of his speech.

"Why, Isabel! Of course!" He turned back and winked at the old lady. "We're authentic southern gentlemen, you know." As if he needed to think about it, he cocked his head and said, "Hmm, don't I remember Ruth cut yours and her pieces first?"

"Humph! Never mind!" Isabel groused. Moving her hand, shooing the twins out the door, she called after them, "Southern gentlemen, I'm sure!"

"Well, we are, Isabel!" Eric answered through her door. "Mama always taught us..."

As Emilyn drove home that night from work her thoughts moved to what would happen on her four day weekend. She was going away. She'd be gone from this place! She'd get to spend those days with her good friends, Jack and Alli, she should be excited. Well, of course she was, but there was one major down side and that was a major problem which took away all the excitement. She was going to Vansville.

She guessed going to Vansville wasn't really the problem, she'd never been to the place before, never heard about it until only a few days ago. But now that her ex-husband lived and worked there, that was a major problem. How did it happen that the man she wanted most NOT to see now lived in the same place where she was going about a job?

She hadn't seen the man in over ten years, not since they'd appeared before the judge about the divorce all those years ago. She'd walked out of that courtroom a devastated woman. Actually, she'd *run* from the courtroom, she didn't want anyone, especially Matt to see her tears that had been scratching behind her eyes the whole time they'd been before the judge. She ran in the closest restroom and into the closest stall. As soon as she locked the door, she grabbed a handful of tissue to blot her eyes and blow her nose.

She'd barely looked at him when the judge's gavel had hit the desk. She didn't remember what expressions he'd had on his face, but she knew she'd been on the verge of tears for the whole time they'd faced the judge. So many times during those weeks she'd tried to think what she could have done to save her marriage and keep her husband. Several times she'd wondered how he could have afforded the lawyer for the divorce. When they'd been together they'd never had any extra money.

She remembered, she'd glanced over at Matt several times, but he seemed to work really hard at not looking at her, at least not when she was looking at him. He had never made eye contact with her the entire time they'd been in the same room. It made her wonder why over the years he'd kept her informed about a promotion or a change in jobs. If he'd wanted her out of his life, why had he kept in touch? She surely hadn't asked him to or kept him informed on what she was doing. Not that things in her life had changed much. She still worked at Barney's

As she turned onto the street where her apartment complex was, she murmured, "Surely the hardware store is on one side of town and the eatery will be on the opposite side! I don't want to see that man. Really, I don't!"

Another thought surfaced. Once the eatery opened she'd have to live somewhere. Were there apartments? "Oh, man! Surely I'll find a place that's not close to where Matt lives."

She turned onto the parking lot for her apartment complex. Most of the parking lot was dark with only one streetlight for the parking lot. The other residents knew she worked second shift, so they usually left a spot under the one streetlight for her, but tonight there was a car she'd never seen before in that spot. She sighed, scanned the lot and finally pulled into a dark spot much further away from the door. Even though it was after midnight she wasn't afraid to walk from her car to the main door, but she would hurry.

As she turned off the key an unwelcome thought crowded her mind. "Oh, no! Alli said this eatery we're opening will be the only one in town.

The place can't be very big if that's so." *So much for keeping away from Matt Thomas!*

Emilyn slowly turned off her car, but quickly grabbed her purse, left the vehicle and ran across the dark parking lot. The light behind the glass door into the hallway was a beacon and she made tracks to get to it. Inside the door, fatigue took over as she climbed the stairs to her apartment. If she were going to stay in this city and keep working at Barney's maybe she should get an apartment closer to work. A fifteen minute drive at midnight was a bit long. If the city kept tearing up roads along her route, making it longer, it was a must.

After a full eight hour shift, these thoughts were just too much to think about. She unlocked her door and sighed as she walked through. She'd worked hard and had hardly a break except her supper break, so she was tired. She wished she wasn't so tired she'd like to take a shower and get rid of the greasy smell she always brought home from the diner. She sighed again. It just wasn't happening.

At twelve thirty in the morning, she closed the door quietly, locked her door and threw the deadbolt, let her purse slide from her shoulder onto her hall table and let her keys drizzle from her hand. They had a spot to hang, but her arm didn't want to move to the hook. It had been a dismal, rainy day and it had only been the regulars who had braved the showers. She made her way to her bedroom and slumped onto her bed. Maybe in the morning over a good cup of coffee things would look brighter. She could only hope. Maybe even the sun would shine, that would help. However, as a single girl, she knew Murphy's Law was alive and well, usually every day in her home town.

Bright and early Monday morning, the day after Fourth of July weekend, Eric and Jerry arrived at the DeLord's house early for breakfast. All the guides knew the routine; Sandy always fed the guides going out the morning before their hiking group arrived. They would eat then print out their hike's itinerary. Unless the group had an extra-ordinary cook who knew how to cook over an open fire, that breakfast was the last good meal they had until their hike was over. Everyone knows those dehydrated packets that hikers stuff in their backpacks that are reconstituted with filtered creek water give a body nourishment and perhaps fill a hollow place, but not much else, certainly not eye appeal.

This was Jerry's last hike as an in-training guide and he couldn't hide his excitement as he left his apartment in Blairsville. He'd been out with Ramon and had learned a lot, but this hike he was going with Eric. Ramon was the owner of the outfit, but Eric was an ex-Marine. In a few short weeks he'd be a deputy sheriff. It made Jerry wonder how differently they approached their jobs of leading a group of people on a hike. After this hike he'd lead his own hikes and he couldn't help but be excited. Eric would be leaving the hiking service soon to take up his new job as deputy sheriff on August first. Jerry was excited to start leading his own hikes, but at the front door he met a very somber Eric.

Eric had to admit he'd had a hard time falling asleep and that was because he missed Carolyn Casbah more than he'd ever expected to miss someone. Of course, Eric knew he'd never been in love before and after spending a long evening with her, then waved goodbye to her Saturday, he knew beyond any doubt that Carolyn was the joy of his life. Neither of them knew what lay in Carolyn's future, they just expected that whatever it was lay in Atlanta. They already knew that Eric's future was meant to be in Vansville as a deputy sheriff.

Eric and Jerry arrived at DeLord's, close to seven. It had to be early, the hikes left at eight o'clock. After Sandy called them in, they plopped down at the dining room table, because Sandy needed all the room she could have to wheel around the kitchen fixing breakfast for the men and Ramon. Ramon was in the little bedroom helping his son get dressed. Jon wanted to be independent, but daddy found it necessary to be handy when Jon tried to dress. After all, he was still only sixteen months old. Shoes were the hardest thing not to put on the wrong feet!

While the two men sat in the dining room, they heard a door open down the hall and Jon's unmistakable toddler walk came on the hallway floor. Momentarily a grinning little boy toddled down the hall ahead of his daddy into the dining room and announced happily, "Ick!"

Ramon went on to the kitchen to help Sandy, but Jerry chuckled at the child. "That child is precious!" Jerry said under his breath.

However, Eric said, "Hi, there fella, how's my best bud?"

"I good! AntiCAR go 'way," he said and his face turned sad.

"Yes, I know," Eric sighed.

Jon patted Eric's arm. "AntiCAR be back."

"Yes, she'll come to visit, I know. She loves your Japa, she'll come back to see him, I know, so we'll see her."

Shaking his head emphatically, he said, "Na-huh, soon."

Eric didn't argue. "Soon?"

"Uh-huh. Soon, Ick, you see."

"Okay, if you say so."

"Uh-huh, soon!" Jon said, emphatically.

Still waiting for the DeLord's to bring breakfast, he wondered if this little child and his mama had the inside track straight to the Throne. Saturday Sandy had told him that Carolyn would be back and when Eric agreed but only to visit, she'd told him that God had a plan and he needed to grow his faith so it was at least as big as a grain of mustard. Today Jon disagreed with him and said Carolyn would be back soon. What did they know that he didn't? As he sat there holding little Jon on one knee he realized he hadn't even prayed about his and Carolyn's situation. Was that part of 'growing his faith'? He felt silently chastised, prayer was a very important part of his life and he hadn't even mentioned Carolyn in his prayers!

All he knew was that Carolyn had been replaced at her job in Atlanta. That establishment had informed her brother of that some time ago and her landlord had also informed him that her rent hadn't been paid in the same length of time. Those two things had caused him to try to locate his sister. In the process, he'd found his dad that he had been estranged from for over a dozen years. They had spent a very restorative weekend over the holiday.

However, Eric was sure there were many more prospects that she could pursue in that big city than in the small city of Blairsville. Vansville was a tiny town in a rural setting, there would be nothing for her here. She was well known in her field in several states. Also, because her brother had paid her rent, she had an apartment there, but no car. Yesterday when she left Vansville, she knew who she was, but she had no identification and would have to spend time getting those identification cards replaced.

All of those problems could be laid at the feet of the criminal who had finally been caught and now sat in jail awaiting trial, not only for what he'd done to Carolyn, but to another young woman who had died and he was charged with her murder. Now that Carolyn had regained her memory, the authorities were sure the criminal could be put away for life in prison without parole. However, Eric was dismal, knowing she'd probably never be back to live in Vansville, unless, of course, Sandy and Jon were right.

As soon as Sandy and Ramon brought all the food to the table and Ramon said the blessing, the men ate then took their refilled coffee mugs to the office. The office opened onto the parking lot where the hikers parked, they didn't have to come in the house that way. Usually, there wasn't much time for the guides to sit around and chat. Eric sat down with Jerry and the two of them went over the route they would take and where they'd stop for lunch and the night. There were other things that both Ramon and Eric wanted Jerry to know.

Not long after Ramon had printed out the hike itineraries for himself and Eric, the two groups of hikers arrived. It was the car doors slamming on the parking lot that alerted them that their hikers had arrived. Eric and Jerry's group left first, but only moments later Ramon shouldered his huge backpack, kissed his wife and hugged his little son. His group had enjoyed one of Ramon's hikes last year, so it was only minutes behind the first group. All the hikers and their guides were glad it was a lovely day.

As the hikers left, Jon stood on Sandy footrest in the doorway and waved as everyone left the parking lot on the trails. That was the routine, Jon loved watching the hikers leave and called out to them. Even new hikers loved the little boy. There was never an unhappy group that left Ramon's parking lot, Jon saw to that.

The house was quiet with Ramon gone. Sandy usually saved several projects because of that. Some of those were in the office, but many more were not. Usually she had a painting for her gallery in Philadelphia or a commissioned painting she was working on. Many of those required a trip out in the country. She and Jon did many things together and Sandy knew she'd get lots of her work done before Ramon got home on Friday. Sandy made sure Ramon's hikes were no longer than five days and only during the week, so he could be home on the weekends. The other hikes could be longer or shorter and could start any day of the week. That was the understanding when they took the guide job.

Matt had taken his brother and gone to Blairsville after Sunday dinner with Isabel and Ruth, so his cupboards were stocked with essentials for supper and breakfast fixings. Like his brother, he wasn't into much original cooking, so his freezer was stacked with frozen dinners. While he was in his bathroom Monday morning, he'd heard Eric's vehicle start up and leave the parking lot. Before eight o'clock, he fixed his breakfast and cleaned up his cabin, as only a bachelor would. The clock over the sink showed a few minutes before eight and he was ready to leave for his first day as a permanent store manager.

He looked outside his sturdy cabin and noticed the sun shining in a deep blue sky. The breeze had to be very slight, he couldn't see any of the trees moving. Because it was such a nice day, he decided to walk the few blocks to the Thomas Complex. In fact, he could see the store from a living room window. That would be a new experience, in Orlando he'd had to either use public transportation or drive his car to work. He smiled, he'd be saving gas, big time!

Of course, he had to wait for Natt to come with the key. Matt could walk, but Natt lived on the new street so he usually drove, rather than walk across people's property. Natt turned on the lot, saw his cousin and waved, but pulled into his usual spot, climbed from his car and turned toward the Laundromat to open it up. Especially over a long weekend he had to check all the fixtures and turn on the main valve for the water supply. Back during the winter he'd found out how important that was. A plumbing bill hadn't been in the budget. Checking through the Laundromat took several minutes.

After making sure all systems were go, Natt left the lights on in the Laundromat and pulled the door closed behind him. He'd obviously left the air-conditioning on, too. After all, it was July in Georgia, a place not known for cool weather in July. Even in the foothills of the Appalachians it could get very warm and humid. He walked across the parking lot grinning at his cousin. Holding the key to the hardware store in front of him, Natt said, "So, I need to make you some keys for this place."

Matt stepped back from the door and grinned at the man only a few years younger than he was. They surely hadn't come from the same part of the country, but he liked Natt, even though he hadn't known him well until only a few months ago. They weren't quite sure what their relationship was, Matt's uncle was Natt's granddad, so they'd decided on being cousins. Who really cared anyway?

"Yup, I'd say that's true if you want me to share in that all important project of opening up and closing down the place once in a while." He grinned at his cousin. "Of course, you wouldn't have to."

 Four

Natt chuckled. "That is one thing about this place I will gladly share with you! Grandad always remembered to open the store, but once he had that first stroke he never remembered to open the Laundromat or turn on the pumps."

Matt made a face and followed his cousin into the quiet store. "I hope to be more responsible than that! I mean, after all! I am not over seventy and I haven't had several strokes. From theme park maintenance to store manager is huge, but I'm on top of it!"

Natt chuckled and flipped several switches that were on the tiny spot between the door and the big front window. "Oh, Grandad was good for a story now and again, as he sat there by the cash register. When he wasn't doing that all important job of checking people out and counting out change, that is. I learned a lot about Vansville and his life here in the last couple of years. Got any of those up your sleeve? I mean, you did just come from an amusement park job surely people shared some of their fun times with you!"

Matt made a face at his younger cousin. "Not that I'd tell you, young fella! Some of my life I like to keep secret."

Natt nodded. "Just as I thought."

Natt's last sentence was nearly drowned out by the huge flatbed semi that down-shifted coming into town. Semi's often down-shifted coming into town, but moved quickly through, leaving only exhaust behind. However, this truck turned the two men's heads toward the street. Right behind the first semi was another flatbed and without another vehicle between, a pickup with a circulating light on top followed. The first semi carried a huge drainage pipe and the second had two large earth-movers. The pickup bed was loaded with smaller items. All three vehicles had the same company logo on the sides. None of them were heading for the open road.

Matt scowled as he looked at the road. Knowing that the buildings on Main Street were all quite close together, he asked, "What are they doing? Are they stopping here?" Watching the trucks slow down even more, he added, "It sure looks like they're stopping."

"Beats me! Usually when something like that comes into town it only downshifts, then heads out. These guys look like they're planning on stopping somewhere."

"That was my thought."

By now the men were inside the store, with the door closed and Matt said, "So turning on the gas pumps is the first order of business."

"Right. As you get that, I'll start the coffee. It takes a few minutes for that big urn to brew and usually our first customer wants a cup."

Matt made a face, as he headed for the switch for the gas pumps that was on the wall inside the utility room. "Yep, that's your department, Cous. I'll be glad to leave that in your capable hands. I remember when I came to cover your honeymoon I never got it right. Even Uncle Brad didn't drink much of my coffee and you know he's a coffee hound! I saw him make a face more than once after I'd fill his cup." Matt sighed, "I used your formula and everything, I followed it to the letter, but it didn't seem to click. My only saving grace was that it was a horrible month and not too many folks ventured out."

Natt chuckled, still heading for the utility room where the utility sink, the other supplies and the all important coffee grounds were. "Guess you never learned the right way to hold your mouth when you start the coffee around here. You know, of course, it's not just in the water and the grounds."

Matt scowled at his younger cousin. "Guess not." Then he grinned. "Guess I'll have to watch you do that some time. Is it something you do on the sly? Will I have to catch you when you're not thinking about it?"

Natt grinned. "Never know!"

After Natt hit the switches for the lights, Matt walked across the store to the back wall where the gas pump switch was and flipped it. It was far enough away it couldn't be confused or accidently flipped at the same time as the electric switches. He looked out the front windows and said, "We got our first customer, he's bright and early for a Monday morning. Glad I hit that switch, he's gonna fill up."

The water splashing in Natt's big urn in the sink covered Matt's comment, so he said, "Guess I'll plug this in and get on with those keys. Did those trucks head on out of town?"

"No, they were nearly stopped when they reached Alex's store. Of course, I can't see beyond that, there's too much of a curve, but I don't think they went on out of town. Say, you'll need to show me again how to open up the cash register. I remember it was a bit tricky and I've slept since I was here before."

"Okay." Looking out the big front window, Natt said, "Ah, I didn't realize we had a customer already. Ted always is an early bird. That man keeps so busy with his handyman business, I'm surprised he doesn't meet himself coming and going!"

"Oh, that's another thing – do you charge for your coffee or is it still donation?"

Natt shook his head. "No, I don't charge. People who come in and want a cup just hand over two quarters. In fact, somebody set a cup on that sideboard. People make change all the time. It's worked since that first cup went out."

Matt grinned. "I guess that's the joy of a small town."

"Yup. Still a bit cynical?"

"A left over from Orlando, I guess."

"Yeah, that entertainment capital of Florida could do that to you, I'm sure."

"I hear you on that! Of course, there are other things."

"Yeah, like putting a fast stop to all you've planned for your life."

"I guess you know about that. You didn't get to finish college."

"Nope and I sure didn't get to be that world traveled reporter I wanted to be, either. Of course, Marcy and I are sort of alike that way. She wanted to be a foreign missionary and her Rheumatic Fever put a stop to that. Sandy always says our plans aren't always what's best for us, lots of times we just barge ahead and don't think to listen to that still small voice. I guess she's right about that. Of course, I didn't know about that still, small voice for a long time, not until I'd been here for a while."

Matt nodded. "Life's like that, sometimes." Then he grinned. "I do know you did get to go abroad, both of you."

"True, but I wouldn't have met Marcy if things had turned out like I figured. She wouldn't have met me either if her plans had worked out."

Matt nodded as the register finally finished its 'wake-up' routine. "I wouldn't mind meeting some cute chick here in town. After all, I am thirty."

Natt chuckled at that. "Well, I wouldn't say you're quite over the hill yet, but you may need to wait on that chick for a while. I think the only single women in town could be your grandmother's age."

"Umm, yeah. I really don't think I'd qualify for the 'over the hill' club yet, thank you very much! Ms Isabel's feisty enough." He grinned at his cousin. "Now Ruth's a bit younger, but still…"

Natt laughed. "I think she's still a good bit beyond you. She's more Ted's age." Natt nodded toward the man coming toward the door from the gas pumps. As Ted made his way toward the door, Natt added in a whisper, "But we don't talk about that." He grinned, "Even though Ted's Isabel's handyman and does lots of work for her. When I lived in one of those cabins it was a bit comical to watch those two."

"You mean Ted and Ruth?" Matt exclaimed, Natt only had time to nod.

"Blows me away!"

The coffee urn was wheezing when Ted walked in from filling his pickup's tank. "Hey," he said, as he reached the counter and handed over his credit card for his gas purchase. "Got any idea what them earth movers are about to do? Had to wait for 'em to get on down the road 'fore I could turn in here." He looked out the big window and added, "But they sure were movin' slow and didn't leave town, I know that for a fact."

"Nope," Natt said, but let Matt do the credit card purchase, since he was closer to the counter. "Far as I know, there's been no gossip around the store. You're the town handyman; I figured you'd be the one to know."

"Not me!" He winked at Natt and said, "You know me, I try to keep a low profile when I do my jobs. That way, I don't get any of them ladies in a snit about me. I mean, I could get into a heap of trouble!"

Natt chuckled. "Yeah, I hear that."

Ted winked at the young man. "Really? You know about things like that?"

"I kinda have that happen around here sometimes. Only it's more men with their gossip than women around the coffeemaker. I guess it's something like those old time pot-bellied stove and checkers corner. Not that I witness any of that around here, of course, Vansville men are much too industrious for that!"

"Yep, I bet that's a fact!"

"Thanks young fella. You'd be Eric's brother right?" Matt nodded and handed Ted back his credit card. As he slid it back in his wallet he raised his nose and sniffed appreciatively. "You got any of that good smellin' coffee ready yet? I know you jes opened up, but I sure could use a good cuppa this early on a Monday morning."

"Ah, there, the light just came on. You'll get the first cup of the day, Ted." Natt held a Styrofoam cup under the spigot then handed it to Ted, who gave him two quarters. Natt grinned. "Man, can't get much fresher than that!" Obviously, Natt knew his customers, or Ted was a regular, because Ted liked his coffee black.

"Fine and dandy!" He raised his cup and took a swallow. "Hey, if ya hear what's goin' on with them earthmovers give me a shout!"

"I'll do that, Ted."

Thinking out loud for a minute, Ted said, "You know, the last time we had them big broozers in town we got that clinic over there by Isabel's, but it rained cats and dogs the day they brought them into town and them machines sat around nearly a week until the ground dried out. Alex said we got two inches of rain in that one storm that day!"

"Yeah, I remember that!" Natt exclaimed.

"But it's July!" Matt exclaimed.

Blowing across his cup then taking a sip, Ted said, "So? This ain't the Sahara, it's the foothills of the Appalachians we get rain in July, sometimes August when the hurricanes come off the ocean. Them things can put a wet blanket on this here town! Well, I'll see y'all again! As always you got the best coffee. Say, ya know, we sure could use an eatery around here!"

"Yeah," Matt said, "had to bum a couple meals off kind neighbors so I wouldn't starve until Alex opens up today."

Taking another swallow, Ted nodded. "I hear that, fella! Been there, doin' that last couple years. Well, I'll see y'all. As a matter of fact; I'm on my way to Alex's now. Since he was gone them three days I plum run outta stuff."

"Take 'er easy!" Natt said, to the closing door.

"Friendly fella," Matt said.

"Yup, he needs to be, people keep him hopping! He's busier than a cat on a hot tin roof. He has several people here in town he does odd jobs for. It's Monday, so I'm sure he's doing his errands early to get done before his first job. You'll see him regularly at Isabel's. He can think of things she needs done on a weekly basis."

"I'm glad somebody in town does that kind of thing. I know lots about repairs, but it's not something I get all tingly about."

"Really? Aw, shucks. Of course, I got a new house so I can't think of any repairs we'd need any time soon."

Matt answered his grin. "That's good to know."

Ted waved at the window before he stepped into his truck, then left and drove off the parking lot. However, since they didn't have any more customers, both Natt and Matt went to look out their front window to see if they could see the big semis and where they stopped. However, there was a moderate curve in the road right in front of Alex's store, so they couldn't see beyond that. If the trucks stopped in town, they'd have to wait for some other branch of Vansville's grapevine to come in and spread the word. As Natt had said, plenty of gossip got spread around his store when people came in for a cup of coffee and sat in the coffee drinker's nook, but he tried not to be the one to pass it on. He might have been a journalism major at the university, but gossip was not his thing to pass on.

Natt pulled the key ring from his pocket and headed to the back of the store where the key machine was. "Well," he said, "since we don't have a customer and we can't see what happened to the trucks, I guess the next best thing is making you some keys. Wouldn't wanna miss that golden opportunity."

Matt chuckled. "Sounds like a plan. As Eric so often reminds me, 'if somebody doesn't do it, it won't get done'."

Natt also chuckled. "You got that right! Say, I noticed he was a bit down and Carolyn Casbah wasn't here yesterday. What's up?"

"As I understand it, Carolyn's brother came looking for his dad, thinking he might know where his sister was. He'd found his dad on the internet. When he appeared at Derek's house, Carolyn's memory came back, so she knew where she needed to be. Her brother took her back to Atlanta yesterday. But you know Cupid! He'd shot his arrows into Eric's and Carolyn's hearts so they were bummed when she had to leave. Neither of them could see how she could stay around here for a job."

"Ah, I see what you mean. So what does she do?"

"Eric says the job she'd started in Atlanta was the director of aqua therapy at some prestigious medical center there. She's got a master's degree of some sort. That institution had pulled her away from the same type of position in Alabama. Still, he's pretty bummed about it."

"Wow! So that'll be that, I guess."

Matt shrugged. "Who knows? It sure does look that way." Matt chuckled. "Can't say as there'd be such a position here in Vansville any time soon."

"Blairsville, either, probably."

Since it was Monday and Alex's grocery store had been closed for three days, Ted's supply of TV dinners was sorely depleted, his favorites especially. Ted was also a bachelor, but he lived by himself in his own house and didn't have family in town or friends who would invite him over for meals. He sure wasn't new in town with empty cupboards for people to take pity on him, so he'd had to survive on the meals he fixed himself or kept in his freezer. He was definitely out of his favorite combinations.

From Thomas's Hardware, he drove down the street and parked in front of the grocery store. From there, he could see that the semis hadn't gone on through the village, but stopped at the far end. When he went in, Alex was leaning against his counter looking out the big window. "Hello, there, neighbor!" he called congenially.

Ted grabbed a cart and started toward the frozen section. "Hi, yourself! So'd you have a good weekend?"

"Yup, wife and I spent it with the kids from down in Atlanta. The weather was so good they talked us into goin' to the beach with them! Spent the whole weekend on the shore in some ritzy hotel. Can you imagine?"

"Yeah, you in a swimsuit? Leaves a bit to the imagination." Ted grinned at his friend. "Don't even see no tan…"

"Hey, look here…"

Ted chuckled at his friend's reaction. He knew how to get a rise out of Alex. After he filled his cart with several packaged meals and fresh fruit, he came up to the counter, and nodded, looking down the road. "Got any ideas about them semis? I know they had to stop close. Had to wait for 'em to get by before I could get gas. They sure was movin' slow."

Alex started ringing up Ted's groceries, shaking his head. "Not one clue! You're the town handyman, you don't know?"

"Hey, give me a break! I work real hard to keep a low profile when I'm doin' jobs. Isabel don't want no gossip around her place, she gets down-right hostile! Don't want any of 'em other biddies to get their dander up over me spreadin' gossip. Besides, I'm not the only one who does small jobs. Some guys do their own 'honeydo' jobs, but I'll work real hard to keep the ladies I got satisfied with my work."

"Well, yeah, I guess that's so. That Natt fella doesn't know either?"

"Nope, him and his cousin asked me. Couldn't tell 'em a thing."

Ted looked at the total, pulled out his money clip and peeled off several bills. As Alex made change, Ted said, "Say, you know, we could use an eatery around here. Natt's got good coffee down there in his nook and you keep your freezer stocked pretty well, but hey, ya both close up five o'clock. Could go with some sit-down restaurant food on occasion. Ya know?"

As he stuffed his money clip back in his pocket, he said, "I make a good wage with all my jobs, but with gas like it is, well, I gotta think twice about goin' someplace else ta eat."

"Yeah, that's true. Gotta go to Blairsville to do that. I hear those critters from the clinic were a bit put out last winter when they couldn't get outta town after it closed and they didn't have no food with them. Isabel put 'em up, but give 'em nothin' ta eat."

Ted nodded. "And us bachelors, we get kinda tired of this fare, too." He reached for the bags holding his groceries.

"I'm sure ya do." Alex grinned at his friend. "Ya could find ya a wife, ya know. 'Course, you buyin' them dinners helps me stay in business." A second later he added, "And lets me take a vacation on occasion."

"Yeah, yeah, I hear ya." Ted grinned at his friend. "Hey, don't hold your breath on that wife thing, I do alright by myself."

Ted grabbed up his plastic bags and Alex said, "Say, when I came in here I saw them flashers goin' on them semi's down there 'cross from DeLord's. Can't think Ramon called 'em. Know who owns that meadow?"

Ted had his hip on the door bar when he looked back. Alex shook his head. "No, not really. Last I heard was a couple years ago old Corky owned it, but I heard he wanted to sell that place. Didn't want the headache of keepin' it up, from what I heard. He don't got no way to keep it mowed, he says." Ted shrugged. "I guess he could get Roger to mow it for him, he's got that mowin' business, as I recall."

"So it could still be Corky's or not."

"Yep, you got that right."

Ted pushed on the door and said, "Well, since it's July, keep cool, old man. I'm on over to Isabel's in a bit, that other twin moved in yesterday, but she got a slow leak in number one I gotta look into."

Alex chuckled. "I got no problem keeping cool! You do the same."

"I'll do that." Ted waved before he stepped into his truck, then started up and drove to the cross street. After all, he needed to put his frozen dinners in the freezer. Since it gave him a better view, it took several minutes to cross the street, even though there was no traffic. By now, the trucks had pulled partly off the road and stopped by the meadow at the end of town.

"What are they about ta do?" Ted muttered. "Is somebody gonna build somethin' on that meadow? Man, it better not be no apartments! But, this place is gettin' built up!" He grinned and turned the wheel. "Still, it'll be a while before we're a booming metropolis! Wonder if Sandy would know what's goin' on across the street from her."

However, the three trucks went beyond Alex's store and stopped across the street from DeLords house, which was on the other end of town from Isabel's. Because the highway made a long curve in the center of town, she couldn't see beyond Alex's store. That meant that Natt and Matt also couldn't see if they'd stopped. The Thomas Complex was on the same side of the street as the grocery store, only a block closer to the east edge of town. All they could be sure about was that they were going mighty slow through town, much slower than any other long distance truckers went through Vansville.

However, Alex and Ted were right when they thought the trucks had stopped by the meadow. The trucks couldn't pull completely off the road because of the three foot drainage ditch between the side of the highway and an empty meadow that was significantly higher than the road. If the trucks had come a half hour earlier they might have caused a traffic jam in the little town of Vansville, because all the hikers' cars were turning into the DeLords parking lot right before eight. But since they were all in the woods now, that wasn't a problem and the cars traveling the highway were sparse enough they could move around the trucks without traffic monitors. Of course, all three trucks left their flashers on as soon as they stopped.

Ramon and the other guides always left the computer running in the office after printing out the itineraries for the hikes going out. Ever since she'd started as Ramon's receptionist, Sandy always spent the mornings in the office and after she cleaned up the kitchen she and Jon worked there for a few hours. It was Monday and she never worked in the office over the weekend if she could help it. She knew there were things to do; the office phone had rung several times over the weekend. She would have to answer those calls and do everything those calls required, as well as enter things into their computer program. She and Ramon had also discussed something over the weekend that she needed to do.

Since her mornings were usually filled with office work, she and Jon filled up the afternoons with errands or went for a drive and Sandy painted. It was not unusual to find Sandy's light blue van parked on some country road around the county and close by a lady in a wheelchair, with a little boy at her feet. She'd be sitting in front of an easel painting beautiful pictures. Her painting was something she loved to do and had for many years.

She did commissions for local people and because her fame was spreading, some of those commissions were going to people who weren't so very local. Even some of the hikers wanted paintings she'd done. She had never completely given up doing paintings for the gallery the library in Philadelphia kept for her. Her beautiful landscapes and still-lifes were very popular among the people of that big city. It was rare that she had a shipment ready to send off before they notified her that the gallery was out. That place had complained loudly and for the entire time she'd been unable to paint when she was hospitalized while she was pregnant.

Of course, two days a week Sandy taught piano to her many students. She was in such demand she couldn't do anything else those days. Twice a year her students hosted a concert in Roger's church. Everybody loved the children's playing. She loved every minute that she spent either painting or at the piano. Usually, about twice a year the town's people wanted her to give a concert, it was always well attended. One of those times was always a Christmas concert and she'd given a summer concert only a few weeks ago. Anyone new who came to town was in awe of Sandy DeLord and her many accomplishments. Of course, it went without saying the people of Vansville would be devastated if Sandy left them.

Jon was Sandy's constant companion he rarely let her out of his sight. The little boy played with his toys close to Sandy's footrest every morning, they were good company for each other. Sandy loved her tiny son he truly was a gift from God. When she'd left Philadelphia to come to Vansville to be Ramon's receptionist, the thought had never entered her mind that she would marry, but only a few months later Ramon changed that, shocking her totally when he told her how much he loved her. At the time she had been speechless by Ramon's confession. She finally realized that her mom's attitude about her chair had rubbed off on her.

Then because she was a paraplegic, they were convinced there wasn't even the remotest chance that she could get pregnant or carry a baby to term. There again, God had a big surprise for them! It had been a very hard time for her, but she rejoiced every minute, thanking God for his precious gift. Now they had Jon, who was the delight of their lives. However, because Sandy had such a hard time with that pregnancy, Ramon and Sandy determined not to have more children of their own. However, they would do the very best job they could to raise Jon to love Jesus. The little boy was only sixteen months old, but he was very smart.

Only a few minutes after Sandy and Jon came to the office Monday morning, Jon heard noise out on the street and ran as fast as his short legs would let him to the long window in the door that looked out on the parking lot. His eyes grew nearly as big as his face as he pointed out the window, but looked back at his mama and exclaimed, "Mama, wuk! Big tar-uck!"

Sandy turned on the motor of her chair and started toward the window. "I see, sweetheart! Wow! There are two big ones and one the size of Daddy's truck! The men look like they're really busy."

"Go see, Mama! Go see!"

"Yes, let's! I'm sure if we don't cross the street we won't be in the way of anything they're planning to do."

"Yea! Yea!"

Jon scrambled up onto Sandy's footrest then held up his hands for her to lift him onto her lap. This was his fastest mode of transportation, besides, he loved sitting on his mama's lap because she could move the chair quite fast and from that perch he could see lots more. Sandy lifted him up and situated him on her legs then she pushed the lever to send the wheelchair into its fastest forward mode. No one could accuse her of being a slow-poke!

Jon was so anxious to get outside he leaned over to reach the doorknob before Sandy arrived and nearly fell off her lap. She quickly circled his waist with her free hand and pulled him back. Soon they were going from the office onto the parking lot.

Just as they reached the halfway point of the asphalt they watched two men climb on the first flatbed and with a good deal of effort because it was so big and long, push the huge pipe off the side of the truck. It made an earsplitting noise as it crashed down onto the gravel, then rolled into the ditch. Involuntarily, Sandy let go of her motor lever.

Jon smacked his hands over his ears and yelled, "Mama, woud noise!"

"I should say!" She shook her head and continued across the parking lot.

One man still stood on the ground as Sandy reached the road. She raised her hand and called him, "Hey, what's going on? What's going in here?"

The man shrugged, as he started across the street. "I dun know! Got orders ta bring that pipe ta put down thar and then move dirt in this here place, then cover that thing up; so that's what them and me's gonna do.

Had ta put that pipe in first, 'course, then cover it up. We'll see what ya think when we get 'er done."

"Okay… You don't know what's going in there?"

The man lifted a shoulder and looked around at the men still standing on the flatbed. "Nope, me and them jest got orders from the boss to come put that drainage pipe in that thar ditch then move dirt in that thar meadow. We was to cover that pipe, then move dirt around. That's my job, what I get paid ta do, so I do it and don't ask no more questions."

Sandy shrugged and smiled. "Well, I guess that's what counts, actually. You do the job you get sent to do."

The man nodded and looked back at the site. "Yes, Ma'am, that's the way I look at it. It'll take most a the mornin', as I see it." He looked back at Sandy more closely, then at her motorized chair and said, "Cute kid you got there, Ma'am."

Before Sandy could answer, Jon pointed to his chest and exclaimed, "I Ja, wuv Mama!"

The man scowled. "*Your* kid?"

"Yes. My husband and I are blessed."

The man cleared his throat. "Yeah, I guess!"

Before he got himself into any more trouble with his words, he hurried across the street. After all, the middle of the highway wasn't a safe place to stand, even if it was a small town. Besides, he was getting paid to move dirt. A woman in a motor chair didn't keep him from moving dirt. Some kid sayin' he loved his mama wasn't some rare thing. He loved his mama, she'd made him biscuits and gravy just this morning and that was his favorite breakfast fare. He had a job to do he'd right better get on with it. Gawkers could stand around – or sit, but not him.

Sandy and Jon stayed and watched as one man stepped up onto the first earthmover and started up. The man who had talked with Sandy moved some long metal pieces from right under the flatbed to make a ramp. They scraped as they came out from under the flatbed and clattered loudly as he let them fall from his hands onto the roadbed and Jon again covered his ears. The men were making the loudest noises the town had heard in several years! The machine started beeping as it moved slowly down the ramp to the ground then headed for the ditch. Jon watched every move that went on; after all, he was an inquisitive little boy.

The two men who weren't running the earthmover went to the barbed wire fence around the meadow and cut it to make an opening right behind where the pipe was in the ditch. With his first swipe the machine operator made a gash in the bank. If what the man said was true there wouldn't be any quiet meadow across the street by this evening. Sandy was glad she'd painted the scene last fall when the colors were the best. Maybe she'd give whoever was putting something in the meadow that painting for a house-warming gift.

As the dozer started pushing dirt into the ditch to cover the pipe, Sandy said to Jon, "Well, Sweetheart, it looks like they can do their work without our help. Let's get back to our work in the office, shall we? I'm sure your toys are sad you went off and left them. I know they want you to come back and play."

"'K, Mama, go pway."

"That's great, Sweetheart!"

However, when Sandy was turned around, the other man started the other machine. It made more noise starting up than the first one did and let out a huge belch of exhaust that floated over DeLords' parking lot. Jon slapped his hands over his ears, but when the noise stopped, he jumped up and precariously turned around, then stood on Sandy's legs, putting his hands on her shoulders. She immediately released the control on her armrest so that her chair stopped moving. "Jon, Honey! You mustn't jump up and stand on Mama's legs like that! I can't see where we're going!"

Contritely, the little boy patted Sandy's cheek and said, "Sowy, Mama. Make noise! Big thing make noise!" His smile was angelic.

"I know, but Mama's got work to do inside. You can watch from the window and tell me what they're doing. Okay?"

"Oh, yahee, Mama!" Jon said, as he turned back around and plopped down on Sandy's legs. "Ja watch Mama."

Sandy smiled. "I'll hold you to that, young man!"

Solemnly, Jon answered, "Yes, Mama."

Sandy was almost positive that Jon wouldn't watch her, but he'd be fascinated by the huge earth movers and the noise they made. Sandy went inside and closed the door behind her. Jon was eager to get down. The closed door blocked out most of the noise outside, however, as Sandy moved to the desk, Jon stayed at the window in the door and watched everything going on across the street. Jon, his eyes shining, started up a constant chatter about the activity.

Sandy went back to listening to the messages on the answering machine then made some phone calls to set up more hikes for the slots left until October. There weren't many. Pretty soon she'd have all the slots filled and have to start turning hikers away until next season. So far none of the guides wanted to chance a winter hike and she couldn't blame them. A reflexive shiver went down her back. She couldn't imagine hiking in the cold all day and trying to sleep on the cold ground or even with snow on the ground. She was sure a canvas tent wouldn't give much protection from the cold and the elements that winter could throw at them. Yes, it was Georgia and they didn't get as much snow as Philadelphia, but it was the foothills of the Appalachians and it did get cold. An ice storm on a trail would be treacherous.

Jon watched through the window all morning and there was plenty of action to watch with both machines working that whole time. Soon the pipe in the ditch was covered with dirt that the machines ran over several times to pack down. Eventually, that would be a driveway from the road. The machines took lots of topsoil off a large part of the meadow and pushed into piles out of the way. Back from the road a good ways, they dug a much deeper hole.

Of course, Sandy learned all this from a sixteen-month-old perspective. That also included not only lots of chatter, but also plenty of animation. When there was something Jon found extremely interesting, he'd run across the office and tell his mama. Sandy was glad when it was lunch time and she could shut off her computer, but she loved the enthusiasm her little boy gave. He was a terrific boost to anyone's day.

From across the street, they couldn't really tell how deep that hole was and it was quite far from the street, but there was a huge mound of dirt in another part of what had been a lovely, peaceful meadow. Jon kept his mama informed in 'toddler talk' of each thing that happened. He exclaimed about the huge dirt piles and Sandy was truly glad he couldn't go play in all that dirt. However, he couldn't tell his mama anything else. No one came around to post a sign telling what would be built there.

When Sandy was finished with her work she shut down the computer and switched the business line to the answering machine, because she had a place in mind to go to paint that afternoon. She knew it would be perfect for painting, there was a gentle breeze to help cool the day and the sun shone brightly from a lovely blue sky. However, before they left the office, she also went to the window and looked out. There certainly wasn't any peaceful meadow across the road any more. All she could see were the piles of dirt and the dirt driveway. She and Jon watched as the men loaded the machines on the truck, then very carefully, used DeLords' parking lot to turn their big trucks around. It was a challenge, since there were so many cars in the lot. Again, the pick-up with its flashing light followed the big trucks back through town.

Even though she had hoped someone would come by and post a sign telling what would be built, none appeared. In fact, she wasn't even sure who owned the meadow. She knew Brad Thomas owned quite a bit of land on the east side of town, but she had no idea who owned that meadow. All she knew for sure was that the quiet place where she could hear birds sing was gone and great piles of ugly dirt now took up the place.

"Well," Sandy sighed, as she lifted Jon to her lap and watched as the first truck started down the street and the second truck pulled onto the parking lot to turn around. "I guess we'll wait until Wednesday when we go for groceries. Probably Alex'll know what's going in there. No one's come around to put up a sign. Now it's time for lunch and then Mama's got a place to go to paint for a while." They reached the bathroom and Sandy took Jon from her lap. She never missed an opportunity to let Jon use his potty chair. Using a potty chair and 'big boy pull-ups' were a whole lot easier than diapers and a changing table!

When he had finished, Jon pulled up his pull-up and said, "Go see Lennie an HiDEE afer lunch, Mama?"

Of course, Sandy had to fix Jon's haphazard attempt to get his pants up, but while she did, she said, "Not today, Sweetheart, maybe another day. The place Mama wants to paint isn't close to Lennie's house. Besides, tomorrow is Heidi's day for her piano lesson, you'll see Lennie then, you know. You can tell him all about your exiting morning while I give Heidi her lesson. Won't that be almost as good? You guys can even look out the window and see all the piles of dirt over there. Probably Heidi'll want to see too."

Jon let out a big sigh. "'K, Mama, I wait for 'mowow." Jon loved to go to the country to see his friend Lennie and his big sister, Heidi. Besides, today he had lots to tell his friend. Never mind that it would be mostly in 'toddler talk'.

Sandy and Jon got back home just in time to fix supper, but she had found a place to paint a beautiful picture. This one would go to her gallery in Philadelphia. Sandy never fixed too much for the night meal when it was just two of them. Since she could never exercise her body, except to move her upper body and Jon was so little, she saved the big meals to fix for Ramon when he was home. The man loved his wife's cooking and could put away plenty. After all, Ramon was a very active man, whether he was on a trail or moving around town.

After setting her wet picture in the place she reserved for her paintings, Sandy fixed two grilled cheese sandwiches for their supper. It was one of Jon's favorite meals, right after macaroni and cheese, of course. She also fixed another of Jon's favorites – chocolate pudding for dessert. The birds were chirping their nighttime songs when Sandy took Jon for his last trip to the potty chair. He was being very good there were hardly any accidents any more. That was something Sandy was very thankful for; it was hard for her to change Jon's diapers. Jon, however, took to the potty chair very willingly. He was very proud of being a 'big' boy.

After he was in his jammies, he climbed onto Sandy's lap so he could listen to his favorite Bible story. Sometimes, he even helped Mama tell the story. Before he left her lap, he threw his arms around Sandy's neck and kissed her then he climbed down and said his prayers beside his bed. Of course, tonight there were lots of things to talk to Jesus about. Number one was Daddy, because he was out on a trail. Of course, the inquisitive little boy talked to Jesus about the big hole across the road. He climbed onto his bed and as Sandy pulled the sheet over him, he gave his mama the best smile of the day. Of course, Sandy's heart turned over.

"Night, Mama," he whispered, sleepily.

Sandy cleared her throat. "Goodnight Honey, sleep well, see you in the morning."

"Yes, Mama." Jon turned over and was sound asleep before Sandy left the room. Still looking at her little boy, her heart thumped. Her little Jon had legs that worked perfectly, that carried him anywhere he wanted to go. She could only thank her Lord for that blessing, even though she knew her paralysis was not something he could inherit.

Quietly, she pulled the door almost closed, then right outside the door, she murmured, "Thank You, Lord for my darling little Jon. You gave me such a blessing in that child. I can't thank You enough for him! Bless him, I pray, may he grow up to be a wonderful Christian young man. Lord God, I also thank You so much, for my wonderful Christian husband, he is my jewel and I praise You for him."

Sandy went back to her studio. She had some finishing touches to do on the painting she'd done that afternoon. She would leave it in its place so that it would be dry by the next afternoon. While she worked with her hands in the quietness of the house, her mind went back several years to the time when she first came to Vansville. She'd come, wanting to be the receptionist for the hiking service. Her life had become so much fuller since then. In fact, it was almost hard to remember what life in Philadelphia had been like.

Tuesday, nothing happened across the street in what was once a quiet meadow. Sandy's students, along with a parent, came for a lesson and those people asked many questions, but there were no answers. Jon played with his toys, but went to the window often. When Raylyn brought Lennie and Heidi for Heidi's lesson, Lennie and Jon stood at the window and talked. Of course, Lennie was only a few months older than Jon, so the 'toddler talk' was rather intense.

However, everything was as it had been when the trucks left. Nothing at all happened all day on Tuesday and because of her many piano students Sandy decided that was a good thing. Trucks constantly coming and leaving across the street would have been a big distraction not only for Jon but also for her many pupils. Many times Jon had gone to a window, but no trucks appeared and no one came around to post a sign. Sandy wondered about that. If there was a building project, didn't whoever was doing the job have to post permits or something to tell the neighbors what was going on? Or was this too small a town to worry about that? Coming from the huge city of Philadelphia where everything had to have a permit, she could only speculate.

Sandy had finished a watercolor on her painting expedition Monday afternoon. Watercolors always dried quickly so after her work in the office Wednesday morning she boxed up a full shipment to send to Philadelphia. As soon as she and Jon finished lunch, she loaded the box into the van and put Jon in his car seat. On her way to Alex's store, she stopped at the post office to mail the huge box. The postmaster always knew when Sandy's van pulled up in front that he needed to go out to get the box for her. After it was safely on its way, Sandy went on to Alex's store.

The pair were some of Alex's favorite people. When they came in the store, Jon was sitting on Sandy's legs. He squealed, "All!"

Smiling broadly, Alex said, "Hi, there! How's my favorite little guy?"

"I good! See big tar-uck!"

"You saw a big truck? I saw them go by here, too!"

"Uh-huh!"

Sandy smiled at Alex and took a cart to fill. "Oh, he was fascinated by those trucks on Monday and all the work they did. We went outside to watch for a few minutes." She chuckled. "Believe me; I got a blow by blow documentary. What's going on? What's going in there?"

"I haven't a clue! I asked everybody who came in yesterday, but all I found out was that Corky owns that meadow."

Ruefully, Sandy said, "Mmm, what *used* to be a meadow."

Alex grinned. "Yes, there is that."

While they talked, Jon, who sat in the seat in the cart, looked out the front window in time to see three huge dump trucks go by the store. He patted her hand enthusiastically and pointed out the window. "Mama! Wuk! Tar-uck! Big tar-uck! More!"

Sandy glanced out the big window to see what could only be called a parade of trucks. "Well, I guess we'll see some more action when we get home. They have to be going to what used to be a meadow across from our place."

Alex nodded. "That you will, Sandy, I'm sure of that. Since it's right across the street from you I'm sure you'll get another blow by blow. Hey, if you find anything out let me know." He winked at her. "I hate being out of the loop, you know."

Sandy laughed. "I'll do what I can, Alex. I did go out and ask one of those men the other day, but they didn't know, either. They said all they got paid to do was move dirt. I agreed, but that didn't tell me much. Say, did you ask the guys down the block? After all, they have that 'coffee drinker's nook', you know how good that is for gossip. That ought to keep them in the loop." Sandy chuckled. "I've heard men gossip just as much as ladies."

Alex snapped his fingers. "Never thought of that. Good idea. Hey, take it easy, Sandy. I'll see you again."

Sandy put her tiny son on her lap and gave him a bag to hold then she loaded up her armrests and smiled at Alex. "I'll be sure to see you again, Alex."

Five

Both Sandy and Alex knew it was almost a forgone conclusion. Alex's store was the only grocery store in town. Since she had her own van, Sandy could go to Blairsville and she often did, but she'd rather spend her money locally. Besides, most everyone in town were friends and they all loved Sandy. She never let it bother her, but sometimes when she went to Blairsville, there were those who stared.

While she watched the dump trucks go by, Isabel held her portable phone in her hand and sat down in her chair to watch out the window. Those dump trucks were loaded, even above the sides, with gravel. She'd never been much of a gossip, but nobody could keep her from watching what went on in town from inside her house. She had just gotten comfortable when the phone rang. She activated the phone and said, "Hello, this is Isaacson's."

"Ma'am," the voice on the other end said, "This is Jack Albertson. I was told to contact you about a place to stay in town."

"Yes, sir. You called the right place. What can I do for you?" Isabel continued to watch out the window, but for now she couldn't see the trucks. Obviously, they were on their way to what used to be a meadow down the road.

"Ma'am, I need a place for three people for Friday, Saturday and Sunday nights."

"Is this a couple and a child?"

"No, Ma'am, it'll be my wife and I and a friend of ours."

"Well, you see, I have one bedroom cabins. These have a large sitting room with a kitchen area. There is a spacious bathroom and a walk-in closet. Would this friend want to rent another cabin?"

"No, not if there is any other possibility."

After a short hesitation, Isabel said, "Well, I suppose I could rent you my number one cabin. It's bigger than the others, it's handicapped equipped. I'm sure there would be space in there to put a cot."

"Yes, that would work just fine."

"All right, we'll do that. Oh, by the way, you need to bring any food with you or be prepared to purchase what you need at our store and Alex closes the store at five o'clock every night but Friday and he's closed on Sunday. He's only open that one evening. There is no restaurant or fast food place in Vansville. The closest place for something like that is Blairsville. Of course, there are several supermarkets in Blairsville also."

The man chuckled. "I'm aware of that, Ma'am. The three of us are coming to meet with the fella who will be building such a place and we'll be running it."

Isabel pulled a paper and pen closer and said, "Ah, I see. What did you say your name is again? I'll get you down right away."

"I'm Jack Albertson, Ma'am. Thank you so much."

"Yes, that's fine. About what time do you expect to arrive?"

"We're from south of Atlanta, so probably in the afternoon."

"Good, that's fine. I'll look for you."

"Your rate is quite reasonable, Ma'am, thank you."

"Yes, well, I'm glad to rent to you. Do be careful, it'll be a good bit of driving to come from south of Atlanta."

Jack was very used to driving, so he said, "Yes, Ma'am, we'll be fine, I'm sure. We look forward to meeting you, Ma'am."

"Yes, thank you for calling."

Isabel disconnected and put her information in the special place she kept reservations for her cabins. She grinned, she'd have that income and she'd use it to fill her propane tank. Before Sandy arrived back home her phone rang. Isabel wasn't afraid to speak to a machine, so when the beep sounded, she said, "I got some real important news. Call me." Isabel grinned mischievously as she disconnected and laid the phone down on the arm of her chair. Yup, she had some important news and probably nobody else in town knew it. She also knew that as soon as Sandy got home she'd be on the phone; she couldn't wait to tell her news! She was also sure Sandy wanted to hear it.

Only a short time after leaving the grocery store, Sandy had to stop on the street, she couldn't pull into her own parking lot. The dump trucks were using her lot to make their turns to dump their loads of gravel. First, they took up most of the roadway to make the first dump over the drainage pipe to make a driveway. After the first two loads, the third truck moved up the drive to dump on the large area where the topsoil had been removed. Of course, the first two trucks never left the street and cars had to wait for them to dump their loads. There were several cars, heading in both directions waiting in line.

From his car seat, Jon yelled, "Wuk, Mama! Wuk!"

"I see, Honey. They're making a driveway."

"Dwyway?"

"A driveway, so cars and trucks can drive on it."

"Oh, a dwyway."

"Yeah, that." Sandy couldn't work on pronunciation from the driver's seat. At that moment one of the trucks was coming dangerously close to the front of her van.

Finally, the first two trucks finished dumping their loads and drove away while the third truck made its turn and backed across the drainpipe. With the two trucks heading back toward Blairsville and the third off the street, the traffic could move, even so, Sandy had to wait for traffic coming into town to get out of her way so she could turn into her own driveway. Quickly, she turned around and backed toward her garage. There was just so much room on the parking lot. Most of it was taken up by all the cars that belonged to the hikers. As she pushed her garage door opener, the truck emptied his gravel and pulled toward her across the street.

Helpfully, Jon pointed and said, "Mama, big tar-uck come." He seemed a little agitated as the nose of the truck pulled onto the parking lot.

Sandy continued to back into the garage and said, "I know, but he won't come this far, Sweetheart. He's only coming to make the turn onto the street."

"Oh, 'K.," he said, dubiously.

Sandy shut off the van, then sat and watched the truck make his turn, then closed the garage door, loaded up again, let herself down on the lift and closed up the van. She headed into the house and in the kitchen noticed the red light on her answering machine. She unloaded her chair and put Jon on the floor. Quickly she put her frozen things in the freezer then hit the button for the machine, glad that the call was on their private line and not another call that came in for another hike.

Sandy grumbled once the short message finished. "Why's she so mysterious? Couldn't she tell me on the phone?"

Because of the activity with the trucks, Jon had wandered into the office and was watching all the activity intently. Soon after the last truck left their driveway another set of three trucks came with more gravel, so Jon was very occupied watching the trucks. Without his chatter, Sandy felt it was a good time to call her friend, so she picked up her phone, hit a number on her speed dial and listened to the first ring. When the older woman answered, Sandy said, "Isabel, what's so mysterious?"

Isabel chuckled. "I know something nobody else in town knows!" she answered, with a bit of a rhythm to her sentence.

"Okay, so spill it!"

Isabel waited just long enough that Sandy had her mouth open, when Isabel said, "I'm pretty sure that hole in the ground across from you will be an eatery."

"Oh? Who told you that?"

"Nobody." She could hear Sandy sigh, but before she could speak, Isabel said, "This guy, Jack somebody, called and wanted to book a room for the weekend…."

That woman can be so obtuse! "Isabel! Come on! I'm on pins and needles!"

Isabel chuckled, then after another short pause, said, "Well, it seems he, his wife and someone else are coming for all that time. Oh, they're meeting somebody to talk about putting some kind of eating place in here in town."

"Isabel," Sandy scolded, "was that so hard you had to draw it out so long?"

Isabel laughed. "It's fun to string you along!"

"So who is it your Jack person's meeting with?"

"He didn't say."

"Great!" Sandy grumbled. "Of course, you never asked him."

"Nope, didn't do that. Didn't think that was my business."

"Why, of course not!" Sandy huffed.

Sandy let out a long sigh. As if Isabel couldn't see the trucks going by her place, Sandy said, "By the way, there're dump trucks unloading tons of gravel across the street! They had the street tied up for a while, but they're using our parking lot to turn around. I had to leave Jon in the office so he can watch. I got a blow by blow all morning the other day from a year and a quarter perspective about all the dirt and the hole."

Isabel chuckled. "I bet that was interesting."

"Oh, it was, believe me." Chuckling, Sandy said, "I can't wait to get back out there to hear this new development from a sixteen month perspective! Oh, gotta run!"

"Sure enough! Hurry on down the hall!"

"I'm on it, Isabel!" After only a second, Sandy added, "Wow! It sounds like another bunch of trucks is on the job! Oh, absolutely! Jon is yelling and telling me to hurry."

Isabel chuckled again. "Well, be about it, girl. Can't miss out on that 'toddler talk', oh, and all that animation!"

Laughing, Sandy said, "Oh, that's the fascinating part!" Isabel laughed with her and they disconnected. Of course, Sandy was on the move. Jon stood in the doorway to the office, his little arms flailing, calling his mama to hurry.

Thursday morning Corky brought his wife to the grocery store to do her weekly shopping, then went on down the block to get a cup of coffee at the 'coffee drinker's nook'. Knowing he'd have plenty of time, Corky sat down in one of the chairs and stretched out his legs while he sipped his doctored coffee. Conversationally, he asked, "So, have ya seen them trucks comin' in town and all that?"

Since they didn't have any other customers, Natt came and sat in the nook, but Matt leaned against the register counter. Natt said, "Yeah, Corky, saw the semis come into town on Monday and the dump trucks yesterday. Got any idea what's going on?"

"Heard tell Ted complained to ya'all that we need an eatery in town," Corky said, but technically, didn't answer Natt's question.

"Yeah, that's what he said," Natt said, tentatively. "Actually, he came to buy gas and get a cuppa. It wasn't just to talk about a restaurant." Natt shrugged. "He did have to wait for those semis to go on by before he could turn in here, though. I guess he was in a bit of a hurry, he sort of complained about those trucks."

Holding up his cup of good coffee to his mouth, Corky said, "So you think we do?"

Matt came up beside his cousin and said, "Well, I wouldn't of had to rush back into Blairsville Sunday afternoon to buy stuff if there'd been a restaurant in town."

"Well, cain't help ya much about that, since Sunday's already a done deal, but someday soon you'll have your eatery. 'Course, bein's it's Vansville, it won't be open on Sunday. Nuthin else is, an ar church, is kinda 'posed, ya know."

"Well, Corky, that's good to know. So you'll build it, but whose gonna run it?"

"My cousin's son's been in the eatery business a long time. He's a comin' up ta take a look-see this weekend. We'll get it goin' after that." Corky shrugged his shoulders. "See, he knows what he wants, so we make it his way."

Corky had taken swallow after swallow and Natt kept track, so he said, "Good to know, Corky. Can I freshen your cup?"

Corky looked at the clock close by and said, "Naw, I'll haveta truck Loretta's groceries in a minute, cain't do that with a cup in my hand, ya know."

Natt chuckled. "No, I guess not. Well, thanks for stopping in, Corky. Get on with that 'honeydo' stuff."

The man chuckled. "I'll get right on that, Son. Thanks for the coffee. As usual, it was a right fine cup." Lifting the cup, he asked, "You use a special blend?"

"Thanks, Corky, but if I told you that I'd be telling secrets out of class, wouldn't I?" Natt said as Corky pushed on the door.

The older man grinned. "Yep, guess you would."

Still with the door open, Matt said, "Cous' says he holds his mouth a certain way to make his coffee taste like that."

As the door closed, the older man raised his hand and waved. He had to take a long step to get into his truck. Matt didn't think men that age liked souped up trucks like that. As the cousins watched, Matt said, "So, now we know what's going in down there!"

"Yup, and maybe Alex knows, too."

"True, if his wife is getting groceries." Of course, Matt didn't know Corky's wife.

Corky started his truck and left the parking lot. Both men stood and watched out the window. "Nice guy," Natt said. "He'd give you the shirt off his back."

Matt chuckled. "He had a real nice truck, but I wasn't too impressed with the shirt."

Natt grinned. "True, but you never know what these old guys here in town have socked away. Sometimes I wonder if some of them don't have their own personal bank buried somewhere out in their backyard."

Matt nodded. "Yeah, I'll give you that. I think some of these old codgers don't put much stock in banks."

"You got that right! Well, around here most of these guys think Derek's a good guy, so they use his bank and sometimes even listen to his advice."

Matt nodded. "That's good to know. With my millions I may have to open an account."

Natt chuckled. "You let me know when you come into those millions, will you?"

"Oh, sure, Cous'! I'll be right on that!"

A block away Alex greeted Loretta, "So, Ms Loretta, you running low on stuff to fill that man of yours up?"

"Yes, that I am, Alex."

Loretta took a cart and started filling it. Expectantly, Alex watched, but didn't follow her. Even if he wanted to talk, he never followed any of his customers. He never wanted to be accused of 'hounding his customers'. However, he was hoping she'd say something about the activity down at the edge of town and his store was small enough they could carry on a conversation from anywhere in the store.

After all, he knew it was her husband who owned the lot where all the activity had been going on for the last few days. Of course he knew most wives knew their husband's business before anybody else did. He was sure Loretta fit that bill, too. However, Loretta never said another word, just filled up her cart. She moved deliberately up and down the rows, consulting her list occasionally and of course heaving packages into her cart. Last of all, she directed her cart toward the cash register like she was a contestant in the Indy 500.

Alex, of course, knew how Loretta was, she was not one of the local gossips, but since it was her husband who owned the lot where all the activity was going on he hoped she'd at least say something about it. When Loretta reached the check-out, she started loading her things on the belt and Alex was nearly beside himself.

When Loretta still didn't say anything, Alex started ringing her groceries, but he said, "So, isn't it Corky who owns that meadow across from DeLords?"

"Yes, he does, Alex. He has for a long time. We thought at one time our Angela would want to build there, but that never happened. You know she's down in Atlanta working in that lawyer group place."

"Yep, I know that. Saw lots of trucks going down there last day or two."

"Probably did, Alex." Loretta watched the display from Alex's register and handed over the proper amount. "Thanks, Alex. You keep a good selection and I'm glad. Since you do, I don't have to make too many trips into Blairsville."

"Yes, Ma'am, I see Corky coming, so I guess he'll load up for you."

"That he will, Alex. You have a good day."

The door closed behind Loretta and her cart and Alex grumbled. "That woman can be as tight-lipped as a tongue-tied deaf-mute!"

As Corky started loading the truck with his wife's groceries outside, Alex noticed that Corky did most of the talking and Loretta hardly said a word. In fact, Loretta only nodded to Corky, then climbed into the cab and let Corky finish emptying the cart. Alex walked around behind his counter again and exclaimed, "I bet that man went down to Thomas's for a cuppa! I bet he wasn't quiet while he was there!" Eagerly, Alex smiled and picked up his phone and punched in some numbers. "Maybe them young fellas will tell me what they found out from that old geezer!"

Natt's phone rang not long after Corky left. After he identified the store, the voice exclaimed, "Was that Corky there?"

Natt chuckled, he wasn't much of a gossip. "Yeah, Alex, he got a cup of coffee while he waited for Loretta to do her grocery shopping at your place."

"So did he talk?"

"Sure, most of the time, between sips, that is. You know he's a good talker."

"Come on, boy! Spill it!"

"What, Alex?"

Letting out a frustrated sigh, Alex said, "You're as bad as Loretta! She never said a blame word. So what did Corky say?"

Natt let the silence lengthen then as if he was thinking about it, he asked, "Oh…, what did Corky say about what, Alex?"

"If your granddad was still in the store I'd get it out of him!" Alex threatened.

Natt's grin spread across his face, even though Alex couldn't see it. "Well, he's not here, Alex, it's just Matt and me. What was it you wanted to know again?"

Letting out a big sigh, Alex asked, "What did Corky say about all that activity we've had in town lately?"

"Yeah, he agreed there's been a lot of trucks coming and going around lately. You know that curve's close to your place. Matt and I can't see where those trucks go exactly."

"It's like pulling teeth with you! Did he say why?"

"Yup, he said, they're moving a lot of dirt down the road from you."

Patiently, Alex said, "And did he say why? What did he say was going in there? Come on, Natt!"

As if he was debating the world's greatest problem, Natt was quiet for several seconds. Finally, he said, "He told us some distant relative's coming to town this weekend to talk about a restaurant he's planning to start."

"In that place?"

"Well, he didn't come right out and say that, no."

Under his breath, Alex said, "Give me a break!" After another sigh, Alex said, "Thanks for your help, Son. Oh, someone just stopped out front I'll have to go be friendly. Say hello to Marcy for me."

A smile stretched from one ear to the other, but of course, Alex couldn't see it. "I'll do that, Alex. She'll probably be in tomorrow, it's her day off and I imagine she'll need groceries. We can't eat hardware supplies, you know."

"Good to know, young fella." Alex hung up and shook his head. Watching another two full dump trucks go by, he said, "That boy is something else! Wonder if they taught him how to do that in those journalism classes at that university?" He sighed, "And just 'cause Marcy'll be in tomorrow won't tell me much more, she's nearly as bad as that Loretta!" As the door opened Alex muttered, "That Marcy sure ain't like her sister."

Natt kept smiling as he hung up, but Matt said, "Man, no wonder you were going to be the world's best journalist! You got that inquisition down to a science!"

"Thanks!" Natt said, with a chuckle. "I have fun with some of these older people in town, but they still tell me their gossip."

"Yeah, I believe that!"

Natt was still in a good mood. Still grinning, he said, "Loretta never told Alex anything, that's why he called here."

Matt also laughed. "And Corky sat over there and never shut his mouth!"

"You got that right!"

Matt shook his head. "How does somebody who doesn't talk live with somebody who never closes his mouth?" He shrugged and answered his own question. "I guess there's a one-sided conversation most of the time."

Natt looked at his older cousin and grinned again. "Beats me! That's what's kind of nice about Marcy. We talk, but not always. I guess you'd have to call it, we communicate. I think actually we're still learning about each other. Sandy's told me Marcy's an intense person. I guess I'd have to agree with that."

Emilyn put the last things she wanted to take on her trip in her one piece of luggage Thursday afternoon. She grinned; one of them was not a uniform! She could wear summer clothes and be comfortable for a change. She was determined not to make her suitcase so full Jack had to carry it. He was sure to comment about that! Of course there were things she'd have to add in the morning, but that wouldn't take long. Toothbrush, hairbrush, cosmetic case, maybe some slippers, but nothing she'd have to hunt for. She must remember she'd be sleeping on a cot in the living room, but that was nothing new for her, except another couple was also occupying the cabin. She'd already put an extra wrap in so she'd be decent.

Unbidden, another thought crossed her mind. The last time somebody else occupied the same place she did was when Matt had been her husband and they'd slept together. Angrily, she said, "What is the matter with me? Why do I keep thinking about that man!"

She stood over the open case a moment. In the foothills of the Appalachians should she put in a sweatshirt? She shook her head, it was July! Surely it wasn't that much different. She'd also listened to the weather forecast; there were no hurricanes or storms in the forecast for the weekend. That was good her rain gear consisted of an old, beat-up umbrella. She hadn't had the thing out in so long she couldn't remember if it had a hole in it or not. Who knew if the thing would keep her dry even if there wasn't a hole! However, that wasn't something too high on her priority list for her next paycheck.

She had to admit she was excited, she would get away. Away from this town, it was an okay town, but still… She'd see more than these four walls of her tiny apartment and much more than the sight and smells of the diner. That alone had to be a plus. Sometimes those smells even got to her and she worked there five days a week! Momentarily, she wondered what a new restaurant would smell like. It wouldn't have months and months of collected grease and stale coffee smells embedded in the walls! That would be a plus, she was sure of it.

Later, she drove happily to work, after all, the sun shone down brightly and it was her last evening to work for four days! At midnight she wouldn't have to think about the diner, or worry about Harry coming in and using his ever-roving hands on her until Tuesday afternoon and that was just fine with her. Of course, she wouldn't have been too upset if Barney had given her a day shift today instead of evening, but she'd live with that. Life was full of little problems, such as an ornery boss…

However, she hadn't even made it to work before her happiness turned to grumbling. That same street department that had closed the street without notice the day after July Fourth had done it again! The street had only been open for a few days, now it was closed again, making her wonder what the real problem was. She slammed on the breaks and pulled in a deep breath. This time, the barricade was only a few feet in front of the hole! Of course, there hadn't been a barricade at the corner or even a sign.

She had to turn around in someone's driveway and find another way to get to the diner. Of course the street department hadn't posted detour signs to tell how to get around the closed street. Again today she was almost late and of course, Barney glanced none too subtly at his watch. Emilyn saw him do it, she sighed, but didn't say anything like she was sure Barney wanted her to. That was one thing she was determined not to do today, after all, it was her last day for four days… and Barney wasn't going along.

Time went by, not nearly as quickly as Emi wanted it to, it never did when you were anticipating something, like a four day weekend away from your place of employment. The noon rush had ended around three o'clock then after an hour lull the afternoon crowd came in for snacks on the way home from work. So coming on at four o'clock, started them right in filling coffee cups and supplying slices of pie to tide the hungry guys coming off shifts over until their wives fixed dinner.

The evening cook came on at five and started right in filling orders, but Barney usually stayed on until six, since that was when the major rush was. Even then he didn't rush off like he usually did. Emi almost wondered if she was supposed to tell him she'd miss him while she was gone. Of course, that would never happen, that was one reason she was glad to get away. She and Barney had never been BFF's.

The usual patrons came in for their dinner, most of them men who lived alone. Fortunately, one of them had not been Harry-with-the-roving-hands. She knew she needed to be thankful for small favors and she was, really. The dinner rush was over by around seven thirty; there were only a few stragglers that lingered with coffee and pie. There were also two men at one table in an animated conversation, even after everyone else left.

Thursday night was never known as a 'pile-'em-in' night and since the boss went home around six, Emi sat with her fellow waitress and watched the clock. Of course, they both knew that to watch the clock never made the time go any faster, but with two patrons eating dessert as their only customers, what else was there? Emi didn't want to drink another cup of coffee, she'd never sleep tonight. However, since both patrons had asked for a refill with their pie-ala-mode, Emi couldn't even empty the carafe.

Barney's Diner, as the place was well known as in the community, had been in the neighborhood for many years and Barney had all the bases covered, his waitresses didn't do any other job in the place. If you were a waitress, that's what you did, you waited on customers. In fact, the man who ran the dishwasher became irate if someone so much as rinsed off a dish! That was his domain and you'd best remember that! She and every other waitress that worked at Barney's learned that within the first eight hour shift.

While she sat her thoughts automatically went to what would happen during the next four days. Her suitcase was packed and waited, still open on a chair in her bedroom. She intended to rush home, shower and fall in bed. She was sure the shower would help relax her and help her fall asleep and of course, it would rinse off the smells from the diner. The suitcase waited for a few incidentals she'd add in the morning. She'd looked at the schedule and knew she'd get off on time, Naomi was on and she was punctual.

Naomi would rather work the night shift than anything else. That was something Emi couldn't put her mind around. Nighttime was the time for sleeping as near as she could figure, but some people had screwed up clocks, it seemed, Naomi being one of them. However, she would gladly leave those hours to her. Getting off at midnight was late enough, then with a twenty minute drive to her apartment and a few minutes to unwind and set up her coffeemaker made it pretty late.

As soon as she got home tonight she'd take her shower and if she had enough 'umph' wash her hair. She was glad she'd made that decision, somebody today had made a mess on the grill and the smell was still really bad in the kitchen. A shower was one thing she didn't want to put off until morning. Besides, showering tonight would make it easier to fall asleep she'd surely go for that. Alli told her they'd stop for coffee and breakfast to go, so all she'd have to do in the morning was get up, wash her face, she didn't even have to put makeup on, she was traveling with friends, so she'd brush her hair and put it in a ponytail, dress and close up her travel case. *Piece of cake!*

She hadn't been out of town in months, or seen her friends in a long time. Both of those things had her grinning, she so wanted to see her friends again. A decade ago Alli had saved her from herself. That was something she could never repay. Jack was a real cut-up! But the one thing that squelched all that excitement and that she couldn't seem to get passed, her ex-husband had just moved to the same little town where they were headed. How ironic was that? Way passed coincidental, for sure. She had to admit it put butterflies in her stomach. What would they say to each other, if anything?

Putting Murphy's Law aside, maybe they wouldn't even see each other. *Yeah, and elephants fly!*

Since she'd never heard of the place until Matt had Emailed her the name only days before Alli had told her about the restaurant prospect, she didn't know if they'd see each other or not. She couldn't begin to figure out her feelings about Matt Thomas. Matt Thomas had been out of her life for a decade, but he surely hadn't been out of her thoughts for nearly that long. How could she put the one man out of her mind who she'd loved so deeply? As an eighteen year old, he'd been her first love. *That is so NOT a piece of cake!*

Since she'd been thinking about the trip and what they'd be doing there, Emilyn wasn't exactly sure what her thoughts about Matt were. As a high school senior her thoughts had been consumed with the handsome guy. They had spent as much time as they could together and felt miserable when they were apart – at least that's how she felt. Years later, she wondered if he'd felt that way about her. She was convinced at the time she'd love the man for a lifetime and beyond. When he'd purposed, that's what he'd claimed, too.

Perhaps she could have loved him forever, if she'd had a chance, but that chance had been ripped away from her by the man himself. She didn't think she'd ever forget that scene when he threw his keys at her. Sure, she'd been fed up with the quarrels they had, but surely they could have worked things out? Sometime in the last few years she'd been able to put the man from her mind… most of the time. However, since his Email and Alli's texts, Matt Thomas had come back into her thoughts with a vengeance.

Since Alli had asked her to go along on this trip, she knew without any doubt that she had not forgotten the man who had broken up their marriage all those years ago and left her a devastated woman. She knew she'd know him if she saw him on the street. To say that the man had hurt her was the understatement of the year! Perhaps it had soured her on men in general – what else could be the reason why she hardly dated? Well, duh, she worked evenings, most men wanted to date in the evenings because they worked in the daytime. She wasn't a goon; after all, she had graduated from high school.

As one of the patrons raised his empty cup, she sighed and stood, after all, Ida was working a puzzle and she was only rummaging around with her thoughts. The person of her thoughts she'd just as soon leave out, but that didn't happen. She grabbed the coffee carafe and headed for the table. The man wasn't Harry, she didn't have to worry he'd try to feel her body parts. That was definitely a plus. With a smile plastered on her face, Emi filled the man's mug and set down two creamers.

The man looked up with a grin and as he opened a creamer and dumped the few dollops into the coffee, he said, "Thank you, Miss."

Emi smiled back. "Not a problem, we aim to please."

"You sure serve good coffee here."

"I'm glad you like it, sir. That's one thing Barney doesn't buy locally, he orders his coffee grounds from a supplier and it's delivered each week."

Nodding appreciatively, the man said, "Good to know, thanks."

Back at the work station, she set the carafe back on the warmer and sat down in the work area so she could watch the diners, but she went back to her thoughts. Of course her side-kick never looked up from her challenging puzzle. Perhaps tomorrow night she'd find out what place the man, Matt Thomas, held in her mind and heart. She had to admit that since Matt had left her, she'd matured. She'd had to grow up a lot and real fast!

Maybe she wouldn't see him – *yeah, right!* As usual, Murphy's Law was alive and well in Georgia, the size of the town or city had nothing to do with it. Life was like that, perhaps the size of the town or city only made the challenges different and Matt Thomas was definitely a challenge. Actually, she wasn't sure if she was up to that much of a challenge. She really wondered how she would react when she saw Matt for the first time in a decade.

She remembered Allison telling her the restaurant they'd manage would be the first in town, so the place had to be small. She was resigned that she'd probably see Matt, but she really hoped she didn't react, Jack would surely have something to say if she was very obvious with her reaction. Perhaps the cabin Jack had rented was far away from the hardware store where Matt worked. Since she was speculating, perhaps Matt's apartment was over that far distant hardware store, too. She sighed, life for a single girl never turned out that great. She'd also learned that a few years ago in the school of hard knocks. Maybe that was the same year Matt had left her a devastated divorcee.

The hands on the clock inched around and as a table emptied, Emi washed it down and set it for breakfast. When her relief came the all-night diner would start serving breakfast food. People who came in during the night were either working the graveyard shift, so their day was just starting and they wanted breakfast food and good, strong coffee, or they were travelers looking to get as far as they could before the caffeine kick ran out and breakfast food seemed to fill that need the best. Emi never questioned how the minds of night-owls worked. She was just glad she wasn't one of them. Her friend, the night waitress, definitely was, she wouldn't work any other shift but overnight. She even hated having a day off! She said she couldn't sleep unless it was broad daylight. *Go figure!*

Not long after she'd cleaned her last table and set it for breakfast, the back door opened and a lady with light chocolate skin, in her mid-forties walked in. She carried no purse, but in her no-nonsense way, she slipped her car key in the pocket of her skirt uniform and grabbed a clean apron from the drawer where they were kept. As she stuffed an order pad in the apron pocket, she found her time card and ran it through the time clock. Satisfied with the *clunk* the machine made, Naomi replaced the card, looked around the kitchen and saw the night cook, gave him a grin and walked into the dining room.

Since she was the only waitress overnight, she came in the dining area and said, "Girls, get your tails out of here! Naomi to the rescue." She looked specifically at Emilyn and grinned. "Girl, you are out of here! Don't even think about this place until Tuesday at four o'clock. Come back tanned and relaxed."

Emi laughed and reached behind her to undo her apron. "Can hardly do that, Naomi. We'll travel tomorrow and Monday, the weekend's hardly long enough to show any kind of tan on this anemic skin. You know, Mom being a Swede, it takes lots more than a weekend to show any kind of tan on this skin. I don't own a tanning bed, so I'll just work on that relaxing part you mentioned. That I could use."

Naomi shrugged. "Probably true, but you can always try. Where is it you're going? You travel all day it can't be too close."

Emi grinned. "Believe me, Naomi I could wish, but it's not to the beach, that's sure. My friend says the town's in the Appalachians."

Naomi nodded. "Yeah, you may have a point. Well, get your tail into your car and get on home. There's always stuff last minute to do, I'm sure. Me, I haven't been out a town in a coon's age, but I got no place I wanna be, either. Even if you travel all day you don't want to be a stick-in-the-mud, I'll guarantee that! Go get your head on your pillow fast as you can, close them blues and get your beauty sleep. Maybe you'll find you a man this weekend, while you're gone to them mountains."

Her excitement building, Emilyn grinned at her friend and exclaimed, "Oh, I'm out of here, Naomi! My friend says they'll come for me about eight and we'll stop for breakfast. You know that's the middle of the night for us late workers. I'm gonna set my alarm first thing when I get home so I'll be up on time." Emi wasn't about to touch that sentence about finding a man this weekend. She'd have enough trouble avoiding the one she'd known a decade ago.

Nodding and looking around at the empty diner, Naomi agreed, "Yup, just the time I'm getting off. I'll be thinking of you while I drive home to bed. You're not going by yourself, are you? If it's not to the shore…"

"No, it's not to the shore and yes my friends are picking me up. Actually, it's my friend, Alli who got me this job and her husband."

"Well, you tell them to drive safe; we need you back here, girl."

"I'll be sure they know that."

Emi and the other waitress rushed to the time clock. Two *clunks* later, while Naomi started her first carafe of coffee, the girls hit the back door, but Emi waved at the night cook before the door closed behind her. The night man only waved his spatula at her. In fact, it was as the door clicked behind her that the realization finally settled in that she was off… off for four full days. She could actually forget about the diner! She would do her very best to do that most important thing. The possibility that this weekend could lead to another chapter in her life sent goose bumps down her arms. Of course, no one at Barney's Diner knew that and she was glad to keep them in the dark, at least for a while. She realized she'd almost told Naomi and her co-waitress was standing right beside her!

In the morning it was the chime from a text message that woke Emilyn up. She opened her eyes, rubbed them a few times, saw some light coming from behind the shade on her window and looked at the digits on the clock. She groaned, knowing what she still needed to do and wondered why her alarm hadn't gone off. She looked at the clock, she hadn't set it!

Disgusted, she muttered, "Man, that's two things I didn't do last night I was supposed to do! I didn't set my alarm or take a shower, great!"

Still with her head on the pillow, she rubbed her eyes and pushed a string of hair from her face. She looked at the words on the screen. *I bet you're still sacked in! Come on, girl, we're on our way! Be there in 30 minutes!*

Her heart beating frantically, she didn't bother to respond, but dropped the phone on the pillow, flung the sheet nearly off the bed, planted her feet on the floor and raced for the bathroom. Again this morning she was glad it was a hardwood floor and helped her wake up. She sighed, last night when she'd left the diner she'd forgotten that they'd dug up the same street again and she had to find another way to get from the diner to her apartment. Of course, since she'd forgotten, she'd gone down the dark street and had to turn around, she felt bad that her lights shone in somebody's dark windows. By the time she unlocked her apartment door she could hardly hold her eyes open. The shower after work went by the boards. She'd barely shed her smelly uniform and crawled into her pajamas.

It took only a few seconds to reach the bathroom, but then she nearly stepped into the shower with her pajamas on. While the water warmed up she managed to pull them off and quickly folded them for her suitcase. Since the kitchen had smelled so bad last night, she had to wash her hair this morning. There was Murphy's Law again, Kurt had burned a steak at dinner time and the smell lasted forever. He'd thrown the back door open, but the humid air outside didn't help much. Thank goodness she could put her hair in a ponytail and Alli had said they'd stop for breakfast. She hadn't had to fix her coffeemaker because of that.

Thirty minutes later, when she heard a horn out in the parking lot she still had her hairbrush in her hand, trying to tame her damp hair. She let out a long sigh, grabbed her purse by a strap, scooped up her keys and juggled everything for a second until she had a free hand to grab the handle of her rolling suitcase. Of course, while she locked her second floor apartment door, Jack sent her another reminder that he was out there. *Of course he would! Give it a rest, Mr. Albertson! I'm coming. It is only eight o'clock on a Saturday!*

As an added precaution, each apartment door had to be locked from the outside with a key and the building was always locked, you could get out, all you had to do was push on the bar, but to get back in you needed a key. Coming home at night from work she was glad for that precaution and also glad the entry hallway was always lighted. As she pulled the key from the lock on her door, her wad of keys dropped to the floor.

She sighed, she couldn't be all the way awake; she wasn't usually this clumsy. As she grabbed them up off the floor, she fumbled the hairbrush she still held and it nearly fell also. Trying to save time, with the same hand she grabbed the suitcase handle and raced down the stairs, the suitcase bumping down behind her. Fortunately the stairs were carpeted, who knew if people slept in on Saturdays! She was only inches from the main door when she heard another blast from the horn!

She pulled her suitcase down off the last step and as she reached the door, she thought, *What is it about men that makes them so impatient!*

Jack had his hand over the horn, but Allison saw her push open the door onto the parking lot, so she reached back and opened the back passenger door of the car. Emi also saw where Jack's hand was, so she gave Allison a grateful smile and rushed across the lot to the SUV. She flung her one handful of things onto the seat, then pushed the handle down on her suitcase and followed it into the back seat, but had to give it another shove with her knee before she could get in enough to close the door. Only moments later she pulled the car door shut behind her and let out a deep breath, as she sank onto the seat.

Breathlessly, as she reached for the seatbelt, she said, "Wish you'd texted me earlier, Alli! Thirty minutes is hardly long enough to get ready for a trip! The kitchen smelled so bad last night I had to wash my hair."

"Thought you had an alarm clock," Jack said.

Emilyn sighed, leaned back in the seat and slipped her purse strap off her shoulder. She pulled the seatbelt far out, then across her body and clicked it before she said, "I do, Jack, I forgot to set it last night. At midnight, after a shift at the diner, it's hard to remember that the street department's dug a hole and you have to take a completely different route, then when I get home I need to set my alarm."

Six

J ack was already pulling out of the parking lot, but he looked in the rear-view mirror and grinned as he said, "Girl, you sure do live dangerously!"

Emilyn leaned back and adjusted the seatbelt across her shoulder. "Not on purpose, Jack. Life just happens."

"Oh, we know that!"

Jack looked at his wife and turned on the street toward a fast food restaurant. "So, first order of business, we go through a drive-thru for coffee and biscuits. Right? That is why we didn't have any coffee before we left."

"That's the plan!"

Emilyn rubbed her eyes and said, "I sure could use some leaded coffee about now!" Much to her embarrassment, it was at that moment her stomach growled. She quickly transferred her hand from her eyes to her stomach and rubbed it. Actually, she'd eaten her supper on break last evening, but it had been a while before she got off and early in the evening both waitresses were running. For a Thursday night it had been busy, the advertised special last night had been chicken and noodles.

"Mmm, so could Jack." Significantly, Allison looked at her husband. "Why else would he work that horn so much? And then, turn this way which is the opposite way to the highway, but close to that place with the golden arches?"

"Good, it's really hard to drive a car without some caffeine under my belt. You know how it is." Jack grinned at Emi in the rear-view mirror. "I heard that rumble, girl. Guess you could use the drive-thru for more than coffee."

Emi sighed. "Jack, just get to the drive-thru, will you? Coffee's the number one necessity right now. But yes, a breakfast order would help a lot."

"Yep, we're about there!"

Even though Emilyn had that leaded coffee and a breakfast biscuit, it wasn't long after they left town on the highway that she made herself comfortable in the corner of the back seat and closed her eyes. Even without a pillow it wasn't long before she fell fast asleep. It was hard to stay awake when she'd gotten to bed at one o'clock and been awakened before eight. Allison and Jack were talking in the front seat, making plans and going over what Corky had told them and didn't notice until they heard a soft snore coming over Allison's shoulder. Jack looked in the rearview mirror, then turned and grinned at his wife.

"That girl's sound asleep!" he exclaimed. "Her leaded coffee didn't do too much for her, I'd say and she had a large!"

Allison turned and looked at the peaceful expression on Emi's face, before she said, "Hey, you gotta remember, Jack, she works the evening shift. Probably she usually sleeps later than seven after she's worked a shift. We did wake her up about then, you know. Still, she's a young thing! She's barely thirty something!"

Jack slid his hand from the wheel and squeezed his wife's shoulder. He'd have pulled her against him if they hadn't been wearing seatbelts. Of course, one had to obey the state law about seatbelts, troopers loved to give out tickets if you didn't have one on. "My dear, didn't you ever work yourself to the bone when you were thirty something?"

Allison grinned at her husband. "Nope, I worked *you* to the bone. You mean you don't remember that, Honey?"

"Mmm, I think I remember that."

Allison swatted her husband's arm. "Cut it out!" Her grin turned angelic, as she said, "Tell me you didn't like it!"

"Mmm, yeah. Yeah, there is that."

"See, I told you!"

Jack looked at the clock on the dash. "Say, it's about lunch time!"

"Yeah, there is that," Allison parroted.

Emilyn slept until Jack pulled off the highway into a convenience store that had a gas station attached. It was nearly lunch time and knowing her husband, Allison knew they'd get lunch to go here. He stepped out to pump gas, but intentionally he slammed his door and Emi jumped, disoriented. "What's going on?" she gasped, her eyes flying open. Her hands also flew out to her sides her right one hit the door.

Unbuckling her seatbelt, intending to get out to go in the store, Allison said, "Oh, Jack's just being his ornery self! He slammed his door so you'd wake up. He stopped here for gas, but more importantly so we could get lunch. It'll be pretty soon we'll be to Blairsville and we'll have to stop for groceries."

Emilyn let out another sigh, "Okay, guess I can eat." She opened her door with Allison, but then fell back against the seat; she'd forgotten to release her seatbelt. After that clicked she added, "I guess I wasn't much on the conversation, was I?"

Allison nodded. "Well, no, but you did get home after midnight, so it's expected. Let's go in and see what they have"

Emilyn rubbed her eyes and said, "Yeah, okay."

The two women left the car, but Jack was fishing in his pockets for his wallet that held his credit card then realized he'd taken his wallet out of his pocket. It was too uncomfortable to drive any distance with it in his hip pocket. He turned back to the door to get his wallet from the console and as she stepped out, Jack gave her a wicked grin and said, "Emi! Did you wake up? Well, I'll be! Here I thought you were dead to the world."

"Jack!" she said, exasperated. "You know you woke me when you slammed your door! For crying out loud! Of course I woke up, you made sure of it!" She also smiled at him. "Alli says we need to stop for lunch here."

Jack grinned at the young woman. "Really? Are you sure it was me?" He nodded around at the huge gas station and at the many parked cars. "You know it could have been anybody here on the lot who slammed their door. You had your eyes closed."

Emilyn huffed and glared at Jack. "Jack, of course I'm sure it was you! Who else? Alli was still in the car."

"Well, I'll be, what do you know."

"Jack," Allison said, "I know you want lunch. We'll see what they have."

Jack had his hand on the door handle; he hadn't ducked back inside for his wallet yet. "Oh, sure! Get lots, after all, you know it takes a lot of energy to drive all this way. That breakfast biscuit didn't last too long."

"Yeah, I'll work on it."

Emi scowled. *It takes a lot of energy to drive? How is that possible?* Not knowing Jack quite as well as his wife, Emilyn asked Jack, "Shall we get a table? It's not quite noon, maybe it isn't packed out yet."

Jack grinned and started ducking into the car for his wallet. He waved his hand and said, "Nah, get stuff to go. It won't hold us back so long. I told that lady we'd get there before dark. Oh, and girl, make sure you get another leaded coffee. Maybe you'll stay awake till after grocery shopping."

Completely ignoring his second shot, Emilyn gave him a beautiful smile. "But maybe Alli won't get what you want. I mean, you know, they probably have a big selection and you'll be missing out."

The gas pump clicked off and Jack was preoccupied with hanging the nozzle up, so Allison said, "Girl, you need a man in your life! You know a man well enough you know that anything fills him up when he's behind the wheel."

Jack called to their backs, "Just make sure it's not pizza with anchovies! Allison, you know I can't abide those things!"

Emi whirled around and grinned at the man. "What, Jack! Aren't those little fishies some of your favorites? I thought you had a fish night at your restaurant every week! I know Alli's told me that."

Jack made a face and turned to put the gas cap back on the tank. "Get on with you, girl! I like my pizza just fine, but them little fishies need to grow up in the water, as I see it."

Emilyn chuckled and followed Allison into the restaurant. Appreciatively she raised her nose and sniffed. "Sure smells good in here."

Allison also pulled in a big whiff. "I do believe they have a good selection. Let's see what they have."

With an angelic grin on her face, Emilyn said, "You wouldn't want to get one of those pizzas with anchovies, would you? I mean, we could get one of those super large with lots of anchovies on it." *Not that I like anchovies; ugh.*

Allison laughed and stepped in line to make an order for her and Jack. "Girl, you might be wearing them if he didn't see them until we were in the car. Believe me, we were at a restaurant the first time I was with him and he encountered them. You never saw fishies fly as fast as those did!"

Making a face, because anchovies weren't her favorite food either, Emi said, "Aw, those poor little things. He must have hurt their feelings."

Allison nodded. "Mmm, I'm sure."

Matt rang up someone's purchase and followed him out the door. It was five o'clock and for Friday, it was the beginning of his supper break. Of course, he'd have to go to his cabin, dig out one of those delicious frozen dinners, rush it through the microwave and gobble down the food that never was as appetizing as the picture on the top. He had a half hour to do all that. Friday evening was the one evening a week they kept the store open until eight o'clock. He knew Natt was anxious to eat dinner with his wife. From what he'd observed, those two were still suffering from the 'newly-wed-syndrome'. He let out a sigh, maybe he'd get to have that, but find a woman his age in this village? *Fat chance.*

He saw a car coming into town and knew the speed limit sign informed people they had to slow down. At the edge of town was a population sign and a LARGE speed limit sign – not that they had any town law enforcement to enforce that speed! However, the store was far enough away from the edge of town he didn't have to worry about being run over. Just before the car reached the clinic he stepped off the curb to cross the street. Surely it was going on through town, most all the traffic did. Instead it put on its turn signal to make the turn into the parking lot he intended to cross to his cabin.

"Well," he sighed, "looks like Isabel has another weekend renter. I'm happy for her, she can use all the help she can get and she's such a good woman. She has Eric and me, but she has to pay utilities for all the cabins even if nobody's in them." His shoulders rose and fell with another big sigh. "If all the signs are right, I'll be by myself here pretty soon."

After five days of being on the job he was getting back in the groove. He'd only been here in February and worked for the entire month, but working in a hardware store in a small town in the dead of winter was worlds apart from being head of the maintenance department in a large theme park in Orlando. That position definitely kept him out of trouble. The thought crossed his mind that he was glad Jason had accepted his resignation so easily. What would Natt have done for another week by himself? There were few times when there hadn't been a customer in the store all week.

Back in February life at the store had been rather dull, since the weather had kept most people inside. Hardware supplies and coffee weren't things that people braved winter weather for very often. As he remembered, it had been area farmers who came for parts or to order some part for their machinery mostly. Of course, there'd been people who worked in Blairsville who'd stopped in for icemelt a lot. He'd nearly run out of the large bags during the month. He'd gotten to know Dr. Miles pretty well; the good doctor used a lot of that icemelt on his clinic parking lot. He would or he'd have to treat an accident victim right there.

Mysteriously, once people had tasted his coffee, they didn't ask for another cup the next time they came in. He had to admit, the aroma had never been what Natt's coffee smelled like now. Maybe that was due to his dislike for coffee. He'd even watched Natt make the coffee the one day they'd worked together before that groom had left on his honeymoon. He grinned, maybe Natt did hold his mouth a certain way when he made the coffee.

He could only be glad he and Natt were working together now, but he felt some satisfaction, they did work well together and they'd had a good week. After he and Natt had had some serious hours of hashing out things they'd settled on what he'd be making and even with all the expenses, they'd come out in the black. For a small town store, that was good. Of course, if Brad came back and did more than just sit in the 'coffee-drinker's nook' they might have to do some more rehashing, but for now they would make it just fine. Saturday was still part of this week and of course, they hadn't lived through that day this week, but usually Saturdays were good sales days at Thomas's.

Natt had told him many people came in on Saturday who didn't come in any other day in the week. Except it was only one day out of six, in the last few months Natt had contemplated getting another coffee maker, even if it was a smaller one that would tide things over while the big one perked more. People really wanted a cup of coffee on Saturday. It kept him on his toes making the brew. Matt had yet to experience that. The store hadn't been like that at all back in February. He grinned; it hadn't been his coffee that drew the crowds, even though the weather had been cold and nasty the whole month. Maybe that's why not many people came in he was not a coffee connoisseur.

That was one way he was a bit like his brother, iced tea was his beverage of choice, even in cold weather. Would there be room to put in a small refrigerator to hold some of Alex's jugs of tea? Hmm, maybe he'd have to think about that when he'd been here a bit longer. Of course, summer was the time for iced tea. He grinned, maybe he'd have to buy double; he'd keep the jugs rotated here at the store. He stepped up on the curb and kept on, stepping onto the gravel parking lot and headed for his cabin. That all important frozen dinner with his name on it for dinner was calling his name.

Inside the car that turned onto Isabel's parking lot, those in the front seat heard a gasp from the back. "Oh, no! That's Matt Thomas! Look, he's coming toward us."

"Thought you told us he was a twin," Jack said, looking at the good looking young man. "Maybe it's his brother."

Exasperated, Emilyn said, "Jack, I lived with the man for two years! That's Matt, I know it. Besides, he just came from that hardware store, it has to be Matt. When I got his Email he told me he'd be working in a hardware store."

Jack shrugged, but kept on across the gravel and slowed to a crawl as the car approached Isabel's house. Of course, Matt kept walking across the gravel toward the cabins. He had no idea who was in the car. "Guess you'll be neighbors for the weekend, girl. Looks like he's heading toward one of those other cabins down that walk."

"This is so bad!" Emilyn wailed. Looking around, looking in vain for the excavation for the restaurant, she asked, "Where is the restaurant gonna be?"

"Don't know, we'll have to wait and talk to Corky," Jack answered. "He said he'd started the ground work already."

"But he's going to one of those cabins just like we are! Oh, man! What'll I do if he sees me? This is so bad!"

Allison turned to look at her friend. Scowling, she said, "Emi, didn't you tell me you were over the man, what's with you?"

Emilyn wiped her eyes with her sleeve, embarrassed that tears were leaking and running down her cheeks. Surely she wasn't crying because she'd finally seen Matt after so long! "Maybe not all the way." She whispered, "I knew he was here, he Emailed me a while ago, but *here*, Oh, man!" Emi's eyes were glued on the handsome man who was only a few feet from the car. She couldn't seem to take her eyes from those wide shoulders!

"Emi, it's been ten years!"

"I know, but really…" she whispered, "but I really loved that guy." Even more quietly, she murmured, "I think he was my first love, too." However, in the closed up car, Emi's words from the back seat carried to her friend.

In a 'no-nonsense' voice, Allison said, "That shouldn't make any difference! The man did you wrong, big time."

As Jack crawled across the gravel parking lot, Emilyn scooted down in the seat even more, trying to be as invisible as possible, never mind that the back windows were tinted. Matt was so close to the car he'd have to see her! Had she thought Murphy's Law was alive and well in her hometown? Oh, my, it was nothing like driving onto the same parking lot that her ex-husband was crossing at the same time! She was in a car, but he was walking and could look in the car and see her at any minute! Emilyn realized her chest hurt. After a second she pulled in a deep breath and felt instant relief. She was sure life couldn't get any worse than this. How could she face the man she'd loved so dearly right here on the same property?

"Emi," Allison chided and turned around to look at her friend. "You must remember, girl, he's your EX-husband, you've been divorced for ten years. You've told me several times you're over him."

After a sniff, she said, "Yeah, I know what I said, but it's different in the nitty-gritty, Alli! I haven't seen the man in that long…"

"Well, girl, you'll have to live with it, at least this weekend," Jack said, helpfully and pulled to a stop in front of the small house. "This is where the lady on the phone told me come to for a key. I saw the sign back there sticking out past that big building, advertising the cabins and I see there are five or six, so I know we're at the right place. If the man's going to a cabin down the walk, it only means he lives here, doesn't mean he'll be there twenty-four-seven."

Still watching the man cross the parking lot, Emi said, "Yup, I understand what you're saying, Jack, but it'll be really, *really* hard."

Noticing her body language, Allison said, "Come on, Emi, give it your best shot! You know life goes on."

Slouched in the seat, her head barely high enough she could look out the window, she said, "I'll try real hard, Alli."

"Yes, I'm sure you will, girl."

As Matt walked close by, Emi bowed her head and looked away hoping Matt wouldn't look in the window and see her. However, Jack mused, "Hmm, is kind of a handsome man. Shall I toot and try to get his attention?" Jack immediately put his hand over the horn, then looked back at Emilyn with a grin.

Her voice muffled a bit, since her head was down, Emi said, "Jack, if I wasn't trying to hide right now I could think of a lot of things I could do to you! Let the man go on by."

Giving a big sigh, Jack said, "Okay, have it your way. But you know, you're bound to see the man up close and personal sometime this weekend. I know you can't hide every minute we're here and besides, you'll want to see where the restaurant's going in."

She flopped back on the seat and laid her arm across her eyes. Perhaps if she didn't see him he wouldn't see her? Maybe that was a possibility. "Mmm, but I could wait for that to happen, later."

Unnecessarily, Jack said, "Well, we're here!"

"Great, just great!" Emi muttered.

Since he only had a half hour, Matt didn't stop to be friendly. He didn't have to check his watch; he'd seen the clock at the store as he walked out. Later, after the store closed and the people were settled in their cabin, would be time enough to go for a handshake. He'd have to invite them to stop in for a cup of coffee before they headed out in the morning. There was no reason not to be friendly and what better way than offer a cup of coffee? It was the beverage of choice to most all red-blooded Americans.

As the car eased up in front of Isabel's house, Matt bounded up the steps to his cabin and pushed the door open. He didn't even have to use a key to open it; this was Vansville after all. That all important frozen dinner beckoned from the freezer and to emphasize that, his stomach reminded him he'd only fixed a bologna and cheese on white bread for lunch, no chocolate chip cookies his wife had made. Oh, the joys of being a single man! Life was so very uncomplicated and he even had his own washer and dryer!

He needed to be patient, maybe that single girl would appear in town sometime soon. She sure hadn't come into the store during the five days he'd been working there. But then, what did he know? Maybe she was lurking just around the corner and would appear in the store while Natt was on supper break. *Yup and elephants fly!*

Jack parked his car in front of Isabel's house, looked back for an instant at Emilyn and grinned. Emi was slouched down, her knees nearly touching Alli's seat and her head was in her chest. "Buck up, girl, he's just a man like me, he surely can't hurt you. He looked pretty innocent walking across that gravel a minute ago. Besides, he's gone inside that other cabin; he won't see you, at least for a little while."

"Oh, Jack, you have no idea how he hurt me! Really, I loved the man, well, the boy he was, really. We'd just turned eighteen when we got married. You know how at that age everything has a silver lining to it."

"Yeah, that sometimes happens," Allison agreed.

Jack turned the key, but left it in the ignition, then put his hand on the door handle and turned his head to look at Emilyn. He smiled compassionately at the younger woman. He and Allison had also married young, but he couldn't imagine life without his wife and they had weathered many tough times over the years. He remembered how much Emilyn had suffered at the hand of her unthinking husband ten years ago.

"Emi, I know for a fact that marriage at that age can last, but often it doesn't. I'm sorry yours didn't and I'm sure it's hard seeing the man you were married to after all this time, but as you know life goes on and we have to live with it. I'm going in for the key. Hide if you must, but if we're this close for the weekend, it'll be easier in the long run to meet up with him and get it over with."

Lifting her head to look at the cabin Matt had gone in, Emi sighed and said, "Yeah, Jack, I know what you're saying. I'll do my best while we're here." Emilyn pulled in another big breath and looked down the row of cabins. "After all, there is a cabin between us. Didn't you say we'll have that first cabin?"

"That's the spirit, girl! I'll go for the key. Yes, she said it was the biggest one and that it'll be more comfortable for three of us." Emi didn't answer, she watched the door close behind the man entering cabin three. Silently, Emilyn shook her head. Yes, she wasn't ill, so she'd survive, but at what cost to her heart?

"Does he know you'll be here?" Allison asked.

Emi pulled in another deep breath and let it out very slowly. "No, I never answered his Email. At the time I didn't think it was any count. I just deleted it and thought nothing about it until your text."

"Shouldn't you have told him then?"

Emilyn shrugged. "I could have but I didn't."

Emilyn looked at the fairly large cabins, the first one was definitely bigger than the others, but none of them were tiny. As Jack closed the car door behind him, Emilyn asked Allison, "Why do we get her handicapped cabin? You did say it was that first cabin we're getting, right? Don't most people who rent places like that try to keep that open? In case someone who is handicapped and needs something like that comes to spend the night."

"Yes, it's that first one. It's the only one that has a ramp and the lady told Jack it was her biggest one and had room to put in a cot."

Emi looked at the large cabin she couldn't remember seeing something that big as a rental cabin. "So there's only one bedroom in something that big?"

"That's what she said."

Just barely in a whisper, Emilyn said, "That's only two doors away from the one Matt went in. I can't very well hide all weekend!"

Allison clicked her seatbelt open so she could turn to look at Emilyn. "No, that's for sure, girl. Get your chin up. Just remember, he'll be working at the store, you won't be in the store where he works. What does a hardware store have in common with a restaurant, anyway?"

Not answering Allison's question, Emi said, "That will be so hard!"

Allison looked at her and said, "Emi, it will be hard, but as Jack said, he's only a man. Maybe he hurt you when you were twenty, but I know you've taken responsibility for yourself since then. Put this behind you and move on!"

Emilyn squared her shoulders and looked back at her friend. "I'll try, Alli, I'll do my best. I won't let him hurt me again!"

"Good, that's the stuff."

Maybe so, but I'm not sure I'm up to 'the stuff.'

Isabel, of course, could see the car out her living room window. Everybody who lived in Vansville knew that Isabel had her favorite chair situated so she could see out her front window and watch everything that went by on the highway or that went on at her end of town. Of course, she'd been waiting for her weekend guests to arrive. The man who called hadn't given her any specific time, but everything was ready for them. These were the people who were meeting with Corky to make plans to build the restaurant at the other end of town.

It didn't matter too much to her, but she knew people were glad Corky had decided to build a restaurant in town. The single men especially were glad there'd be something different, a place where they could socialize with other people and didn't have to always eat those frozen dinners they bought at Alex's store. She could understand that. As she watched her two renters, she knew, she'd lived alone for several years, how lonely life could be for a single person.

She'd had her husband for many years, but these boys didn't have anyone they could come home to and confide in. That had to be a lonely life. Before Ruth had moved back home life had been nearly that way for her. She was glad that over the years she'd made many friends in town, those friends kept her occupied. They could always get together and have coffee and cookies if they wanted to.

Jack got out of his car and as he walked the few steps to her porch steps, Isabel came out her front door onto her porch. She smiled warmly at Jack, who smiled back and said, "Hi, I saw the sign out on the highway saying this is Vansville. I assume I'm at the right place, since you said the cabins were very close to the edge of town. Are you Mrs. Isaacson?" Holding out his hand towards Isabel, he added, "I'm Jack Albertson."

Giving the younger man her no-nonsense smile, Isabel waited for him to climb the steps, took his hand, shook it and said, "Sonny, I'm Isabel and you're at the right place. As I told you it's a little town, so there's no other cabins. Come in and let's finalize everything. That number one cabin is all ready. I got my handyman to bring in a cot and it's set up and made up. I sure do hope you folks are comfortable for the weekend. As I told you, it's a one bedroom cabin, so with a cot it may be a little cramped. We put the cot against the wall, so there's as much open floor space as possible and it's away from the kitchen area, so there's room around the table."

Jack looked back over his shoulder and said, "Ma'am, that's actually a huge place! I'm sure we will be just fine."

Isabel nodded toward the next two cabins. "I got a set of twins in the next two cabins. They live there fulltime. One of them's gone a lot. He's a hiking guide on the trails around this place. The other one just came home for his supper break, but he'll be going back to the store to finish out Friday night hours. Believe me, they're both good men. Feel free to introduce yourselves. I sure hope you folks will be comfortable."

Jack looked at the large cabin. "Ma'am, I'm sure we'll be just fine. This is a cute little town. I'm sure we'll get to know some of it before the weekend's over with."

Isabel grinned. "Believe me, Sonny, you'll have to sleep the weekend away not to know this little place. All the businesses are along this street and people live on the other streets. But yes, we work real hard to make folks feel welcome." She grinned at him. "Now if you were an apartment house developer, nobody would like you!"

Jack grinned back at her. "That's not something I'm known for! Nighttime's the time for sleeping, as I see it. I see there's a grocery store just down the street. When's he close on a Friday evening? When's he open?" He scowled. "Really? You folks don't want apartments in this place? Wow!"

"At eight tonight and tomorrow at nine o'clock, Sonny. He's not one of these high power places that stays open for all hours! He runs the place himself, so he closes up most evenings, only Friday night but he may be on supper break. Got a good selection, though, I'd recommend it. Now the hardware store's open until eight tonight and he's got a bottomless coffee pot. I hear it's really good coffee. I've never tried it out myself, but I've heard many people in town say it's the best they've ever tasted." She chuckled a bit and shrugged. "What reason would an old lady like me have for going in a hardware store? And yep, no apartments in town!"

"Good to know, Isabel, thanks. Being in the restaurant business, my wife and I do a lot on the caffeine we consume." Looking up and down the street, Jack asked, "By the way, where is this place where the restaurant's going in? Corky told me he's started working on the property already and had some earthmovers come in."

Waving vaguely toward the grocery store, Isabel said, "Down that way at the other end of town. The place used to be a large meadow, but you can't see the place for the curve in the road, not from here, anyway. From what I've heard, it'll be a good sized place when it's finished. My friend lives across the street."

"Ah, good to know." Still looking out at the road, he asked, "By the way, what's in this town to live in once we get here to open the restaurant? Is there any place to rent or houses for sale? This girl we brought along, she won't want to live with us."

Isabel waved her hand toward her cabins and said, "Ah, well, that's why those two cabins have long term residents. We don't have empty houses or any apartments here in town. There really isn't much turnover, either. The people who work at the clinic live in Blairsville, except for Marcy, who's married to Natt and Nancy who's married to Duncan, that is." Putting her thumb over her shoulder, she added, "Those two houses back there on that new street belong to them. Had them built last year or two. After the clinic, those two houses been about it. And it was because Natt's Brad's grandson he got that street extended for those two houses." Isabel shrugged. "It's the way it is in a small town, you know."

Jack stroked his chin, not that he cared about who was married to whom, or that there were new houses on a new street in town. "Hmm, interesting. Gotta build your own place if you wanna live here."

"Yup, that's the size of it, Sonny. Of course, that's why I have two long term single guys as renters. My cabins are the only other option for living here in town. I really don't think three of you'd want to live in them long term."

Jack nodded. "Yes, Ma'am, that is good to know."

Isabel stepped back toward the door and put her hand on the knob. "Well, come on in. I have some papers for you to fill out."

Jack followed Isabel inside and she handed him a clipboard with the papers she had for him. He sat on her couch and quickly filled out the necessary information and handed them back to her, along with his check. She grinned at him and handed him two keys. She said, "Thank you, Sonny, I hope your stay is comfortable. I'm sure you'll want to be on the road kind of early on Monday, but check out isn't until eleven. As I say, the grocery's open every day but Sunday. From what I understand the church down the way is good for a Sunday morning." Isabel chuckled. "If that doesn't suit you, the church bell'll bring you around. Roger rings it for Sunday school and also for church, as I understand it."

Jack chuckled at that, then they both went back to the door and as Jack turned away from Isabel, he asked, "So I can park over there closer to the cabin? I see that one car there. Didn't you say that next cabin's occupied, too?"

"That's right, Sonny, but the one fella's gone till later. Since his job headquarters is at the other end of town, he drives there. Anywhere you see gravel it's fine for you to park. Since it's my handicapped cabin you get a bigger space."

Jack shrugged. "Just one car, but thanks."

Isabel smiled at him. "I'm glad you got here while it's still light." She nodded at the pole in the middle of her parking lot. "I got a security light, but the parking lot isn't too bright at night, but my renters never have complained about that. Since it's such a small town, folks turn in early. TV's sort of popular around here."

"When we started out this morning we weren't too sure of that." He grinned at Isabel and continued, "The girl we brought works second shift and had a hard time getting on the move this morning. Still, I'm with you, I'm glad we got here now; it'll give us a chance to relax in this nice little place. We'll get right on that move in. Thanks, Isabel." He held up the two keys on the ring and jiggled them together.

"You'll have that quietness, Sonny, I guarantee it," Isabel said

"Yup, can't beat it!" Jack said and walked down the steps, as Isabel went back inside and shut her door. She was happy enough to watch the activity from her chair and Ruth was getting dinner. She could see a head in the back of the car, the person didn't look very big, but she guessed it could be an adult, at least that's what Jack had told her.

Soon, Jack had his car backed up right in front of the walk that led to the ramp into cabin one. Even before Jack shut off the car, Emi grabbed her things from the seat and the handle on her suitcase and opened the back door. She was determined to be inside the cabin before Matt left his cabin, if he was going to any time this evening. She'd put off the inevitable until tomorrow if she could. Surely Murphy's Law would leave her alone for tonight. Maybe if she thought positively about that it would happen. Then again, she was a single girl…. She sighed; it seemed Murphy's Law was very adept at finding single girls and making their lives extra complicated. Or was it just her?

As Jack went to the back to open the hatch to the cargo area, he said, "Well, it's a good thing we ate along the way and brought our snacks with us. Isabel told me the grocery store isn't open now not until nine in the morning." He lifted out two grocery bags then as the three walked up the walk to the first cabin, Jack said, as he sauntered along, "We could go down the street to the hardware store and get a coffee, though. Isabel said they're open until eight this evening and they have a bottomless coffee urn. She said people in town say it's the best they've ever tasted." Jack looked at Allison and said, "Yeah, I think I could use a coffee after we finish unpacking. How 'bout it, Alli, wanna go with me?"

Emi quickly passed Jack and Allison and ran up the ramp to the porch. Before Allison could answer him, she said, "I'll pass."

Jack laughed. "Thought you said you were a coffee hound? At least that's what you told us at our meal stops all day. 'Course, couldn't tell after breakfast, though. I heard you snoring in the back seat there."

"Umm, yeah, usually, but I'm a bit tired tonight, so I don't want a reason not to sleep. With a different bed and all, it may be a challenge." She gave Jack a disgusted look. "Besides, how do you know I snore!"

Jack chuckled at Emi's belligerent tone. "Heard you after breakfast, Girl. That car's a good sized SUV, but the backseat isn't too far from the front, so me and Alli both heard you. Kinda pronounced, you know?"

Emilyn turned red she could feel the heat on her cheeks. It was the bane of a fair-skinned blond. "No, no way! I… I'm too young to snore!" She knew Jack was taking his time, so she said, "Come on, Jack open the door!" She stood right beside the door, shifting from one foot to the other. She even held the handle of her suitcase, instantly ready to barge across the threshold as soon as the door opened.

Allison, walking beside Jack and carrying one of the grocery bags, chuckled. "Oh, but you did, girl! Jack and me didn't talk all the time, you know. He does stay awake when he drives during the day."

Still sauntering along, Jack moved one foot to the bottom of the ramp. He looked up to the porch and grinned broadly before he said, "Ah, I get it. It's nothing to do with that good lookin' guy we saw a few minutes ago, is that it?"

Anxious for Jack to use his key, Emilyn looked at the closed door and said, "Well, maybe just a little...."

Jack sauntered up the long ramp, making Emi wonder if he was just being ornery. "Jack," she whispered, even though the three of them were the only ones in sight, "come on! Open the door!"

"Oh, yeah, I'll get right on that as soon as I get there. Achally, I'm workin' out the kinks in my legs, it was a long drive, ya know," he drawled. He actually stopped, set down the bag of groceries and rubbed the middle of his back. "There's a kink right there, you know? Alli, maybe that new-fangled thing you got me for my birthday would be a good thing in the car." Emilyn didn't say anything, but both Allison and Jack heard her long sigh.

Finally, reaching the door and pushing the key into the lock, Jack still didn't turn the key. Instead he looked around and said, "Why the rush, girl? We aren't meeting with Corky until tomorrow. Besides, it's not too hot and the sun isn't close to setting yet, maybe we can sit out here on the porch for a while and drink something and eat our snacks out here. It's a quiet little place, I'm sure there'll be a breeze off that meadow. And wow! Look at this really nice wicker furniture here on the porch! After that car ride it would sure feel good. Could kick back and listen to all the night sounds. I can hear some night peepers singing. Oh, and Alli brought along a six pack of cola."

Letting out a long sigh, Emi said, "Jack, I'd just as soon *not* see Matt right now."

"Ah, so that's it."

"Yeah, that's it."

Finally, Jack turned the key and gave the door a shove. "Well, you know, we'll be here for four days, we're bound to see those twins sometime. Isabel said the one only works across the street."

Emi barged inside and muttered, "As if we didn't know that already! Jack, you are so impossible and that's a fact!"

Working on that incredulous look, Jack said, "Surely not me!"

Matt knew he only had a half hour. Natt waited for him to get back so he could go home to eat with Marcy. Marcy left the clinic on Friday at five, so Natt usually left the store around five thirty on Fridays. That gave Marcy time to get home and start supper, since Natt only took a half hour on Fridays. Being newlyweds made that time very special for them. Matt had no wish to be the ogre in that situation. In fact, he hoped it would happen to him someday. He didn't know how or when, especially here in Vansville, but he hoped the where would be here in this little town. After all, Natt had moved here and so had Marcy.

He made a beeline for his refrigerator, opened his freezer door and looked through the pile of dinners on the shelf, thankful he'd stocked up when he'd shopped in Blairsville on Sunday. He still looked at each package in his freezer and pulled out the one that looked the most appetizing. After five days he pretty much knew the instructions, so he put the dinner in the microwave and set the timer. It gave him just enough time to get some silverware and pour a large glass of tea before the machine dinged. Threading his hand into his mitt, he pulled the steaming meal from the microwave then sat down to eat.

Matt ate quickly, then threw away his supper remains and headed back out his door. He only had a few minutes left of his half hour. There was no sweet little lady wanting to spend a quiet evening with him. He sighed, wondering if that kind of thing would ever happen to him. After all, he was thirty years old. By the time he bounded down his steps and was on the walk he only saw two people by the first cabin – a man and lady. The man had the hatch of the SUV up and was putting a suitcase down in front of the lady. As a gentleman, he pulled the handle up on the rolling luggage for her and she was smiling at him. Matt didn't want to be jealous, but he sure could be a whole lot happier if there was a pretty woman who smiled at him like that.

Matt scowled a bit, he saw the door open on cabin one, so he knew they were unloading into the handicapped cabin and neither of them looked like they were handicapped at all. At the park in Orlando he'd seen enough handicapped people to know all kinds. The SUV wasn't like Sandy's wheelchair equipped either. He knew Isabel usually guarded that cabin pretty well. There was always the potential that someone who needed handicapped accommodations could stop for the night. All the other cabins had four steps; she'd have to turn someone away if they had any problems at all. Why had she rented them that cabin when there were three others that were empty? It wasn't like it never got used. He knew somebody with a walker had rented it back the first of February. He shrugged, that wasn't the kind of question you asked people who rented overnight accommodations. Besides, he only had minutes to get back to the store before his half hour was up.

Deciding to be friendly, Matt smiled and said, "Howdy folks! Welcome to Vansville, Georgia, gateway to the Appalachians!" he added expansively and throwing his hand out toward the mountains close around them. "I know there isn't much time to settle in before we close, but we have some really good coffee over at the hardware store until we close at eight. You're always welcome. You folks just here for the night?" Matt walked up to Jack with his hand out. "Good to have you folks."

"Thanks, no, we're here for the weekend, until Monday, actually." Jack took Matt's hand and shook it warmly, then looked at his wife. "I think we're here to settle in, with groceries and all. Still, may come for that coffee in the morning, though." Jack shrugged. "All sorta depends on Corky, actually, he's the one who wanted us to come up."

Allison looked at Matt. "Thanks for asking, though."

"Well, sure. Gotta get back so my buddy can go eat supper with his wife." He grinned and jauntily headed across the rest of the parking lot. He didn't look at the cabin again, so he didn't see the young woman standing just inside the doorway.

Seven

Emilyn had come to the door, but as Matt walked up to Jack she faded back inside. She didn't close the door she didn't want to draw attention to herself. Besides, she could get a good look at him without anyone commenting about it. "Why does he have to live only two doors away?" she muttered to herself. She had to admit, the man hadn't gotten any uglier in ten years! "Life has just gotten way more complicated! Why on God's green earth did I have to come and why does he have to live only two doors away?" A little voice on her shoulder chuckled, *Get used to it girl, life's like that. Murphy's law, remember?*

Oblivious to the third person who had come and was watching every move he made, Matt walked on, came to the sidewalk, but had to stop to let the car go by on the highway, then crossed and sauntered down to the hardware store. Emi stood inside the unlighted cabin and watched Matt stop to talk with Jack, then watched his progress across the street, down the sidewalk and into the store.

He was a handsome man, from a distance he hadn't taken a turn for the worse! He had filled out very well from the young man she remembered. It made her wonder what he'd think of her after ten years. Maybe she'd put on a pound or two since they'd divorced, she couldn't quite remember. Actually, she could remember, right after he left she'd hardly had an appetite. One meal after another came and went and she never cracked the refrigerator door. A drink from the faucet was about all she put in her mouth, but when Alli had discovered what she was doing, besides getting her some employment, she'd made her eat, too.

119

By now, Jack had pulled another suitcase from the back and Allison walked up the ramp pulling the suitcase Jack had given her. As she came inside, Allison grinned at Emi, who had taken some things from her suitcase to put in the closet and said, "Whew! That guy could give a woman a heart flutter! My, my!"

"Stop it, Alli!" Emi reprimanded. She started to walk toward the closet that was across the living room.

"Well, it's true!" she exclaimed with a grin, totally ignoring Emilyn's reprimand. "Those broad shoulders, that dimple in his left cheek…"

From the doorway into the closet, Emi pulled in a deep breath and let it out with, "Stop!"

Jack came through the door and stopped. Looking around at the room and then at the empty closet doorway where the word had come from, he scowled. "Did you say to stop, Emi?"

Pulling in a deep breath, Emilyn moved back to the doorway and said, "No, Jack, I didn't tell you to stop! I was talking to Alli. You guys are driving me insane!"

Jack cocked his head, took another step so he could see Emi in the closet, then he headed across the living room for the bedroom with the suitcase. "Girl, you don't look insane. Well, maybe a little, but then, I think all women are just a little. Well, I guess we'll go get our coffee at the hardware store in the morning. That's something you won't have to fix, my dear."

Emilyn raised her foot, as if to stamp it; then put it down silently, after all, she wasn't a kid any more. "Will you guys stop it! I'll fix my own coffee!"

Acting truly perplexed, Jack asked, "But why, Emi? That really nice man said they open at eight and they serve really good coffee. By the time we sleep in a little, eight o'clock'll be just right. Besides, did we even bring coffee with us, Alli?" he added, with a twinkle in his eye.

"Jack! You. Know. Why! You're just being difficult!"

Walking behind his wife into the bedroom, he said, "Why no! Why did what I say make you think I was being difficult? I like a good cup of coffee to start off the day and that guy said they have a really good cup down at the hardware store. You know, that's a good idea, we'd be patronizing the local enterprises that way. No time like the present to start making friends with the local business owners."

"Mmm, and that guy just *happened* to be Matt Thomas," Emi grumbled and watched the couple disappear into the bedroom. She noticed the huge dresser in the closet and was glad she could put some clothes in it. She listened as Jack put their luggage on the rack, so she went back to the cot and zipped her suitcase closed. While Allison started unpacking, Emi took her suitcase to the closet and put it under the things she'd hung up.

"Really? He never did say his name. You're sure it's not his twin? Isabel didn't say which twin lived in which cabin. She did tell me that one of them's gone a lot, maybe that's the one you're worried about."

Emi pulled in a huge breath and let it out very slowly, intent on getting her things settled. Maybe it was her mind that needed to be settled. "It doesn't matter, Jack Albertson, that man that stopped to talk to you was Matt Thomas and you know I know that," she grumbled. "Like I told you before, I lived with the man for two years and he hasn't changed that much."

From the door, on his way back to the car for another load, this one of groceries, Jack winked at Emilyn and said, "Nice looking guy, if I do say so myself. Young, too. Alli, wouldn't you say he's about Emi's age?"

Emi made a face and knew she was telling a lie, she said, "Really? I hadn't noticed." Of course she knew Matt Thomas was good looking. He'd been good looking in high school she'd been thrilled he'd even looked at her. Her age? Of course he was!

"Never mind, Emi," Allison said. "We'll get through this weekend."

"Promise nobody'll get hurt?" Emi asked.

Grinning, Allison said, "No, I didn't say that."

Emi turned toward the comfortable looking couch. Maybe if she didn't say anything more they'd drop the subject. She let out another sigh, she could only hope! As Allison walked some things into the walk-in closet, Emi decided that, no, nobody could promise nobody would be hurt. Maybe not physically, she was sure, but she'd been hurt ten years ago when Matt walked out of her life.

Surely, they had both changed in ten years, but how much, she didn't know. It was up to her to make sure she wasn't hurt again by the same man, since they were now both in the same town. At least when he'd left her he'd moved away far enough she didn't see him anymore. As Allison hung up something on the low rack, Emi decided that fortunately for her, she was only here temporarily. Maybe between now and when Allison and Jack moved back to open the restaurant she'd have a much better, much higher paying job and she could happily turn down their offer of coming to work with them. She nearly snorted. *Yeah, and elephants fly!*

Jack walked an armload of grocery bags inside, kicked the door closed behind him and walked to the counter in the kitchen area. Watching Allison put away something in the refrigerator, he said, "I'd say we've got the car emptied and it's still plenty light out. I'm for a glass of iced tea or one of them cola cans and a relaxing hour on the porch. That wicker furniture looks downright inviting. One of 'em's callin' my name. Can't say I've sat down to do any relaxing in a good long time. You gonna join us, Emi?"

"I guess," Emi sighed. After all, she'd heard Matt say he was at the store until eight.

"Oh, I'm for the iced tea! I do believe it's some cooler here than it is back home. The porch sounds fantastic!" Allison exclaimed. "Let's get everything put away first, then we'll have the rest of the evening to relax on the porch. Is this all there is to the town? Didn't you say Corky has started working on the place where the restaurant's going in? I didn't miss it when we came in town, did I?"

"Yes, he's started and I asked Isabel. She said it's on down past the grocery store and we can't see it from here, because of the curve in the road down there. Hopefully Corky'll take us there tomorrow. I'm really excited to see the place!"

"So it's dug out like you asked?"

"That's what he said the last time he called."

"Well, good, he's even got the builder hired?"

"Don't know about that, my dear. All I know for sure is he's got the hole dug. Hopefully, it won't rain enough to fill it up before he pours the slab."

"Yeah, I guess that is a possibility."

"I heard there's a tropical storm off the coast, so it could turn this way and give us a beating here soon."

"Don't say that!" Emilyn said from the couch. "I really was hoping we'd have a nice weekend, since I haven't had four days off in so long." She chuckled. "My friend, the night waitress, told me to come back rested and tanned."

Allison laughed. "I hope you told her we weren't visiting the shore! Now the rested part, if this is all the entertainment in town, you may find yourself more rested than you want. Now the tan part, with your blond, fair complexion, I doubt you'd be tanned in two days."

"Yup, but all she changed was to say I should come back rested. I guess if it rains much we'd have to rest; there wouldn't be much else to do in this little place."

"I'd say you got that in one, Girl!" Jack exclaimed. "Got that iced tea, Alli?"

"It's right here, Jack!" Allison opened the cupboard and pulled out three huge glasses. The refrigerator was large for just a rental cabin; it was a full size side by side and had an ice maker. Happily, Allison pushed the glasses under the spout and the ice bounced into the glasses. Soon, the dark amber filled the glasses and they were heading out the door.

Matt walked back in the hardware store and said to Natt, "I'd say Isabel got some weekend renters. Maybe they're Corky's folks. Actually, that's what the man said, that Corky had asked them to come up."

"You mean to be the restaurant people?"

"I think so. Anyway, that's what the guy said. Still, it's a bit of a mystery, they're going in Isabel's handicapped cabin and neither of them looked the least bit handicapped."

"Wow! She guards that one almost with her life." Natt scowled. "What happens if somebody with a handicap comes by?"

Matt nodded and said, "I know, that sorta surprised me. Hey, you're out of here! Go get supper with Marcy. Did she tell you what she's fixing for Friday night?"

Natt grinned. "Nope, but I know it'll be better than that frozen dinner that you had! I had my share of those, they're okay, but hey. I'm out of here! You becha! You don't have to tell me twice. See you later, Cous. Oh, I'm pretty sure the coffee'll last until I get back. We don't usually have a huge run on it after supper on Fridays." Natt chuckled. "Hey, I'll be back in a half hour… if I'm not detained."

Giving his cousin a grin, Matt said, "I'll guard it until you're back, Cous. Don't worry, anybody who comes in would know you didn't make the coffee if we ran out." Matt made a face. "Even the smell's different."

Natt grinned at his cousin. "Yup, there is that!"

He rushed out the door, jumped into his car and started up. He whirled his car around and was off the parking lot in a flash, making Matt grin. Matt had no customers and watched out the front window, but Natt barely stopped to look for traffic. He chuckled at his younger cousin's actions, that newlywed spirit hadn't worn off yet, that was pretty obvious. He slouched into a chair in the 'coffee-drinker's nook' and sighed. Briefly, he wondered if he'd ever find someone he could love. At eighteen he'd thought he'd gotten it for a lifetime. The girl he'd snagged was pretty and always smiling. "You idiot! You were the one who threw her away!" At thirty, life was getting lonely and here he was stuck in a two-bit town, for the duration, as Roger had said on Sunday.

He thought at eighteen he'd found his soulmate, but couldn't there be another woman anywhere in the world for him? He leaned back in the chair and crossed his ankles. Why hadn't he tried a bit harder to make it with Emilyn? She'd been pretty enough, well, that wasn't really it… not any more. He guessed if she wasn't a believer that was the most important reason. Back when they were married she surely hadn't been.

He thought about his life back then. He'd pretty much relied on his faith as the son of George and Lynnette Thomas. Actually, as a nineteen – twenty year old, he hadn't really let his faith affect his life in the least. He'd gone to church, leaving his wife behind, because his mom would have gotten after him if he didn't show. He hadn't really listened to the preacher much at all, and his Bible had collected dust for weeks – from Sunday to Sunday. Feeling a bit uncomfortable, he realized it had collected dust for years after that, too. Until last Sunday. Now he read a verse or two each day.

He'd been at the amusement park for years and had moved up into management in the last few years. As he'd told his brother, he'd never told Jason not to put him on the schedule for Sunday. In fact, he'd worked more Sundays than most and hadn't given it much thought. Nobody much had asked for Sunday's off. You worked it just like any other day. Life happened you lived it and went on. Vansville was totally different; the town rolled its sidewalks up Saturday night at five o'clock. Sunday, in this town, you went to church!

There'd been a lot of women his age who'd come to work at the park and he'd dated several a time or two, but never long term, but none of them had sparked any long lasting interest. Most of the time he just hadn't called them for a second or third date. None of the women had ever sparked a bad feeling, just not any interest.

Natt had found his life's love here in this tiny town and his brother had also found his love here. Eric's love had left, but much to his surprise, he'd heard on the village grapevine that Carolyn Casbah would be moving back to town soon, she'd found a job in Blairsville! As he'd heard it, God must have opened it up, she was professor intelligent material. When Eric returned from his hike he'd be ecstatic! Matt was happy for him.

Matt sighed, switched legs and pushed the chair back on its back legs. He put his hands together behind his head and let out another sigh. He'd been here a week and so far, he hadn't met another single woman close to his age. Well, duh, not everybody in town had come in to the store! Usually single girls didn't wear a sign saying, *Hey, I'm single, ask me out!* He grinned, no; single women were a bit more subtle than that – usually. And come to a hardware store? Just to see him? Not so much. Life just didn't happen that way. So far, since he'd come, he and Eric were the only ones who'd rented a cabin until tonight.

Matt was still alone, since it was still Natt's supper break, when Corky walked in. Matt immediately straightened up and said, "Hi, there! What can I do for you, Corky? You got some 'honey-do' job lined up?"

The older man stopped just inside the door and looked at 'the nook'. He seemed to take an extra good look around the little area. "Uh, no, no 'honey-do' job. Achully, just came for a cuppa. Got any left? The wife fixed a good supper, but I felt like a good cuppa to wash it all down, know what I mean? I usually take my constitutional in the morning, but got tied up doin' that honey-do stuff today, so I gotta take it now."

No wonder the man walked on the parking lot. Looks like he could use more than a 'constitutional' really. Matt swallowed that thought and said,

"Sure do, Corky! We keep it on hand as long as we're open. Help yourself, I know it's pretty fresh. When I went on my supper break I saw the couple for your eatery."

"Should of been another woman. My nephew, Jack, said they'd be bringing a friend of theirs that'll be working with 'em."

When Corky didn't act like he'd be getting his own coffee, Matt stifled a sigh, stood up and stepped over to the big urn, pulled a Styrofoam cup from the stack and put it under the spigot. As he handed Corky the full cup, he said, "Huh, maybe that's why Isabel put them in her handicapped cabin just now. That cabin of mine could accommodate a couple easily enough, but three would be a crowd."

"Yep, that could be." After accepting the cup of coffee Matt held out, Corky absently handed him two quarters, blew across the top of the cup, but then walked over to the side of the little stand that held the creamer and sugar. He dumped in a large dollop of creamer and two spoons full of sugar, then sat down as if he was settling in for a 'long winter's nap' and looked around the 'coffee-drinker's nook' again.

No wonder he needs more than a 'constitutional' once a day! Matt thought.

Corky rubbed his chin, blew across the top of the cup and said, "Hmm, this here's pretty small. I kinda hoped I could bring a card table here in the mornin' so we could sit around and make some plans while we drank your coffee. Ya know? Bein's it's the only place in town we could do somethin' like that, ya know?"

Matt walked up beside him and also looked at the small space inside the half-moon of dining room chairs that made up the small nook. "Yeah, it is kind of small. If you want to bring that table by in the morning we can check it out, though. No harm in that."

Corky nodded and took another swallow of coffee. "Yeah, I'll do that, Matt. There just ain't no other place in town. Saturday's the wife's day to clean, so my house ain't the best place to meet, ya know? Now after church on Sunday, I think Loretta'll have 'em over for dinner, but that'll mean she'll be a stickler on cleanin' the place tomorra. She gets that vacyum out first thing, ya know? She's a bit on the finicky side a things with her cleanin' you understand? Says them antiques gotta be jes so." Corky shook his head. "Ain't much like anti-ques, they look like jes old furniture ta me."

Matt grinned at the older man. "Yeah, my mom had some of those. She'd guard them with her life against my brothers and me."

The older man grinned. "Yeah, I hear ya!"

Taking another sip of his coffee and finished, he threw the cup away. Corky walked out, obviously he didn't need any hardware goods for his 'honey-do' jobs tomorrow. Then again, the people for his restaurant were in town, he'd be dealing with them, maybe right here. Matt sat back down and wondered if he might interest Natt in adding iced tea to his 'coffee drinker's nook'. He sure could use a big mug full of his ice cold tea right now. He knew Natt could buy a small apartment size refrigerator when he made an order, but he'd be willing to supply the tea, just so he could have some. Listening to Corky say he'd probably bring his meeting here in the morning made Matt want a drink.

Not long after Corky left, Natt wheeled back into his spot. Since they were open only one evening a week, it was a busy evening. Many people came in that Matt had never seen, probably they worked during the time they were open during the week, so they came Friday evening so they'd have all day Saturday to do whatever.

At any rate, Natt and Matt hardly had a minute to talk in the two hours after Natt came back from supper. As the last person walked out at eight o'clock, Matt followed them, locked the door behind them and turned the sign from open to closed. Natt took the urn to the big sink in the back to dump out the dregs. He washed out the big urn so that it would be ready to fill in the morning. While he did that, Matt quickly shut off the gas pumps, then stopped at the counter to count out the money that needed to go in the safe and pushed the buttons to send the register into sleep mode.

As Natt finished cleaning the urn, Matt walked up holding the money to go in the safe in the back office. After Natt turned off the water, Matt said, "Corky came by and looked at the nook up there. He's bringing a card table by to see if he can have his meeting with those folks about the restaurant here. There's three of them, plus him. I told him it looked pretty small, but he's coming by with his table."

Natt emptied out the water, left the urn in the sink and walked around the wall to look at the front of the store. "Hmm, it's pretty small. Never thought about somebody having a meeting here. It's never happened before.

On a Saturday morning?" He walked across the entire store to have a better look. "If he put in a table…. Wow! I don't think so!"

"I wondered. Guess we'll see when he brings it."

Natt still looked at the small space and shook his head. "I sure hope we can convince him it's not gonna happen."

"Well, I knew he'd listen to you more than me on that one."

Still looking at the small space, Natt shook his head. "You know how much that would cramp that entryway on a Saturday? Nope, won't happen."

"That's what I thought."

While Matt worked his first evening, his brother came home from a hike. Except that he drove onto the lot and looked very scruffy, with a five day beard, those people sitting on the porch of the first cabin nearly thought that it was Matt coming home from the store early. Emily jumped up as she saw Eric for the first time, but then she didn't run, because he stopped to take his backpack from his passenger seat. She did wonder if Eric would remember her from that fateful day of her wedding to his brother. He had been Matt's best man, after all and a very handsome one at that. She hadn't seen him since then and she wondered if she'd changed enough he wouldn't remember her. However, there was no reason to run away.

"Good evening," he said, as he approached the porch of the first cabin. "I'm Eric Thomas. I see you're here for the weekend?"

"Yes," Jack answered. "We're Jack and Allison Albertson and our friend Emilyn…"

Eric didn't let Jack finish. He exclaimed, "Emilyn! So good to see you!" He looked at Emilyn for a moment; then he asked more quietly, "Does Matt know you're here?"

Shaking her head, she whispered, "No, he doesn't know."

He smiled at her and took another step toward his cabin. "I won't tell him, Emilyn, that'll be your department."

"Thanks, Eric." Emilyn remembered how very polite and considerate Eric was, even back in high school.

Eric saluted them, then moved to his cabin, which was right next door. Giving the huge backpack a yank, he said, "I gotta get a bit more presentable in short order. See you."

"Yep, glad to meet you," Jack said.

After he dragged his huge backpack up the steps to his cabin and across the porch, Allison asked in little more than a whisper, "Emi, why didn't you latch on to him? Even as scruffy as he is, man, he's a real hunk and so polite!"

Emilyn watched him cross his porch and enter his cabin and again shook her head. "I don't know, I've heard he's done a lot more with his life than his brother. I still have a friend in my hometown and some of what he's done was reported in the paper. I knew him in high school. It was hard not to since they're twins, but it just didn't click with him as it did with Matt. Eric always seemed to be so far beyond me at the time." She shook her head. "No, he wasn't interested in me either."

She raised her hand and let it drop. "I mean, he was the quarterback in football and captain of the basketball team and a class officer all four years. He took every hard academic class there was and was on the dean's list. You know the type."

Jack also watched the man enter the other cabin. "What's with the huge backpack? Man, that'd weigh you down! If he had to cross a river, he'd sink to the bottom and never come up! He dragged it, too, didn't carry it."

"Jack," Allison said, as Eric and his backpack thumped across the porch of his cabin. "Don't you remember what's all around us here? It's the Appalachians. I imagine he leads hikes or he's a hiker in the mountains."

Leaning back and crossing his ankles, soaking up the peaceful evening and the nature sounds from the meadow, he put his glass to his lips for another swallow of tea and said, "Yeah, you're right. I remember now, Isabel said he was a hiking guide. He sure was scruffy enough!" He nodded toward the parking lot. "Still, he drives a decent car though!" He turned to Emilyn and asked, "So he did all those things in high school. What's he done since then?" Jack shook his head. "Being a hiking guide doesn't seem too challenging to me, not if he was all those things in high school."

Emilyn shook her head. "My friend back home told me he went to college and spent time in the Marines in the middle east. She told me what he's done overseas; at least what he's willing to talk about. She said the hometown paper told about some heroic things he's done." She grinned at her friends. "My friend said they even named a street, 'Eric Street' after their hometown hero."

"Ah, explains a lot! Maybe he's just taking a break and doing something that's not so heroic or challenging for a while."

"That could be." Allison added.

While the three still sat on the porch, a light blue van pulled onto the lot and as the trio watched, the big side door slid open and a lift moved out, then down, but nobody appeared from inside the van. It sat that way for a few minutes until a transformed Eric came from his cabin, rushed down the walk past them, but didn't acknowledge them again and stepped onto the lift, then took himself up and went inside.

Emi gasped her eyes wide as saucers, "What was that? Why did he ride a lift? He's sure not handicapped!"

"I imagine someone in that van needs a lift and it was the easiest way for Eric to get in," Jack said and watched the empty lift move up and the big door close. "That's a nifty thing for someone who's handicapped!"

As if talking to herself, Emi said, "It's a tiny town. Somebody lives here who's handicapped? That's unusual, isn't it?"

"Honey," Allison said, "It's a free country, anybody can live anywhere, even if they're handicapped." Allison turned to Jack. "You know, we better remember to make the restaurant and parking lot handicapped friendly."

Jack set his glass down on the little table, leaned back and put his hands behind his head. After crossing one ankle over his knee, he nodded. "Yeah, hadn't thought about that before, but you're right. Of course, state regulations have that stipulation. It wouldn't pass code otherwise. You gotta have so many handicapped spaces for so many that aren't. Whoever does the striping of the parking lot'll know what's required."

"Yes, that's true, of course. But inside, we'll have to make the aisles wide enough a wheelchair can get through."

Allison looked across the meadow at the end of the street behind Isabel's house. "Honey, if these guys live in these cabins, are there places to rent or where would we live once we moved here? Those two houses look pretty new."

Jack nodded and picked up a cookie from the plate on the little table. How did he tell these ladies, especially Emi, there were no apartments or anything besides these cabins to live in in this town? Giving himself some time, he stuffed the whole cookie in his mouth, chewed and swallowed, before he said, "Isabel said there aren't any apartments or empty houses in town. There aren't any rentals at all – houses or apartments. She called that a new street and said those two houses had only been built recently. It sounded like they both have newlywed couples in them. She said they all lived in her cabins at one time. She said that's why these two guys live in her cabins that's the only alternative."

"No apartments? Not even any duplexes or condos?" Emilyn exclaimed.

Jack shrugged. "That's what she said. She told me that's why she rents these two cabins to these guys there isn't any other place to rent in town."

"Maybe we should think about making the restaurant building two stories and having our place upstairs. What do you think?"

Jack nodded. "It's something to think about. Actually, I drew up plans for a second floor it would be more convenient that way. Right at first we won't have much help other than us, so that was my thought."

Emi looked at the couple and scowled. "Where would I live?"

Jack's eyes twinkled, as he nodded toward Eric's cabin. "Looks like there's another cabin or two on down the way. Isabel said she's had several people live in these cabins over the years. Could think about that, girl."

Letting out a long sigh, Emilyn said, "Jack, you are so not funny! I really don't want to live next door to my ex-husband."

"Actually, I wasn't trying to be." He put his large glass to his lips, then looked at her over the top and added, "'Course, you could marry one of these guys… That Eric guy seems just as handsome as his brother."

"Ohhhhhhhh!"

Jack chuckled. "Just a thought…"

Surprising all three of them, Emilyn's eyes clouded up with tears. She leaned back against the straight back of the kitchen chair, stuck her thumb and forefinger into the corners of her eyes to try to stop the tears. So softly that the other two sitting only inches away could hardly hear her, Emi whispered, "I really loved that man. When we were first married, I thought he was my soul mate and we'd grow old together."

Thinking he'd put the tears in her eyes, Jack cleared his throat and whispered, "Sorry." He looked away he didn't do women's tears too well.

Seeing how upset she was, Allison got up immediately and bent over the younger woman. She put her arms around her and hugged her for several silent minutes. Finally, she whispered into her ear, "I know you did,

Emi. I know it's hard for you to see him again. We didn't realize when we committed to Corky."

Emilyn nodded. "Yes, it's so hard. You have no idea. Before we got here I didn't know how hard it would be."

It was quiet in town, there wasn't much traffic on the road and the three on the porch relaxed with their iced tea. Friday nights weren't like this on either end of the town where they lived. Emilyn usually worked Friday nights and it was one of their 'pack-'em-in' nights. Sometimes they even had a waiting line. Friday night was very rowdy with people yelling across the restaurant and Barney stayed. Even without serving alcohol he had to act as the bouncer sometimes. Usually she was washing down the last table at midnight when Naomi walked in. Fortunately by that time of night it wasn't families, just single folks.

Breathing in the clean, mountain air, Emi realized Vansville and where she lived were like night and day. There might even be people still leaving their cars in the parking lot heading into her apartment building from a movie or late night stop at a restaurant when she got home from work, but as they sipped their tea on the cabin porch all they heard were birds twittering in the trees across the meadow and a bullfrog grumping off in the distance, in some quiet stream they couldn't see. A car going through town really broke up the stillness.

They lost track of time in the quietness. The late evening sun was still bright in the western sky and the three friends had settled into a comfortable quietness. They'd finished their snack and Allison hadn't gotten up to find more. They were glad to be away from the hustle and bustle of their everyday lives for a few days. Jack especially didn't miss the heat of the sizzling grill and its smells at all.

They were unaware when a much more quiet man walked across the parking lot later. Being on foot didn't make much noise on the gravel parking lot, his footsteps only mingled with the car going by on the highway. He had decided he'd stop and be friendly when he came home from the store, so he stepped from the gravel and started up the walkway in front of the cabins. He saw the people sitting on the porch and before any of the three noticed him, he turned up the ramp for cabin one. Corky had told him there were three people, he'd only met two earlier.

Confidently, he started up the ramp because he saw the three people sitting together around the wicker table. The woman he hadn't met before had her back to him. Just before he took the last step onto the porch, he put on his best smile and said, "Hi, folks, glad you're…" his mouth fell open, he couldn't continue. He stared at the second woman on the porch, because she had turned her head at his voice. He couldn't say anything more. Not that it was too hot, but he felt a drop of sweat trickle down his back.

Two other heads swung around immediately and all three people noticed him swallow, then swallow again. He took his index finger and rubbed across his upper lip, then let his hand drop. Finally a squeak left his mouth, as he whispered, "Emilyn?"

Well, maybe I'm not the only one who hasn't changed too much. As soon as he spoke her name, Emi dropped her eyes and stared at the floor, but she felt the heat work its way up her neck onto her cheeks. Why did she always blush when she was embarrassed? It surely was her Swedish background.

After an extended silence, Jack looked from Matt to Emilyn. "You two know each other?" Of course he knew that.

Matt was the first to answer, because every faculty that Emilyn possessed seemed to be frozen except, perhaps, her eyes. He cleared his throat and in a voice that still sounded unnatural, he said, "Umm, yeah, ten years ago."

Jack grinned and watched the pink creep up Emilyn's neck onto her cheeks. "Well, how about that! What do you know! Guess maybe you'll see lots more of each other in the near future. Seems Emilyn's gonna be a waitress in that restaurant my uncle Corky's building for the town here real soon."

Emi could have died! Not only was she here now, but now Matt knew she'd be here for a long time in the future. Maybe there'd be an earthquake while they were here and it'd swallow her up! Why did Jack always have such fun teasing her? When she raised her head, it wasn't to look at Matt, but her eyes glared at Jack. He knew if looks could kill he'd be at least ten feet under. Of course, Emilyn didn't say a word. It felt like a ball of cotton the size of Georgia lodged in her throat.

Matt cleared his throat again, turned so he looked at Jack and not at his ex-wife and said, "So you're the folks Corky's planning on talking to around a table in our 'coffee-drinker's nook' in the morning. He came by the store after I went back to see if he could fit his card table in the spot. We couldn't be sure."

Did he really have to say that? The other three on the porch heard the strangled groan that left Emilyn's throat and her chin hit her chest again.

She couldn't very well run and hide in the cabin, the door was shut and Matt only stood a few feet away from her. She raised her head and let her eyes peek at him for an instant. *Is that hunger in his eyes as he looks at me?* NO! IT IS NOT!! *No, it can't be! He was the one who skipped out, who threw his set of keys at me!*

Only a few minutes later, after another time of silence, Matt cleared his throat and turned, anxious to leave the porch. Just before he escaped, he said, "Well, folks, umm, have a good evening. I'll be getting on home, big day at the store tomorrow." Matt cleared his throat. "Umm, neighbors, you know, probably see you again."

Cheerfully, Jack answered, "We plan to, you do the same. It's good to know something. Uncle Corky never did tell us what to expect.

Matt didn't answer Jack he hurried off the porch for the number one cabin and took long strides to his own cabin. They heard two decisive steps on the porch two doors away and Emilyn let out a long sigh. She knew she'd made a complete fool of herself in front of three people. What in the world did Matt think of her after so many years? Another thought hit her. *Tomorrow? Their meeting with Corky would be at his store? Oh, man!*

"So," Jack said, "like I said before, nice looking man." Jack upended his glass for the last swallow, then grinned at Emi and said, "He's even polite! He welcomed us to his little town. When we were emptying the car he invited us over for coffee. 'Course we can't go now, but it seems like Corky's taking us over to his store for coffee in the morning."

Allison got in the act. With a smirk, she asked, "Was he always that quiet, Emi?"

Slowly, with great precision, Emi set her empty glass on the wicker table. Bringing her hand back to her lap, the fingers curling into a fist, she looked at the two people who sat opposite her and said, "Jack, Allison, I don't want to talk about Matt Thomas. Can we do that? Please?"

Allison took pity on the girl. "Okay, Emi, we'll stop teasing you."

"Thanks. I really appreciate that." She let out a long sigh. "Life will be way too complicated if he's here and I'm here."

Of course, Jack never said he wouldn't tease her anymore and he said, "Say, if he's here and you're here, would you ever marry him?"

"Jack! You are so *not* funny!" Emi exploded.

"But hey, just think, you could be neighbors until you got married. You could build you a nice house back there and be neighbors with those other newly-weds, it'd be great! You know the restaurant's at the other end of town." Jack pointed across the street. "His hardware store is just down the block, but you can't even see where the restaurant's gonna be. Your hours, well they'd be a little off, but we could work on that. A restaurant isn't usually open at quite the same time as a hardware store. Still, he could come for dinner then hang out until you got off." Grinning, Jack leaned back in the chair. "He could walk you home, wouldn't that be romantic, especially in the winter when it's dark."

"But you just said there's no place else to live but in these cabins!" Using her hand to demonstrate, Emilyn continued, "If he lives there and I live in another one, we'll see each other all the time! How could we not?"

"Yeah, see, that's what I'm saying," Jack agreed. On the end of that statement all three of them heard the distinctive click of the closing door two doors away. "Guess he wasn't gonna bring some iced tea out to enjoy the evening. Too bad, as quiet as the man is, he'd be a good one to have for a visit."

"Jack, please…" both Allison and Emilyn said the words together.

He sighed, "Yeah, yeah, I get it."

"Thanks," Emi said.

Matt had planned on sitting on his porch with a mug of iced tea until dark. When he left the store he felt the balmy breeze, knew his brother was gone, although his SUV was on the parking lot. He really had wanted to listen to the evening sounds of the meadow as he unwound from a fairly busy day at the store. He had no desire to watch TV, why learn what part of the world fell off while he worked? However, he never even opened his fridge, or turned on the TV, but collapsed into his favorite chair in his living room and put his face in his hands. He didn't even think to turn on a light. All at once, Matt Thomas knew he didn't have life by the tail! In fact, it had him by the tail.

Emilyn was as beautiful as she'd ever been! In fact, he was sure she was more beautiful than the image he'd kept in his heart all these years. He'd thought he was over his wife. He'd moved on, changed jobs, moved from Georgia to Florida ten years ago. However, one look at her and he knew she was still that beautiful first love he'd never forget. Was she having as much trouble seeing him as he'd had seeing her? After all, she hadn't said a word to him while he stood there strangled from seeing her for the first time in many years.

Before he left the chair it turned dark outside. Finally, he pulled in a deep breath and turned on the lamp beside the chair, then went to the counter and opened the cookie jar his mom had given him and he'd carted everywhere with him. At dinner time he'd forgotten he had cookies. The TV dinner at five o'clock hadn't stayed with him long, he felt like he hadn't eaten in a week. Besides, seeing Emi had put a hole in his belly. He pulled out three cookies and scarfed them down. Life as he knew it had just changed drastically. That woman he'd loved all those years ago was going to be part of the restaurant operation on the other end of town! It wouldn't be that long from now, either.

Wow! Can I handle that? It didn't matter. He'd committed to working the store with Natt, he had no job to go back to in Florida. He was thirty years old, way past time for running from his troubles. This was life you took it as it came at you. You took the pleasure ride, but you also took the hard knocks as they came along. There was no throwing keys in anyone's face, not now, not ever again. Even though he'd tried so hard to forget that moment, he knew he never would forget the look on Emi's face when he did that.

After the cookies, he went in the bathroom and got ready for bed. However, before he climbed into bed he sat in the chair in his bedroom and picked up his Bible. Yes, he'd been reading a verse or two every morning while he ate his breakfast, but this was something a whole lot different, a whole lot harder. Emilyn would be living here in Vansville! *God! How do I handle that? After how I treated her, she couldn't love me again, could she?* Even before he had the Book open a verse popped into his head: '… we know that in all things God works for the good of those who love him…' (Rom 8:28)

"Really, God? Really? Are You saying having Emi here is for my good?" He didn't expect a lightning bolt to come with an answer. Actually no answer came at all. However, the verse repeated itself in his mind. '…*in all things God works...'* God had brought him here to Vansville only a week ago. He was sure of it. In a few months Emilyn would be here – *'in all things...'* He sighed, they'd both be here long term. There wasn't another place to live for a single person except Isabel's cabins.

After reading his Bible for some time, Matt slowly closed the Book, placed it in slow motion on the table beside the chair, turned off the light and stood up. In the semi-darkness, because the security light in the parking lot was so far away, he made his way to the bedroom door and slowly closed it. Even though he was the only one in the cabin, he liked it dark to sleep and with the light in the parking lot shining in his front window, he always closed the door to block out the light. Tonight perhaps it would block out the thought that his ex-wife was sleeping in the cabin only two doors down. How could her living here be a plus in his life? In his Bible reading tonight he hadn't noticed it, but maybe God had a sense of humor?

"In all things God works for the good of those who love him." Matt sank onto the sheet and sighed. *Emilyn, why did I ever leave you?* **You were a stupid fool, that's why**! He nodded, agreeing with the little voice. He'd been so full of himself, so full of number one, that what happened to his best friend and the woman he loved hadn't even entered the equation. As he pulled his feet up onto the bed he realized he'd mourned that decision many times over the years. Probably every time he Emailed her about some change in his life. Had he wanted her to know because somehow, if she knew she'd think about him? *Really?* Was he still so full of himself he'd put her through such agony?

Oh, God, I'm sorry!

However, after the light went out in cabin one, Emi lay between the sheets. The cot was comfortable enough, actually, it was a fold up bed and more comfortable than her lumpy mattress in her apartment, but her eyes were wide open, even though she hadn't had any coffee since lunch time and she'd been sleepy for most of the trip. She was in the big room of the cabin and there were windows on three sides. Since the cabin was the closest one to the parking lot, that also meant that the security light in the center shone directly in one of those windows and she had pulled the drapes on all of them before she climbed into bed.

Eight

Even as she pulled the drapes she knew the light in the parking lot wouldn't keep her awake, it was the man down the walk who would do just fine in that department. Did she think that closing all the drapes would keep his image from barging into her thoughts? She sighed and closed her eyes, *no, closing the drapes or closing my eyes won't keep his real live image away.*

He'd told her only days ago that he was moving to this town, but she had no idea how small the town was or how close they would be while she and the Albertson's were here. *Since I knew he was living in this town before she asked, why did I tell Alli I'd come with them?* That was a question she had no answer for. She pulled in a long breath, turned over so she faced the wall and closed her eyes. It was comfortable in the cabin, but she still pulled the sheet and light blanket up around her ears. Life had definitely become so much harder for this single girl! And Murphy's Law? It was here in Vansville in spades!

Instead of going blank like the wall a foot from her eyes, her mind relived the few minutes when Matt had been on the porch. When they'd seen each other, neither of them said much. Actually, she didn't say anything to him! As she thought about it, she knew she couldn't have said a word, it felt like her tongue was glued to the roof of her mouth. *No,* she decided, *I am definitely not over Matt Thomas!* And Matt? Well, he didn't say a whole lot either, in fact, he ran away really fast!

A cynical little voice whispered, *'Wasn't that kind of like what he did a decade ago? He ran away, didn't he?'*

She whispered, "He threw those awful keys at me on his way out the door. Would I have gone with him if he'd asked me?"

Even though it made her feel like a ninny, tears welled up in her eyes. When they had come to her earlier she'd felt like a first class fool. The tears had come in front of Jack and Allison! It made Jack think he'd caused them. *Oh, my!* At the time she'd gotten Matt's Email she was sure she was over him, but she hadn't seen him in a really long while. Now she had, now she knew she wasn't over him, not even close. She'd bragged to Allison several times over the years she'd known the lady that she was over Matt.

She turned over again and buried her head in the pillow, surely she wouldn't cry over Matt Thomas! The man had left her! He'd thrown the keys to their apartment at her and walked out, telling her she wasn't welcome to come with him to his new job. She'd had no idea he'd even applied for a different job! They'd been working at the factory, but somehow he'd made an application to a job out of town and she had no clue.

At the time, she'd wondered what she could have done differently to keep him, but other than being a better cook, dutifully going to his church, then to dinner with his parents to suffer through those looks his mom could give her, etcetera, etcetera, she'd had no clue. She'd been a young woman, barely twenty years old. She didn't know how to lure her husband back. She wasn't pregnant; she couldn't have put him on a guilt trip about being a daddy. She had loved the man and as he walked out the door she was so broken, her mouth had fallen open and her feet had glued themselves to the floor.

She remembered as the door closed behind him it felt like her heart had broken also, into a million pieces. With the snick of the door shutting her knees became water and she fell on the threadbare carpet, her arms went out, but her elbows buckled and she'd collapsed with her face into the carpet. Tears had blinded her eyes and rolled down her cheeks. She remembered, she'd cried and sobbed for hours and used a full box of tissues.

Realizing she was still crying, she wiped her eyes on the pillowcase, but the tears kept coming. She tried to swallow and turned her face away from the light reflected onto the ceiling from the window. She was a big girl now. Just because they were in the same town didn't mean she had to fall apart. She pulled in a deep breath and closed her eyes.

Willing the tears to stop, she picked up the edge of the pillowcase and wiped the bridge of her nose where she could feel the tickle of one tear that still leaked from her eye. She wondered how long she'd been laying here having this pity party with herself, but there was no clock to look at. She knew there wasn't enough light in the room to illuminate the clock on the wall a full room away. She turned once more, lying on her stomach; she put her face into her pillow and willed the tears to stop.

Maybe something would happen; maybe they wouldn't have coffee at his store tomorrow morning. Maybe Murphy's Law had done enough for this trip. It sure had done a number! Finally, she fell asleep, but her dreams were full of Matt Thomas – the strangled way he'd said her name and the look he'd given her, before he'd run away - again.

During the night, something woke her. It wasn't a groggy wakefulness, she was wide awake. She lay still for several minutes trying to decide what had wakened her, but came up with nothing. The air conditioning was already running it hadn't just kicked on. She didn't have to go, but she still threw back the covers and went to the bathroom. In the dark, she found her glass and took a drink. She hoped that the cool water would sooth the parched feeling in her throat. The water tasted good.

With the light off, she shuffled back to the cot, stretched out and covered up, hoping to get back to sleep, however, that didn't happen. She lay there for quite a while wondering what had brought her out of sleep. The cot was comfortable, although it was a single it was similar to the daybed/sofa in her apartment. The cabin was the right temperature and it was as dark as her apartment usually was, so it was nothing inside that had made her wake up. She couldn't remember if she'd had a dream. But then, she rarely remembered a dream, just knew one had wakened her.

She listened: listened to the silence that was both inside and outside the cabin. Even the clock on the wall didn't make much noise. This tiny town was so in the sticks, there wasn't any traffic going through on the highway! She could never remember being in a place that was so profoundly silent! Even the two people behind the closed bedroom door weren't making any noise. *Don't men usually snore?*

As she lay there in the darkness her thoughts turned again to the man who had left her all those years ago, but who had crashed into her existence only hours ago. *Why? Why do things like this happen to girls like me? God, if You really are there, why?* However, there was no answer to her question; she hadn't expected one. Besides, why should she be asking God anything? She'd never done anything about a god before, why now? In a hoarse whisper, she said, "Girl, are you that desperate?"

Emilyn scrunched her eyes shut and willed the thoughts and the well defined image out of her mind. Ever since she'd seen him when they pulled into town, Matt Thomas had occupied front and center of Emi's mind. She sighed and turned over, putting her face toward the wall. She snuggled down under the sheet and light blanket, but only minutes later decided it was too warm for that, so she threw off the light blanket. She tried to get comfortable again under the sheet, but the blanket hadn't gone all the way off the bed, the double thickness still covered her feet. At this point, it was too heavy. She sighed, knowing it wasn't the covers, it wasn't the darkness, but the man who haunted her thoughts. Obviously, those were heavy.

It was dark in the cabin, because she'd pulled the heavy drapes across the windows in the living room before she lay down. Back home she needed darkness where she slept because she wanted to sleep later in the morning, but now she wished she'd left a little light. The tiny glow on the ceiling wasn't enough to see what time it was and she'd left her phone in her purse across the room. She sighed, this trip had really been a bad idea. She sighed knowing that she'd really wanted to come to get away from Barney's place.

Of course, this was the living room and wasn't set up for people to sleep in it, there was no illuminated bedside clock, only the large wall clock hanging on the tiny arch separating the kitchen and the living areas, but it was ten feet away and too dark to see it. She wiggled around in the bed, but her eyes wouldn't stay closed.

As she thought about the place, the cabin seemed like a miniature house and Emi wondered if the lady kept any books on a bookshelf for people to read. After Matt had made his hurried exit several hours ago and the three of them came inside, they'd sat around and talked for few minutes, but she hadn't really looked around too much. All she knew for sure was how to get to the bathroom from the cot. *Been there, done that, don't need to do it again.*

After she'd turned every way she could think of and even turned the pillow over, she still couldn't make sleep come. She let out a long sigh, threw back the sheet again and sat on the edge of the cot. She put her feet down this floor was carpeted, unlike her apartment with its hardwood floor. She looked around the room trying to remember where things were. However, even though there was a light in the parking lot, the drapes were so heavy she couldn't even see shapes in the big room. The only light was the dim reflection on the ceiling. These drapes weren't like ones she'd known about in most hotels where there was a small strip between the two drapes that covered the window. She sat for several minutes looking around in the dark, but couldn't make out anything.

"Where's the closest light?" she grumbled. It certainly was not close to the cot! She'd had to fumble around in the dark after turning out the light for bed, but then Jack and Allison still had the light on in the bedroom and some had filtered out under their door. Of course, their room was dark now she knew they'd turned the light out not long after she lay down. Surely now they were asleep. She wasn't about to wake them.

Finally, after sitting on the side of the cot for several minutes looking around, she decided to feel her way along the wall, since she knew for sure the cot was up against the wall. Maybe she'd find a piece of furniture and maybe there would be a lamp close to it. She could only hope. She stood up and turned to put her hand on the side of the cot and knew how a blind person felt as she shuffled along. Just as she reached the end of the cot and as she raised her hand to find the wall, a loud snort came from the bedroom. Instead of putting her hand out to feel for the wall, she stuffed her fist in her mouth to hold in the scream. That was definitely something she didn't have at her apartment. However, no other noise came from the bedroom.

It took several seconds for her heart rate to settle back to normal. She took another shuffling step and found the wall. It was cool and felt good to her very warm skin, so she kept her hand on the wall. Several steps later, her bare toe connected with something solid. Again she yanked her hand back and stuffed her fist in her mouth. Instantly, her heart began to pound, but her toe hurt like crazy. It was a good thing she'd brought open-toed shoes, that toe might be too swollen to stuff in a tennis shoe when it finally became morning! Why were nights like this so long? However, when she investigated the object she decided it might be a small table. Perhaps there might be a table lamp on it.

Carefully, she reached out and found the edge of the object then even more carefully, she moved her hands onto what she thought was the surface of the object. "Yes!" she whispered, "it's a table! Surely a light isn't too far away."

However, just as she moved her hand onto the surface of the table, another loud snort came from the bedroom. Her hand jerked and something fell to the floor, but struck her already sore toe. "Awww!" The tears that wouldn't stop when she first went to bed started again. This time, there was reason, her toe hurt like crazy!

She slammed her hand over her mouth, hoping her cry wasn't loud enough to wake Alli or Jack. She put her other hand down on the table and raised her foot, trying to ease the pain in her toe. At least she hadn't hit the light that might be on the table. That would have been much louder and more painful when it fell. It could even have broken and if the glass would have been everywhere in the dark room she couldn't have seen it. She sighed, if she'd broken a lamp she'd have been in the dark, with glass on the floor and not have any idea where another light could be in the room. *Thank goodness for small favors!*

Finally, it registered that what had fallen was some kind of book and the edge of it had landed on the toe that was already sore from striking the table leg. The tears that had been falling since she'd hit her toe made rivers down her cheeks. She knew these tears weren't just from her hurting toe. It didn't matter, she still couldn't see.

Pulling her lower lip into her mouth to keep from making enough noise to wake Jack and Alli, she started sweeping her hand back and forth on the top of the table, but she did it very slowly and very carefully. She put her foot back down on the floor, but kept her hand on the edge of the table. She didn't want to send anything else onto her poor toe! If there was a lamp and she sent it to the floor there would be much more than a hurt toe, there'd be lots of noise and maybe even some cuts to show for the catastrophe.

Finally, her fingers touched some cool metal. The tips of her fingers felt for the shape. That had to be the base of a lamp! Slowly she moved her hand up the base; she was determined not to send this object onto the floor. Finally, six inches up the shaft and at the back, she found the switch. She put her fingers around it and only seconds later she had light in the room! She decided that was quite an accomplishment!

The first thing she did was look at the object she had sent to the floor. It was a Bible. A red Bible! Was that the only thing the lady had in the cabin to read? Still standing beside the table, with the red Bible only centimeters from her hurting toe, she looked around the room. With a great sigh, as she looked at every piece of furniture in the subdued light from the table lamp, she could find no other piece of reading material in the room. There was no coffee table and therefore no magazines on it. There was another table at the other end of the couch, but there was nothing on it, either. Now that the light was on, she also looked at the clock. It told her there were still several hours before daylight. She thought she'd slept longer than that.

Why of course! What made you think dawn was just about to break? Actually, I thought the night was long enough it should be over.

With another sigh of defeat, she swung around the little table and sank onto the couch it was beside. She looked at her toe, but of course, it hadn't started to swell or turn black, perhaps it wouldn't anyway. She still determined to wear her flip flops if she could. At least that would keep her toes from hurting inside a tight shoe. Besides, she was on vacation! Flip-flops were the footwear of choice in the summer. She let out another sigh, reached down and picked up the Bible. She looked at the cover for several minutes. The Book itself was bright red, but the letters and the emblem were even brighter, they were shiny gold. *Red and gold? I thought the Bible was some ancient book. This isn't old! It's bright and sparkly and looks almost new.*

Still holding it closed, she remembered vaguely from when she and Matt were married that he'd told her two things about religious things. They needed to go to church, so they'd been married in the church he went to. He'd showed her a Bible, but he'd told her not to start reading it at the beginning of the Book, but as she racked her brain she couldn't remember if he'd ever told her where to start! She sat and stared at the bright gold lettering and the gold emblem and wondered where to begin reading.

She shook her head, still staring at the cover. *If you don't start at the beginning of a book where do you start?* She'd never been that interested, she hadn't asked him where she should start. All she remembered was that he'd said the beginning of the Bible wasn't the best place for someone who knew nothing about it to start to read it. When she'd asked why, he'd only answered, 'trust me'. She had and look where that got her! Looking back, she realized how much she had trusted him – with her life – with her happiness.

However, someone else had read the Book before her. As she held the Book loosely in her hands, it fell open. Under the heading; Genesis, chapter one, the next four words seemed to leap off the page at her. "IN THE BEGINNING GOD..."

Emilyn stared at those words. She couldn't seem to go beyond them. She remembered her silent words from a few minutes ago. *Yes, there must be a God! Who is He? Where is He? How do I get to know Him? Is Matt the only one who knows Him? There has to be somebody who knows something! Why did the lady have one of these in her cabin?*

It was the middle of the night, no one was awake. Really, not much time had gone by, maybe only five minutes since she'd sat down. Emilyn stared for a long time at those words and the same questions kept circling in her mind, but there were no answers. Finally, still holding the Bible in her hands, the page still open to the front and the lamp beside the couch still on, her eyes closed and before she realized what was happening she toppled onto the couch. Her hands cradled the red book to her chest, her feet came up and wedged into the tiny space between the arm of the couch and her bottom. She heard nothing else.

That was how Allison found her in the morning, with the Bible clutched to her chest and still open to Genesis 1:1.

In the morning, when Allison entered the bathroom through the closet, she poked her head around the open door of the bathroom into the living area. She knew Emi had pulled all the drapes, so she knew a light had to be on, it was too bright in the living room. When she looked, she saw that the table lamp was on. Just before she closed that door between the bathroom and the living room she glimpsed Emilyn on the couch.

She didn't go out to investigate, she was sure the girl would wake up with the noise she made taking her shower, flushing the toilet and brushing her teeth. Jack came in while she was still putting on makeup and he definitely wasn't quiet, but when Allison opened the bedroom door a half hour later, Emi still lay on the couch, holding a Book and the light was still on. She didn't look all that comfortable, either. Her legs were smashed into the tiny space between her bottom and the arm of the couch. She also held that hard covered Book to her chest. That couldn't be comfortable.

Allison scowled as she approached the sleeping girl. *What's Emi doing holding a Bible to her chest?* "A Bible? Emilyn? What gives?" she murmured.

"Emi?" Allison said, quietly. "Why aren't you on the cot? Emi, it's morning, it's time to get up. Why's the light still on?"

Emi still didn't move. She didn't even stretch her legs. The couch was big, with three cushions, but Emi's body only covered two of them. While Jack went to open the drapes, Allison walked up to the couch and stood right in front of the sleeping girl, but Emi never moved. Allison looked down at the Bible she clutched in her hands. It looked like Emi had opened to the first page, found she couldn't make any sense of all those names and fallen asleep. This made no sense to Allison. Emi didn't do church, she admitted she didn't know that much about what went on in church, but she was holding a Bible?

Allison reached down and started shaking her shoulder. At the same time, she said, "Emi? Come on, wake up! You can't be comfortable!"

Emilyn didn't wake up right away. Allison kept shaking her and talking to her. Finally, her bleary eyes came open, but didn't focus. She didn't even move before she asked, "Alli, is there really a God?"

Sucker-punched, Allison stammered, "Well… well… of course there's a God! Why?"

Slowly, still clutching the Bible, Emi's legs left the couch and she sat up. Her hands fell away from her chest, but the Bible came with her hands. Emilyn looked up at her friend and pointed to the top line. "See, look, it says here, 'In the beginning God…' How come I never knew about Him?"

Perplexed, Allison, scowled. "Never knew about Him? How can you say that? Didn't… didn't Matt…?"

Emi looked up at her friend and shook her head. She looked down at the page still open, then back up to Allison. "Matt said we had to go to church." Looking down at the still open page in the Bible, she scowled at the page, pointed to the first line again, then looked up again at Allison and said, "This says; 'In the beginning God…' there was a beginning? It didn't just… you know…just happen? In school they always said stuff just

happened, or maybe there was some big bang, or some gunk somehow ....
I don't know… but right here it says, 'In the beginning God…'"

Allison moved her head slowly back and forth. "No, I don't know, Emi. I… I know there's a God, but I don't know what that means." Contemplatively, Allison repeated the words; "'In the beginning God…' Wow!"

Emi looked at her friend and asked, "Who would know? Why was this Book here?" With her free hand she pointed to the little table. "It was here on this table. I… I started to read it, but I guess I fell back to sleep."

"Well, I guess those men; you know, it says on there, 'placed by the Gideons'. I guess those guys put Bibles all over the place."

"Why?"

Allison shrugged. "I… I guess they think it's important."

Even as Allison left her to start their breakfast, Emi sat staring at the first page of the Book she was holding. "'In the beginning God…'" she murmured. "God, who are You? How can I know You?"

Matt had to get up in the middle of the night to use the bathroom, something he never needed to do, but the urge had been on the tail end of a very vivid dream. In fact, he left the bathroom and instead of going back to bed right away, he went to the kitchen and pulled his jug of tea from the refrigerator. He felt he needed something to wash the dream out of his mind. He wouldn't get back to sleep if he didn't do something! He didn't take a mug, just took the jug to his living room and slumped into his favorite chair in the darkness to drink. The only light came from the far distant security light in the parking lot three cabins away. He unscrewed the top and took a long slug straight from the jug, letting the cold liquid slide down his throat. Actually, it was so cold it sent a shiver down his back. That wasn't enough, he up-ended the jug again for another long swallow.

Many things went through his mind as he took swallow after swallow. Some of those thoughts were about the young woman he hadn't seen in ten years, but was in the cabin only a few yards away from his. The dark of very early morning seemed to be a good time to think heavy thoughts. He had treated her so badly.

"Why did I leave her?" he heard himself ask. "In my own way, at twenty years old, I loved her. I… I admired her spunk. She stood up to her dad. Well, yes, she stood up to me, too. If she didn't know something, she asked. I quarreled with her because I didn't know the answer or because I didn't want her to think I didn't... I don't know!"

He swallowed another mouthful of tea, but also a gasp. "She... she loved me," he said brokenly. "She loved me, she was devastated when I walked out."

He closed his eyes, the look on her face as those keys came at her flashed vividly across his mind. *"Oh, God, why did I do that to her?"*

It was at least fifteen minutes later, maybe longer, he didn't look at the clock, before he set the jug down on the coffee table, screwed the top on and closed his eyes. Many things passed through his mind as he dozed in the chair. In fact, the dream that woke him had been about Emilyn. His thoughts, while he sat in the living room were all about his ex-wife. A tear escaped and slid down his cheek.

Perhaps the first ray of dawn brightened the sky when he went back to bed. He pulled the sheet over him, but even then found it extremely hard to get back to sleep. As he lay in the bed and closed his eyes, he murmured, "God in heaven, why did I leave that woman? I know, I remember, I loved her, I loved her even as I walked out that door! I was such a fool at twenty years old! God, my Father, why is she back in my life? Will she be coming here to live? If she is, I'll see her nearly every day! How do I survive that?" His last words were a cry of anguish. On the last sigh before sleep claimed him, Jack's words came back. 'She'll be living here.'

Later that morning, when it was already light, Matt's alarm woke him. That was very unusual, most of the time he woke up, raring to go, only minutes before the alarm went off. As he showered, he thought about the young woman he'd seen last night for the first time in ten years. She hadn't lost her figure, in fact, she was still a beautiful woman. If anything, she was more beautiful than he remembered her when he'd married her. At the time, he'd seen her as the most beautiful girl in their graduating class. He felt so important because the most beautiful girl had decided to lavish her affection on him! Him! The younger twin that wasn't much to speak of, just one who squeaked by and didn't have much ambition.

He'd been proud to take her to their senior prom. He'd bought her the best corsage he could afford on his limited money. He'd been ecstatic when she accepted his proposal and his tiny engagement ring. At the time, he didn't listen or care what his parents or even his twin said. If he remembered right, even her parents weren't that keen on them getting married right out of high school. Of course, their reason was very different from his parents' reason.

It didn't matter at the time, he wanted his own way! He was intent on marrying the girl who had captured his heart no matter how old they were. One thing that had stuck with him of his parents' teaching, you didn't go to bed with a woman unless you were married to her. He'd stuck to that teaching they were still virgins when they were married.

He remembered he'd been a horny teenager when they'd married. They'd been eighteen and he couldn't wait for the honeymoon! To satisfy the in-laws, he'd agreed to wait a week after graduation to get married, but that was all. He remembered his mom had cried at the wedding. She said it wasn't that he'd married Emilyn; she liked the girl well enough, but that he'd married her so quickly, they were so young and as far as anyone knew, she was not a Believer.

He never heard her say a cuss word, she didn't smoke and heaven forbid, she didn't drink or do drugs. The fact that she didn't do church or know anything about God was what concerned his mom the most. Of course, at the time, that didn't concern him at all. He'd only been doing the motions for most of his high school years. Now, looking back, he understood why. From the time he had married her they'd quarreled about going to church. He wondered if she'd become a believer since he'd left or if she still didn't know the Lord. He shook his head, he hadn't been much of a help to her.

He wondered what she was doing now. At the time, they'd both had flunky jobs, jobs they could get only because they were high school graduates. They couldn't qualify for anything better. Their jobs only provided a small apartment, clothes and the food on the table, no money for savings – no college fund. Was she still doing that kind of work? Had she gone on to get more education? He shook his head, even as the thought crossed his mind. As he remembered it, they'd both been wrapped up in each other and just squeaked by in school, so of course, there was no scholarship money for either of them to go for higher education. That certainly would have been the only way either of them could have gone on to college. That was how Eric had gone, but he'd been the valedictorian and had gotten several local scholarships, as well as the major one to Clemson University where he'd made application.

When they'd married there was no money that came from her home, they had footed every bill for their wedding themselves. That's why it was a bare bones affair. They'd gone to a cheap hotel two towns away for their honeymoon night and why they'd rented a furnished apartment. They'd barely stocked their kitchen cabinets.

Her dad was an alcoholic, he'd drink up nearly all his paycheck every Friday. How could she have gotten more education? There surely wouldn't have been any help from her folks. For each of them it had been the march down the aisle in the multipurpose room of the small high school and a diploma. After commencement, they'd gone out with a bunch of friends and cuddled in a booth in the all night diner in town. Some of the rich kids had gone to a lounge or the country club if their dads belonged, but kids who weren't rich hung out in the diner. After a couple of hours at the diner, some of their friends had urged them to park down by the railroad tracks, but he'd told them no. Thinking about it he knew now that it had only been his parents' influence, not his own heart-felt decision.

Thinking about the decision he'd made last Sunday during Sunday school, he wondered if she was a believer now. Back then, she'd had no clue about anything in the Christian life that he'd talked about, in fact, she'd said she'd never been in church! Come to think of it, he hadn't been all that helpful in changing that, either. He'd told her she had to go to church, but didn't tell her why or that knowing Jesus as her Savior was all important. Would that have changed? Had someone come along side and showed her the right way? Probably not.

He'd been so overwhelmed from having seen her on the porch of cabin one, he hadn't thought to see if she wore any rings or even to examine how she dressed. Well, that was a bit snobbish, wasn't it? Still, if she was here with those people to be part of the staff for a restaurant, if she was alone with them, very probably she wasn't married. But why not? They'd been divorced ten years. She was still a beautiful woman, any man would be happy to have her on his arm. *So why aren't you?* Some little voice asked. *I think it's because I really never stopped loving Emilyn and I couldn't find anybody like her to suit me,* he answered himself.

When he sat down to eat his breakfast, he bowed his head. "God in heaven! Did You bring Emi back into my life? Did she just come along with those people to have a short vacation, or is she going to move here?" He didn't hear an answer, but '...in all things God works for the good of those who love him...' circled through his mind again. He feared she'd be moving here with them. He took a deep breath, put a mouthful of cereal in his mouth and shook his head. Life as he knew it had just gotten way more complicated!

However, he knew one thing for sure! "Thomas, you *will not* run away!" He couldn't and he wouldn't! He might have just worked in an amusement park, but he'd grown up in those years. He'd made a commitment to Natt and he would keep his word!

What would he ever do if she moved here to Vansville? Would they build her an apartment close to the restaurant? Or maybe she'd end up being a neighbor in one of Isabel's cabins. He shuddered and the milk he'd swallowed with the cereal seemed to instantly curdle in his stomach. He'd been so flustered he didn't even remember if the man had said why Emi had come along! Maybe he hadn't said, maybe he'd fled too quickly for anyone to say anything. He'd sure acted like the biggest ninny in the world! *Yup and you ran away - again!*

When he finished the cereal he looked at the clock and was shocked that it was time to leave for work, in fact, almost past time! He must have dilly-dallied through his thoughts! He didn't even finish his last few swallows of the one cup of coffee he always drank at breakfast. He nearly threw his dishes in the sink and rushed out the door. It was the first time there was a possibility that he'd be late! Before he closed the door completely, he felt his pocket and stepped back inside. He hadn't even picked his keys from the basket, he certainly wasn't thinking about going to work! He grabbed up the ring of keys and rushed out the door. He didn't put the keys in his pocket he kept the wad in his hand.

As he went by he was glad to see that the door to cabin one was closed and the drape was still closed. He hurried down the walk and ran across Isabel's parking lot. Ever since Natt had given him his set of keys he'd been the one to open up and today would be no exception. He'd open the store, but Natt would do the Laundromat. He'd hurried so fast he was a bit breathless when he reached the edge of the store parking lot.

When he looked up from stepping onto the curb at the Thomas Complex, Corky's truck sat in a close parking spot and Corky stood beside the door of the store, leaning on the frame, with his arms crossed across his ample chest, a card table leaning against his leg. Seeing the man slowed him down, he had temporarily forgotten Corky was coming.

His feet felt like lead. Automatically, since he was sure who would be sitting around that table, Matt's heart hit overdrive, he could feel it banging against his breast bone. That bowl of cereal he'd stuffed into his mouth felt like a chunk of cement in his belly. It was nearly the same reaction he'd had when he'd seen Emilyn sitting on the porch with the unknown couple last evening. In fact, that little bit of coffee he'd drunk wanted to exit the way it went in a lot faster. He swallowed hard and took another step.

He couldn't even remember if those people had introduced themselves, noise was clanging in his head the minute he saw Emi. Her presence on that porch had sucker-punched him, that was for sure! He didn't remember exactly how he'd acted, but surely like a tongue-tied ninny! All he remembered was that he'd beaten a hasty retreat. He couldn't remember if he'd jumped from the ramp or run down it to the sidewalk! He might as well admit it, he was sure it had been a dream about Emilyn that woke him last night.

Like he'd told the man last night it had been a decade since he'd seen Emilyn, but only a few weeks since he'd communicated with her by Email. "Why didn't she let me know she'd be coming to Vansville when I sent her that Email?" he grumbled to himself. He might have been a little better prepared and not acted like a ninny when he saw her. *Really?* A voice on his shoulder said, *You hadn't seen her in so long? If you knew she was coming you'd have done what?* He sighed, he hated that voice of his conscience. It usually knew him much better than he wanted anyone to know him.

As he hurried across the parking lot, he had the key ready. He stopped beside the older man, then inserted the key in the lock and said, "So, Corky, you're going to try to see if that'll fit with four people around it in the 'nook'?" Matt eyed the square leaning against the man's leg. "It sure looks bigger than I remember a card table!"

Corky picked up the table and turned, ready to follow Matt inside. He nodded, held out his hand to let Matt in front of him and said, "You betcha, fella! I thought on it all night 'cause Loretta told me last night she was runnin' that vacyum this mornin'. Got no other place in town. Like I say, the wife has her vacyum out already this mornin' ya cain't hear yourself think around that house! That's for shore!"

Matt pushed the door open and pulled the key from the lock and reached around the corner for the light switches, then cleared his throat. Not anxious to have these people, but specifically, Emi in his store for so long, he asked, "Wouldn't there be room around the table in Isabel's cabin where they're staying? I happen to know they're in the big one. If I remember right, that table's got places for four people to sit around it."

"Yep, thar probly would be." However, he waited for Matt to step clear of the door, then followed him in the store and immediately turned toward the 'nook' with his table. Without saying anything else he started unfolding the legs. Before the door closed behind them, Matt heard a car come on the lot and knew that Natt had arrived. Of course, he'd go first to the Laundromat to open it up. With Corky so determined to have his meeting here, he wondered how Natt would handle the situation.

Matt took several steps out of the way, but stood silently watching Corky, not even remembering that he should be turning on the gas pumps. Fortunately, no one drove on the lot except Natt. Of course, he saw Corky's truck, but he still went to the Laundromat to open it and turn on the lights. Even though he had a mission, there were some things that had to be done when you ran a business. Who knew if someone would come early to do laundry? Lots of people did chores on Saturdays and laundry sure was a chore.

As Corky opened the fourth leg and reached for the top to set the legs on the floor, Natt walked in the store. He took one look at the small space that was being made even smaller by the table and shook his head. "Corky," he said, moving up beside the older man. In a non-judgmental voice, Natt said, "I can't let you do that."

The four table legs thumped onto the floor, probably Corky had put the table down much more forcibly than necessary. With the table out of his hands he straightened up and for a man his size, whirled around and demanded, "And why not! It'll fit!" Now that his back was turned Matt silently shook his head.

Very reasonably, Natt said, "Corky, look." He laid a hand on Corky's shoulder and moved the other hand around in a circle to demonstrate.

"When you put four chairs with people in them around that table no one will be able to get to the coffee urn, since its place is on that back wall and can't be plugged in anywhere else in the nook.

"Not only that, the fourth person will be stuck out in the walkway from the door. I know you can see that, too. If someone's not watching exactly where he's going when he comes in, he's libel to run into that person and then your conversation'll be interrupted." Natt looked directly into Corky's face to see if he was listening. "Besides," he continued, "Saturday's my best day for business and also for sending out coffee, your meeting would be disrupted all the time. I'm sure of it."

Not to mention somebody could get hurt. That thought went through Matt's mind and Natt had probably already thought of it.

Lifting his eyes to look where the urn usually sat, he sighed. "Yeah, might be," Corky said, grudgingly. He still stood, one hand on the table, and looked at the tiny space on the three sides inside the 'nook'. The fourth side leaned against Corky's legs and he was standing in the aisle. The chairs in the 'nook' still sat around the edge of the not-too-large space, not pulled up to the table and certainly didn't have people in them. Corky didn't move, he continued to look first at Natt as if he expected him to say more, then looked at the 'nook'.

After a moment when all three men looked at the 'nook' without saying anything, Natt said, "Say, did I hear right or was it Matt and I talked last night, aren't these people staying in Isabel's big cabin? They got table and chairs there. Is it a big enough table four people could sit around it? It would be quiet there with no interruptions from all my customers. Whadya say, Corky? Could ya work with that?"

Corky looked around at the small 'nook'. While he looked, neither of the other two said anything. With his table mostly sitting in the small space, no one could get to the urn even now, without any people sitting around it. Matt wasn't sure if the man thought about his own size and that he'd probably be the one sitting in the aisle.

After several minutes, Corky heaved a sigh, "I suppose you're right, fella. I recon it would be a bit cramped."

"Thanks, Corky. I appreciate your cooperation," Natt said with a smile, then helped Corky take the table down. "I tell you what, though. I'm pretty sure Isabel has some kind of coffee maker in the cabins. Suppose

I send some coffee grounds along with you and you can make some there at the cabin. How's that sound?"

Corky gave the young man a brilliant smile and patted him on the back. "That sounds perfect, young fella. I'll take ya up on that idea." It was obvious Corky wanted Natt's good coffee. It made Matt wonder if someone beside Natt could make the coffee smell and taste like he did. Surely it wasn't the coffee grounds that did the trick! He'd used the same coffee and people didn't rave over it!

Natt nodded, gave Corky a smile and patted the shoulder he'd had his hand on then straightened away from the older man. "Thanks, man. You know I really appreciate that. I'll go round up some coffee grounds for your meeting. I'm sure you'll have a good one over there. I know it'll be a lot more quiet than here."

"Yeah," Corky grudgingly answered. "Yeah, it jes might at that. Probly got some drawin' ta do. Mebe need a bigger space than this."

It finally occurred to Matt that he had a job to do, so he rushed away to another part of the store to turn on the gas pumps and get the cash register out of sleep mode, all the while silently congratulating his cousin on his diplomacy. Natt, without being obvious about it, folded the legs of Corky's table and leaned it against the chair closest to the door. Without saying anything else, he started for the back room to measure out some coffee grounds to send with Corky and also to start fixing his urn for his first batch of the day.

Corky followed more slowly behind Natt. As he did, he remembered something his wife had asked him to pick up some time. He saw it on the shelf close by and picked it up. He turned it over, inspecting it more closely, looked at the price and balanced it in his hand, then closed his hand around it. Matt said nothing, but moved quickly behind the cash register. He hurriedly brought the register out of sleep mode then waited for Corky to come to the counter with his purchase. Corky didn't move very fast.

While Matt rang up the purchase, he was impressed with his younger cousin's diplomacy. He would have made a good journalist and Matt was sure he wouldn't have thought of anything like that to say. Chagrined, he realized he might even have had a few harsh words to say to the older man. He guessed he had a bit to learn about retail sales. Being head of maintenance at a theme park didn't give you much opportunity to practice people skills.

Corky laid his purchase down on the counter. Matt rang it up, after a short wait for the register to ding, Corky collected his change from Matt and Natt walked up with a little baggy that held coffee grounds. As Corky collected his purchase, Natt held out the bag and said, "Here you go, Corky. Thanks so much for being understanding that way. You have a good meeting with those folks and get us a restaurant built real soon."

Nodding at his single cousin, still with a grin on his face, he said, "Way I understand it, guys like him gotta eat Alex's frozen dinners all the time or rush off to Blairsville to fill their hollow legs at a drive-thru or something." He nodded to the front of the store and said, "Gas prices the way they are, that second isn't much of an option, as I see it."

Corky chuckled, as Natt hoped he would and said, "Sure enough, Natt! I'll get them guys right on that as soon as we get some thoughts lined out. I have all the confidence in that young fella that he'll come up with a real good place. He's a whale of a cook, too. I et some of his pulled Pork BBQ one time and thought I'd died and gone ta heaven! I'll see ya'all again. Hey, and thanks for the coffee!"

"Sure, Corky! Have a good meeting," Natt said. "You get that place up and running before the snow flies, you hear?"

Corky gave Natt a silent salute, all the while guarding the little baggy of coffee grounds as if it were gold. He moved toward the door, collected his card table and walked out. Both Matt and Natt heard him start to whistle as the door closed. They watched and saw him carefully lay the little baggy of coffee grounds on the tailgate before he hoisted the card table into the bed, then laid the bag with his purchase on top of it. Treating it like gold, he picked the baggy up before he closed the tailgate. Holding it carefully in front of him, he opened his driver's door and gently put the little bag on the seat. He slammed his door and started up, but he turned toward Isabel's cabins instead of going home.

Matt gave his cousin a big grin and said, "You're great, Natt! I'd a never thought of sending coffee grounds with him, although, as he kept standing there, I realized it was your coffee he wanted to offer those people."

Natt shrugged, but watched Corky get in his pickup. Anyone could tell it was a major undertaking for him to step that high. Probably the truck was more a status symbol rather than a need. It looked to be only a few years old and probably had every bell and whistle the dealer could legitimately include. Corky's children had left home years ago and most of his 'jobs' were 'honey-do' things or jobs he volunteered for. He had retired several years ago, but he obviously had money for the things he and Loretta wanted.

Without acknowledging the compliment, Natt said, "Saturday's one of our busiest days, always is, and if he'd be the one sitting out in the aisle, people coming in would trip over him all the time. He's not a spring chicken and no gust of wind would blow him away. It's no telling who might get hurt and I'm not too excited about having to pay a hospital bill. Insurance might pay, but why risk it? It's lots better sending coffee with him than letting him have his meeting here, wouldn't you say?"

Matt let out a long sigh, "You have hit the nail on the head, Cous. I was not looking forward to having that meeting here. Not for your reason, though. I didn't know about it until after I left here last night after we closed up, but my ex-wife, Emilyn, is the third person who came. I'd have felt really strange with her in this store for so long." After a moment's thought, he added, "Actually, I can't figure out why she had to come along. I'm sure it won't be her money or her ideas that'll get a restaurant up and running in Vansville."

Natt shrugged again. "Think it could be that God's putting you to a test?"

Matt sank down onto one of the 'nook' chairs. After looking at his hands, he raised his eyes to Natt and nodded slowly. "Cous, that could be a good possibility. You know, ten years ago I was a cocky, self-centered so and so. Had no reason to be, other than I was only twenty and I was trying hard to live up to some invisible expectations, 'cause my twin brother was such an over-achiever. I really didn't think too much about anybody else but me."

He swallowed and cleared his throat. Natt was sure Matt's eyes glistened with unshed tears. Finally, he whispered, "I wasn't thinking about the most important person in my life, my wife. I left her devastated."

He shook his head and was quiet for several minutes. He stretched out his legs and crossed his ankles before he said, "Emilyn and I got married right after graduation and our parents didn't think too much of that. We got a tiny apartment and both of us took flunky jobs. All we could get, really, as high school graduates. Both of us worked ourselves to the bone for not much money, but hey, we both had a job! We'd come home worn out, her especially, but right off when we talked it wasn't some nice stuff and me lovin' on her, she and I got into constant fights. Instead of trying to work it out and listen to her side, I threw in the towel and walked out. Somethin' I'm not proud of."

Leaning up against the end of the counter, Natt said, quietly, "I wondered if that was it. I didn't know you back then and I think I was only in middle school, so I couldn't see what was so all fire important about getting married so young. Grandad, well Gramma Joyce really, sorta kept us informed about his twin nephews. Mom and Dad, mostly, but I'd listen sometimes. Believe me, they were really disappointed when they heard about your divorce. I think Gramma even cried about it a time or two."

Matt shook his head, then put his hands behind his head and rested them on the window frame. He didn't look at Natt, but looked at the ceiling, while he said, "What she informed you about me wasn't much to brag on! Believe me! Mom and Dad were really disappointed that I threw in the towel and didn't try to work anything out with Emilyn. I wouldn't even do counseling, even though they all said we should, but instead I said it cost too much. And no, I wasn't about to take somebody's money to go see a counselor. As you know, older Christians don't look too highly on divorce and mine was the first divorce in my family!"

He shook his head, pulled in a deep breath and continued, "It was me who did it, too. My first job after I left her I saved every penny for that lawyer and all the stuff he wanted paid for. Man, now I can't believe how self-centered I was!"

After a minute's thought, he brought his hands down and crossed them over his chest. He glanced around the nook, then back at Natt before he said, "Now Eric, ever since he graduated high school he got on a roll. 'Course, he was something in high school, too. Made a name for himself there. He got a scholarship, went to college, got a degree in criminal science. Uncle Brad was so proud! Man, he was a hero, with all he did overseas on his tours in Afghanistan with the Marines. Yeah, stuff he's done, but won't talk about, he's a hero all right."

Natt didn't comment on the hero statement, instead he asked, "What made the difference? You're the same age and all."

Matt took a deep breath, stuffed his hands into his armpits and rested his ankle on his knee. He looked off to the back of the store for several long minutes and finally answered, "I think it was that blond. She had eyes for me and not him, so I tried real hard to impress her without doing much. Maybe you don't know too much about that, but well, it was all I could think about. I mean, she really was beautiful and I fell, like leaves in fall! But when we started having words, I couldn't handle it, so I quit." Taking another deep breath he said, "Man, I can't believe how immature I was! Even at twenty years old, this job I just left really grew me up."

After a pause, Matt pulled in another long breath, dropped his eyes to look at the floor, then back to his cousin and said, "Saw her last night there on the porch. She's pretty as she ever was, only more mature. If it's them three that'll be running the restaurant, I may still be eating Alex's frozen dinners even after that restaurant opens."

Natt moved away from the counter and turned toward the back of the store, but not before Matt saw him smirk. Two steps later, Matt was sure he heard, *"Bawk, Bawk."*

Matt couldn't help the grin that moved across his face. "Hey, are you calling me a chicken, Cous?"

Looking at Natt's back, he saw one shoulder lift, as Natt said, "If the shoe fits…."

"Thanks, I needed that."

Natt spun around and grinned at his cousin. "Hey, I just thought of something! Wasn't it you that said he wished for some young female flesh to grace this town? She'd be your age, right? You did say you'd graduated together, right?" *Of course, he knew that!*

Matt pulled his ankle off his knee, then brought his feet back under him and slammed his fists on his knees. He cleared his throat, but the words he said were much quieter, "Umm, yeah, it was me who said that.

But you know, I hadn't really thought that the next one to come to town would be my ex, though. I mean, what are the odds on that?"

Natt stepped into the utility room, then brought the big urn from the back and walked into the 'nook'. As he set the urn on the small piece of furniture where it usually sat, he said, "Think she'd have you back?"

Matt gulped and looked at his cousin. "What?"

Natt took the end of the cord lying on the table to plug into the back of the urn and said, "Hey, we're the only ones in here. I don't hear any big semis going by on the road. I'm three feet away from you. There's no other noise in the store. I think you heard me."

"Marry my ex-wife?"

"Yeah, I've heard such things happen. From what you've said, it sounds like you're both still single. You know, Eric and I read in our Bible studies back before Marcy and I married where God said when a man and woman marry God considers them one flesh. Do you think that changes when they get divorced?"

Intensely, Matt grabbed his knees and leaned forward. Finally, he said, "I don't know! Wow! That's something to think about!" He sank back against the chair. "She'd kinda need to take me back. I don't know if she'd forgive me. It was my fault, you know. I threw my set of house keys at her and walked out."

Natt shrugged. "Yeah, that's true, but it is something to think about, really. I never heard you say that God could work things out for His good."

"Yeah, I guess so."

"Hey, I'll catch you later. I got orders to send in for supplies."

As Natt walked away, Matt grumbled, "Thanks a lot! You're walking away, gonna work in back and you leave me with this heavy stuff to think about."

As if he read his mind, Natt said, "It is kinda heavy stuff to think about."

Before anyone else came in, Natt disappeared into the tiny office at the far end of the utility room that he'd cleared out since he took over. Where his granddad had stacks of unusable, nondescript items and stacks of ledgers he'd kept his accounts in for years, Natt had cleaned out and thrown away piles of things and brought in a used desk and office chair and his computer. Of course, his granddad hadn't used a computer at all. Natt wondered how he'd ever kept his accounts and his inventory straight. The inventory changed from week to week!

Last Saturday, when he was alone, he'd made a very abbreviated order, so today he must make up for that. He had to send in an order for things he needed, not the least of which was the weekly supply of coffee he had to order. Not long after starting his 'coffee drinker's nook' Alex had suggested that he order his coffee direct, so that was the top item on his list every week. After coffee, there were things like sugar packs, creamer... screws, hammers... all that tedious stuff.... stuff any hardware store runs out of constantly. This wasn't his most favorite part of the job, but he knew it had to be done. He was glad he only had to do it once a week.

Of course, the first thing he did was turn on the computer. He knew, with Matt out front that he wouldn't have to be disturbed for a while. Saturday usually started slow then picked up mid-morning. He'd have at least an hour to work on the orders. He guessed most people liked to sleep in on Saturday mornings and get a late start on those 'honey-do' jobs. When the screen came up, he typed in his supplier then put a check mark by the brand of coffee he ordered each week, then sat and looked at the rest of the items on the screen, but didn't see much, there were other things crowding into his mind.

He wasn't much of a Bible scholar, so he wondered how it worked. He'd asked a question of Matt he didn't know how to answer. How did God look at divorced people? He knew God allowed people to divorce and he knew God could forgive sin, but the image that came to him was ghastly. A man and wife made one flesh, but if you tore them apart...?

> 'For this reason a man will leave his father and mother
> and be united to his wife, and the two will become one flesh.
> So they are no longer two but one. Therefore what God has
> joined together, let man not separate.' (Matt 18:5,6)

But man did separate husband and wife all the time.

Matt sat on the chair in the 'coffee drinker's nook' for several minutes thinking about Natt's question. He was a believer now, he knew it. Back when he was twenty years old – well, maybe he hadn't been, but ever since he'd prayed that simple prayer as he sat beside his mom he'd thought he was a believer, but he'd divorced his wife ten years ago. What did that make him now? He remembered what Pastor Allen had said way back when he was eighteen and so full of himself. "What God has joined, let not man separate."

"Oh, God in heaven! I separated us! I threw those keys at her, she was devastated! I've never forgotten that look on her face. God, forgive me!" he murmured the words. Now he was devastated. He had separated something sacred, something God had joined. As he sat in that chair, tears welled up in his eyes, but he swallowed. "I was such a fool!"

Finally after Jack had left the bathroom door open and come to the table, Emilyn left the Bible on the couch, but it still stayed open to the first page of Scripture. She gave those four words another look before she slowly made her way into the closet for some clean clothes and headed for the bathroom. She felt in need of a shower.

The towels in the bathroom were soft and fluffy and the shower looked like pure luxury in the very nice bathroom. It was a much nicer bathroom than the one in her own apartment, she luxuriated in the warm spray, but all the time she kept thinking about those four words. Who would know about things like that? Obviously, Alli couldn't tell her. She knew if Alli couldn't tell her there was no sense asking Jack! She wasn't even sure the man knew what was between the two covers of a Bible.

A shiver went down her back, because there was one person she wouldn't ask. She hoped she could make it this weekend not to see Matt again. Could that be possible? "Probably not," she grumbled. "He lives two doors away. Life couldn't be that good to me." Emi dressed slowly, gave her teeth an extra good brushing and because the smells from the nearby kitchen were so tantalizing she opened the door into the living room.

Allison had breakfast ready several minutes before Emi showed her face and Jack was already eating when she left the bathroom. She made a detour to the couch and closed the Bible. For some reason Alli had left the light on, so she turned it off. Reluctantly, she took a seat at the table and mechanically ate the food Allison put on a plate then placed in front of her. However, she seemed to be deep in thought and never entered into the conversation that Jack and Allison were already carrying on.

Reading those words in the Bible weighed heavily on her mind. They had ever since she'd read them in the middle of the night. If there was a god and according to that Book there really was, why hadn't she known about Him? She'd heard her dad say God's Name all the time, but that was to curse someone! Matt had talked about God and somebody called Jesus quite a few times and said that she needed to know about Them, but mostly he'd told her she needed to go to church, she'd learn about Them there. To say she was confused was the understatement of the year!

"Hey, girl!" Jack exclaimed, once he and Allison finished the subject they had been discussing when Emi appeared at the table. "What's the long face? You're never this quiet! This isn't like you at all!"

Emi jumped, when Jack spoke to her, her mind was far away from those at the table with her. She looked at Jack and wondered if he'd said something to her before and she hadn't heard him. She had to swallow before she could say, "Jack, I got a big dose of reality check since we got here yesterday. Not just seeing Matt, but it's made me think some deep thoughts, some I've never thought before. Some of them kept me awake for a while last night."

Not really into reality checks himself, Jack shrugged. "Okay, I guess you're entitled. But you know, we're here and it's a mini-vacation for you. That means you need to lighten up!"

Emi smiled. "Thanks, Jack, but I'll try to get my head out of the sand."

He grinned at her. "Oh, that's good; I've heard that sand's kind of stifling."

Neither of the women had anything to say, they both shook their heads at the man. If he was trying to lighten Emi's mood he seemed to have failed miserably. Emi guessed that was sort of how a man thought, but it didn't help her much. She finished eating and washed the last mouthful down with a swig of coffee.

Jack, Allison and Emilyn sat around the table in the cabin after eating their breakfast. Being long time restaurateurs, Allison had fixed a big pot of coffee, glad that Isabel supplied such a large coffee maker in a rental cabin. Of course, she'd fixed an excellent meal, she and Jack knew how to make people come back often to their restaurant. Even the good smells lingered in the small living area of the cabin.

Now all three were nursing their second cup, when Jack said, "Sort of strange that Corky didn't come around last night to say what was going on today. He did know we were coming yesterday. Surprises me, you know? Wonder if he'll show up or what? He was the guy who was so keen on us coming up here. He wouldn't hear of doing this by phone or fax or Email! We had to come here. Said he wasn't into that high power technology stuff. He didn't know too much about computers and all that new-fangled stuff, he said.

"I mean, this is a little town, but who knows if that's the only building that's going up in town." Looking out the large picture window, he added, "Can't see anything that looks like a new building from here."

"Couldn't tell you, Honey," Allison said. She looked at the phone on the wall behind Jack and wondered if it even worked, perhaps it was there for those long term renters and they had to activate the phone if they wanted service. As an after-thought, she said, "Actually, he could have called, I should think. At least there is a phone in here. He has called you on your cell, right? He knew we were coming last evening. You don't even know where he lives, but I guess, the town's small enough you could drive up and down the streets…" Knowing before he spoke what Jack would say, she grinned at him.

Jack let out a loud huff, took another swig of the dark brew, then set the mug down on the table and looked at his wife. Shaking his head, he said, "Alli, come on, get real! I'm not that much into Uncle Corky, haven't seen him in a good many years. I have no idea what he drives and as small as this town is, he could have whatever he drives in a garage. And if we can't see the building site, who'd know how many streets are in this place!"

"Well, yeah, there is that…"

Jack looked at the clock over the sink and said, "Sure wish he'd come around! This waitin' for stuff to happen gets me."

Allison rested her hand on Jack's arm and said, "I know, Honey, if it doesn't get done as fast as a hamburger on the grill you're ready to kick something." She grinned at him.

Jack let out a long breath and shook his head. "Alli, I swear…"

Still grinning, Allison said, "Just sayin'…"

Just then, a huge extended cab pickup truck pulled in next to their car and Emilyn said, "There's a truck. Maybe that's him."

The older man, who, as Natt had said, wouldn't get blown away by any breeze, worked his way out of the truck. With his size he couldn't jump out, so he 'slithered' out until his feet reached the ground. The people in the cabin watched as the legs appeared under the door and dangled in the air until they finally reached the ground. He reached back into the truck for something and as he slammed the door, Jack said, "Yep, that's him."

Allison was also watching out the window and scowled. "Wonder what's in that little bag? He sure is treating it like gold!"

Jack chuckled as he stood up to open the door for the man. "Kinda looks like coffee grounds, Alli. Maybe he thinks we didn't bring any ourselves."

Allison whispered, because Corky was so close, "That's crazy! Why in heaven's name wouldn't we bring coffee with us? I mean, we run a restaurant; we serve coffee, gallons of it! Give me a break!"

Maybe we don't have to go to that store for our meeting! Emilyn thought. Wow! Murphy's Law wasn't working against her this morning! She would take that as a good sign.

She swallowed a sigh as the man slammed his truck door and walked the ramp onto the porch. Emilyn didn't know what she'd expected as she looked at the older man. He didn't look like a dashing tycoon, but more a grandfatherly gentleman. She shrugged, people with money could come in any size, age or denomination, she guessed.

She was still wondering why Jack and Alli had invited her along. It couldn't be for any special skills she had. She was no professional architect and definitely was not someone who knew how to cook or run a restaurant. Absolutely, she had no money to sink into a new venture. All she really knew how to do was wait tables and that time was still months away. She'd sit by quietly and listen, glad to be away from Barney's Diner for four days.

Jack pulled the door open and saw the baggy Corky held out in front of him. "Well, uncle Corky! Sure is good to see you! It's been a while maybe five years, you think? So whatcha got there, Corky?" He gave the older man a smile and stepped back, opening the door wider for his uncle to enter. Corky stepped inside, grinning at the younger man.

For a minute Corky didn't say anything, he looked around the nice accommodations and nodded. "Ben a while since I been in one of Isabel's cabins. She shore got this one lookin' good. I'll give her that."

Being the congenial southern gentleman that he was, Corky held out his hand to shake his nephew's, as he said, "Well ya know the wife, she always does her cleanin' on any given Saturday, so meetin' there ain't an option. Went over to Thomas's first thing to see if his 'coffee drinker's nook' would be a good place, but the place ain't big enough for a meetin'. Took my table and all, but jes' wouldn't fit. The young guy makes the best coffee, so I was kinda wantin' to have our meetin' there, but we decided the place was too small. Still, he was good enough ta give me some of his coffee grounds. He knew we was havin' a meetin' so he sent this along." He held out the baggy to Jack.

Taking the baggy, his eyes twinkling, he said, "Well, come on in, Uncle. Alli fixed a big pot for our breakfast and there's still some left, but I'll bet if our meeting goes into extra innings we'll be using that, too."

Corky nodded. "That'd be good, right good. Yeah, I see Isabel does have a right good sized table in here, don't she?"

Allison jumped up, found another mug and filled it with coffee, then brought it to the empty place at the table. Corky grinned at her and pulled out the empty chair from the end of the table. He slouched into the chair and let out a long sigh. "Mighty kind of ya, Allison. Your stuff smells right good." He saw the evidence of clean dishes on the counter and added. "I guess Isabel warned ya 'bout our lack of food stuffs around here." His grin widened. "'Course, that's why you're here, achully."

"Thanks, Corky. Yes, she did warn us." Allison also sat back down after she warmed up the three cups already on the table.

After Corky took a swallow, Jack said, "So, you know Alli, but we brought along the gal who'll be our right hand. This is Emilyn Willard."

Corky held out a hand and smiled at the young woman. "Good ta meet ya, Emilyn. Welcome to Vansville. Right pleased ta know ya. Them's a good couple, you join up with them and you're on the right track."

Feeling unsure of herself, Emi took the older man's hand and gave him a tentative smile. "It's good to meet you," was all she said.

"Same here, Lassie, you'll probly do 'em a good job."

"Thanks," she whispered.

Before Jack sat down, he picked up a briefcase from beside the couch and asked, "What do we do today, Corky?"

Nodding at the briefcase Jack held in his hand, Corky said, "You tell me whacha need, young fella, we put some lines on paper and a friend of mine changes 'em into blueprints. We go from there and before snow flies we got us a restaurant. Like I said, this here town's growin' and we ain't got no eatery here." Nodding toward the rest of the cabins, Corky continued, "Them two bachelors and a couple others in town get kinda tired of them frozen dinners all the time. Now mind you, Alex alays keeps a good supply o' them dinners, but I hear they get kinda old on occasion. Know what I mean?"

Jack nodded, "Uh huh, I hear ya."

Jack came back to the table, placed the briefcase in front of his place, slid into his chair, unlatched the case, opened it and said, "Sounds good, Corky. What do you say we make a second story on the place for a good size apartment?"

As Corky took another long swallow and nodded, Jack pulled out a roll of parchment and some papers from his case. Pensively, Corky said, "Yeah, now thar's a good idea, since thar ain't no empty houses in town. These here cabins be the only place ta live on the short term. Isabel, she's a good landlady, but she only rents by the month. Besides, these cabins is only good on the long term for single folk. They're great for weekend travelers, but not long term livin'. This here's the biggest one and she usually keeps it for handicapped folks. She rented this here cabin to Ms. Sandy for a while 'fore she married Ramon." Not that that made any sense to the others sitting at the table.

"That was what Isabel told me last night. So this restaurant we're talking about can get started right away?" Jack asked, wanting to get to the point.

Corky took another long swallow of Allison's good coffee. He let out a long sigh of satisfaction and set the mug down on the table. Before he said anything, he stuck his hands behind his suspenders and said, "Yep, I had that piece a property down the street. Now Ms Sandy, she done a paintin' of it. I seen it and it's real pretty, but it's jes' settin' there and ain't doin' nobody no good. I couldn't think what ta do with it for so long. Then it hit me!

"I called ya and ya said you could work with it. Ya said how big ta make the hole, so that's what it is and I got all the gravel spread. That company I got ta do that follered them directions right well. I was real glad of that. Got a good entryway onto the place, too. Got right on it the day after we talked back a few weeks. After lunch we can go on down there and have a look see. I'll let ya give it the onst over, see whacha think, ef it's up ta snuff."

Jack grinned. "So it isn't filled with water? Haven't had one of those 'gulley-washers' since the hole's been dug?"

Corky grinned at the younger man. "Nope, rained a gully-washer back in May or so, but not here lately. Haven't had much rain since I had 'er dug out. I even had 'em take off topsoil for the parkin' lot and spread gravel there. I'm pretty shore it be ready ta pour cee-ment, ef it meets yore approval."

Holding the roll up, Jack said, "Well, Corky, I'll surprise you. I already got blueprints made. I even got the second floor laid out, too. It'd be lots easier for Alli and me to live real close. We do now where we are."

"Well, well! I declare." The older man gave his nephew a big smile. "Yore a man after my own heart! Yore a real go-getter! Gotta admit, I really love it when a plan comes together. Know what I mean?"

Slapping the rolled up blueprints on his palm, Jack said, "Yup, I do and I'm anxious to get started. Like you said, I want this to be up and running before the snow flies. Thanksgiving, Christmas – that's a great time of year for business." As if realizing what he said for the first time, he asked, "It really snows around here? This is Georgia, you know. Last year in our town we got some sleet, but snow?"

"Well, it is the foothills of them Appalachians, ya know," Corky countered immediately. Hardly taking a breath, he said, "That's them mountains you see out that winda. Achally, that's why that one cabin's rented. That Eric fella, he's a hikin' guide in them mountains out thar, but I hear he's gonna be a deputy sheriff one day soon." Corky nearly snorted. "Like we need a deputy here in this here town! Only one bad thing happened here in years! But, hey, I ain't into that law enforcement stuff."

"Yeah, but snow?"

Corky rested his mug on his belly and nodded. "Hey, we have snow, don't last long, usually, but we had the ice this past winter. You better believe we did! It come in – lasted three weeks or more!" Nodding at the back wall of the cabin, Corky added, "Them people at that clinic back there, they talked kinda mean about this here town, since we didn't have nothin' but Alex's store ta git food. He closed up the same time they quit workin' too. They got in them cars and slid all over the place. Couldn't get outta town no how!"

Jack shrugged. "I'll believe it when I see it, Corky. So, how 'bout another coffee? Can we take a run down to the site?"

"Shore! I got a king cab, we can all fit." Corky looked at the clock over his head. "How 'bout we do that after lunch? Since I went to the store first, it's ben a while since I et breakfast. I'm one of them three meals a day guys, ya know?"

Jack also looked at the clock on the wall. "Great. We'll fix some sandwiches and watch for you to come back, Uncle."

"Good idea. Loretta's probly got some fixed for us, too." Corky shook his head. "'Course, she could still be runnin' that ear-splittin' vacyum, ya know?"

Jack took the last swallow of his coffee and nodded. "Yeah, Allison does that once in a while at our house, too. So we'll see you later."

However, Corky didn't leave right away. He seemed fascinated with Jack's blueprints. Since he wasn't leaving, Allison emptied the coffee carafe and sat back down. Corky took another sip and said, "These here are good, fella. I think my contractor can use these right off. I'll give him a call."

"Good enough, Uncle. I was hoping he could use them right away."

"Shore enough, fella! Shore 'nough." Then he heaved himself from the chair.

Corky worked his way to the door and Jack said, "See ya later, uncle!"

"Yep, I'll be back!"

Jack grinned at the older man. "Okay, we'll be waiting."

Joyce Thomas took advantage of Brad's trip to the physical therapist and used the restroom, but then came back to sat in the chair in her husband's room at the rehab center in Blairsville. She watched as the physical therapist walked her husband back into the room. Brad had a belt around his middle and had his hands on the handlebars of a rolling walker, but his left leg was noticeably dragging behind him. Not long after he'd been allowed up he'd been fitted with a hard plastic device that went around his left foot and ankle that was to help him move better. Joyce still wondered if he'd ever be back close to normal.

However, as soon as he crossed the threshold into his room he made a beeline for the bed. He gave the walker a shove and it went careening across the room as he plopped onto the bed and swung his good leg up in one move. The other still hung off the side, it didn't move with the other and that definitely put him on the edge of the bed. However, Brad's head hit the pillow he let out a long sigh and closed his eyes. The therapist hurried to the bed, swung Brad's left leg up beside the other and did a little maneuvering to get Brad more centered on the bed, then reached to loosen the belt.

The man undid the buckle on the front of the belt, pulled it from Brad's waist and said, "So, Brad, you did pretty well today. It seems like you're really trying to get that leg working again so you can walk better."

"Yeah…" Joyce was surprised he answered she thought he was already asleep.

"So he's doing better?" Joyce asked.

Diplomatically, the man said, "He has good movement in the limbs that weren't affected, ma'am. There is some weakness on that right side, but those on his left side are still quite sluggish. As he keeps on with his therapy it should keep improving." The man pointed to Brad's left leg. "You saw his left leg… The fingers on his left hand want to curl, which is normal, but isn't good at all. I asked the doc to order a squeeze block. I'm hoping he'll use it so that won't happen."

Joyce shook her head, looked over at her husband and whispered, "I hope he'll use it, I can see where it would help, but he's a stubborn man, you know. He's been a stubborn man all his life. Seems he's worse now."

Trying for diplomacy, the man said, "Yes, we in the department had that figured out. How's his speech therapy coming?"

Joyce let out a loud sigh, shook her head and said, "Very slowly, he doesn't talk much when I'm in the room, but what he does say I can understand, usually. Still, it's not coming back anywhere as good as the last time he had a bad stroke. After only a day or two he was talking in sentences really well."

The therapist nodded in understanding. He'd been the one working with Brad for several times now and had read much of the notes in his chart. "Probably because he's older and this stroke was much worse, the very worst one he's had, from my understanding. Even a year or two can affect someone's ability to snap back from something like this. As I understand it, this stroke was quite a bit worse than his last bad one."

Joyce nodded, still looking at her husband. "Yes, that's probably true."

She shook her head and continued, "The doctor told us he could have died from this one. It's a good thing he was in the store with Natt. He called 911 right off and got the ambulance there in a jiffy."

By now, the therapist had the belt wound up and put away, so he said, "Well, we'll be back for another session on Monday. Take care."

"Thanks for all you folks do," Joyce said. He turned at the doorway and smiled, then hurried down the hall. Into the quietness Joyce heard a familiar sound; Brad was snoring.

Since she knew he was asleep and that lunch trays would be along soon, Joyce slipped out of the room and went to the cafeteria for some things she could bring back. Often Brad's doctor came while he ate lunch and Joyce didn't want to miss his visit. Brad never told her anything the doctor said. He rarely talked to her any more. She knew he was frustrated by his inability to make himself understood as well as before.

After a short nap, a nurse aid brought in Brad's lunch tray. She talked to him as she raised the head of his bed and adjusted his rolling table with the tray across his lap. She raised the cover from the plate, but there was nothing to cut up, however, Brad only grunted at her. Most of the staff knew Brad's personality, so they didn't hold his attitude against him. They all knew that stroke victims often had a personality change. The aid smiled at Joyce, then left the room and met the doctor on his way down the hall. The doctor saw the girl come from Brad's room and gave her a sympathetic smile. Before he entered the room he pulled the chart from the pocket on the wall and carried it in the room with him.

While Brad ate lunch, the doctor came in and smiled at Joyce. The minute he saw his doctor Brad dropped his fork onto the plate with a clatter so loud that the doctor immediately turned to look at him. Brad was staring at the man. "I… go home…"

"Brad," the man said patiently. "You aren't recouped yet. We brought you here to the rehab center so we can work on that."

Brad pounded his fist on his rolling table beside his tray, angrily enough that the plate bounced and the fork fell off. Fiercely, he said, "Go home!"

The doctor shook his head, opened the chart in his hand to the last page where the therapist had written his note and said quite emphatically, "You have a few more sessions with the speech therapist you need, Brad. Not to mention you need more physical therapy before I can feel good about sending you home."

Brad shook his head and pounded his fist again on the table. Fiercely, he said, "Go home… store… Natt need… me!"

The doctor looked at Joyce for explanations. "Natt? Store?"

Joyce said, "Natt's our grandson. He's running the store Brad's owned and operated for years. Brad likes to go sit in the store with him."

The younger man shook his head. "That can't happen!"

Joyce shook her head and whispered, "Don't tell him that!"

Becoming quite agitated, Brad said, "GO HOME!"

The doctor stood at the foot of the bed, but shook his head emphatically. "Can't let you, not today, Brad. Besides, that's why you're in this rehab place, they're the experts to get you back to your full potential."

Brad had lost some of the strength on his right side, but when he moved his hand neither Joyce nor the doctor was prepared for what happened next. Brad pushed the edge of the table. It turned sideways and kept rolling. With the momentum of the rolling table, the tray flew off and everything on it flew in all directions. However, none of it went on the bed, but some of the food hit Joyce, not only on her face, but much of it clung to her clothes. Her face instantly showed her surprise and her hand came up automatically to wipe her face. The glass was full of iced tea and that went all over the doctor, while the ice clattered to the floor, followed instantly by the glass that broke with a crash and tinkling glass.

Brad tried to move in the bed. Of course, his left side did not cooperate, but he yelled, "I GO HOME!!! TODAY!!! NOW!!!"

Looking sternly at the older man, the doctor immediately shook the chart in his hand to get the liquid off before it stained the paper. While he wiped the liquid from his face, the doctor said, "NO!!! YOU WILL NOT GO HOME TODAY!!!"

"YOU… STOP ME!!!"

The doctor pushed his lab coat back and pulled his handkerchief from his back pocket. Still looking at the man in the bed, but wiping his face, he asked his patient quite sternly, "Do you want me to tie you down, Brad? I mean, I can put an order in your chart. It's right here and the nurses know I'm in here now."

Brad hadn't moved but perhaps an inch with all his efforts. Momentarily he fell back against the bed in defeat. Grumbling, pulling his right hand down his face, he glared at his doctor and mumbled, "No... not... now."

Still wiping at the tea droplets, the doctor nodded and said, "I didn't think so, Brad. You still have several sessions more with the speech and the physical therapists. If you cooperate with them, you'll gain lots more, especially with that speech therapist. I know you get frustrated, but I hear you did quite well in your physical therapy session this morning. I ordered the ball for you. Just think, maybe you could be a pitcher on your church softball team if you work it right."

Brad pounded his right fist on the bed beside him, looked daggers at the doctor and grumbled. "Humph! Got no ball team!"

The doctor shrugged, still swiping his handkerchief across his clothes. "We'll think about letting you out of here late next week, but not before, Brad. You have a lot more work to do before I'd even consider it."

"Yeah... I... hear ya." Brad leaned back into his pillows, sighed heavily and closed his eyes. The sound was that of a totally defeated man.

"Brad, dear," Joyce said, as she came to the bed and picked up one of the napkins, "shall I order another tray?"

Brad's eyes popped open, as he said, "Leave... me...alone, Woman! I... sleep." To validate his words, Brad squirmed around in the bed for more comfort, laid his head back on the pillow and closed his eyes.

Wiping her face, she said, "I'm sorry, doctor."

As the doctor pushed his damp handkerchief back in his pocket, he said, "Hey, it's par for a stroke victim, Joyce. We'll all live through it."

"Still...."

With all the clatter that Brad had created, the nurse aid came running in the room. "Oh, wow! What happened?"

"Sort of had an accident, Michelle," the doctor said. "Since you're here and Brad's about to rest, I'll leave so you can get it cleaned up."

"Yes, Doctor, I'll get right on that."

The doctor pulled his pen from his pocket and opened the chart to a clean page. "See you tomorrow, Joyce. As my granddad used to tell me, 'Keep a stiff upper lip'." The doctor smiled at Joyce, glanced at Brad, then at the mess on the floor and shook his head at the CNA.

"Yes, Doctor." Joyce shook her head. "I wish he'd be a little more cooperative!" She looked around at the disaster he'd created and sighed.

The doctor shrugged. "Yes, it'd be helpful, but then he wouldn't be Brad Thomas, now would he?" He grinned at Joyce and walked out.

Joyce slouched back into the chair and let out a long sigh. As the nurse aid brought back a broom to start cleaning up, Joyce said, "No, he wouldn't be himself if he wasn't cantankerous." The aid silently agreed, but she only smiled at Joyce. Joyce watched for several minutes and then said, "Thank you, dear, I'm sorry for the mess."

Very sympathetic, the nurse aid said, "It's okay, Mrs. Thomas, sometimes accidents happen. I'll get this cleaned up in no time."

After another cup of coffee and looking over Jack's plans, Corky slapped his hand on the prints. "Them's good, boy. I be back after lunch. We'll get to that site and have a look see."

Jack stood up with Corky and said, "Sounds good, Uncle, since it's such a pretty day today. What, about an hour?"

"Yep, see ya then."

Corky climbed into his truck and went home for lunch. Allison fixed several club sandwiches for their lunch and filled glasses with iced tea to wash them down. Allison laid her hand on Jack's shoulder as she put his plate in front of him. "I didn't know you had all that done, Jack! Even a second floor!"

"Hey, I'm a go-getter, you know that! Even Corky said I was!" he boasted, but chuckled and winked at his wife.

"Well, sure, I know that, but I didn't know you were that excited to get away from home. I thought you liked it there."

Jack took a large bite of his sandwich and said, "Well, Max sort of wanted to be his own boss and I let him stew in it for a while. Then Corky called me and it seemed the thing to do, both to start up this new place and to let Max buy me out. It's a good deal I'm using that money to get this up and running and used some of it to get those blueprints done. We'll have us a good restaurant here in no time."

"Wow! Great! I didn't know that." She turned to Emilyn and grinned. "Just think, girl, you'll get out of that Barney's place real soon!"

"Yeah, there is that." She still had no idea why they had wanted her to come with them. She'd never had anything to do with management. She hoped Allison would be the one to make a menu or hire people and make schedules. Another thing she didn't have an idea about was how she would handle the situation with Matt and her in the same town. Obviously, he still affected her and if last night was any indication, she affected him, too. She was positive she could wait a long time to come back.

When Corky drove back on the parking lot and pulled up to the edge of the walk closest to cabin one; the three inside walked out and down the ramp. Corky's truck didn't have four doors, so he had to get out of the driver's seat to let Emilyn in the back, but several minutes later he drove across the gravel parking lot, then turned on the street through town and drove away. Of course, Isabel watched from her chair. Corky and Isabel weren't buddies, so he, along with the other three were not aware that Isabel saw them. The three passengers were excited to see more of the town and especially where the restaurant would be.

However, as the truck left her parking lot, Isabel pushed a button on her phone and a minute later a voice said, "Hello, DeLord's"

Without saying who she was, Isabel said, "Corky just left with those three people from my cabin. Probably they're on their way to that hole in the ground across from you. At least that's what the man said they'd come to town for."

Ramon immediately turned and grinned at his wife, but said into the phone, "Thanks, Isabel, but being the fine, upstanding, non-gossiping folks that we are, we'll let them take a look, but we won't bother them. I mean, we aren't really that nosy, you know." Ramon chuckled and added, "Of course, we don't have a chair that faces the street and all…."

Ten

sabel chuckled. "Sonny, you better watch it! But I guess that's so. But then, you got that baby, he's a bit inquisitive. If you find anything out, though, let me know. Probably that single girl'll be living in one of my cabins…"

"Yes, that's a thought." Chuckling, Ramon added, "Take it easy, Isabel. It's Saturday and tomorrow you're making that long trip to Blairsville for church, when you could go here. I hear Derek's a really good Sunday school teacher for your age and all…and you know, I tell you every week, how good Roger's gotten over the months."

"Sonny, one of these days…!"

Innocently, Ramon said, "What, Isabel?" He hung up before she could respond. However, he was chuckling; he loved to torment the older lady.

Sandy also grinned at her husband and said, "Honey, you are something else! You goad that lady endlessly."

Still chuckling, Ramon said, "Oh, I know, but Isabel's so much fun to tease."

Sandy nodded. "And you do such a good job of it, too."

Only a few minutes later, Corky's truck turned onto the gravel driveway onto the large graveled area. Of course Jon saw the activity from the living room picture window and toddled as fast as his short legs would let him, down the hall into the office where he could see out the window to the parking lot, the street and across it to the large open area. Only seconds after he disappeared into the room, he screamed, "Daddy! Come see! Cor, tar-uck! Watza pee-pa! Come see now!"

Sandy and Ramon looked at each other and smiled. Together, they followed Jon into the office and Ramon asked, "So what's going on, Jon?"

"Cor, tar-uck!"

"Really, what's Corky's truck doing?"

"Da-no, Daddy!" He came to his parents and climbed up on Sandy's footrest. With his arms in the air, he said, "Go see!"

Ramon scowled, but watched Corky's truck stop on the gravel and asked the little boy, "You think we should go out there and bother them?"

"Yeah! Now, go see!"

"But maybe it's a secret and we shouldn't know."

"Na uh, no seket!" Still waving his hands in the air, he said again, "Daddy, go see now! Cor tar-uck. Now, Daddy!"

Since Sandy wasn't reaching for Jon as quickly as he thought she should, his little hands grabbed hold of her slacks and started to pull himself, first onto her feet, then he raised his leg as high as it would go, trying to climb onto Sandy's lap. Wanting to keep things from getting discombobulated, Sandy reached down and pulled her little son onto her lap. She kept her hands on him as he squirmed around to sit on her legs. Sandy was always glad she had no feeling in her legs when Jon plopped down on them. It made her grin because Ramon usually winced when Jon did that, with any normal person Jon crashing down on their legs would hurt. Of course, as he got bigger the crash was heavier.

From his perch, Jon gave his parents an angelic smile and said, "Now, go see!" Letting out a long sigh, Jon pointed toward the door and said, "Daddy, door!"

Chuckling, Ramon reached for the doorknob of the door onto the parking lot. He hesitated and looked at his son before he opened it. "So, Corky won't be mad if he sees us coming across the parking lot? Are you sure, Jon?"

Shaking his head emphatically, Jon said, "Nope! Cor good." He bounced a few times on Sandy's legs and pointed at the door again. "Now, go!"

Ramon let out a long sigh. "Okay, I guess we'll go see."

As if he'd won a major conflict, Jon let out a big sigh. "Good!" Sandy, with her son perched on her legs, followed her husband out the door.

By now, Corky had extricated himself from the cab and the other three stood on the gravel. Jack wiped his shirtsleeve across his forehead, then looked around at what once was a meadow, then started walking around, taking in everything that was graveled as well as the large mounds of dirt sitting in different parts of the lot. The meadow had been quite large, so there was still some grass at the back in front of a row of trees and on the side away from town. Still looking at the trees standing at the very back of the lot, Jack said, "Looks good, Uncle. So you can get a contractor in here pretty quick?"

Jack grinned at the older man. "'Member, it'll be hurricane season here pretty soon. Rain like that can fill a hole like this up in a couple of hours. I'd hate to think all this work would end up as a puddle of mud before we really got going on it."

Corky also looked around and folded his arms across his ample chest. "Yep, talked to that Casbah fella. He's the bank president back in Blairsville and knows lotsa folks. He's got the inside track on them contractor types, so I got me a good guy lined up. I called him over lunch and he said he'd leave right away. Takes a half ar, so he'll be along here any minute now. You show him yore plans, we get on this 'fore them hurricanes come ashore and fill that there hole up with water 'stead of cee-ment."

"Yeah, that would be bad. We need that slab real soon. Gotta let a slab cure for a bit, too. It'll be a week or more 'fore things happen around here. It'd be the middle of that hurricane season about the time the frame was going up."

"Yep, that's what I figger. Get that slab poured now, we get this here restrnt up and runnin' 'fore Thanksgivin' mebe."

"Hey, that'd be a good thing. The holidays are always a good time for people to eat out. Alli, she sure likes to decorate for the holidays, too."

Allison and Emi climbed out of the short seat in the cab, but hung back to let the men talk. Putting up a building was not in Allison's realm of expertise and Emi was still wondering why Jack and Allison had even brought her along. Of course, she was happy to enjoy the beautiful day. It was definitely cooler than Barney's kitchen. Emi was walking even more slowly than Allison, looking back at the road and saw the little family on their parking lot across the street. "Who's that?" she whispered.

Allison looked behind her and shrugged. "Don't know, but it's probably the same people who came for that other twin last night. You know, had the blue van?"

Jon was waving from his perch on Sandy's lap. "Look at that cute little boy!" Emi said.

"Oh, he's adorable!"

Drawn away from the excavated site because of the little boy, the two women walked down the driveway toward the road. Ramon gave the ladies his best grin and called from across the street, "So, what's Corky got up his sleeve?"

Allison looked back at the two men, then in front of her to the little family and said, "Oh, he and my husband are getting things in the works to put in a restaurant. He's been telling us this place is growing and needs a place for people to eat out."

Jon was nodding at the ladies. He put his thumb in his chest and said, "I Ja, wuv Mama'n Daddy." Then he pointed beyond the women. "Cor tar-uck."

"You're Jon?" Allison asked.

"Una huh," Jon answered importantly. He pointed behind him and added, "Mamandaddy good, too."

The two women had sauntered across the street by now. Emi couldn't take her eyes from Jon. Softly, she asked, "How old is he?"

"He's sixteen months."

"He's precious!"

"Yes, we think so."

Importantly, Jon said again, "I Ja. Mama go fast! See Cor tar-uck."

"I know!" Allison exclaimed. She looked at Sandy and said, "He's only sixteen months? He talks so well."

"Yes, he does and we're glad."

Just then, another pick-up truck slowed, then pulled off onto the gravel driveway and drove up beside Corky's truck. "'Nuda tar-uck!" Jon screamed and bounced on Sandy's legs.

Ramon nodded, seeing the name of a construction company displayed on the side of the truck. "Probably Corky's contractor."

Allison looked back over her shoulder, as the man left his truck and walked toward Jack and Corky. "Yes, I'd say that's so. Jack wants to get the place open before snow flies." She scowled. "It snows around here? Down where we live we don't get snow that sticks, it's mostly sleet and freezing rain."

"Yeah, we get a few flakes each winter, but doesn't last long. Of course, we have the potential, since we're so close to those big hills back there. Up in those mountains it does snow and can get pretty bad. Last winter we got the ice really bad around here. People from that clinic down near where you're staying couldn't get out of town." Ramon raised his hand and added, "That's when those folks wanted an eatery really bad! They sort of bummed out when Alex closed his store about the same time they closed the clinic."

Allison nodded. "Yes, that would be bad. The ice was so bad they couldn't leave?"

"You got it!"

Sandy hadn't spoken while Ramon spoke. She smiled at the two women and said, "Say, will you be here tomorrow?"

"Yes, we planned to stay until Monday. Emilyn has to be back to work on Tuesday and it took us most of yesterday to get here."

"After church tomorrow, why don't you folks come back and have lunch with us?"

"Una huh, lunch." Jon nodded emphatically.

"Oh, we couldn't impose…"

Sandy waved her hand, dismissing Allison's comment. "It's no imposition! I make the best spaghetti sauce in town, just ask anybody." Sandy's smile was so broad her eyes twinkled. "The church is real close there to where you're staying, there at Isabel's. Please do come for Sunday school at nine o'clock. My husband's a teacher for one of the adult classes and my brother-in-law makes the best coffee. You are most welcome!" Of course, she had no idea whether the Albertson's or Emilyn went to church.

Knowing that Emi and Jack didn't do church, Allison said, "We'll think about it." Emi still looked at the little boy, but didn't comment.

Chuckling, Ramon said, "By the way, we're Ramon and Sandy DeLord and of course, you already met Jon."

Allison smiled. "That's Jack and I'm Allison Albertson and our friend Emilyn Willard. Emi'll be part of our crew when we open up."

Smiling broadly, Ramon said, "We're happy to know you! I can vouch for my wife's spaghetti! You'll be in for a treat, I'll guarantee it. After church and all, it'd probably be close to twelve-thirty for lunch. Our pastor, Roger, isn't long winded, but he packs a powerful message. Everybody loves him."

"Could we bring something for lunch?"

"Alex sells a good loaf of Italian bread, but you'll have to get it today before five o'clock. He closes right at five and he's not open on Sunday."

"Yes, Isabel already told us that."

"Yes, I would expect that she did. After all, she likes people coming back to her cabins and eating's sort of important if you stay in them. She's a really nice lady. She rented that cabin you're in to my wife when she first came here to Vansville. That is until I convinced her she should be my wife." He winked at the ladies, "I had a job convincing her, though. She came from Philadelphia. Big city, small town, you know."

However, Allison stepped back and looked across the street and saw that the men were deep in conversation. The man from the construction company was intent on looking at Jack's plans. "You know, maybe we ought to hold on that dinner. Jack and Corky may be cooking up something. Let's clear that Sunday dinner with them first."

"Sure, that's fine, but you're very welcome. We always love company, especially Jon loves people."

Allison smiled at the little family. "Thank you so much. Corky's told us how friendly everybody here in town is."

Ramon looked away from Allison and grinned at Emilyn. "Say, you folks are staying at Isabel's cabins. Have you met the guys in the next two cabins?"

Emi pulled in a sharp gasp, but Allison said, "Yes, they both introduced themselves last evening. One of them only stayed a few minutes then got in a blue van, but the other one came by on his way back to the store from his supper break and invited us for coffee. He seemed really friendly. Since we had our meeting with Corky this morning at the cabin, we haven't gotten there yet." She smiled and said, "We may stop by there when we leave here on Monday."

Emi looked daggers at her friend and for her ears alone, she hissed, "We won't be going there for coffee, either."

"You say you'll be leaving on Monday?" Allison nodded and Ramon continued, "Well, they open at eight o'clock. As I understand it, Natt makes his coffee first thing, while Matt opens up, so you'd get a real fresh cup right away. Stop by on your way out of town and get you a cup. His coffee is second only to my wife's and it's quite popular."

Allison glanced at Emi, but nodded at Ramon. "That sounds like a plan."

Sandy added, "They're twins, you know. Eric's one of our guides until the end of the month, then he'll be a deputy sheriff. Matt's just come to town to work with his cousin at the store. They both go to our church." Sandy looked from Allison to Emilyn. "They're both single, well, Eric probably won't be for much longer. As I understand it, the love of his life came back to live here, so it could be we'd only have to stretch our spaghetti sauce and invite Matt for our dinner tomorrow."

Emi gasped again, but her hand flew to cover her mouth. Allison grinned and waved her hand. "Oh, don't put yourselves out on our account, please! We've still got that on hold until we know Corky's plans."

"Yes," Sandy chuckled. "I won't try to twist his arm. Loretta compliments her husband quite well. They are quite a couple!"

Ramon looked across the street and said, "Looks like the men are deep into it. Now that Jon's got his little eyes satisfied, maybe we'll head on inside."

"Good to meet you folks," Sandy said and started her chair motor.

"Yes," Allison said, "Thanks for inviting us for dinner tomorrow. Spaghetti does sound really good. We can probably decide this afternoon on that."

"That's great! Hope we see you at church in the morning." Neither of the ladies answered that statement, they only smiled. Allison didn't know Emi's thoughts and she wasn't about to say her husband hadn't been to church since their wedding! However, she did remember that everyone so far had told them that the stores all closed up Saturday evening.

Meanwhile, the three men talked and walked around the hole in the ground and Corky filled Jason in on what had been done, since the contractor hadn't seen the place before. After walking all the way around it, Jack went back to Corky's truck and pulled out his briefcase, while the contractor went to his truck and opened the tailgate. Jack walked up, swung his briefcase onto the tailgate and Corky came puffing up to stand beside him. Jack pulled the rolled up plans out, then spread them on the tailgate and Jason looked over the plans carefully.

Finally, he turned the page to look at the second story plans. After a few moments, Corky said, "So, Jason, whadaya think?"

"Could get right on it, Corky, right away."

Both Jack and Corky grinned and Corky exclaimed, "That's my man! I knowd ya'd git right on it, Man! Jack, here, was kinda worried 'bout beatin' them hurricanes. It'll be about that season here real soon."

"In fact, he couldn't come today, of course, but I'll give my cement supplier a call right now so he'll put us on the schedule for a drop on Monday. We'll get that slab poured and get it curing so we can get this show on the road."

Jack grinned at the man and said, "That'll be good! Like I told Uncle, we don't want that hole filled up with water any time soon."

"Hurricane season coming here soon, we'll want to be ahead of it." Looking at Jack, Jason said, "You'll leave me your blueprints today?"

"Sure! That's why I brought them. I got my own version back home. I'm sure getting excited about this. See, I have all the people in place to take over my restaurant down where we're living now. This'll be my first expansion and I'm excited about it."

"Well, I'll get my whole crew on this as soon as the slab cures. Like Corky says, we'll have this up and running before the snow flies."

Jack pointed to the page still turned to the second floor. "So you're okay with putting on that second story?"

"Sure am! Not a problem at all. We'll get 'er done just like you want it, man. I live in Blairsville, but I may come on out and sample your menu when you're up and running. I'll bring the wife along she's a good one to test out good food."

"Sounds good to me. Thanks." Jack held out his hand to Jason and they shook on the deal. The two men grinned at each other. Corky took a step, reached across in front of Jack and took Jason's hand in his beefy one.

Jason rolled up the blueprints and headed for the cab. "I'll see you guys again!" Jason said and climbed in his truck. He barely sat down when he put his phone to his ear. Jack knew he was calling the man with the cement truck. He was pretty sure the cement would be poured before any rain filled the hole.

Jason was barely off the gravel and Jack started toward Corky's truck when Corky asked, "You folks have plans for dinner?"

"Don't think so, Uncle, but let's ask Alli. I just don't like to leave her out of the loop, you know? Especially when we're out of town."

"I don't blame ya none."

The two men turned and saw the two ladies still talking with the DeLord's and Jack asked, "Who are those people?"

As they started walking toward the road, Corky gave Jack a grin and said, "That there's the DeLord's. 'Member I told ya about Sandy livin' in that first cabin a while? They do the hikin' and campin' thing here in town. They're busy all during good weather. She's the pride of Vansville, I garuntee it!"

"The lady in the wheelchair?" Jack asked, totally surprised.

Corky nodded enthusiastically. "Absolutely! She come here and Vansville got on the map. Buleeve me!"

"Is that so!"

As the men reached the road, a little voice shouted, "Cor-ky!"

A grin from one ear to the other accompanied the words, "And that there is the sweetest little fella a body could know! Hi, there, Jon-nie!"

"Cor-ky, tar-uck!"

"Yep! Got my truck. You good boy?"

Nodding enthusiastically, Jon said, "Uh huh, Ja good!"

"Corky," the lady in the wheelchair said, "we were just talking with these fine ladies and wanted to know if they could come for spaghetti after church tomorrow. They said they could unless you and Loretta have plans."

Corky grinned at Sandy and said, "Ms Sandy, them folks better get your recipp fer that spaghetti fer their diner. If you invited 'em, they'd better get your spaghetti and no escuse! No, the wife she run the sweeper all mornin' and wants 'em for dinner tonight afore I git the place all messed up, so you kin have 'em tomorra, jes fine."

Sandy looked at Allison and said, "Okay, it's all set. We'll see you folks after church."

"Thanks for the invite, Mrs. Delord," Jack said, graciously.

"Oh, please, it's Sandy," she said with a grin.

Sandy turned on the motor of her chair and Jon, his little face angelic, started waving. "Bye, bye, Cor, bye mis-ter."

Emi waved back to the little boy. "Bye, Jon, see you."

"Uh-huh! Bye, lady!"

"What a beautiful child!" Allison exclaimed.

"Yep, that he is!" Corky agreed instantly. "She had a really tough time havin' that baby, but he's as right as rain and the best little kid."

"She's okay with us coming for spaghetti?" Jack asked. "I mean, her in a wheelchair?"

"She'd be miffed effin she heard you say that! 'Course it's fine!"

"So we must stop for a loaf of Italian bread."

Corky chuckled. "Yup, she won't letcha do nothin' else."

"Okay, we'll do it."

From the doorway, Ramon said, "See you folks tomorrow!"

After the little family disappeared inside their house, Allison asked, "Corky, why's she in a wheelchair? She's not mentally challenged, that's for sure!"

Corky watched the door close behind the little family and said, "She don't talk about it much, but it ain't no secret. She were dropped as a baby, never walked a day in her life. But she shore is somethin' else! She's the life of this here town!"

There was a collective gasp from the three new people, but Allison asked, "Oh, my! How do you mean, Corky?"

"Hey, don't be surprised effen she gives you a paintin' tomorra after dinner. She got her own galry up in Philly and she's played with the Atlanta band or somethin'."

"Wow!"

"Yep, she's good! She's a wonder! I tol' ya, she put Vansville on the map."

"I can't wait to go there!" Allison exclaimed.

"Well, you'll have a great time. I knowd that for shore."

"Is she from here?"

"Nope, she's from Philly. Came here ta hep that scallywag, Ramon. She even made sompin outta him."

"What do you mean?" Allison asked.

Corky was always happy to talk about his hometown and said, "Hey, fore she come he run that there hike stuff hisself. Now they got a half dozen men workin' fer 'em. Fore she'd marry him he got converted, though. Now he's a Sunday school teacher. That preacher we got, he got on fire fer God 'cause a her. I tell ya, she's a marvel."

"Wow!" Jack said.

Do I really wanna go to dinner there? Emilyn asked herself.

Corky looked up at the sun and said, "Well, I better take ya back. Loretta said supper's gonna be ready 'bout five-thirty or so."

"So where do you live, Corky?" Jack asked.

"On the way back I show ya."

Jack nodded. "That'd be good, uncle."

"Yes," Allison said, "We told Mrs. DeLord we'd bring a loaf of bread to go with the spaghetti and she reminded us we'd better get it before Alex closes." The four people slowly made their way toward Corky's truck.

"That'd be right, Allison. Yep, that'd be right. This here's a little town." He grinned at the visitors. "We tend ta roll up the sidewalks after Alex and Natt close up on Saturday. Only thing's open on Sunday be the church."

"Really?"

After they were in the truck and Corky turned around, he said, "You'll wanna go to our church tomorra. That preacher fella, he's right good. Sandy, she plays fer church, too."

Jack hesitated a minute before he said, "We'll think on that a bit, Uncle."

"Yep, you do that. That fella rings that bell 'fore Sunday school and then agin 'fore church. Cain't sleep through that much anyway."

From the highway, Corky pointed down the next street. "See that gray house three doors down? That'd be where Loretta and me lives. Could walk it, I guess, from Isabel's."

Jack looked from Corky's house down Main street to see Isabel's cabins and said, "Okay, Uncle, we'll do a bit of freshening and we'll be there real soon."

Corky grinned at Jack. "Don't forget that bread for Sandy's dinner."

"We'll do that. In fact, drop me off and I'll get it to go."

Allison let out a long sigh. "Jack, you'd better let me get it."

"Oh, right."

Since both Allison and Emilyn sat in the back seat, when Corky stopped his truck across the street from Alex's store, Jack got out, but both Allison and Emilyn slipped out. Corky looked as if he'd wait for them, but Jack watched the women enter the store. "Corky," he said, on a deep sigh, "you might as well take me back to the cabin, they'll be a while. For some reason my wife likes to browse in grocery stores." He shook his head. "Who knows what she'll have in grocery bags when she comes out!"

"Sure, not a problem!" Corky pulled the stick down into drive and headed back to Isabel's cabins. "Usually, when Loretta goes grocery shoppin' I get me a cuppa down at Thomas's. Good place to relax and the coffee's good."

Jack nodded. "I better sample that coffee before I leave town. Maybe I'll get a recommendation for where to get good coffee. Ya'all seem stuck on his coffee."

"Yep, it shore is good! Well, we'll see ya later."

"That you will, Uncle. We'll work to be on time."

It was late evening. Jack, Allison and Emilyn had just said goodnight to Corky and Loretta and Corky had closed the door behind them. Loretta had served a good meal and some really good coffee. During the meal, then in the conversation afterward the younger people had found out a lot about the little town of Vansville. During the evening's conversation, Loretta, then Corky later on invited the Albertson's and Emi to church in the morning. Jack had never refused them, but he hadn't made any commitment either. He'd never been a church goer. He made a habit of sleeping a bit later on Sunday. It was a day for a restaurant to be open, but not as early. People went to church in the morning.

Jack had been a cook in a restaurant since he could reach the grill and run his own restaurant for many years. For many of those years he'd been the chief daytime cook and had never closed the place on Sunday just so he and Allison could go to church together. Allison didn't always work on Sunday, there had been times when she'd felt she should go to church, so for some religious holidays she made the effort to go to church. However, Vansville was different. Both Corky and Loretta let the Albertson's know that to open a restaurant in Vansville meant that that eating place was closed on Sunday.

After leaving Corky's house the three walked the sidewalk of the quiet little town back to the cabins and realized how quiet it was. Nothing was open, even the houses they passed were dark or only had one light on. Really, the only noise they heard were nature noises - tree toads, bullfrogs and several whip-poor-wills in the meadow behind Isabel's house.

As they walked they talked about how unusual it was for a public place to eat was expected to be closed on Sunday. "Why would they insist the restaurant be closed on Sunday? It's the day most people want to eat out!" Jack exclaimed, truly puzzled.

"I don't know, Honey," Allison answered, "but we'd better stick with the program."

Pensively, Jack nodded. "I suppose we should, after all, Uncle asked us to come and he expects the place to be closed on Sundays, so we'd better. Still, it makes no sense! All the restaurants I know about it's their best day, people flock to a restaurant right after they go to church. Lots of times they'll entertain their friends, meet family – it's a good day to relax over a meal. And frankly, most restaurants stay open and profitable because of Friday night dinner and Sunday afternoon and evening dinner."

"That's true, Honey," Allison agreed.

They were ready to step onto Isabel's parking lot when Emi surprised herself by saying, "I think I'll go to church tomorrow, if it's okay with you guys." Even as she said the words she scowled. *Where had those words come from?*

Both Jack and Allison were quiet for several seconds, perplexed that Emi, who had always told them how Matt had been about church when they'd been married and how opposed it had made her, would say what she said. Finally, Jack cleared his throat and said, "Well, sure, Emi, if that's what you want to do. The first thing we have on is that dinner date at... what were their names again?"

"Sandy... and little Jon. I just want to go..." Emi answered.

Jack went ahead of them and unlocked the door to the cabin, but Allison smiled at her friend. "It's fine, Emi, I'll have coffee on. We still have that baggy of coffee grounds Corky brought this morning. I'll use it."

"Okay, thanks."

"Not a problem, Emi, we're here to see about this restaurant and you're here to get away from Barney's for several days."

It was quite late when Jack opened the cabin door. Isabel's house was dark and the other two cabins showed no sign of life. Jack reached in and flipped the switch inside the door, but Emi immediately made her way to the lamp beside the couch and turned it on. As soon as Jack locked the door, he again flipped the switch and turned the central light off.

Allison sighed, "Corky wore me out, so much talking! I'm heading for bed. See you in the morning, Emi. I hope you sleep well."

Emi nodded as Allison went straight to the bedroom and Jack hurried behind her. When their door was shut, Emi ran in the bathroom with her night clothes and finished in record time. She hardly remembered brushing her teeth. She left the bathroom and closed the door behind her and momentarily heard Allison and Jack go in. She looked at the cot in the corner, but shook her head. It held no appeal. It was late, the clock on the wall told her that, but she wasn't sleepy, she had other things pressing on her mind and she knew only one place she could look. Those four words had been with her all day. No matter who was talking, if her mind wandered the words, "In the beginning, God..." were there.

Instead of sitting on the cot she sank onto the couch and reached for the Bible she'd put back on the little table beside the couch. Holding it in her hands again, she looked at the bright gold emblem and the lettering on the front cover. The color of the cover was bright red, not some drab brown or black. Everything about the Book seemed to draw her. She'd been thinking about those first four words that had captured her during the night.

She scooted very close to the arm of the couch close to the light. This time, the Book didn't fall open. She took extra care and opened the front cover. She didn't expect to see anything, but to her surprise, there were several lists there. The very first word was a word Matt had said to her several times while they were married. "Salvation," she murmured. "What's it mean?" There beside the word was a page number listed. Eagerly, she turned to the page, maybe she could learn what he'd meant all those years ago.

She read the words out loud, "'Jesus answered, "I am the way and the truth and the life. No one comes to the Father except through me."'" (John

14:6) Emi looked up from the words on the page, but then she looked back at them and read them again. "The word 'salvation' wasn't in those two sentences. I still don't know what 'salvation' means."

Still, she realized there was a place inside her that ached to read more. "This is the middle of the book. Chapter fourteen means there are thirteen chapters before this one. What will they tell me?" She turned back the pages until she found chapter one of the book of John. It started almost like the words she'd read last night. Hungrily, she started reading, her eyes darting back and forth on the column. Instantly it captured her heart so much that she kept reading and read the words of the book of John for hours. She was oblivious to the time. It became a new day, but she didn't notice. Her eyes read ravenously, but her heart soaked up the words she was reading.

The clock on the wall told her it would soon be daylight. She looked back to the words on the page, but instead of reading more, again tonight her eyes closed and she toppled over, her head hit the arm of the couch and her feet automatically pulled themselves up onto the second cushion. The light shining down on her never registered, but she was holding the red Book with the shiny gold lettering on the front open against her chest. This time, however, the Book was open to the gospel of John.

Again in the morning, Allison saw the living room light shining under the door into the bathroom. She scowled, curious, wondering why Emilyn had left the light on two nights in a row. As quietly as she could, she turned the knob, pushed the door enough to stick her head out and peeked into the living room from the bathroom and unable to understand she shook her head.

"What is with that girl?" she murmured. "She can't be comfortable! In fact, did she even use the cot?" Allison pushed the door further open so she could see the cot. It looked like Emi had made it Saturday morning, like she hadn't slept on the cot at all. However, Allison didn't want to wake her yet so she closed the bathroom door quietly.

However, this morning, the snick of the bathroom door closing woke Emilyn. Still clutching the Bible, Emi sat up, put the Bible down on her legs and rubbed her eyes. "I fell asleep!" she whispered. "I can't believe it!"

The Bible was open to the first chapter of John. As if she was a woman on a desert and the words in front of her were the best thirst-quenching drink, Emi read;

> "'In the beginning was the Word and the Word was with God, and the Word was God. He was with God in the beginning…. The Word became flesh and lived for a while among us. We have seen His glory, the glory of the one and only Son who came from the Father, full of grace and truth.'" (John 1: 1,2,14)

When Allison left the bathroom and left the door open, Emi was ready with some clothes. She hadn't packed any dress-up clothes, but she had some better looking clean clothes. She ran in, started the shower and was ready for coffee when Allison had it ready. Without a word, Emi doctored her coffee then sat and grabbed a muffin Allison had set out, then ate and drank quickly. She couldn't remember the last time she was so excited to do anything, but she was going to church! She gulped down the last mouthful of the muffin and chased it with the last swallow of coffee, took the cup to the sink and rinsed it out, then dashed to the couch for the Bible, while Allison sat watching, dumbfounded.

"I'm leaving, Alli!" she said and rushed to the door.

"Well, okay," Allison said, dubiously.

Jack hadn't made a sound from the bedroom and Allison was still in her housecoat when Emi clutched the Bible to her chest and dashed out the door. Running down the ramp she collided with Matt who had just turned the corner on the walk. He was dressed up, his Bible under his arm, obviously on his way to church. To keep the two of them from toppling onto the pavement, Matt grabbed Emi's upper arms and held on.

"Oh!" Emi whispered, embarrassed. "Oh, I'm sorry, I didn't see you."

Hesitantly, Matt asked, "Are… are you, um, going to church, Emi?"

"Yes!" Emi exclaimed and held up the Bible. "Um, I read this all night…," her words petered out as Matt stared at her incredulously.

"Really? Wow!" Matt licked his lips and looked down at the pretty woman. "Wanna go with me? I'll introduce you around."

Emilyn looked at Matt, then swallowed and whispered, "I guess it's alright, thanks." Even so, she knew there was only one person she wanted to see.

"Okay…" Matt said, tentatively.

However, Emilyn was on a mission. If Matt thought he could saunter along leisurely with Emi beside him, he was mistaken! Once Matt had them back in balance, Emi took a long step away from him and nearly ran across the gravel parking lot. Matt turned and hurried after her. He'd never known Emilyn to move so fast. He had to lengthen his stride, walking normally he couldn't keep up with Emi, it was like something or someone was chasing her.

Sandy and Ramon did their usual routine for Sunday morning. Now that they went to church in Vansville, they didn't have to get up quite so early. After fixing her good, nutritious meal, Sandy brought the bowl of scrambled eggs to the table and right behind her Ramon set their mugs of coffee down in their places. Jon was already in his booster seat whacking his spoon on the table, anxious to have Mama and Daddy sit down and pray so he could fill his little tummy with their good breakfast.

Ramon said a short blessing, then reached for the bowl of eggs and put some on Jon's plate, then took a strip of bacon from the small platter and also put it on Jon's plate. The little boy dug in immediately and Ramon placed a large helping of eggs on his own plate then turned to hand the bowl to Sandy. "Eat up, Love! It looks good as usual."

However, Sandy didn't take the bowl right away and Ramon looked up to see where she was looking. She was looking at him, but the expression on her face was one he hadn't seen in a long time. "What is it, Sweetheart?" he asked.

"Honey, we must hurry! We must get to church!"

Ramon looked through the archway into the kitchen to see the clock over the sink. "Sweetheart, it's nearly forty-five minutes before Roger rings the bell!"

"I know! I know, but that girl… the girl we saw yesterday… what was her name? The one who came with the couple for the restaurant… Anyway, we need to get there as soon as we can," Sandy said, intensely. "Emilyn – that's it!"

Ramon put the bowl of eggs down on the table because Sandy had not taken it, instead, he took her hand that she was holding out. She bowed her head, closed her eyes and whispered, "God in heaven, that girl needs You! May she come to church today and please, give all of us the right words to lead her to You!"

From experience, Ramon knew it wouldn't be 'all of us' but his darling wife who would need the right words, but his part was to pray for her to have the right words and for the girl to have an open heart. It was quiet around the table at DeLord's while all three concentrated on the task that was before them – eating that nutritious breakfast.

From that moment on everything at the DeLord's house happened in double time. Jon never complained, he also seemed to have a sixth sense about what his mama would do. As Sandy headed for the garage, Jon held up his hands to his daddy to take him. Well before nine o'clock Ramon fastened Jon into his carseat, as Sandy fastened herself down in the empty spot behind the wheel. She had the garage door up and the engine running as Ramon slid into the passenger seat. Sandy left their parking lot, turned on the street and headed for church. Here was another lady on a mission – God's mission.

Sandy pulled into her spot in front of the church and as she shut off the ignition she raised her hand to activate the controls for the door and the lift. She looked back out the windshield and said, "There she is! She's nearly running! Matt's trying to keep up with her!"

"I see her! Wow!" Ramon exclaimed.

Sandy hurried to release her chair from the spot behind the wheel, whipped around and headed for the lift that was slowly extending from the side of the van. Of course, the mechanism wouldn't hurry and Sandy waited while the lift groaned before it reached the horizontal position. Ramon waited for Sandy to cross the open space in the van and smiled at her as he climbed out of the passenger seat to get Jon from his carseat. Ramon went behind her and squeezed her shoulder, giving her his support, then took another step to release Jon from his seat, but didn't say anything. He knew that in her heart Sandy was praying for the young woman who was nearly running toward them. Ramon knew that Sandy had a sixth sense about someone who needed the Lord. He'd prayed all the way into the church building for the interaction he knew was about to take place.

Emilyn never slowed down, once she stepped away from Matt, she nearly ran across the parking lot, onto the sidewalk and down to the corner where the church was. Matt was trying unsuccessfully to keep up with her, but couldn't seem to catch up. Before Emi reached the van, Sandy took herself onto the platform. Ramon was still releasing Jon from his carseat.

Still clutching the Bible close to her chest, breathlessly, Emilyn ran up, looked up at Sandy and exclaimed, "Please! I need to know!"

Sandy started the lift down towards the ground and with her beautiful smile in place, asked, "Emilyn, what is it you need to know?"

"Oh! Everything! About God, salvation, all of that!" She pulled the Bible from her chest and held it out to Sandy. "Here, can you tell me?"

Sandy smiled at the young woman. "Honey, I'll be glad to," she said.

When Ramon realized that Sandy would probably be talking to Emilyn right there on the sidewalk, still holding Jon, he moved to the front of the van, picked up his Bible and Sunday school things and went out through the front door. Once he was on the sidewalk, Jon wanted down, so Ramon put him on the ground but kept his hand. The little boy wanted to run, but Ramon held him back. Matt was only a few steps behind Emi, but he came up panting to stand a few steps behind her so he wouldn't distract her.

"This is amazing!" he whispered to Ramon. "I… I never saw her this way! Goodness, she ran all the way from the cabins!"

Ramon motioned Matt to come with him, so Matt turned beside Ramon, who asked, "You know that lady?"

Immediately, Matt's chin fell on his chest. With no more volume than he'd had with the first words, he whispered, "Yes, more than ten years ago she was my wife. I divorced her after two years and moved on without her. I was a long ways from her; never saw her until last night when I came home from the store." He cleared his throat and said again, "I've never seen her like this before!"

Trying not to show his surprise, Ramon said, "We're early, come on inside, we can talk." Matt nodded and followed Ramon and Jon up the steps to the front door.

Eleven

Still on the lift that had finally made it to the ground, Sandy took the Bible that Emi held out to her. Looking compassionately at the young woman, she said, "Emilyn, I have a most favorite verse that will tell you all you need to know. Have you ever heard of John 3:16?"

Nodding eagerly, Emilyn looked at the Bible, then at Sandy and said, "Yes, I… I read that whole book of John last night. I remember reading that verse. Still I don't know what it all means, it's all muddled in my brain! But Sandy! I need to *know*!"

Still with that loving smile on her face, Sandy took Emi's hand that had held the Bible and said, "But I bet you didn't read it like I'm going to right now!"

"Really? How?" Emi asked, intensely, leaving her hand in Sandy's. "Oh, my! I… I need to know!" she whispered. Looking expectantly at the lady in the wheelchair, Emi danced back and forth from one foot to the other nervously.

Sandy seemed to know exactly where in the Book to look, so only seconds later, she said, "'For God so loved' Emilyn 'that he gave his one and only Son, that' if Emilyn 'believes in him' she 'shall not perish but have eternal life.'" And verse seventeen says, "'For God did not send his Son into the world to condemn' Emilyn, 'but to save' her 'through him.'"

Sandy looked up from the Bible. The smile was still on her face, but her eyes were full of compassion. "Emilyn, that's what you need to know. God loves you so much that He sent His beloved Son, the Lord Jesus, to die on a cruel cross to take away all your sin and make you a new woman who can go to heaven when you die to live with Him forever."

Her voice filled with awe and tears running tracks down her cheeks, Emi said, "Really? Really and truly? God will do that? For me?"

Still with the Bible open on her lap, Sandy pulled her hand from Emi's, but put it on her shoulder and said, "Yes, He will, Emilyn. All you must do is tell Him you're a sinner and you want Jesus' blood to wash away your sin and make you a new person. Absolutely, that is all you need to do!"

"I can do that now?"

"Yes, right here, right now."

Right there on the sidewalk, beside the edge of the lift, Emi collapsed to her knees, tears streamed down her cheeks and her chin hit her chest, but Sandy kept her hand on Emilyn's shoulders and gently squeezed and put her head down on the back of Emi's head. After a few seconds of silence, Emi cried, "God! I'm a sinner! But, God, Sandy says You'll take it all away because Jesus died for me!"

Seconds later, Emi raised her head, her smile stretching over her face, but tears slid down her cheeks. "Sandy! I feel it! I feel it in here!" she slapped her chest. "That awful weight… it isn't… it's gone!" Without thinking, Emi threw her arms around Sandy and hugged her tightly.

Sandy pulled Emi so she could put her other arm around her, but she said, "I know! Jesus took it all away, washed it away with His precious blood. Now you're a new woman, Emilyn. You are God's child, because Jesus is God's Son. He gave His life, shed His blood, so you could be saved – that means you now have His free gift of salvation. Does that answer your question?"

Emi slowly stood up, but held Sandy's hands as they left her shoulders. Her tears still making tracks down her face, Emi looked at Sandy and a smile burst across her face. "Lots of them. Oh, Sandy, thank you, thank you! I am a new woman! I have never before felt like this. I have peace in my heart. It's… it's amazing!"

Sandy gave her another smile and handed the red Bible back to her. Of course she could see the emblem on the front, but she said, "Emilyn, do you have a Bible of your own?"

Emi shook her head. "No I don't. I never had one. Until this weekend I didn't think a Bible was important."

"Isabel can get another from a Gideon to put in that cabin. You can take this with you so you have your own. Please read it every day, it'll help you grow as a Christian and make sure you find a good church to go to in your hometown. Of course, when you come back, you can go to this church, but it's important to go now."

"I'll try to find a church, Sandy, thanks."

"Great!" As she took herself off the lift, Sandy said, "I need to stow this in the van, then let's go inside. Probably Natt has the coffee going already. I saw Matt trying to keep up with you. Do you know him?"

"Ye-es, he, um, used to be my husband a long time ago."

"Oh, my!" That was something Matt had never shared with anyone any of the times he'd been in town. No one, except for his family, in Vansville knew he'd ever been married. Other times it hadn't been important, now he was ashamed of his behavior.

The door on the van closed and Sandy said, "Come, let's go inside for Sunday school." She took the key from the outside mechanism and held out her hand to Emi.

"Okay," Emi said and took Sandy's hand, "I'm ready."

Once they were inside and made it to Ramon's classroom where he put his materials. He looked at Matt and asked, "What did you say?"

Matt nodded, "I married Emi right out of high school. We were married two years, but I couldn't take the fights we had all the time, 'course, they were mostly my fault, but I got a job in Florida, divorced her and left."

"Wow!" Ramon swallowed. They reached Jon's classroom, but they had to go in, since the teacher wasn't in the room yet. He let Jon's hand go, so the little boy could play, but he turned and looked at Matt again. "Wow! So she'll be here soon to live?"

Matt shrugged. "I don't know. I didn't know she was coming."

"We saw them at the worksite across the street from us yesterday. The lady she was with said she'd be coming to work in the restaurant when it was built."

"Oh, my!" Matt whispered. "Oh, my, that means she may be living in one of Isabel's cabins once she's here."

Ramon nodded. "I'd say that's a good possibility."

All color drained from Matt's face. After a strained silence of several seconds, he said, in a strangled whisper, "Oh, my! Oh… my…"

The church bell had rung twice when a very groggy Jack came from the bedroom. He'd just crawled out of bed, so his feet were bare. He scratched his bare chest, ran his hand through his mussed up hair and looked up at the wall clock over the sink. He scowled as he pulled up his nearly worn out sweats and looked at the clock again. Allison still sat at the kitchen table in her housecoat nursing her cold cup of coffee. Her fingers were around the handle, but she didn't raise the mug to her lips.

Shaking his head, as if to clear his eyes so he could see the clock hands for sure, Jack muttered loud enough for Allison to hear, "What's with this town? Why do they gotta wake a body up on a Sunday morning with that confounded church bell? I mean, it's so loud a body could hear it all over town! Can't a body sleep?" Jack pulled his hand through his hair again. "What'll we do when we get here to live? This is ridiculous! I work hard all week and do lots of extra hours, I wanna sleep in on Sunday!"

Allison shifted in the chair, let out a long sigh and said, "I guess 'cause it's a small town and lots of people go to church here. Maybe they like hearing that church bell, it's part of their Sunday." She picked up the cup and looked into the black liquid and continued, "I guess when we get here we could go to church, we're supposed to keep the restaurant closed on Sundays, you know. That's what Corky said."

"Us, go to church?" Jack looking quite dazed, shook his head, as if that was a foreign thought. The sweatpants Jack used to sleep in were nearly worn out, so he hiked them up, but they started back down immediately. "What? Us go to church? Why would we do that?"

"Well, lots of people still go to church, especially in small towns, Jack. Some people think it's the thing to do, you know."

Jack cleared his throat. Just talking about it made him uncomfortable. "Yeah, I guess." Still looking around the living room, he pulled his hand through his hair again, scowled and asked, "Where's Emi? She's not here?"

"She went to church."

A perplexed look spread across Jack's face. "Did what?" Jack took another step into the living area. "What did you say?"

"Jack, I said she went to church."

Acting totally perplexed, Jack said, "Emi doesn't do church!"

Allison looked into her mug at the half cup, made a face and left her chair, dumped out her cold coffee, then filled both her mug and another and returned to the table. She set both mugs down and Jack sauntered forward toward his place at the table. Allison brought out the rest of the large muffins and set the package on the table between her place and the one Jack slouched into. Nodding as Jack took a hefty slurp of his coffee Allison also sat down and said, "She did today!"

"What's with the woman?" Jack pushed nearly half of a muffin in his mouth, then croaked, "She doesn't do church! What is going on?"

"I don't know, but yesterday when I got up the lamp was on by the couch and she was asleep on it hugging that red Bible to her chest. When I finally got her awake, she asked me some weird question I couldn't answer. She told us yesterday she was going to church today. Again this morning I found her asleep on the couch, the light on and she was clutching that Bible to her chest. After a coffee and a muffin she raced out of here with that Bible. She must have gone to church because I haven't seen her since then."

Jack opened his mouth wide for another bite of muffin and shook his head. "I don't get it! Not at all! She's never done church, she said Matt turned her off to it. Now she's in the same town he's in and she goes?" He barely swallowed that mouthful of his muffin, then put his mug to his mouth and took another long swallow of coffee. "And now you say we oughtta go ta church. Woman, you're scarin' me!"

Allison picked out a muffin, took a large bite, chewed and swallowed, then took a swallow of her coffee. "I know," she said thoughtfully, "she did a really fast number in the bathroom, swigged down her coffee in nearly three swallows, scarfed down a muffin, grabbed up that Bible and tore out of here like something was chasing her! I mean, I've never seen that girl move so fast!" Allison hadn't seen her run into Matt.

Jack finished his muffin and grabbed another, while he shook his head. "Really, it makes no sense to me, not a bit."

Allison looked at the clock over the sink and sighed. "Since that was the church bell, and it's rung twice, I guess we'd better get a move on. We're supposed to be at their house by eleven thirty." She watched her husband snag the last muffin from the package. She swatted his hand and exclaimed, "Jack, cut out eating the muffins, already. You heard them ask us! We're supposed to eat spaghetti for dinner." Allison looked up at the clock over the sink. "It's only another hour before we're to be there."

Stuffing the last of his third muffin in his mouth, Jack said, "I can still eat spaghetti. My mama wasn't from Italy, but she knew how to make spaghetti and us boys knew how to eat it! If it's any good I'll put away my share."

Allison sighed and pulled the empty package toward herself. "Oh, I know you will! You'll have to run extra hard at the restaurant to wear it off."

The still in shape, middle-aged man grinned at his wife as he put the empty mug back on the table. "Oh, no worries about that, my dear!"

The lady who was about the same age, but had had three children and couldn't seem to lose any extra pounds sighed, "Oh, yeah, I know that."

Monday morning Matt sat at his kitchen table swigging down his last mouthful of coffee and thinking about his weekend. It had been nothing like the weekend he'd thought would happen to him. After all, he'd been in his new life for only days! He'd changed places to live by hundreds of miles, he'd changed careers... what more? However, changes he'd never, ever dreamed of had happened to him this weekend. They had blind-sided him, to say the least he was still reeling from the impact.

Life as he knew it had changed drastically Friday evening after the last customer left the store. He'd left the store thinking he'd greet the people who rented Isabel's cabin one for the weekend, invite them to the store for coffee and wish them well. Just to be neighborly, of course. He'd seen the couple after his supper break and hadn't known them at all.

In fact, he'd wondered as he went back to the store after his supper break why Isabel had rented her handicapped cabin to them when neither of them seemed handicapped at all. Every minute he wasn't busy until the store closed, that fact bugged him. However, they would be his neighbors if only for a few days and he wanted to give them a friendly impression of Vansville. Even if it did bug him, he could still be neighborly. As a store manager that seemed to be to invite them to come in for a cup of coffee. Ever since he'd started working with Natt he'd been glad they closed the store promptly on time, so that's what happened Friday night.

Instead, as he'd started up the ramp to cabin one on his way to his own cabin, he'd gotten the jolt of his life! After a decade he'd seen someone he'd never fathomed he'd ever see again. It had been such a shock he'd nearly tumbled off the porch of cabin one. From that moment on he knew life would never be the same. Instead of the couple he'd seen before and had expected to see again, his eyes only saw an older version of the woman he'd once loved. A decade before she'd been a pretty high school graduate. Now, she was still young, but she was the most beautiful creature he'd laid eyes on in a very long time.

They had obviously affected each other nearly the same, she hadn't said a word to him, but only stared. It felt like there was something, some invisible rope between her eyes and his that wouldn't let them look away from each other. Finally the man had cleared his throat and it had broken the connection, but he'd scrambled off the porch without saying a word about coffee.

As he sat at his table and up-ended his mug for the last drop of his instant coffee to finish his breakfast, he realized one very important thing, the wife of his heart, the lady that he had rejected out-of-hand a decade ago, was in town and was temporarily living two doors away in Isabel's cabin one. As he sat there in the quietness he realized that, although he hadn't really thought specifically about her in a long time, now that he'd seen her, that love for her, that craving to have her close that had motivated him to marry her, to come home at night to a loving wife, who was Emilyn Thomas, hit him like a ton of bricks.

He thumped his empty mug down on the table in front of him. Only yesterday for sure, he had also come to find out that this same young woman was undoubtedly returning at some point in the near future to work and live in this town. Where she would live at that time would be a major concern not only for her but possibly for him as well. After all, where was there for a single person to live in this town if they didn't live in Isabel's cabins? That would make them neighbors whether they liked it or not!

Saturday he hadn't seen her. He'd worked and had been relieved that Corky would not be having his meeting, that Emi would be a part of, at his store. Seeing her Friday evening had definitely unnerved him, to say the least. After he'd found out that they wouldn't be meeting at the store, he'd gone about his day, knowing she'd done whatever with the couple she'd come to town with and Corky. He'd more or less dismissed her from his thoughts.

However, on Sunday, they'd spent nearly the whole day together. It all started when she collided with him at the bottom of the ramp up to cabin one. Even though he'd put his hands on her arms to steady them he'd made her uncomfortable. However, it didn't take him long to realize she was on a mission. She'd agreed to walk with him, but then she'd taken off so fast even he couldn't keep up with her. It was amazing! Because he had collided with her he'd nearly witnessed her conversion. Ramon had kept that from happening.

At first, he knew her discomfort with him was palpable and to be near him wasn't by her choice, but as the day wore on and their nearness was forced upon them throughout the day, it became easier for both of them. He'd sat with her in Sunday school and church, been invited to dinner with her and spent the afternoon listening to Sandy play her piano with her and at her insistence had helped her pick out one of Sandy's absolutely awesome paintings. A very foreign thought crossed his mind and sent his heart into spasms, *Would one day that picture grace the living room of their reestablished home?*

As he thought that thought, he pulled his fingers from the handle of his empty mug and looked down at the empty plate in front of him. Had he really eaten his breakfast? He couldn't remember pushing a single mouthful into his mouth! But the plate was empty after all. He stared into the mug and saw the almost dry bottom. Had he really drunk even the last dreg? Amazing! He looked at the clock, grabbed up his plate and mug and made a dash for his sink. He was about to be late for work, again and that wouldn't do! He was single after all; he wouldn't let his married cousin show him up!

However, on a Monday morning in July, in Georgia, he wouldn't leave dirty dishes in his sink for any bugs to even sniff a delicious morsel. Quickly, he washed his breakfast dishes, nearly threw them into his dish drainer and dashed out the door, then just as quickly, he pushed the door back open and grabbed up his wad of keys, thanking heaven above that this was Vansville where most people didn't lock doors! Thank goodness the thought hadn't even crossed his mind to push in the lock.

"Thomas," he grumbled and slammed the door, "get your head out of the clouds and back on the work day! For crying out loud!"

He walked out onto his porch just as three people also walked out onto their porch two doors away. All three of the travelers had the handle of a pull-behind suitcase in one hand and a small grocery bag in the other. Jack was the last one out and pulled the door closed behind him. Matt knew he didn't have the time to stop and be really friendly. He had a job to get to, but he should at least speak to the people.

Actually, he had to admit, what he really wanted to do was give Emi a hug – whoa! *Where had that thought come from?* He shook himself, no… no. He could stop long enough to look Emilyn in the eye - just to memorize her lovely face - and invite them once again for a cup of coffee to take them on their way. He was sure he could make his face muscles work that much on a Monday morning. After all, he hadn't just jumped out of bed after not hearing his alarm and over sleeping.

He walked up just as the first one, a lovely blond, reached the walk. "Emi, have a good trip this morning."

She gave him her sweetest smile and his heart turned over. "Oh, we will. We're planning on coming in for coffee after Jack's loaded up."

He smiled back at her, his blue eyes twinkling. "That's great! I'll see you then. I need to rush over to the store and get it open so Natt can get coffee going." He held up his handful of keys, then turned to the Albertson's and gave them a rather strange looking salute. He said, as he started to walk on, "You folks take care and have a good trip back to wherever. Emi says you're coming in for coffee in a few minutes. Natt'll have that going real soon, but I need to open up the store, so he can do that."

From behind the two women, Jack tramped down the ramp and his booming voice said, "Yup, we'll be there in just a few minutes! Allison fixed us a small pot to wake us up, but there's nothing like a good coffee to go, as I see it! I gotta take this key back to Isabel first, though. Say, you're coffee's leaded, isn't it?"

As he walked on, Matt said, "That's great! Yep, the coffee's leaded. From what I've heard, Natt's granddad, who started the store, wouldn't have it any other way. Natt makes sure his shipment has lead in it each week." Matt exclaimed, "We'll see you soon!"

Jack saluted Matt's back and called, "Sure will!"

Matt rushed on, the keys dangling from his hand, as the travelers stopped at their SUV. Jack beeped the storage door open, but Emi stood back, as Jack and Allison put their luggage into the vehicle. Even after that, Emi watched the man she had once loved rush from the parking lot, down the block and cross the street. The man had aged well, ten years had made a man of a teenager and it hadn't hurt him at all! He hadn't gone in the military as his brother had done, but what he had done had given him a masterful physique. For just a minute Emi wondered what her ex had really done with his life after he'd left her. Surely he hadn't gotten stuck in a rut as she had at Barney's.

Of course, she'd known what they both worked at while they were married. When she'd finally gotten a new job, it hadn't been what she'd been doing. Had Matt worked the same kind of job only moved away when he divorced her? Come to think of it, he'd told her when he'd moved, but he'd never told her about his job or what he was doing. All she'd known for sure was that he'd moved out of town, divorced her and hadn't so much as told her where. *Not that you did! You never even answered his Emails.*

Emi didn't sigh out loud, but the Albertson's were well aware of Emi's actions and where her eyes rested. In the early morning stillness they even heard the keys rattle as Matt worked them to open the hardware store door, then they heard it close, but Emilyn's eyes still stayed looking at the same place. Allison looked at her husband and grinned, but she shook her head, she knew what Jack was capable of doing and saying. Much to her surprise, Jack kept his mouth closed and his thoughts to himself.

"Good for you, Jack, I'm proud of you," she whispered.

"What?" Jack asked, rather loudly.

Only moments after he left them, Matt pushed the door to the store open and disappeared, but Emi didn't move immediately. However, only moments later the lights blinked on on the gas pumps and another car whirled onto the parking lot from the other direction and another young man jumped out and headed for the Laundromat.

Finally a voice penetrated, "Emi, are you gonna stand there and drool all day or will you put that suitcase in here before I slam the door?"

Emi pulled in a long breath, pushed the handle down into her suitcase and let Jack hoist the case into the cargo space. "Yes, Jack, I'm with you."

"Uh huh. I could tell." As Allison and Emi moved from the back of the car toward the passenger doors, with the plastic bags Allison had given them to carry out, Jack added, "Gotta take the key back to Isabel, then we'll go for coffee."

Allison turned back, took Jack's plastic bag and assured him, "That's good, Jack, that's what we planned. Emi and me'll wait in the car."

Jack took long strides across the parking lot towards Isabel's house, but both Allison and Emilyn moved up the side of the vehicle and slid inside. Emi sat in the back, but she kept watch on the hardware store. She knew the man had gone inside for a day's work, and didn't know why she kept watch, but her eyes didn't seem capable of looking anywhere else. Finally, she sighed, laid her head back on the headrest and closed her eyes. That didn't seem to stop her mind from bringing a clear image to her mind's eyes, however. Instead of dismissing it, as she would have done last week, she let Matt's image linger in her mind. She had loved him all those years ago, did she still love him like that?

This weekend had turned out nothing like she'd thought it would, but well… so much better! No matter what happened in the future, she knew her life had changed she was now a child of God! As she thought about it, it seemed like God had brought her here, had chased her from home all the way to Vansville. Maybe it had started when, even though she'd known Matt had moved here, she'd felt compelled to come when Alli texted her with the invitation. Maybe He'd sent that Bible onto her toe during the night to get her attention! It seemed like the minute she'd taken the Bible in her hands she'd felt a compelling force. *Did God do stuff like that?* Emi shook her head. This was all so new!

Allison pulled her from her reverie by asking. "So, was the weekend a good vacation, Emi?" Emilyn and Matt's actions at dinner and during the afternoon yesterday hadn't slipped by the Albertson's. After their split ten years ago, Allison and Jack were astonished with how they acted together yesterday. Even after they'd left DeLord's, they'd spent all evening together. However, the Albertson's had no idea how God could work in the lives of ordinary people. The 'idea' of God had never been part of their adult lives. Even as children He hadn't been an important part of their existence. Now they were content with how life was treating them.

Emi opened her eyes and looked at Allison in her cosmetic mirror. "Alli, you can't imagine! It was totally different from anything I'd imagined that would happen, but it sure wasn't a bad time! I think in many ways it's turned a hundred and eighty."

If nothing else, Emilyn knew her heart was free and the load she'd carried for the thirty years of her life was gone. She had to admit, seeing her ex-husband hadn't turned out nearly as badly as she'd thought it would. In fact yesterday afternoon had been really great! Matt had acted totally different from what he had done as a new high school graduate.

With a twinkle in her eyes as she looked in her cosmetic mirror, Allison said, "And you were so worried about Matt Thomas!"

"Yeah, I know, but things turned out so much better!" Actually, Friday night, all day Saturday until she'd talked with Sandy on Sunday had been such an all-consuming time with God she couldn't understand how Alli could still be as she was, so non-committal. Emi was almost convinced that God had chased her – only her - to Vansville.

Jack spent a few minutes talking with Isabel before he came back to the SUV and slid into the driver's seat, stuck the key in the ignition and said, "Isabel wished us a good trip. Actually, she even invited us to come spend time here again and in her cabin."

"That was nice of her."

"Yep, she invited us back so you wanna come, Emi?"

"I would if I could, Jack, but I don't think Barney would let me off until I quit."

"Yeah, you probably got a point." Tongue in cheek, he added, "Umm, I could put in a word for you, tell him about building this new place up here. I do see him on occasion, you know. Could let him know he'll be losing a waitress…"

Emi let out a long sigh. "Jack, just get on over to the store. It's getting late. I know you don't wanna be too late getting home. After all, you still have that restaurant down there to work at. You've not left that yet, have you?"

Jack put his hand on the wheel, but turned and looked at Emi. "No, we're still there, just took a few days off. I could still help you out with Barncy…"

"Jack! I'll do my own dealings with Barney, thank you very much!"

"Just sayin'…"

Meanwhile, Matt started the early morning routine by rote. Inside he flipped on the lights and headed for the gas pumps switch. While he threw that switch he heard Natt wheel onto the parking lot and knew he was headed for the Laundromat. Only moments later the young man pushed the door open and strode in, heading directly to the back to start his first urn of coffee for the day. One thing, that coffee always made the store smell good.

"Mornin'!" Natt said, as an afterthought.

By now, Matt was bent over the safe, working the combination, to bring out the money that normally went in the cash box, but spent Sunday in the safe. "Mornin'," he mumbled. He straightened up and with the cash in hand, he moved up to the counter to start the process to bring the cash register out of sleep mode for the day. His mind might be filled with a certain blond, but life's day to day happenings kept coming on schedule.

"So, your temporary neighbors are heading out soon," Natt said, over the water splashing into the big urn.

"Yes, Emi told me they'll come in for coffee on their way out of town."

"Oh, she did? You had a chance to talk on your way over?"

Matt grinned as his cousin appeared with the big urn in his hands. "Yup. Had to walk right by the lot of 'em. Got to wish them all a safe trip." With an even broader smile, Matt continued, "The single one told me they'd be in for coffee."

Natt put the urn down on the little sideboard in 'the nook' and reached for the cord to plug in. "Hmm, never can tell, you may snag you a single girl here in Vansville yet."

"Yup, might just do that!" Matt answered enthusiastically. Natt noted how different his attitude was from only the day before.

With his newly returned faith Matt knew he'd pray that's what would happen. Actually, he wouldn't pray in the abstract, he'd pray specifically that he would snag a lovely blond single girl in the near future. He'd had plenty of time yesterday to notice that her left ring finger was bare and during their conversation it had come out that she was still single, with no prospects, since she worked the afternoon shift.

Since all the instant chores were finished, both men sat down in the 'nook'. It was close to the door and they could watch a medium sized SUV leave Isabel's parking lot and head for the store. It stopped at a gas pump, but the three doors opened at almost the same time. The driver went to the back to pump gas, but the two women headed for the store. He'd never admit it to his cousin, but Matt's heart started banging in double time. As he watched, Matt knew that the blond-haired lady was the most beautiful woman he'd ever in his life laid eyes on. She'd matured from a pretty high school graduate to a beautiful single woman. *Why hasn't someone snagged her up in ten years?* Almost out loud he said, *I'm sure glad nobody did!*

Natt stood up and said, "Well, I think I'll see if any messages came in over the weekend. I'm sure you can handle the coffee situation just fine."

"Thanks," Matt muttered, as the women headed ever closer. His eyes glued to the lovely blond, he wasn't sure what he was thanking his cousin for. Just as Natt was turning to go to the back, he winked at his cousin.

The door opened and Matt heard the urn let out its normal wheezing sounds. He knew the brewing stage was nearly finished, so he said, "Hi, ladies! Come for that fresh cup of coffee? The urn's about to let us have some."

Allison had two travel mugs with lids in her hand and raised them to show Matt. "Yes, we did. I'll have to admit my husband and I are coffee hounds. Could we have them to go? I'll need two, my husband's out there filling our tank for the trip back."

Rather than keep his eyes where they wanted to be, Matt deliberately turned his head and said, "Sure, we'll have those for you in a second." At that moment the huge urn stopped wheezing and the light came on.

"Do you charge?" Allison asked.

"Well, no, but most everybody leaves a fifty cent tip."

"Wow! I sure don't have a problem with that. That's the cheapest cup of coffee I've had in a long time and it smells delicious! It sure smells and looks a lot better than that little 'to go' cup of sludge we had Friday at that drive-thru down home!"

Matt gave her his mega-watt smile and said, "We aim to please!"

While both women fumbled in their purses, Matt turned away and started filling a mug with the rich smelling coffee. Allison handed Matt a dollar and he handed her first one mug then the other. As she snapped the tops on both mugs, Allison said, "You know, this is a sweet little town! We've really enjoyed ourselves here over the weekend and believe me I'm looking forward to coming back to live and work."

"Thank you, ma'am for the compliment. We'll be looking for you again." Patting his flat stomach, Matt continued, "It'll be a pleasure to eat a meal or so in a restaurant. Our good friend at the grocery keeps those frozen dinners stocked, but a good meal at a restaurant would be a really nice change."

Allison grinned at the young man. "Hey, I hear that!"

Allison left with two mugs of black, unadulterated coffee, but Emilyn took her place and Matt filled the mug she held out. As he turned with the mug, Emi held out her hand with the two quarters, but Matt gave her the mug and engulfed her other hand, his fingers pushing the money back against her palm. She looked up into his eyes that twinkled as they looked down at her. "On the house," he murmured, giving her a smile, the smile that used to send her heart into flutters. "You want a cuppa, you come back any old time you want."

Emilyn giggled and set the mug down on the little table to add creamer and sugar. Still with her eyes twinkling, she said, "Sure, Matt, I'll just do that! Umm, I only live two hundred or so miles away. It'll be no problem to come by."

He sobered immediately and said, "I'm thinking that won't be forever? Isn't that what I heard Corky say yesterday?"

Emi finished doctoring her coffee, but left the mug on the little stand and didn't put the lid on it. "You may be right, Matt. One never knows about things like that." Emi nearly shook her head. Why was she being so obtuse? She and probably Matt, knew she'd be coming back when the restaurant opened. Finally she understood Albertson's reason for bringing her was to get her on the same page. However, she knew that God had had a different agenda and had brought her here to put her on His page.

Matt wasn't sure if he said the words out loud, but the words that he definitely wanted to say were, *I could wish very hard that you would come back and that you would consent to be my wife again. I was such a fool ten years ago to walk out and leave you behind!* He could hope and pray that would happen. At this point in time it was too early to voice what was truly on his heart. In matters of the heart he knew women, especially women who had been jilted, were very gun-shy of men like him. However, he knew that each day from now on he would fervently pray that there would be a wedding soon in his and her lives. He knew that nothing with God was impossible and he would be sure to pray that way.

Since both of Matt's hands were empty and Emi only held the quarters in one hand, Matt lightly placed his hands on Emi's upper arms. He was extremely happy that she didn't pull away, which she could have easily done. He looked into her face and realized - the feeling almost overwhelmed him – that he wanted so much to kiss her. For an instant he glanced at those lips, they still looked very kissable, but just as quickly he brought his eyes back to hers. Still he waited until she looked up into his eyes.

Into the silence he whispered, "Emi, please, will you forgive me? I was such a stupid fool all those years ago..."

The door opened with a whoosh and Jack strode in. He looked around the store that was very much like any hardware store that was in any small town and not a franchise in a chain. Briefly noting the two standing in the 'nook' and how they stood in front of each other, with Matt's hands on Emi's arms, he said into the room, "Well, I see ya gotta come in to pay for your gas. Will ya ever get some modern pumps so a body can pay at the pump?"

Matt looked up at the intruder; after all, he was a store manager and said, "There's a possibility that'll happen one of these days. We're kind of hoping it'll be sooner rather than later. Right now, though, the company doesn't think we sell enough gas in a month for the extra expense of putting in new pumps. I'll be glad to run your credit card, though." Still holding Emilyn's shoulders, he smiled and said, "Of course, it gives folks the opportunity to 'need' something else while they're here."

Jack took another step into the store away from the 'nook' and toward the cash register. Finally taking his focus off of Emilyn and Matt and looked toward the cash register. Nodding, he said, "Yeah, guess that's so, sorta like my special display case in my restaurant down home that I keep stashed full of pieces of pie that my pie maker makes special every day. It 'helps' people decide they want dessert before they leave. Anyway, I'll letcha do my card. Boy, that coffee smells good!"

"Jack, Allison took yours out with her," Emi told him.

"Yep, I know that, she even let me take a swig before I came in, but I can sure appreciate that good smell. Say, you couldn't give me a heads up on the brand, could ya? I mean, some day soon I'll have that restaurant up and running and I'll need to supply coffee to my customers to go along with that pie."

Of course, Natt had been listening from the back, with no doors, just openings it wasn't hard. He'd heard the door when Allison walked out and he'd heard the door when Jack walked in, but he'd also heard the silence in-between and was pretty sure what that was all about. He'd finished checking the Email, so he chose that moment to saunter toward the counter. He gave Jack a grin to beat all grins and held out his hand.

Natt took Jack's credit card to do his gas transaction. "I'll do that credit card for you, sir." His eyes twinkled at Jack and as he ran the card, he said, "I could tell you my coffee supplier, but then I'd give away my secret and I might lose customers that way. I mean, even in Vansville life's full of rocks and hard places."

Jack laughed and stepped to the counter. "But I ain't gonna be here for a few months. Probably fall or so, you'd keep your customers, easy, I should think with winter and all." He looked out the door, knowing, of course, he couldn't see the worksite. "We're at opposite ends of town, you know." He waved his hand around the store and added, "They'd come here for hardware stuff and to my place for food. Blocks apart. So we'd serve the same blend, it ain't no crime as I see it!"

"Well, I could hope so." Natt handed his card back. "Say, you folks travel safe." Matt, and probably both of the others in the store, realized that Natt didn't give his supplier's name.

"Will do our best!" Jack assured him.

Matt still stood in the 'nook' with Emi. Now that Natt had taken Jack's attention and moved him away from looking at Matt and Emi, Matt looked back at Emilyn. He had asked his question, but Emi hadn't had a chance to answer it. He continued to look into her eyes, he was sure his heart was in his own as he looked at her.

Emi pulled in a deep breath, but allowed Matt's hands to stay on her arms. After several seconds, she looked back into his eyes and saw the sincerity in them. As the air came slowly from her mouth, she said, for his ears only, "Matt, for a long time I was devastated. You knew then as well as you know now that I couldn't have gone home, that was not a choice." She shook her head. "By then it was only my mom and little sister who were there with Dad, but oh, my! You know I couldn't have dealt with Dad." Matt bowed his head and an anguished groan slid from his throat. It hit him, possibly for the first time, what he'd really put Emilyn through. He nearly shook his head. What a jerk – a number one jerk – he had been! Without knowing Matt's thoughts Emi added, "Actually, I stayed in our apartment and cried nearly all the time. I lost my job, I couldn't pay the bills, I couldn't eat…."

She nodded toward Allison's back outside and said, "Alli had to come along and pull me up by my bootstraps. She talked to me like some grouchy, spinster aunt, then she fed me, making me eat when I didn't want to because I'd lost so much weight. She took me to the employment office, I got the job I have now and then I was really mad! Mostly at you, but I think I was mad at the world, too. As you know, I never answered your Emails, I'd read them then delete them. I'll never figure out why I told Alli I'd come here with them, since I'd only gotten your Email a few days before that about your move here."

Perhaps it was God? They didn't know it, but they both had that same thought.

She had to stop and pull more air into her lungs. She felt his hands on her arms and looked into the blue of his eyes. She'd heard the groan, but she saw the anguish in his eyes. Finally, she sighed out the words, "I don't know, Matt. I know I'm a Christian now and that's something Christians are supposed to do. I'll have to say I'll work on that in the next few weeks and months. It still doesn't come easily. I do plan on coming back with Jack and Alli, I'm ready to get out of Barney's diner. Jack and Alli have already offered me a spot working with them in this new restaurant."

"I'm glad," Matt whispered. "I'm so glad, Emi. I'll be looking forward to that day, believe me." However, in all her speech he realized she hadn't said the words he so longed to hear. She hadn't said she'd forgive him.

She broke away from Matt's hands, looked down at the table and reached for her mug of coffee. She hadn't put the top on it and steam wasn't coming off it any longer. It was a way to get her out of Matt's hands and away from those eyes, so she reached for her cup and took a sip. Looking at the young man over the rim of her cup, she said, "I'll give your question some thought, Matt. See you sometime." She picked up the cap and made a production of putting it on the travel mug.

"Yes, Emi, I'll be looking for that day." Since Emilyn didn't look back at Matt she didn't see the moisture in his eyes. Her response was definitely not what he'd wanted to hear. The look on her face as he'd left the apartment so many years ago had stayed with him for days and he'd had a momentary twinge of conscience, but now it was not hard to remember it, but he had no idea about what she'd gone through after that, in fact, he hadn't given it much thought. As a twenty year old it had been all about number one.

Matt shook his head; he'd been such an arrogant jerk! He swallowed a sigh. As he thought about it now it hit him like a two by four to the head. He'd left because of all the fights, but he'd been the one who started most of them. Knowing Emilyn, as he remembered her, he realized she'd been anxious to try to talk things out, but not him. She'd even asked him to go with her to see a counselor, but he wouldn't even consider it! Remembering all the fights, he knew he'd been unfairly comparing her to his mom. His mom! What eighteen year old bride can compare to a lady who has raised three boys to adulthood? He shook his head and looked at Emilyn's back as she turned away. She was still the loveliest woman he'd ever known. The thought hit him he still loved her, so much more now!

His gas transaction finished, Jack looked mischievously at the couple and said, "Emi, you ready to head out? I see you got your coffee. You know it's later than we left down home, so it'll be later when we get back. Might even be dark."

Emi took a deep breath the last few minutes with Matt had been very intense, very hard. It took a second to change gears and answer Jack. "Jack, it's no later than when we went through the drive-thru for breakfast last Friday and you know it! You are just being difficult! But, yes, I'm ready and I'm coming!"

Being the man that he was, Jack winked at Matt and said to Emi, "Oh, I'm sure glad to hear that! I wasn't sure you weren't gonna skip out on Barney and leave him in the lurch for his Tuesday afternoon shift tomorrow. I mean, you know, I'm sure those tips really will make you a millionaire one of these days!"

Taking another sip from her cup, Emi shook her head incredulously. "Jack, don't remind me! I've sure been glad to be away from his place for four days. Millionaire? At Barney's? In which lifetime? Give me a break!"

Jack pulled open the door and Emi took a step toward it, but Matt whispered, "See you, Emi, have a good trip."

Twelve

Emi did look at him then and grinned. That smile turned Matt's heart over, he remembered all those years ago that it had then, too. "Thanks, Matt. If I can put up with this crazy guy, I'll be doing well."

Jack held the door making a sweeping motion with his free hand, as he said, "What was it you called me?"

"A crazy guy?"

"Well! And I'm to take you home? Humph!"

"Oh, Jack, I know you wouldn't give up that lovely opportunity!" She held up the coffee mug. "Thanks for the coffee, Matt, it's sure good!" With that, both she and Jack were out the door and Matt breathed out a long sigh.

However, it was hard to swallow the great lump in his throat. He wished Emi had answered his question differently, but then why should she? He'd been a real jerk! He hadn't thought about what would happen to her once he'd left he'd only been thinking about number one. Even though he'd said he'd loved her, he realized now he'd loved number one way more than he should have. He'd done most of the quarrelling, most of the criticizing…

He quickly sank onto a chair in the 'nook'. He wasn't sure his legs would hold him up if he'd tried to stay standing. He dropped his head and put his hands between his knees. He couldn't watch as she walked out of his life. It wasn't nearly as dramatic as his exit had been, but he felt bereft. Still, what did he have to offer her? He had a bit of savings from his former

216

job… A new job in a tiny town and he lived in a weekend rental cabin that he rented by the month. That was a whole lot of, well… nothing.

The Albertson's car pulled away from the gas pumps, but Matt didn't hear it go. A car pulled onto the parking lot, but Matt didn't move. Natt watched him silently for a few minutes. Then he crossed in front of Matt and filled his own mug with coffee, then crossed again and leaned against the counter and crossed his ankles. Still holding his mug in one hand, he crossed his arms across his chest and looked at his cousin, he asked, "You gonna stay there and mope all day, man?"

Matt pulled in a long breath, looked out the window and saw the people leave the car. "Well, no, I hadn't planned to, sorry."

Natt took pity on his cousin, took a swig from his mug and said, "It'll be alright, Cous. You know she'll be back one day not too far off. Things'll change, I'm sure. I do believe she even smiled at you as she left."

Matt pulled in a deep breath and as he let it out, he stood up, preparing to be ready for the customers and said, "Yeah, I believe you're right. I believe she did smile at me. But man, I really did a number on her. I was such a jerk! As I think back – man, I threw my set of house keys at her – almost hit her in the face!"

As the door opened, Natt pulled away from the counter ready to greet the new customers, but he said, "Yeah, I believe you did, Man."

A little boy stood in the office close to his mama's chair early Monday morning as he usually did. He had just waved off his daddy's exuberant hiking group and right before that Jerry's group had left. His group had been a bunch of teenage boys along with their leaders. The only reason Ramon's group had left last was he'd lingered over a kiss for his wife and little son. All the hikers loved the little boy. He was so sweet and joyful, even someone with a chip on his shoulder had to smile at Jon.

Jon loved to play the part of a big boy, so Sandy backed away from the opening and let him close the door to the parking lot. It was big and heavy for the toddler, but he got behind it and pushed with all his might. Sandy left him to the chore and went back to the desk she had work to do that had waited all weekend. The little boy had barely reached his mama's side when he heard a loud noise outside.

He couldn't open the big door he'd just closed, so he left his mama and toddled as quickly as his short legs would carry him back to the door to look out the window in the door. The window was long, so Jon could look out on the parking lot to investigate. So now, instead of his toys, he stood gripping the door handle. His eyes were huge as he looked across the parking lot to the street. Again today there was more activity in what used to be a quiet meadow.

He started jumping up and down and screaming frantically, "Mama, Mama, wuk, BIG tar-uck! BIG tar-uck come!" Momentarily, he left the window and toddled so fast that his short legs nearly tripped him up, back to her desk. Gripping the armrest of Mama's chair he looked up at her, his eyes nearly as big as the truck he'd seen and pointed out across the parking lot and pleaded, "Mama, peese, peese, go see, NOW!"

Sandy smiled down at her little boy and looked out the same window from where she sat. A huge cement mixer wobbled its way very slowly from the highway onto the gravel driveway across the street. The circular body slowly rotated as it leveled out and moved toward the back of the large lot. Corky and Jack's mission was actually coming to pass.

For now the telephone messages, the notes that sat on the big blotter on the office desk and the computer, with its program waiting for the entries were forgotten as the huge cement truck made its way slowly over the gravel onto what used to be a peaceful meadow. Before she moved, the huge truck moved inch by inch nearly out of sight before it stopped. Little Jon kept jumping and pleading beside her chair.

Jon also watched the truck. From his short perspective he probably couldn't see it. Sadly, he said, "Mama, tar-uck a-most gone." Finally, when the big truck stopped all he could see was the very top of the circulating body.

"Sweetheart, it has a job to do and that's in the back part."

"Go see, Mama, peese?" Jon pleaded and patted his mama's leg, even though he knew she couldn't feel it. "Tar-uck a-most gone. It big tar-uck!"

"Yes, it is, Sweetheart."

Sandy backed away from the desk, let go of the chair control and held her hands down to Jon. Eagerly the little boy did what he did many times in a day; he pulled himself up on Sandy's footrest, then waved his hands for his mama to pick him up onto her lap. "Sweetheart," she smiled and lifted the little boy to put his feet on her lap, but continued to watch the truck's progress, "that's a cement truck. The driver's taking the truck to where he needs to put the cement, back in that deep hole. Daddy took us to see the hole yesterday. Remember how deep it was? Now that truck's going to fill it up! That's the first thing a builder must do before he can start to build the building. That cement will make the building really sturdy. Come on, we'll go see what we can. Remember, Mama can't go on that gravel, we must stay on our parking lot."

"'K, Mama," he sighed, once he stood on Sandy's legs. Sandy gave her little son a smile and a quick kiss on his cheek. He smiled and gave her a slobbery kiss, then quickly turned around, plopped down on her legs and waited for his speedy mode of transportation to start. Almost immediately the motor of Sandy's chair started to hum. Jon turned his head and gave his mama his angelic smile, of course, Sandy's heart turned over as she smiled back.

Sandy put her free arm around Jon and squeezed. "Mama loves Jon. You are my special gift from God, Sweetheart."

His eyes dancing, Jon said, "Ja wuvs Mama!"

It had been a beautiful weekend and Emilyn had enjoyed the weather. It had been a relief to be gone from Barney's and not had to smell the odors of stale burgers and coffee, but she'd enjoyed it even more because the sun had been shining and the temperature had been just about perfect. It had been a weekend like none other. As they traveled south Emi realized how much she had needed this time away, not only the R & R but to see Matt again. This time with him had been so different from any experience she'd had with him.

She even remembered what the night waitress, Naomi, had told her 'Come back tanned and rested.' She smiled and looked out the window as Jack competently took them over the miles from Vansville to her hometown. She wasn't even sure she'd rested! Sunday night, though, she'd slept like a log. Alli had some trouble waking her this morning.

However, the later in the day it got to be on Monday and the closer to home, the more clouds covered the sky and finally hid the sun completely. With not much else to do over the miles she watched as the clouds grew darker and darker. It was rather dismal as Jack pulled onto her parking lot.

At her apartment complex Allison, as well as Jack got out with her. Jack opened the cargo place and set Emi's suitcase and picture out, but Allison said, "We had a good time, didn't we, girl? We'll keep in touch." She reached over and hugged Emi. "Of course, we'll let you know when we leave and when we'll open so you'll have time to quit and stuff."

"Oh, I really had a good time! Lots better than I thought. What'll we do with our pictures if we're moving so soon?"

Before Allison could answer, Jack said, "You can hang it in that cabin next to Matt in just a couple of months, Emi."

Emilyn sighed, she could feel the heat on her cheeks, so instead of looking at Jack, she reached for the handle of her suitcase. "Jack, you can be such a hassle!"

Jack shook his head. "Oh, not me. Just see it like it is, girl."

"Yeah, Jack. Actually, I'm talking about here, now." She waved vaguely at the big apartment building, which, of course, included her apartment.

Jack grinned at the young woman whom he loved to tease. "Oh, Alli has her place all picked out, I'm sure, but we'll be packing up soon."

Emi scowled. "You mean you'll go back before it's open? Why would you do that? What could you do?"

"Probably. Need to be in on the building end of things. I'll need to see that things are going like we want them, sometimes contractors miss-read blueprints and Max is on top of stuff here at this restaurant. Alli and me'll feel like a fifth wheel pretty soon. Guess we'll be living in another of them cabins for a while."

He winked at Emi. "'Course you could go along and get right in on the ground floor and live in another of them cabins, ya know. Still, I know you gotta stay here and let Barney see your charming face for a while yet."

"Mmm, thanks. I'm sure he's really thrilled about that! Of course, it's not my charming face it's that I'm not independently wealthy."

"Yup, I hear that! Hey, take care!"

"Oh, I will!"

The Albertson's left her. She watched their nearly new SUV pull from her apartment parking lot. When it was gone, her eyes found her own vehicle, it wasn't near as new nor near as sporty, but then again, it was paid for, it did run okay and it was hers. She knew it could get her from here to work or even from here to… where was that? Vansville? Hmmm.

She shook herself, that trip was off in the future somewhere, lots of things could happen between now and then. She was a sensible girl she needed to keep her head out of the clouds. She also knew she shouldn't be envious of someone else's things, but she could wish…. A millionaire? From tips at Barney's? Doesn't happen!

Emilyn pulled up the handle on her suitcase and carefully lifted the picture up that Jack had set on the ground and headed for the main entrance to her apartment building. She was amazed at how much the weather had changed from when they left this morning. It felt like it could rain at any minute and with the clouds so thick it seemed like a good possibility. However, she hoped she could get inside she didn't want anything to ruin her beautiful painting.

There was an announcement board in the entry-way and since she hadn't been home to look at it for four days, she decided to take a look before she went to her apartment upstairs. There were several new announcements, but there was also another small paper she hadn't seen before, so she stopped to read it. The title was: 'Forgiveness'

> People think of forgiveness as chopping away at something, hacking at a suffocating wild grape vine until you are sweaty and exhausted and there is nothing left, not even the roots. An afternoon's work followed by a cold lemonade on the back porch.
>
> I always thought of forgiveness as a seed, something you plant in the best spot in the garden. A place with neither too much sun nor too much shade. A delicate seedling you fertilize and water and protect from an early frost. A plant you nurture through drought and flood, carefully guarding the first fragile blooms from encroaching weeds and voracious rabbits.
>
> Until one day you realize your patient labor has borne fruit, the roots have grown deep enough, and the stem is stout enough to survive the strongest wind. Even then you must tend forgiveness through the seasons, through harsh winters and dry summers. Like any garden, forgiveness is something you must never neglect for long.

There was no author listed, but the words spoke to Emi's heart and before she finished reading tears clouded her vision. In fact, the little piece spoke so loudly to her that she tore the paper from the board and held it in her hand as she made her way to her second floor apartment. "Oh, God, You put that there just for me! I know You did! I didn't forgive Matt, even though he asked me. I didn't tell him I would," she murmured as she closed the door and let the silence of her apartment greet her.

She looked around, it was as she'd left it, of course it would be. She sighed and looked out the one window she had in the tiny apartment. It looked out on the back empty lot. Fortunately there was a little grass, but it looked like nothing she'd seen and appreciated over the weekend. She couldn't help but remember the lovely walk she and Matt had taken in the quiet meadow behind the landlady's house. And Matt… he had been great!

Emilyn knew she needed to get up early Tuesday morning, so after emptying her suitcase on the bathroom floor and making a bologna and cheese sandwich on white bread for her supper, she turned on the TV to watch the weather, then set her alarm Monday night. She wanted to get up a bit earlier in the morning to read the Bible she'd brought home.

She had laundry to do in the morning, an unusually big load, because she needed to wash uniforms from last week, but also regular clothes from her four day vacation. So much had happened it seemed like many more than four days had gone by since she'd been at Barney's. Sunday had been a day like she'd never spent before in her life. She had to admit, the time she'd spent with Matt had been so much better than any she remembered spending with the same guy as a teenager. She knew they'd matured, of course they would. People didn't stay the same for ten years, but now they were both Believers, too. Could that be what they needed to make a marriage work between them? *Oh, God in heaven, please make it so!*

However, before her alarm went off Tuesday morning she was jolted awake by a brilliant streak of lightning and then a loud clap of thunder. They seemed to happen right outside her window and nearly one on top of the other. "Great!" she grumbled and pulled the extra pillow over her head, but even before she could pull her hand back under the covers another clap of thunder roared. She'd closed her eyes, but under the pillow, she hadn't seen the lightning. She had never liked thunder storms even though her dad had made fun of her fear even as a little kid all those years ago. Of course, now she was wide awake.

She sighed, there was no reason to lie in bed she'd never fall back to sleep, not with that crashing thunder just outside her window. A look at her clock told her the alarm would go off before she was sound asleep anyway. As she headed for the bathroom, she heard her coffeemaker click on. Ah, a good cup of coffee would be waiting for her. She went to her bathroom and decided to start with a shower. She hesitated for just a moment. Back when she was a little girl she remembered her gramma had warned her not to have anything to do with water during a thunderstorm. Well, nothing had happened back then… Surely, this building was well protected from lightning strikes.

She'd get an early start on that pile of laundry she'd dumped in the middle of her bathroom floor. However, she'd rather have the hot water run out in the wash load than while she was under the shower head. It might be July, but she didn't appreciate a cold shower, even in the heat of summer. Besides, her apartment was air conditioned.

While the shower ran, a smile, that seemed to come from inside, spread across her face. Life as she knew it was not the same any more! Her decision for Christ had been two days ago, but the change she felt in her heart was still fresh and wonderful. She hoped and prayed it would never fade. She must find a church, just as Sandy had told her to. It was quite a few months before she'd be back in Vansville to go to that church. However, she wished she could be going to that church right away.

Sunday had been a day she'd never forget! She had thought about it several times when no one was talking on the drive back yesterday. She had wondered how Sandy had known to be at the church when she was. She realized later that she had come quite early, but Sandy had pulled her van up to the parking place only minutes before she had come barreling up.

She was sure Sandy somehow knew to be there! Even though she hadn't known what to say or what to ask, Sandy knew exactly what to say and what she needed to know. It was like Someone had told her! Emi shook her head, baffled. *Would God do that?* She'd always thought of God as some big force that sort of was around somewhere, not Someone who knew her! Her! Her, who only had a high school diploma, who waited tables at a neighborhood diner.…

That afternoon had also lived up to… way beyond… any expectation she'd ever thought could happen! It wasn't because she and the Albertson's ate with the DeLord's for a fabulous spaghetti dinner, either. She couldn't believe it, Ramon had asked Matt to join them for the spaghetti dinner and instead of feeling so terribly awkward, they'd sat side by side at the table and had a meaningful conversation. It had been so much different from when they were married. Of course, little Jon had added so much to the meal. She loved children and had hoped to have several by this time in her life, but no one had ever interested her except for Matt.

After dinner, Sandy had played for them. It had been the best music she'd ever heard, even though she'd never heard most of it before. She was totally in awe of the lady in the wheelchair. Some of the music Sandy had said was classical, she'd even played something that started out with <u>Twinkle</u>, <u>Twinkle</u> <u>Little</u> <u>Star</u>. That was cool! After that she'd played many other pieces that were songs and as soon as she'd started playing them the Albertsons had excused themselves and left. She couldn't understand that.

Emi didn't know the songs, but Ramon, Sandy and Matt had sung the words and now they meant so much to her, because they were Christian songs and Sandy especially had made sure she knew what the words meant.

Some of them were from what she called a hymnbook and she'd lent her one to follow along. While they sat in the living room, Sandy had told her how important it was for her to go to church now that she was a Believer. She would try to do that. She knew she could, since she worked in the evenings. Sandy had even told her how to find a good church and she would. Even if she had to work on a Sunday, she'd have plenty of time to get to work on time.

After dinner, Sandy had given her a painting and Matt had helped her pick it out. There had been so many to choose from and Alli had Jack to help her… It was an awesome picture from somewhere around Vansville. It was a place where Sandy could drive her van, but there wasn't time for Emi to find it, perhaps she could once she moved to Vansville. After they left DeLord's, Matt had taken her for a walk in that lovely meadow behind the cabins. At first, the sun was shining on the hills and mountains behind the town. She hadn't realized how many different shades of green there were! They had stayed away from town so long that before they returned to the cabins the sun had sparkled off the peaks of the Appalachian Mountains.

They had walked so far they couldn't see any of the houses in town, but the country sounds had been all around them and they had found a crystal clear babbling brook. Matt had taken her to a huge rock right beside the brook and they had taken off their shoes to put their feet in the water. The water of the brook was just cold enough to be totally refreshing. While they sat with their feet in the water, several tiny fish had nibbled at their toes. Emi had laughed and wiggled her toes at them.

Interrupting their quiet conversation had been a deer family who came silently to the brook for a drink. She couldn't remember ever being so close to deer. While the doe and her baby had stepped in the water to drink, the stately buck had stood alert on the opposite shore keeping watch. She and Matt had sat like statues to watch them. It had been the highlight of a wonderful afternoon. She'd enjoyed every minute of it.

Rather than spend the evening with Alli and Jack, she'd chosen to go with Matt to evening church. Pastor Roger had a Bible study and she had listened to every word. After that, she sat on Matt's porch and drank iced tea with him. Maybe it was because they'd both matured ten years, maybe it was because they seemed to have so much in common or maybe it was because now they were both believers, but they had spent several hours talking, something they'd never done before. She couldn't remember a time while they were married when they'd spent time talking together instead of fighting with each other. It had turned out to be one of the best days of her life.

Monday morning, with tears in his eyes Matt had asked her to forgive him for how he'd treated her when he left. She knew in her heart that she had, but the words just wouldn't make it through her lips just then. She'd left him up in the air and walked out of the store, using loud-mouth Jack as a buffer. *Chicken!* She knew that was true. She sighed, maybe she ought to look up Matt's Email address and tell him. The little piece of paper she'd snagged off the bulletin board downstairs still sat on her dresser and seemed to prick her conscience. It would be months before she went back. Even though the Albertson's were going back soon, she had no reason to leave her job yet.

Yesterday, rather than bring out things for a big breakfast, Allison had brought another box of huge muffins into the car and they had stopped at the hardware store for a coffee to go. As he had held the mug under the spigot for some of the delicious smelling coffee, Matt's eyes had glistened. When he'd handed her the mug, he whispered for her ears only, "Stay safe, Emi until I see you again." She could almost feel those two quarters he'd pressed back in her hand as he'd said those words. In fact, she glanced at her palm just to be sure they weren't there, it was such a strong sensation. Then as he'd put his hands on her arms she'd wished he'd keep them going… she could have used a hug… She'd looked into his face, had that been love she'd seen there? Could she hope? She pulled in a deep breath and let the water run through her hair once more, it felt so good. God was good, too. He loved her!

As she shut off the water in the shower and grabbed her towel, she also whispered, "I'll try real hard, Matt. It'll be Thanksgiving, but I plan to be there." She toweled off, drying her hair at the same time. She sighed; today it was back to Barney's Diner at four o'clock, with all its smells and ornery people. She shook her head maybe Harry wouldn't be one of them.

Before she hung the wet towel up there was another loud clap of thunder. Emi jumped, she'd forgotten about the thunder storm outside, since her bathroom didn't have a window.

As she started the washer and sorted clothes, she wondered if she and Matt had changed too much so that they could only be friends or had they matured so that they could take up where they'd left off only a few weeks after their marriage. She remembered how truly like heaven that had seemed. She thought at the time it would never end. She sighed and pushed in the starter on the washer. That time surely had come to an end.

Yes, now they were both true believers. Back then she hadn't known what that was, but now she knew, she knew it without any question. Matt had confided in her as they sat on that rock by the brook that he'd only made his decision to let Jesus' blood wash his sins away the Sunday before she had.

She knew, Sandy had told her, God could do anything, anything but fail! She would hold Him to that promise. As she examined her heart she knew deep inside that she would be happiest as Matt's wife again, but would he be happy as her husband? At this point, she could only hope and pray that could happen. At that moment it hit her, she could have help with that question coming true. She smiled because now she knew He could.

"God in heaven, I really would like to be Matt's wife again. Please, could You make that happen?" Outside, the rain was sheeting down, but Emi couldn't see it or hear it. It didn't matter she had peace in her heart as she'd never had before.

Emi started her washer, added the detergent and the clothes then headed for the kitchen and that good smelling coffee from her highly sophisticated coffee maker. She was glad to realize that the coffee smelled nearly as good as Alli's had smelled yesterday. However, she had to admit, the coffee at the store had smelled and tasted better. Maybe that was because of who had poured it for her? Who knew!

She poured a cup and set it on the table where she usually ate, then pulled out one of the muffins Alli had insisted she keep for breakfast. Another snap of lightning and boom of thunder happened right outside her window. It sent a shiver down her back and made her look out. When she did she saw the rain sheeting down. Outside it looked almost white it rained so hard. She was very glad she didn't have to leave for work just yet. Even with an umbrella she'd be soaked to the skin before she reached her car and Barney would have some comment.

Tuesday morning, Matt sat at his table washing down his breakfast muffin with a dismal cup of instant coffee and looked out at the dreary day. Yesterday had started off nice and he and Natt had watched the big cement truck come into town just after the SUV with his first love had left the gas pump. He didn't want to admit it, but as that vehicle pulled out of sight, Matt felt something like a beating heart leave his chest. After that it felt like a cold lump in its place.

There was no question where the big truck was headed. No grapevine had to spread the word anymore. Everyone in town knew that the new excavation was going to be a restaurant. Several of the town folks were hoping they could eat Thanksgiving dinner at the new restaurant. At church on Sunday Corky had bragged that's when he was sure the place would be open. Matt was a bit excited about that – it meant his first love would be back in town.

Just after Matt put his mug in his dish drainer on Tuesday, there was a loud snap of lightning and almost instantly, a loud roar of thunder. It seemed like they happened right over his cabin. If there'd been warning grumbles off in the distance, Matt had missed them completely. Matt looked out the window, it had been calm. When he'd gotten up he'd looked out and seen the clouds, but trees were barely moving. Now with the lightning and thunder there was an instant gust of wind that sent the trees into a writhing mass. Some of the smaller trees back across the meadow seemed to bend nearly to the ground.

"Great! Just what I needed to get to work," he grumbled. He really didn't want to start his car for the short distance and he wouldn't if he didn't have to. He knew he could run the distance, after all, he'd been on the track team in high school!

Matt was ready for work, so he grabbed his keys, ran out the door and slammed it. He took the four steps off his porch in two and ran down the walk toward the parking lot. At the moment it wasn't raining, but the sky was dark as midnight and the air was very heavy, but he hoped to beat out the rain. He ran full out across the parking lot and across the street. On the opposite sidewalk he could hear the rain coming, but he couldn't go any faster. As it was, his chest hurt from running so hard, his breath came out as labored pants and he felt a cramp coming in his right calf, but he didn't stop to rest.

He could hear the raindrops plopping on the asphalt behind him. At that moment he remembered his friends the track runners from high school who seemed to have a little burst of speed at the end of the race, but, for him today, it didn't happen. It couldn't be because he was now thirty instead of eighteen and not nearly as in shape, could it? Maybe it was because he hadn't been all that good at track back then, his major interest had been... well, Emilyn!

He made it onto Thomas's parking lot before the first drops hit him. However, before he made it across the short distance to the door he was soaked. It felt like a huge tub had dumped its contents on him. The water dripped from his hair onto his shoulders before he could get the door unlocked and get inside. Today, for the first time, his key decided to stick in the lock and Matt turned it the wrong way. Natt would also be soaked, since he had to open the Laundromat. Thank goodness the store roof was sound and he wouldn't have to round up any buckets to catch any drips! As he shut the door behind him the storm sound diminished more than half. He let out a sigh. At least he could dry out now that he was inside.

He hadn't thought about it much since he'd moved, but this wouldn't be a very nice day for the people wanting to visit the theme park he'd worked for. Those workers would be drenched too. Eric was out with a hiking group! Oh, my! Would they be wet!

Five minutes later Natt burst through the door. "Whew! That came up awful fast! Marcy was gonna walk and she hadn't left yet. I'm glad because she'd have been soaked!" Letting the door close behind him, and therefore shutting out the sound of the rain again, he shook off any extra dampness that would leave his clothes just inside the door. Looking at the empty spot in the 'nook' where the urn usually sat, he said, "Sure could wish the coffee was already finished so I could have a cup to warm up!"

"Sorry, that's your department."

Grinning at his cousin, Natt said, "As if I don't know that! So, have you heard from the travelers yet?" Another snap of lightning and clap of thunder nearly drowned out his question. However, Natt started back toward the utility room to fill up the urn.

Wishing he had heard from Emi, he shook his head and said, "No, I don't expect to, really. Say, with this rain does that put the construction back?"

"I doubt it. The slab had all day yesterday to dry, now it only has to cure and that'll be for a couple of days, even a week. The contractor wouldn't be planning to start his construction yet anyway. Did anybody say when they think the place'll be open?"

Matt grinned and said, "I guess since you spend so much time tending the nursery on Sundays you didn't hear, but Corky wasn't quiet about it at church, believe me. I think he thinks he has bragging rights. He's saying it'll be open for Thanksgiving."

Natt turned the corner into the utility room to start the coffee and picked up the basket to fill with the filter and grounds, Matt followed him. However, even before Natt started water running into the urn, he said, "That'll be good. Maybe the in-laws would come down. We could have this big feast at a restaurant all together. Mother-in-law could try to convince her daughters to go on back home for the millionth time. She could snag 'em both at the same time."

Matt turned toward his cousin and with a scowl looked at him directly. "Really? They're both married! Sandy has a little boy! They've been here how long?"

Natt shrugged, as if it happened every day. "Yup. Every time they come or every time we go or Ramon and Sandy. Her especially. It doesn't seem to faze Mama that the girls have been married and their husbands are standing right there. Actually, it even happens when their mom calls, believe it or not! Sandy lets it run like water off a duck's back, she just whirls around and leaves, but Marcy gets really angry. I mean, she's given her mom 'what for' several times." Natt shook his head. "It doesn't do any good, really and I've told her that several times. Now of course, their brother stayed there in Philly. He's the good child of the family and Mama never lets the girls forget that."

"That is unreal! Why does she do that?" Matt asked truly perplexed. "You'd think the girls were still kids or something!"

Natt set the basket with the coffee grounds inside the urn and set the lid in place, then started for the 'nook'. He shrugged. "I know, but it's the way she is. Now Dad, he loves his wife, but he'll try anything to keep her from saying those words. Why? Well, ever since Sandy was born she's tried to keep her first child hidden because of her chair. She's never acknowledged that Marcy got well from her Rheumatic Fever, either."

Matt shook his head. "That is truly unbelievable!"

"That's true, but that's how Colleen Bernard thinks. When does your brother start his new job for the sheriff's department?"

"August first. I guess he's to pick up his stuff the day before and the car, but I sure can't see where we need a deputy sheriff around here!"

Natt reached for the cord to plug into the big urn and said, "Nope, me neither, but then, it's a good thing they don't ask me about a lot of things. Of course, there was that awful thing that happened to Carolyn Casbah back in the spring. Maybe that's what the high officials are looking at. Who knows?"

"I guess that's why the sheriff asked Brother to be the new deputy." Matt shook his head. "I'll let him have that with my blessing!"

"I hear you on that! Didn't he get some kind of degree in that?"

"Yup. Four years in Criminal Justice."

"So this is right up his alley."

Matt nodded. "You could say that."

"So Carolyn's back in town?"

"Yup. Those two took up right where they'd left off. I mean, you should see Bro! If that isn't puppy love, I don't know what it is! He looks at her like he wants her to scratch behind his ears or something."

"Good, I'm glad to hear it!"

There hadn't been any electrical activity outside for several minutes and Natt looked out to see that Corky was at a gas pump. When the man came in to pay, he laid down his cash, but there was an extra fifty cents. Natt was closest to the cash register, but held up the quarters so Matt could see them, so he turned to fill a cup for Corky.

As the older man sprawled in a chair in the 'nook' and gave the guys his huge grin, Natt said, "So, is Loretta at Alex's?"

"Yep. Affer that Jack fella done et her outta house and home, she gotta fill back up. Didja hear my nephew's plannin' on openin' his restrnt fer Thanksgiving?"

"Yes," Matt said, "you told us at church on Sunday."

Corky took a swig from his cup, slapped his thigh and exclaimed, "That's right! We'll have us a celebration that day!"

"Free turkey dinner?" Natt asked, tongue in cheek.

Corky back-peddled immediately. After a long draw on his cup of coffee, he said, "Ah, probly not the whole dinner, I'd say mebe dessert and coffee. After all, the man's gotta make some money right off ta pay some of his bills. But, buleeve me, it'll be a humdinger whatever he got on the menu! That man can cook and his wife ain't that bad a cook neither. She jes' leaves it ta him, 'cause he's so good."

Natt left the cash register and walked around the counter to be closer to the 'nook'. "Could go for that, Corky! A piece of pumpkin pie and a coffee? Man, could go for that. I'm a true believer in pumpkin pie and coffee on Thanksgiving, for sure! Ah, with a dollop of whipped cream? Umm, that'll be some treat. This rain'll put that curing process a bit behind, won't it? I mean, it's been coming down like cats and dogs!"

"Yeah, that's true, but he got it poured yezzerday, early, so it'll cure real good. Think he's plannin' on construction startin' next Monday."

"I'm glad," Matt spoke up. "Us single guys can really use some food besides those frozen dinners Alex keeps in the freezer. Where'll these people live once they've moved here? Will they build a house around here?

Will they be coming to Vansville before the place is finished? If they do where would they stay?"

"Naw, they're buildin' a second floor on the restrnt fer a place ta live. Jack thinks it's better that way, anyhow. Where he is now ain't that close and he's had some trouble a time or two, so he tells me and whatever was a mess by the time he got there. Said it'd be easier for 'em ta get there effin there's a problem, in the kitchen or what not." Corky shrugged. "I ain't up on stuff like that, ya know."

Corky looked at Matt and asked, "Say, didn't I see ya sittin' with that purdy girl that come along with them? Set beside her in church?"

"Yes, Corky, she used to be my wife a long time ago."

Corky pulled his cup away from his face and looked – wide-eyed at the young man. "Wow! Small world."

"You could say that." Matt knew that wasn't common knowledge around town, Ramon had nearly fallen over a kid's chair on Sunday when he'd told him, but with Emilyn moving to Vansville soon, he knew it would eventually come out. He wasn't embarrassed that he knew Emilyn, he was embarrassed how he'd treated her and divorced her. He'd wished more ways than one since Sunday that he could have a do-over. Maybe a do-over wasn't the right word, this time they needed divine direction and that would be a first. As he watched Emi walk out the door yesterday he knew he'd pray to that end. The question Natt had asked him came to mind. "What God joins together, let not man pull apart." He had failed exponentially, he'd pulled them apart. It had been that way for ten years!

Corky finished his coffee and straightened up. Throwing his empty cup in the trash he stood up and said, "Well, I'd say Loretta's probly done with shoppin'. Best get down there so's I can load her stuff in the truck. See you boys."

"Yes, Corky, you have a good day and thanks for your business," Natt said to the door, as it closed behind the older man. At that moment a snap of lightning and another roll of thunder echoed through the store. Corky tried to move faster, but… well… maybe it was that cup of coffee that weighed him down. The heavy cloud overhead dumped more rain at that moment and Corky was soaked.

Natt shrugged. "Guess he'll be wetter before he's drier loading Loretta's groceries."

Matt chuckled. "That's for sure!"

The timer on the dryer went off and Emi knew it was only a short time until she must dress in a uniform and be on her way to the diner. Being the single woman that she was, she wondered how Murphy's Law would work for her today. Would the street be closed on the way to work as it had been for several weeks already this summer or would 'long-armed-Harry' be in for his usual 'all-you-can-eat special' and leave her, 'keep the change' tip? It was good not every one of the customers left only the change as tips. She never could have afforded her sophisticated coffee maker on that little.

The thunder storm finally passed, but the drizzle persisted on into the afternoon. Her dryer had shut off and she'd put the clothes away. She had already dressed in her uniform, so she grabbed an apple and a glass of iced tea for a snack only a few minutes before time to leave and her phone alerted her that she had an Email message. She grabbed her phone out of her purse and sank onto a chair at the kitchen table. Her heart skittered in her chest and her mouth went dry, so she gulped down a long swallow of tea. Only a few people sent her Emails, so she was pretty sure who this one was coming from. She activated her phone and looked at the sender, then opened the message.

Hi, there, good lookin'! Did you get back OK? Have been wondering. Matt

She grinned she would not delete this message as if it were spam. She took another bite of her apple and typed in, *Yes, good old Jack brought me right to the door. I guess he's planning on opening for Thanksgiving. Umm, I don't think I can stop in for that coffee until then. Dear Barney won't let me off that long. He's sort of a stickler for the schedule he posts every couple of weeks. Life in a 24/7 diner is like that.*

Let me know, we'll make a fresh pot!

She took a deep breath, now was as good a time as any to say what she knew she needed to say, something she hadn't said when she should have. She'd admitted to herself many times what a chicken she'd been when he'd asked her. She'd thought about his question and how she'd answered all the way back home from Vansville.

Matt, I forgive you for leaving me back then. I know we were really young.

Immediately the words started forming, *Thank you, dear heart! I know we were young, but that's no excuse. Bottom line, I was a jerk! Again, you can't know how sorry I am for that awful time in your life. Thanks. Gotta get back to work. Talk to you again and see you in November, if not before for that coffee. Matt.*

She held her phone in her left hand and had the apple in her right, but nothing moved, only her eyes went back to the words he had just sent. She whispered, "He called me 'dear heart'! 'dear heart' oh, my! Oh, my!" She did not delete that Email! She let out a long sigh, perhaps there was hope for them as a couple. She'd prayed that would happen, now she knew she needed to believe that God had heard her prayer. The time for her to quit at Barney's to go to Vansville could not come soon enough!

Finally, she finished her apple and iced tea. It was a chore, because all she wanted to do was stare at the little words on her phone screen. However, only moments later she hurried to her bedroom to make sure she was dressed right. After all, she'd been gone for four days and she wanted Barney to have nothing to gripe about after that long. Quickly, she looked in the mirror at her uniform. Of course, it was missing the apron, but she'd get that at the diner along with an order pad. Sandals, not flip flops, were good footwear.

As she stared at herself, she murmured, "Will Jack and Alli expect the waitresses to wear uniforms?" She'd never been in their restaurant, it was across town and completely out of the way for her to visit, besides, she didn't know when they opened; it could be for the afternoon shift when she was working. However, as crazy as Jack was it was anyone's guess how he ran his operation. She guessed it would be a few months before she found out and that would be in Vansville. She knew he'd be leaving town soon and the other man was taking over, he could be running the show already. He must have been running it while Jack and Alli were gone. Somebody had to be in charge, most likely the new man. She knew, she'd trained enough new wait staff to know that you learned best by doing it yourself.

When it was time to leave, the sky was gray and ominous, but there weren't any raindrops. Her hair was frizzy enough with the humidity. She was glad she'd left plenty of time to get to the diner whether there were problems or not. When she came to the street that had been closed, she found it open and there was even new paving over what had been a hole. For just a second she thought about complimenting the street department for doing such a good job, but of course, it was only a fleeting thought, she'd had enough inconvenience with that street, why compliment the city? Now all she had to wonder about was Harry-with-the-long-arms. It was Tuesday he could very well come in for dinner. Was it chicken and noodles night? She wondered for just a minute what the house special usually was on Tuesday and how much it cost, but then put it out of her mind.

As usual, she had left her apartment in plenty of time to arrive at the diner on time. After nine years it didn't take a rocket scientist to know how long it took to drive the route. She pulled her phone from her purse and stuffed it, along with her keys in her uniform pockets, walked in the back door and Barney looked at the clock.

Making a big production of looking at it a second time, he said, "Wow! Wouldja looky that! She come back and she's on time! 'Course, her hair ain't up."

Thirteen

Emilyn sighed and also looked at the clock. "Yes, Barney, I'm back, I didn't tell you I wouldn't be. My hair isn't up yet, when it's humid it's hard to manage and I'm on time, even for your ridiculous clock-in rules. I wasn't gone that long that I can't remember how it works. I'll have my hair up when I leave the break room, don't worry." She held up her arm. "See, I even have my scrunchee right here."

"Well, I could wonder, ya know."

"Yes, of course you would."

Her co-worker came in the back door just then, but of course, Barney didn't say anything to her. Minnie didn't look anywhere but at Emi, but she did with a grin. Immediately, she said, "Naomi said you should be tanned. You're not!"

Emi shook her head. "Minnie, come on! I only had four days off and we traveled two of them. We didn't go to the shore and I didn't even take a swimsuit." Raising her voice just a little, she said, "Believe me, the next time Barney gives me four days in a row off I'll be sure to come back tanned."

Barney flipped a hamburger and gave a loud snort. Without looking at Emi, he groused, "Won't happen!"

Emi gave him a wide grin, even though he hadn't looked at her. "I knew it wouldn't, Barney, that's why I said that. You are so predictable!"

"Humph!" he grunted again and opened a bun to spread on the grill and smacked it down with his spatula. Before he removed either the bun or the burger, he slapped another burger on the grill. "Order up!" he yelled, slapped the burger on the bun, picked up a plate and slapped the bun in the center.

Today was not the day to inform him she definitely planned to leave. It was July and Thanksgiving was several months away. Besides, most of the workers didn't give Barney any notice when they left, they just told him some Friday when he gave out pay envelopes they wouldn't be in anymore and walked out with their money. She's seen it happen many times. She didn't think it was fair to Barney and she wouldn't do it, but lots of people did. She guessed nobody who worked in a diner expected to have to give references at their next job. She wouldn't need them, but she still wouldn't just walk out without giving notice. Murphy's Law might be heavy-handed in her life, but she wouldn't be the cause in someone else's life.

It was only a few minutes before midnight and Harry-with-the-long-arms hadn't come in for dinner, but Emi wouldn't complain about that! Even without having to avoid his extra attentiveness, she'd had a fairly busy evening. She also knew that if the clock hands were anywhere close to being one on top of the other and straight up, Minnie was out of there! Usually, she gave some flimsy excuse she needed to get home to her better half. Emi never cared to learn who her better half was. She left the dining area, untying her apron as she went.

Minnie was never one to overdo in anything, certainly not work and yet Barney never called her on it. It made Emi shake her head. If she didn't have customers at her tables and took a break before Barney went off, he'd want to know why she was sitting in the booth by the coffee maker not doing anything. She'd learned some time ago not to sit where he could see her. If she took a break she made sure she went to the break room and closed the door.

With Minnie gone, that left Emi dumping out the old coffee and rinsing out the carafes. People said she made good coffee, but it didn't smell anything like the coffee at Matt's store. She turned off the warming machines, Naomi insisted on doing her own coffee, she said nothing that anyone else made was good enough. Emi didn't argue with that, but she also had to wipe down the counter at the coffee center. Naomi was a stickler for having a clean work place. There would be no spills left, whether it was from the shift before hers or the one before that! Emi was all for the clean workplace, she kept her spills cleaned up all evening, but then to have to wash it all again - with bleachwater? A bit much!

Emi was alone in the dining area when the back door opened and Naomi walked in. She didn't do her usual routine; she never looked at her co-workers or even greeted them, but walked right through the kitchen and into the dining area. That was so unusual, the cook put his spatula down and watched her, his mouth slowly dropping open, because she rarely deviated from her routine. However, he never said a word, even to the closed door.

When she spotted Emi in the big empty eating room, she walked right in and the kitchen door whooshed closed. She marched right up to her, jammed her fists on her hips, glared at her as if she'd done some major thing wrong and said, "Listen, girl, I told you to come back tanned and rested! You didn't do either one!"

Emi chuckled, patting her blond hair. Since she had finished wiping the work place, she hung the cloth on the hook and grinned at the older lady. "I told you I wouldn't get tanned, Naomi, I said we weren't going to the beach, besides, it usually takes me all summer to tan. Still, how do you know I'm not rested?" That was one thing Emi hadn't looked for in the mirror at home was dark bags under her eyes.

Naomi took another step closer to Emilyn, pointed her finger nearly into her nose and exclaimed, "Girl, with those bags under your eyes how can you be?"

"Because the storm woke me up this morning and I've been working here this afternoon and evening. Wouldn't that do it?"

"So what'd you do?"

The diner was empty, there were no customers and of course, Minnie had left, but Emi looked around, before she said, in a rather soft voice, "I went with some friends to this little town north of Atlanta. My friends are opening a new restaurant there and they wanted to see about it. It's being built from scratch and my friend wanted to give his plans to the contractor. They wanted me to go just for a vacation." She wouldn't even tell her good friend about leaving just yet. Walls were known to talk.

"That all? That's it?" Naomi scowled at her younger friend. "You just went along for a vacation? You went through all that to get Barney to give you a four day, just so you could get a vacation that was in the mountains?

"Naomi, isn't that enough?"

Naomi breathed out a sigh. "Well, I kinda hoped you'd meet some devastatingly handsome man, fall hopelessly in love and get out of this place. You know 'love at first sight' does happen here in Georgia sometimes."

Emi laughed. "Didn't happen, Naomi." Emi shrugged. "But, hey, it's like most other small towns, I did see some good-looking single men, though. But love at first sight? Really, is there such a thing?"

Naomi took one hand from her hip and waved it around, then sighed dramatically, "So why are you back here?"

"Because it's my job?" Emi stated, as if it was the most obvious conclusion. "Because I need the money?" she added.

Naomi let out a huff. "Well, yeah, I suppose, but you know how it is, some of them critters just up and leave."

"I know. I think that's the pits, too. I mean, Barney's not the most easy boss to get along with, but still….. I just don't think it's right to just walk out on him. If and when I quit, he'll get some notice, I guarantee it."

Naomi sat down in the booth by the coffee maker and motioned Emi to the other side. After Emi moved toward the bench, Naomi asked, "So, didn't you just say your friends are opening a restaurant in that place?"

Emi looked around the empty room again before she said, "Yes, they are, they're planning on Thanksgiving weekend for their opening."

"So will you go there to work in that new place?"

Emi lowered her voice, leaned toward her friend and said, "Naomi, there's a good chance, but I don't want Barney to learn about that yet. Can you keep that inside your hat?"

Naomi didn't answer her, but asked, "So these good-looking single men – is there some possibility for some romance there?"

Realizing her face was growing warm and therefore, she was probably blushing outrageously, she folded her hands demurely in her lap and smiled at her friend. Emi grinned. "Naomi, I swear! You're like a dog with a bone! Umm, yes, there is a possibility. One of those good-looking single men is my ex-husband…." Here was another place where that statement was news, but only Naomi heard it.

Naomi had been leaning forward to get any tidbit of information, but with that she reared back, as if she'd been slapped. However, a grin as wide as the Atlantic spread across her face and her white teeth sparkled. "Whoa! What was that?"

Emi nodded her head, her own grin spreading. "At first I thought it'd be awful and I'd just gotten an Email from him that he was moving to that place when my friend texted me to go on that four day. Still, I told her I'd go. Friday I saw him first thing and that was hard, but really, it was great! In fact, I can't wait to go back again."

Seriously, Naomi asked, "You think it could work this time?"

"Naomi, I think with the Lord's help it could be great!"

Naomi sobered immediately. "What did you say?"

"I said, I think with the Lord's help it could be great. Why?"

Naomi laid her hand on Emilyn's arm and said, earnestly, "Woman, that's the first time I've ever heard you talk about the Lord and that's a fact!"

Emi glanced at the clock, saw that it was minutes after twelve and said, "Naomi, don't you need to clock in?"

Naomi waved her hand, but stood up and answered, "Yes, yes, but don't you move! I'll be back in a flash and I gotta hear about this!"

"I'll stay."

Naomi jumped up, but Emi still sat. As Naomi rushed back to the kitchen and the pass-thru door closed, Emi leaned her head back against the wall and wondered at herself. Normally she wouldn't talk about something that happened when she wasn't at work, but she realized this was something that had changed her life and she wanted to talk about it to anyone who would listen. Naomi was the closest person she had to being a friend here in this town.

Momentarily, Naomi came back, fell into the booth and said, "Okay, now shoot! Those words you just said are something I never heard you say – ever!"

As seriously as Naomi had ever seen Emi, she said, "Naomi, I met this perfectly awesome lady who lives in that town…"

"A lady?"

"Yes, she's never walked, she sits in a wheelchair. She was dropped as a newborn and it severed her spinal cord, but that hasn't kept her from, well… anything!"

"O-o-o-ka-ka-ka-y… tell me more."

"Naomi, she paints awesome pictures, better than I've ever seen in my life and she gave me one. She plays piano like nobody I've ever heard and… well, she's… she's, I guess I gotta say, I don't know… she's joyful! It's written all over her! But the most awesome thing… she knew exactly when to be at a certain place when I was there. I mean, nobody called her! She drove up in front of the church just as I got there! And… and she knew exactly what I needed to hear even though I didn't know how or what to ask! All I did was hand her that red Bible and… I'm amazed even now as I think about it and that happened on Sunday."

Naomi scowled. "She's from that little place where you went?"

"Well… ye-ye-ah," Emi said, hesitantly.

"Always? She's lived there all her life? What's her name?"

"I don't know if she's lived there all her life… well, no, maybe not. Her name's Sandy. Now that I think about it, she couldn't have lived there all her life, she talks like a northerner."

"Sandy… Sandy what?"

"I don't remember. She has a husband and a little boy."

"How old is she?"

"A few years younger than me, I think."

Emilyn watched as Naomi sat back in her chair and put her hands together on top of the table. She was quiet for several minutes, but then she swallowed and looking off into another time in her life, she said, "I knew a lady once who came home from the hospital with her first baby. She was in the hospital longer than most because a nursery worker had dropped her baby and as she tried to stop the fall, the baby hit against the edge of the changing table. The doctor determined that it severed her spinal cord. Before the doctor let them go home he had a neurologist check the baby out. They said the injury was permanent, the child would never walk. Believe me; I know that was a hard pill for that young couple to swallow. Naturally, the lady and her husband were devastated with the news.

"After they left the hospital, someone called me and asked if I'd go and help this lady with the new baby, she was distraught and she cried all the time. She and Charlie had named the baby Sandra, but they lived in Philadelphia, that's where I lived then. As soon as I saw them for the first time I knew they were Believers."

Excited, Emi nodded and exclaimed, "Yes! It has to be the same person! I remember now, she has a gallery for her paintings in Philadelphia because that's where she was from."

Naomi snapped out of her thoughts, leaned forward and looked at Emi. Again she pinned her with a look and said, "What do you mean 'she knew exactly when to be at a certain place… and what I needed to know'?"

Emi pulled in a deep breath and as she exhaled, she said, "I don't know, Naomi. It was just so weird! When we went to that little town, Jack had rented a cabin for the weekend. That's where I saw my ex-husband for the first time. He lives in a cabin two doors from where we were to stay. Anyway, there was this red Bible on the little table beside the couch. Well, during that first night I woke up and then couldn't sleep, so I got up and that Book fell open to the first page. All I could see was; 'In the beginning God…' Those words stopped me, I couldn't see anything else. They kept going through my head all the next day. On Saturday, we went to see where the restaurant was going to be and met Sandy and her family, because they live right across the street. She was in a wheelchair, but oh my! She was amazing! She invited us to Sunday dinner after church at their house.

"Saturday night I couldn't sleep at all. I opened that Bible, but I saw the word, 'Salvation' inside the front cover. My ex-husband had said that word a lot, so I looked up where it said, but that word never showed up in what it said to read. I read the whole book of John a couple of times, but I still felt so empty and I never found the word 'salvation'. Anyway, on Sunday morning I ran to the church that was only a couple of blocks from where we stayed. It was early, but Sandy was just pulling her van up in front. She… well… it was like she knew I'd be there! When I gave her that Bible she seemed to know just where to look and showed me John 3:16 and… and read it with my name in it. Naomi, I fell to the ground and cried out to God! But how did she know to be there?"

Tears were streaming down Naomi's cheeks. Brokenly she answered, "Honey, God told her. That lady is so in tune with God she knew you needed her to be there and she was."

Contemplatively, Emi nodded. "Yes, that has to be it. It has to be! That afternoon she told me to find a good church to go to here. I told her I'd try."

Naomi slid her hand down to Emi's and covered it. Grasping it tightly, she said, "Honey, you can go with me to my church. I'll write out directions before Sunday and you can meet me there. I would love to have you go with me to my church. It's a great place to worship!" After a few seconds, she asked, "Are these people you'll work for gonna need another waitress or another worker?"

Emi scowled. "Probably, why?"

The tears were still glistening on Naomi's cheeks, but she looked seriously into Emi's face and asked, "Could you put in a good word for me? I'd love to get out of Barney's, but more than that I'd love to see my most favorite baby all grown up!" Reminiscing again, Naomi said, "That baby was the happiest child I've ever cared for, she was paralyzed but she never seemed to mind and did everything she could, even though her mom was such a wet blanket. Believe me, she was totally amazing even as a baby!"

"I'll put in a good word for you, Naomi, but I'm sure their restaurant won't be open twenty-four hours a day."

Naomi waved her hand to dismiss Emi's words, "Oh, that's not a problem, girl, but see what you can do, okay?"

"I will, Naomi."

The door into the diner from the front opened and Naomi got to her feet. "Girl, get your tail outta here! You should be home in bed by now! Still, what we had to talk about was really, really important. I'll talk to you tomorrow."

"Sure will, Naomi. Thanks for listening."

"Hey, what we talked about? It was awesome!"

"I know. It sure was for me."

The person who came into the diner must have been a regular Naomi knew because she jumped up and ran to the kitchen for something, even while Emi still sat. Emi should have been punched out twenty minutes ago, but she slowly stood up and made her way behind Naomi into the kitchen. What Naomi had said about Sandy gave her pause.

Once she was in the kitchen, Emi moved in slow motion. She pulled her order pad from her apron pocket then pulled off her apron. Slowly she took care of them and moved to the time clock. What she and Naomi had talked about was truly amazing. Of course, nothing she'd ever dealt with in her life had ever had anything to do with God. It was something completely knew.

She pulled her card from the slot, but when Naomi had punched in, she'd punched Emi out. Emi breathed a sigh of relief, Barney would never have tolerated an extra twenty minutes on her card and he'd been really suspicious if she'd written in a time. That was something he had to initial and he'd give the person the third degree before he'd do that. Still, as she slowly replaced the card in the slot what Naomi said still moved through her brain. *That lady was so in tune with God, she knew to be there and she was.* "Yes. She was there, she came to me and she said just what I needed to hear," Emi whispered. "God knows EVERYTHING!!!"

Emi walked out of the warm kitchen into the cool night air and shivered. It had rained much of the day, but now there were stars in the dark sky. She stood in the darkness and looked at the stars, something she rarely did after work. Amazed, she watched a bright star seem to pluck itself from its spot and streak across the expanse, then stop and disappear. Had God done that just for her? Maybe; she was the only one on the parking lot.

Finally, she used her key to unlock her car door, opened it and slowly slid behind the wheel. "Could it be? Did God tell Sandy I needed her?" She pushed the key into the ignition and started up. "It had to be! Sandy pulled up just as I came. She even came from the opposite direction." Before Emi pulled the stick into gear, she dropped her head and murmured, "God, You are so awesome!"

The days inched on, July became a hot, dry month, but inevitably it became the last week of the month, time does march on, after all. Brad Thomas's doctor at the Blairsville Hospital Rehabilitation Center decided that Brad wouldn't benefit much more from the physical and speech therapies the rehab center was doing with him. It had been a very hard stroke and had left quite a bit of damage, but he finally agreed to send Brad home. Brad was ecstatic, he had wanted to be home for a good long time. Once he was home, Joyce silently wished she'd left him at the rehab center. His disposition didn't change much and with her, he was downright surly.

The Sunday after he came home Natt's dad and his aunt and their families all brought things for dinner and gathered at the Thomas home in Vansville after church for Sunday dinner and the afternoon. Joyce had to help Brad several times with his meal and the family watched. Immediately after dinner Brad wanted to lay down for an afternoon nap, Nathan had to help him to the bedroom. Brad's major complaint was how low the bed was and Nathan agreed. Of course, Brad being Brad, hadn't wanted to get a new mattress and box springs, even though Joyce had said they needed one, until now when he was unable to get up from his bed at all.

Nathan decided immediately that he would remedy the situation as soon as possible.

Once Brad was in bed, the rest of the family gathered in the living room to decide how to proceed. Everyone had watched him during the meal, so they agreed that there hadn't been enough improvement in Brad's physical capabilities that he could go back to the store, not even to work the cash box. Everyone knew that he would need help to get there and back home and only sit in the 'coffee drinker's nook' all day long. The family wondered if he would be content if that's all he could do or would he be frustrated and cause a scene, therefore drive customers away, but the stroke had really done a number on him this time. None of the earlier strokes had affected his speech as much as this one had.

They felt sorry for Joyce, they had witnessed him making her the brunt of his bad attitude and she'd be there with him 24/7, but they saw no alternative. Neither of his children or their spouses could give up their fulltime jobs. They did agree with his doctor's order, she would need some professional part time help. That had been arranged before Brad left the center. However, he wasn't too nice with the professionals.

Later that afternoon, after Brad got up from his nap with his son's help, his two children reluctantly told him their decision, quickly said their goodbyes and left with their families. Natt and Marcy and also Matt hurried out, hoping that Brad wouldn't try to corner them and get them to say he could come to the store in the morning. That left poor Joyce to deal with Brad's attitude alone. She was nearly in tears when she helped him into bed hours later. However, Nathan had convinced his dad that they would be getting a new mattress.

With the attitude he'd had at dinner, both Natt and Matt knew that if Brad insisted on coming back the store wouldn't run nearly as well as it had for the last several weeks while Brad had been gone. Brad's attitude was downright surly when the family was there. It made them wonder what he'd act like with customers. They were afraid that people would be reluctant to come once they encountered Brad's new attitude. Natt knew for sure people wouldn't sit in the 'nook' if Brad was there.

Not only at Thomas's store, but other things were changing. Jerry enthusiastically took over a spot of fulltime hiking guide for DeLord's

Hiking Service. He had trained well and been an eager learner when he went on his 'in training' hikes. As a newbie he watched all the other guides to see what they carried in their backpacks and decided what he needed. He worked really hard to get all the equipment he needed to be the best guide he could be. He was very excited about his job. Duncan and his other long-term associates were sure he'd reform his opinion some day soon. After all, sleeping on the ground, in a one man tent and often eating reconstituted meals surely had to become old after a while. However, for now, they'd let him have his euphoria. They were sure that those March hikes would cure whatever ailed him. They would be patient!

Sandy didn't assign Eric a hike once he brought his group back on the last Saturday of July. Ramon and Sandy were sure he and Carolyn were excited to be back together and they were both starting new jobs August first. This time off for Eric would let them have a few days just to enjoy a bit of vacation together. Carolyn would be working in Blairsville as the Director of Allied Therapies at Blairsville Hospital and Rehabilitation Center. It wouldn't be near the scope of the job in Atlanta, but Carolyn was happy for it.

Eric had a large rural area in which to work around Vansville as a new deputy sheriff. No one, not even the sheriff, knew how much work Eric would have, usually until someone started in the new area no one did know. However, there were acres and acres of undeveloped land in the county. That was great for the hiking service and they were discovering new trails all the time, but also those many acres were a potential for things not so legitimate and therefore, lure undesirable people to live in the area.

He would be getting that snazzy white Sheriff's car that Isabel thought was so obvious and would keep people away from renting her cabins once it was parked on her parking lot. However, because he still had his own vehicle and would be keeping it parked on the lot, Eric planned not to park his 'snazzy white car' on Isabel's lot. However, he didn't tell Isabel that, he let her continue to fuss about it being on her lot.

Without even a hint to Isabel, he made arrangements to park the car on the back side of the clinic where very few people had to park, even though the area was paved. It would be out of sight while it was parked there and also it wouldn't be in the way of anyone using the services of the clinic. Eric was fairly sure the car wouldn't even be at the clinic when it was open.

However, he never told Isabel any of this. The first she'd know about it was when he brought the car to Vansville.

That car appeared the last day of July. The sheriff had asked Eric to come in to get everything in order, get his gear, including the standard issue revolver, the uniforms the sheriff had ordered for him and pick up his sheriff's car, get last minute details worked out and any new questions answered. Eric had thought of several since he'd seen the sheriff last.

Since Carolyn was in town, but hadn't started her new job, they went together to Blairsville, Eric was happy for her to ride along. She also wanted to check in at the hospital and talk with the administrator, just to be prepared for her first day. Eric drove the white car back to Vansville and Carolyn drove his SUV.

Isabel was surprised to see his SUV come on the lot, but the sheriff's car went to a place close by but didn't park in a conspicuous spot on her lot. She was on her porch when Carolyn parked his SUV, but Eric walked onto the lot. She stood on her porch with her hands on her hips as he walked toward her. "Well, why did you park that white thing back there?" she called to him across the gravel. "Why didn't you tell me?"

Eric kept walking toward her, but he grinned. "Isabel, I heard by a short grapevine that someone on this property didn't want 'some snazzy white car with big letters on the side' cluttering up her parking lot." Eric's eyes twinkled. "Know anybody who'd say that?"

"Humph!" Isabel said, quite emphatically and shaking her finger at him, she said, "Fella, you are putting words in my mouth!"

Eric chuckled at the older lady. "Really?" He scratched his chin, still grinning at her and continued, "I didn't think so, Isabel. You started off telling my boss you didn't like his car parked on your lot, even when it was only for ten minutes. He chuckled when he told me." He came along side Carolyn and added, "I'm sure you even said it to me."

Very typically Isabel, she scolded, "Get your tail in here for supper, fella! I see you roped that girl of yours into driving your wheels back here. You and Carolyn have lots to celebrate and us old gals are gonna do it up right! We got a roast from Alex and Ruth made your favorite kind of pie. We also got a big tub of ice cream for the top of that pie, so you're gonna have to help us out. Besides, you haven't been around much for us to see."

Carolyn walked beside Eric. They looked into each other's eyes and smiled. When neither of them moved for several minutes, Isabel huffed and said, "Girl, you and that boy get in here for our celebration!"

"We're coming, Isabel! You know Eric, he's hungry all the time." Carolyn exclaimed. "What about Dad, is he in on this celebration?"

"'Course not! I left a message though, he knows you won't be there for dinner. Now then, get your tails in here!" she groused. "That roast's been done a good while and if we don't eat it soon it'll get hard and dry." She stuck her finger nearly into Eric's face. "I know you you'd eat it hard and dry or moist and tender."

"We're on it, Isabel! Wouldn't miss a dinner like that! Why waste good food?" Eric exclaimed and ushered Carolyn up the steps of Isabel's house.

Carolyn smiled at the older lady and said, "Isabel, thanks for inviting us."

As they sat down for dinner, Ruth said, "So there's enough work for a deputy here?"

Eric shrugged. "Seems so, Ruth, I got my orders today. Sheriff's kind of excited about me taking this job." He made a face and continued, "I sure hope there aren't too many off road requirements, that sheriff's car doesn't have four wheel drive. Goodness knows there's lots of trails in the county but not so many paved roads."

"Humph!" Isabel groused. "I was sure there was some reason I didn't think it was a practical thing for that white car for the sheriff's department, not in this county."

Eric grinned at his landlady. "Isabel, Sheriff thought of that while I was there. He said he'll think about it some more and maybe, after seeing how much I need to drive around, he'll put in an order for an SUV that's white with SHERIFF on the side, but has four wheel drive."

"Humph! Why can't they make their cars black and make those words little?" She held up her thumb and forefinger an inch apart.

Eric laughed. "Isabel, that's part of law enforcement. You show who you are and it helps to get law breakers back in line."

"Mmm, yes, I'm sure!"

Satisfied, Eric let out a long sigh. "But of course!"

Isabel waved her hand nearly in Eric's face. "Youngun, you be sure to keep that car parked over there. There's only room for one car for each cabin, you know."

"Really? Well, sure I'll keep it parked over there."

However, the biggest news in Vansville happened the next day after the deputy sheriff had fulfilled his duties for the day. Still dressed in his impeccable uniform, his last official duty for August first happened at the intersection of the last country road just before entering the town of Vansville. He stopped a car that was trying to make the turn off the highway onto the country road. Perhaps he thought the driver was trying to go off into the hills to do some of that illegal activity. Of course, there was always that possibility. Being as new as he was in this jurisdiction, he needed to establish his authority.

In fact, his 'snazzy white sheriff car' was blocking the intersection, making it impossible for the driver to turn, so she pulled to the side of the road. The driver of the car had a scowl on her face until she saw who got out of the sheriff's car then she let out a huff. When the deputy left his white car, he didn't have his gun in his hand, or even his citation pad, but he held something even smaller, something the driver couldn't see.

When he reached the driver's door of the car he'd stopped, opened that door, but much to the surprise of the driver, he knelt on one knee on the road beside her and grinned up at her. Carolyn was speechless, but Eric was not. Quietly, for only her ears, he said, "Miss Carolyn Casbah, will you do me the honor of becoming my wife soon?"

Carolyn had been fussing in her purse, intent on finding her driver's license when her door opened. Tears glistened in her eyes, when she heard those words, but her smile was devastating as she turned and threw out her arms. Quickly she replied, "Eric! Of course! Of course! I want to be your wife, as soon as possible. Oh, Eric, you wonderful man!"

Eric captured her left hand and slid the lovely ring on Carolyn's finger, then their arms went around each other and Eric stood up, bringing Carolyn with him out of her car. However, before they moved their cars another car came up behind Carolyn's. When the driver of the BMW saw who was blocking the intersection, he swerved to the side of the road, stomped on the brake and stalled the car. It rocked back and forth as he jammed the gear stick into park. Unmindful that the vehicle was still rocking, he flung the door open and jumped out.

"Is this what I think?" Derek exclaimed, a grin spreading across his face. He was nearly running as his feet hit the pavement and he ran up to the two people embracing. Before he even reached them he opened his arms as wide as he could. "Oh, kids, this makes me so happy! So very, very happy!"

Carolyn turned happy eyes his way, but stayed in the circle of her fiancé's arms and said, "Dad, Eric just asked me to be his wife!" She turned her left hand so he could see the ring. "Look, isn't this beautiful?"

Throwing his arms around both young people, happy tears moistened his lashes as he exclaimed, "Oh, perfect! Terrific! Let's all go home right now and figure out how we can remodel that monstrosity to suit us all! Believe me, that place is much too much house for me. It needs a family and right now I'm holding the two most super people snug in my arms!"

"We're with you, Dad!" she exclaimed. "We'll follow you home."

The grinning deputy looked at his father-in-law-to-be and asked, "Could I call you Dad?"

Derek squeezed the young man's shoulder and said, "Young man, you had better start that habit this instant! You found my darling daughter in those woods back in the spring and you've done nothing but grow on me."

Pleased with the man's response, Eric also put an arm around Derek's shoulders. "Believe me, it's a pleasure, Dad." Only moments later the road block disappeared, the deputy leading the procession on towards the great house several miles away. Mrs. Beecham was setting the food on the table, but Derek rushed into his office and brought out pencils and paper even before they sat down to eat. He was determined to do a remodel job and soon.

By now, the foundation had been laid and there was framing on the concrete slab on what used to be a meadow just before the open road on the east side of Vansville. In that time, after the slab cured a sturdy foundation was laid in view of the fact that Jack wanted two floors to the building. The plans called for a cozy upper floor that nestled into the roof for an apartment, but it was still a second floor and quite large.

Each day, when his mama was in the office, Jon would watch what he could from the window and of course give his mama a toddler version of the going's on. However, as far back from the street as it was, his running commentary could only be about what happened several feet off the ground. Sandy never had to worry that she'd be left out of the loop. Jon kept her well informed about the events going on across the street. Of course, it was in toddler-talk, but Sandy could understand fairly well.

Usually, since Jon couldn't see everything, he insisted that after Mama was finished with her hiking service work that they had to go out to find out more. At about the same time each day, the wheelchair and its two people were a familiar sight to the construction workers and they loved seeing the pair. Usually, Sandy brought some iced tea and cups with her and the workers were happy to take a break. August in north Georgia was turning out to be a very hot month to be working construction. So far, none of those hurricane rains had materialized.

The first Monday of August Sandy finished her office work, then she and Jon went to the kitchen for her pitcher of lemonade and disposable glasses, then they made their daily trip onto their parking lot and watched as the workers laid their hammers down and jumped off the wood frames they had up. It was time for their morning break after all. They all decided it was the best time to take a break; they all loved both Jon and Sandy.

Jason, the contractor, saw the pair, left his truck and walked across the street first. Jon waved to the man and grinned. "Mizzer Ja-son!"

"Hi, there, master Jon! How's my friend today?"

"Ja good. Work hard!"

Jason chuckled. "You or me?"

Obviously, not getting an adult joke, Jon pointed across the street as all the other men came toward them. "Lozza wood!"

Jason chuckled at the toddler. "Yup! We gotta work fast! Corky thinks we may get stopped by hurricane rain."

Jon scowled. He'd been too young to remember hurricane rain from last year. "Cor-key here now?"

Jon scrambled off Sandy's lap as she began to pour glasses full of lemonade for the workers who started to come around. When he was on the parking lot, Jason held out his hand and said, "No, Corky's not over there now, but you want to see what we're doing? Today we're putting up lots of wood!"

Jon shook his head and looked at Sandy. "Mama no come on rocks."

Jason smiled at the sweet child. Even less than two years old, he thought of his mama first. "I know she can't, but you can walk on them with me, can't you?"

Jon looked from his mama, who was busy handing out lemonade, back to Jason and slowly nodded. "Guess so." Jon trustingly placed his tiny hand in the big man's large hand.

"Mama, busy now."

"Well, come on, big man! Let's go see what we're building."

"Yea! Okay!" Jon happily grabbed Jason's hand and skipped along beside him.

Of course, he made Jason stop at the street. "Mama say stop, mizzer Ja-son."

With a twinkle in his eyes, Jason asked, "Why?"

"Gotta wuk for cars."

"Oh, sure!"

Sandy heard the exchange, but she continued to pour cups of lemonade. She had no worries that Jon would be fine with Jason. She smiled at the contractor who had made a point of introducing himself to her the first time he'd come back to the construction site. He had known her from her concerts she'd given in Blairsville. She also had no worries that she would get left out of the loop. After all, with Jon taking the tour with Mister Jason, he would tell her all about it in toddler-talk while they ate lunch… and until he took his nap… and probably tell her many more things after his nap… and maybe even through a yawn before he reluctantly said his prayers before bedtime….

Something else happened that Monday morning. Eric had been instructed to check in with his boss in Blairsville each Monday morning. Since he was so new at his job he was anxious to do that. That meant he must be on the road before eight o'clock. Quickly he finished his breakfast, checked his reflection in his bathroom mirror to see that he positively reflected the Sheriff Department of his county. Last of all, he clipped his cellphone onto his belt, picked up his personal keys and stuffed them in his pocket.

Since he only wore his sheriff's hat on the job with his uniform, it sat on the front seat of the sheriff's car. He took the sheriff car key from its special place on his hanging key rack and headed out the door. Knowing that Isabel had her favorite chair situated so she could see her first few cabins, the parking lot and the street out front, Eric didn't look that way, but waved at the window as he headed the other way for his 'snazzy white car' parked behind the clinic. She, of course, huffed out a sigh. The man was incorrigible, but she thought the world of him.

Twenty-five minutes later he parked in the cage beside the justice building and headed into the sheriff's office. The office door was open, but the dispatch officer who usually sat behind the front desk wasn't there yet. The sheriff sat behind his desk and motioned Eric to a seat across from him. Before Eric had a chance to voice any questions, Sheriff Winslow picked up an envelope that lay in front of him, tapped the edge on the desk and said, with a grin, "Eric, know anybody by the name of Matthew K. Thomas?"

Eric scowled and looked at the envelope the sheriff was holding, but couldn't see much because of his hand. "Well, sure, Sheriff, he's my twin brother! What's the deal? You know I see him nearly every time I'm home."

Still holding the envelope, Sheriff Winslow turned it so Eric could see that the front was nearly covered with slashes and bold magic marker writing, along with several yellow sticky notes. "It seems some not-so-bright folks in the next state south couldn't enquire from the post office about a forwarding address. Since your brother left his former home and place of employment, this letter has traveled many miles. Since it's registered, it couldn't go in a dead-letter office, so we finally got it. During your travels today could you see that he gets it?"

Eric grinned. "Sheriff, you know it won't be a problem. I know where he works and he's my closest neighbor. I'll make sure he gets it today before I finish my official duties." He put the last words in air-quotes.

The sheriff grinned back and his eyes twinkled. "I had that figured out, too. Thanks, Eric." Eric had his hands on the arms of the chair to stand, but before Eric stood up, the sheriff scratched his head, as if he had a baffling situation and asked, "Ah, did I hear some rumors since I saw you last?"

If possible, Eric's grin spread even further. "What would those rumors be, Sheriff?"

"Well, I guess it's possible it was wind blowing through the trees, but I heard by some grapevine that a lady you know received a lovely ring the other day. Some lady you stopped, was that what happened? Was there some infraction?"

Eric chuckled. "Yup, you got it right! I asked a special lady to be my wife. I stopped her so I could give her that sparkly ring."

Sheriff Winslow held out his hand and Eric grasped it. "I'm happy for you, Eric. Best wishes to both you and Carolyn. That rescue back in the spring turned out very well, didn't it? Who would have known at the time?"

"You have no idea, Sheriff!"

Still holding the sheriff's hand, Eric leaned over the desk and said, "Yes, Sheriff, we're very happy and yes, that rescue turned out great in the end. Derek came upon us in the throes of a passionate embrace and trotted us right out to his house. After a very hurried dinner, we spent the whole evening working on plans to make several self-contained units out of that place. Of course, we're to get the biggest one and he's expecting his third grandchild within a matter of months, no longer than eighteen months – and I quote."

The sheriff let out a belly laugh. "No subtlety there!"

"No, none what-so-ever!"

"Got a date set?"

"Probably around Thanksgiving or between Thanksgiving and Christmas. It seems Carolyn must consult several of her buddies as to details."

"Yes, as I understand these things, it's the lady of the pair that has the right to tell the man what to do *before* the wedding. Let me know, I'll make sure you have time off."

"And you will come?"

"Is that an invitation?"

"It sure is, but you'll get a formal one when it's time."

"Good! I'll be sure to be there."

Eric let go of the sheriff's hand, but reached for the envelope. "Thanks, Sheriff. I'll make sure this gets delivered today. I can't imagine…"

Sheriff Winslow shook his head and said, "Nor can I. Did you get such a letter in the mail some time ago?"

Fourteen

Eric looked down at the much abused envelope to see that it had the letterhead of a large attorney group in Atlanta and that the postmark was only days before Matt had moved. He shook his head. "No I didn't, but Matt and I haven't been in the same circles since we graduated from high school back in the dark ages."

Rubbing his hand over his own salt and pepper hair, the sheriff chuckled and said, "Ah, yes, a man turns thirty and his high school days turn into 'the dark ages.'"

Eric chuckled. "Yup, you got that right!" He held up the envelope and said, "I'll see that he gets this today."

Sheriff Winslow chuckled. "I guess there's no rush, after all the time it's been in transit."

Matt finished off his coffee, looked at the clock, sighed and took his dishes to the sink to give them a good wash. So far, he'd managed to keep those bugs at bay, not a stray one had found his cabin. August was proving to be just as hot and dry as July had been. He was glad for the sturdy cabin and the well-modulated cooling system that kept his place so comfortable. That was not the way it had been in Orlando. That building had been newer than Isabel's cabin, but the heating/cooling system forever needed repair. Matt was convinced that Isabel's husband had spared no expense to make sure the six tiny houses that made up his weekend cabins for rent were built to high standards. Another advantage of this job over the last one, he worked in an air conditioned store, the job in Florida had been mostly outside.

He and Emilyn had traded Emails on several occasions since she'd left Vansville. He'd learned that the couple she'd come with back in July was getting ready to close up their home, sell it, and soon would move to Vansville. Since the restaurant wouldn't be anywhere near finished he suspected they'd rent a cabin until it was. Emi, of course, had no reason to move with them. She was not independently wealthy so that she could live without a job to pay her expenses. Of course, in Vansville there was no place to live except Isabel's cabins. She couldn't afford to rent one without a job for any time at all and no one of her acquaintance could step in to rent it for her. She must stay at Barney's Diner for a while. Matt had wished on several occasions since they'd started Emailing that he could rent her a cabin so he could show her his true heart now that he was a sensible adult and a true Believer.

When the clock on the wall told him it was time to head over to the store to open up, he took his wad of keys and headed out. He'd heard his brother leave some time ago. He now was a deputy sheriff, so he was living in his cabin, but he'd heard rumors over the weekend that that situation would change in a few months – about the time that the restaurant opened. The lucky man would marry the daughter of a wealthy man and after a honeymoon would start living in Derek Casbah's house, which really was easily classified as a mansion.

Matt sighed and pulled the door shut behind him. He grumbled, "My brother, my twin brother, has everything. He went to college, he's a decorated hero, he has money in the bank, he's marrying a lady, also a college graduate and has a very prestigious job and whose dad is a wealthy man and going to live in a mansion."

He sighed again, still holding his keys in his hand and tossing them from one hand to the other, he said, "What about me? Well, let's see... I squeaked through high school, didn't go to college, I'm a divorced man, I'm sure no hero, I don't have money in the bank and the lady I love is as poor as me and her dad sure doesn't live in a mansion. End of story." He sighed, "I think all of those things are due to poor choices on my part." He pulled in another deep breath and continued on across the parking lot for the street and the hardware store. Life went on; you took the peaches along with the pits. "Actually, those poor choices were mainly because I thought too much of number one and acted like a stupid jerk in my teens and early twenties."

Emilyn woke up from the noise from her phone that sat on the night stand beside the daybed. It was the chime for a text message that came from Allison - *Emi, who is this lady you asked about wants a job at our new restaurant?*

Emi sat up, pushed the hair out of her eyes and replied, *She's the night waitress at Barney's, but she says she's good at about anything in food service.*

When could we meet her? You know we're moving at the end of the week.

She gets to work at midnight and her shift's over at eight. She's very conscientious and I know she'd do you a good job. I guess I could find out where she lives. I never saw her with a cellphone, I don't know if she does texting or anything.

Talk to her and find out what you can. Maybe we could meet her at a restaurant besides Barney's some morning.

OK, I'll do it tonight. We're both on.

That'll be good, let me know as soon as possible.

Will do.

When Eric returned to his car from the sheriff's office his radio was squawking. It seemed there was something in his jurisdiction that needed immediate attention. He guessed that most law enforcement work was in the 'immediate attention' category. From the minute he started the car he was busy with his duties for the rest of the day. Before he put on his deputy uniform for the first time he'd wondered if there'd be enough work to keep him busy. Ha! He'd been busy each day since he'd started. Obviously, today was no exception. He liked being busy, he never liked to read a book while he was on the job.

The letter the sheriff had given him to deliver first thing in the morning sat in his car all day. Every time he saw the envelope he pondered why a law firm in the big city of Atlanta was contacting his brother, but each time he shook his head. He had no idea. Except for the two years after they graduated, Matt hadn't even worked in Georgia, let alone lived there. After his divorce he'd moved to Florida. Why a law firm from Atlanta?

He and Carolyn were to meet at the mansion to eat with Derek for dinner, but he knew he must deliver the letter before he called it a day. The earliest postmark said it had been posted July first in Atlanta, Georgia. That was over a month ago. What had taken it so long to get delivered not to Vansville, but to the sheriff's office in Blairsville? He shook his head, he could only speculate. Of course, his speculation was interrupted by yet another immediate need. He drove to the end of the road they sent him on, but it ended in a hayfield.

When he finally finished his last duty for the day, the clock on the dash told him it was after five and he still had Matt's letter. He must find Matt at his cabin before he left, if he planned on doing something else for the evening. He and Matt never kept tabs on each other, they never had. Right after graduation from high school he had been best man in his brother's wedding, then they'd gone different ways. He had gone to Clemson and Matt had taken his wife to a tiny apartment and started a factory job.

Of course, he must deliver the letter before going to the country for dinner and the evening with Carolyn and Derek. He sighed and drove past the road leading to Derek's house. That was the life of a deputy sheriff. It didn't matter how long he'd been a deputy, duty always came first he knew that.

He pulled on Isabel's parking lot only moments later to see Matt turn from the walkway onto the small walk to the steps to his cabin. Eric breathed out a sigh of relief. Rather than toot the horn and therefore, call Isabel's attention to his 'snazzy white car', Eric quickly put the car in park and opened the door. "Hey, Matt!" he called. "Wait a minute, I have something for you." Eric quickly stepped from the car, leaving it running and the door open and hurried toward his brother. He held the envelope out in front of him.

Matt stopped where he was and didn't climb his steps. At the base of the steps to his cabin, Matt turned, but waited until Eric was only a few steps away before he asked, "So the deputy wants to see me? What's up? Do you still have stuff to do after five?"

Holding out the abused envelope, Eric said, "Seems you're an important person. This has followed you for over a month and ended up at the sheriff's office. He asked me to deliver it."

Matt stared at his brother, "What? Me important?" He took the envelope. When it was in his hand, he stared at it for some time, then looked at Eric with a scowl. "What in the world?! It's a mess! You can hardly see my name on here. It's been all over God's creation!"

"Yup, I'd say it has."

There were only two places on the envelope that were still clear, one was his name, the other was the official looking return address of a rather prestigious Atlanta attorney. Besides the slashes and bold markings were several sticky notes with other instructions on them. Still staring at the return address, Matt shook his head then looked up at his brother again. He scowled and shook the envelope, as he said, "What could some attorney from Atlanta want with me? Goodness, I haven't lived in Georgia in nearly ten years until a month ago! This is totally absurd, I can't believe it!"

Eric shrugged, looked back into eyes the same shade as his. "Don't know. You won't find out until you open it, I guess."

"Yeah, guess you're right on that score." With Eric standing silently beside him, Matt turned the envelope over and slid his finger under the sealed flap. Of course, it had been sealed so long it didn't want to budge. "Man! It's giving me fits! Whoever did this must have used some heavy-duty glue on it."

Eric nodded. "Yeah, I can see that."

Finally, Matt had the envelope mangled and ripped enough so that he could pull out a single sheet of very shiny, embossed paper. Matt stuffed the envelope under his arm then looked at the letter a long time. With Eric reading over his shoulder, Matt finally read the bold print from the heading on top out loud:

Elton G. Messmerson Attorney at Law

"Who is Elton G. Messmerson?" Matt asked. "He must be something special, it looks like he's on his own, not in a firm."

Eric shrugged. "Beats me. Never heard of the man."

Matt pulled in a deep breath and read on:

"'Dear Mr. Thomas.

I am the attorney who drew up The Last Will and Testament of Effie May Tindal of Atlanta. Unfortunately, she passed away on June thirty at the age of ninety-two. She stated in her will that you, Matthew K. Thomas, her great nephew, was to receive a certain CD, held in the First Bank here in Atlanta. That CD also names you as the beneficiary. If you could contact me at your earliest convenience it would be appreciated....'"

Incredulous, Matt stopped reading and looked at his brother. "Eric! Did you get something like this? What, a month ago?"

Eric shook his head, still looking at the letter. "No, I never and I've lived here for some time, so there'd be no reason it would take over a month to find me. It is amazing! That lady was Mom's aunt. I guess she always lived in Atlanta and worked for some huge conglomerate all her working life. She was the president's executive secretary. At least that's what Mom said. She never married, but she kept in touch with Mom once in a while, but that's all I know about her. Why would she leave you something? Surely, she has other relatives closer kin than you."

"I know, did we ever visit her?"

Eric shook his head. "I don't think so. I think Mom said she visited her as a kid, but I can't say I remember ever seeing her. She and Mom weren't close and she was always busy."

Shaking the piece of paper, perhaps to see if it was real, Matt said, "This is unbelievable! I wonder how much the CD's for. A CD, I just can't get my brain around this, it's unreal!"

Eric shrugged. "Don't know. Guess unless he says there in the letter you'll have to call that attorney to find out."

"Yeah, guess I will, but it'll have to be tomorrow. Don't attorney's offices close at five?" he asked, looking at his watch.

"Yup, I think they're in the same category as bankers."

"Yeah, probably..." Matt said cynically.

A hot breeze blew down on them and rattled the paper in Matt's hand and messed with his hair. "Whew! Sure can tell it's August!"

Eric nodded. "Thank goodness for AC in that car! I've been in it all day. So, how's it with you and Emi? Have you heard from her since she left?"

The official letter was forgotten. Matt's face burst into a grin. "Real fine! Real fine, Bro. We've been Emailing since they left. I've almost got her convinced she can quit her job a week before the restaurant opens and come here." Matt took a deep breath and as he let it out, he said, "I haven't asked her yet to marry me, but I… I plan to." His voice not quite so confident, he said, "I think things have progressed that far – at least for my part, I'm convinced I love her." His voice lost even more volume, as he said, "Really, I don't think I ever quit loving her."

Eric slapped Matt on the shoulder and grinned right back at his brother. "Well, super! That's terrific! Be sure not to rush her, though."

"I know, I was a jerk back then and ruined a good thing. You know, I've regretted what I did many times, especially after I saw her here that weekend."

"Perhaps so. I'm not wanting to rub salt in a wound, but I really felt bad for Emi."

"I know, I'll never forget her face that morning, she had no clue." Matt took a deep breath and said, "So when are you tying the knot?"

Eric couldn't help the grin on his face, as he answered, "I'm pretty sure our date's the Saturday before Thanksgiving. Anyway, that's the last I heard, but you know how it is. The groom's usually the last to know. We really don't want to put it off; after all, we aren't getting any younger. Man, I want you for my best man, you know that."

Matt pulled in another deep breath. He cleared his throat, before he said, "Bro, I asked you for that once. It didn't turn out so good. You're sure?"

"Yes, I'm sure. All of that's under the Blood, Brother. 'Old things are gone, the new has come.' You know that."

"Thanks, I'll be glad to. Count me in."

"Okay, as I get the info I'll keep you in the loop." Eric looked at his watch and sighed, "Well, I'm late for dinner and I have a few miles to go, so I'll see you again. Don't forget to call about that. See you again." Eric patted his brother's shoulder then turned to walk back to the 'snazzy white car' still running with the driver's door open.

"I will. Thanks." Matt pulled the letter up to look at it again and as the same time slowly mounted the steps to his porch. He didn't watch to see what his brother was doing. The content of the letter was enough to give him pause. He stood on his porch to finish reading the rest of the letter, but the amount of the CD was never mentioned. He shook his head. "This boggles my mind! It's unbelievable!" he muttered.

Just to torment Isabel again, Eric took several long strides back to his 'snazzy white car'. When he was beside the driver's door, he turned toward the house across the parking lot, smiled as broadly as he could and waved at the window. He mouthed the words, 'See you later, Isabel!' Of course, then he hurried and settled in the car and drove away.

In the morning Matt watched the clock and as soon after nine when they didn't have any customers he walked to the 'nook', pulled out his cell phone and called the number listed in the attorney's letter. His heart was hammering as if he'd run a marathon at full throttle. Some sweet voice answered and Matt asked to speak with the attorney listed on the letter. After several clicks a man's deep voice said, "This is Alton Messmerson."

Matt pulled in a deep breath and said, "Sir, this is Matt Thomas. Sorry I'm just getting back with you, but I only received your letter late yesterday afternoon."

The man cleared his throat and said, "Matt Thomas… oh, yes. Miss Tindal's nephew. Why did it take so long to reach you?"

"Sir, the envelope spoke to its taking many side trips along the way to my new place of residence. I now live north of Atlanta. I really don't understand why it went to so many places. I did leave a forwarding address there in Florida."

"My, my. Well, let's see what I can pull up on my computer about that transaction. It's been a while, so it's not fresh in my mind."

"Yes, I really have no idea how this came about."

After Matt heard several clicks in the background, the man said, "Ah, here we are. My goodness, that letter was generated weeks ago!" After another short silence, the man said, "You say you have no knowledge of this?"

"Yes, that's true. I can't even remember ever seeing the lady. In fact, my brother said our mom only saw her as a little girl."

On a long breath, Alton said, "That is most interesting."

After more clicks, the attorney was momentarily silent, but then he said a number and Matt's legs instantly felt like water. Fortunately he was by a chair in 'the nook' and collapsed suddenly onto it. He had to swallow before he could whisper, "What?! What did you say?"

Without answering directly, Alton cleared his throat and said, "Mr. Thomas, I'd say you're a rather wealthy man. Since I wrote to you that CD has matured and they're holding it at the bank awaiting your instruction."

Matt had to swallow, his throat was suddenly as dry as the Sahara. "Mr. Messmerson,…" he started, but had to clear his throat. "Really, I don't know what to say! This is amazing!"

The attorney hit a few more keys and said, "Yes, I'd agree with you, especially if you've never seen the woman. However, that amount is clearly marked on the bank information. The bank sent us all the information they had of Miss Tindal's dealings as soon as we notified them of her death. If you wish, I can contact the bank and have them send you information as to getting this placed into your own bank account."

"Actually, I haven't set up a local bank account as yet, but I'll do that as soon as possible. Yes, I'll give you my present address so please send me that information. Surely I can get an account set up within a day or two."

"Yes, that'll be fine. I'll get this into the mail as soon as we're off the phone. It is amazing that it took this long to reach you!"

"Yes, I agree. Thank you. I'll do that."

Matt disconnected and sat staring silently at his dark phone in 'the nook' for several minutes. He had to swallow and he shook his head, for just a minute his brain didn't seem capable of computing anything. Thankfully, the store was quiet no customers had come in while he was on the phone. As he'd dialed, Natt had disappeared into the office so he could be alone. He definitely liked that about his cousin.

However, he was too overcome to think straight. Suddenly, without doing anything himself, he'd become a man of means. He'd never seen as much money as the attorney had mentioned he'd now inherited. What he couldn't do with that money! Instantly, he knew that was his immediate problem. He had no idea how to use what he now had in a wise manner. Now that he was a Christian man he didn't want to squander that money.

"Derek Casbah… I need to talk with him," Matt said, just under his breath. "I'm sure the man can help me do what I need to do. Besides, I need to close out that account in Orlando. People don't like to get out of town checks."

Matt jumped up and hurried to the back to the office. "Natt," he said, "I need to see Mr. Casbah today and open a bank account. When could I have some time to go to Blairsville?"

Natt looked at the clock on the wall that they could see from the whole back part of the store and said, "Well, it's Tuesday morning. Usually Tuesday mornings are pretty quiet around here, why not go now? Take until lunch time if you need to. I think I can probably hold down the fort until you're back."

"Great! I need some advice as well as opening an account, but I'll hurry as much as I can. Thanks, Natt, I'll see you later."

"Better call ahead." Natt said to Matt's retreating back.

"I'll do that."

By ten o'clock, Matt was walking into the downtown office of the bank on the square in Blairsville. Matt had taken the time before he left Vansville to look up the number of the bank and Derek's secretary had confirmed that the man would be there all morning. The president's office door was open and Derek met him as he walked around his secretary's desk.

Smiling at the young man, he said, "Come in, Matt, thanks for calling ahead, at least I was prepared to see someone. What can I do for you this morning, at this early hour?" Derek chuckled. "You are Matt, of course. I saw your twin for some time last evening and you definitely look alike. Did you play any pranks on your teachers when you were in school?"

Matt chuckled as he remembered their elementary school days. "Oh, yes, some, but Eric was much more studious, he'd give it away every time."

Derek nodded thoughtfully. "Yes, I can believe that."

After Derek had showed him to a seat and closed the door to his office, Derek asked, "So what do you need my advice on?"

Matt had brought the attorney's letter with him, but he didn't pull it out. Instead he said, "Mr. Casbah, just this morning I learned I had inherited a large sum of money, so much that I'm afraid I have no idea how to handle that amount."

Derek took his seat behind his desk and leaned his elbows on the desk. Looking earnestly at Matt, Derek asked, "Matt, please call me Derek. How much are we talking about?" After Matt told him the amount, Derek swallowed and said, "Wow! That is something! You say you don't… well… didn't know this lady? How is it you are remembered in her will?"

"I have no idea! Eric brought me the letter that had finally gone to the sheriff's office. I asked him what he knew about her. He said he thought our mom had seen her as a little girl. Why should she leave me a CD? Eric's the older twin, none of this makes any sense!" Matt rubbed his chin and added, "Hey, not that I can't use a few extra coins now and then, but this! This is beyond incredible. I got the letter last evening and learned the amount this morning!"

"I guess that makes no difference now. It's your name on the CD, so you need to take care of it. Let's open an account for you so there is somewhere to have the bank send the money. There'll be time after that for us to figure out what to do with it."

"Okay. I really have no idea how to handle this."

Derek chuckled. "You mean you don't make this much working at Thomas's store?"

Matt grinned. "Not hardly!"

Derek helped Matt handle the paperwork for a savings and checking account where the money could be deposited, then helped him close out his account in Orlando and bring that money to Blairsville. When they finished that transaction, he asked, "Is there anything significant in your life coming up?"

Matt pulled in a deep breath, held it momentarily, then said, "Well, I'm hoping to ask a lady to marry me in the near future. However, that's still up in the air at this point."

Derek raised his eyebrows, but said, "Okay, how soon?"

"Well, she's my ex-wife, but she's moving to Vansville to work in the new restaurant. I saw her over that weekend when she and her friends were here just before the work started on that building and we've been Emailing since she left. I'm afraid she may still have some trust issues with me, but up to this point there was no way we could get together to do more than send Emails back and forth."

"Hmmm," Derek said. Without saying anything, Derek put his hands together as if he was praying and rested his chin on his fingertips. "Hmmm," he muttered again.

While Matt was gone and Natt was alone in the store, the back door opened and Natt heard his gramma's voice even before he saw her. His heart took a nose-dive, that had to mean his grandad had persuaded his gramma to bring him to the store. How long would the man insist on staying and how many people would he run off before he left?

Pasting a cheery smile on his face, Natt waited for his grandparents to appear. He didn't get up to meet them, but it was only a few steps from the back door to his tiny office. Soon the couple appeared in the utility area and Joyce said, "Brad, here's Natt."

"I see him. I ain't blind, ya know. That there stroke didn't take my eyeballs." He looked at Natt and said, "So ya run out on me the other day! Been wantin' to get back here."

"Hi, Grandad. It's good to see you."

"Yeah, jes' came by to see the old place. Joyce tells me doc says I can't come back ta drink your coffee. Sure smells good, though."

"It's still the same stuff you drank before you got sick, Grandad."

"Can we sit a spell and I get me a cup?"

"Sure, let's go up to 'the nook' and get us a cup. I was just thinking I could use a cup myself. Maybe a friend of yours will come in while we're up there."

Natt stood up and walked around Brad's back. He grinned at his gramma and said, "Gramma Joyce, do you have a bit of shopping at Alex's to do? Why don't you take a break while Grandad and I get a cup of coffee? You come on back after you get it all put away." Affectionately, Natt put his arm around his grandad's back.

The gratitude showed on Joyce's face as she let go of Brad's arm. "Bless you, Natt, I did have some things I needed to get from Alex. I never thought it could be this easy. Sure, I'll take a bit and do that, but I won't be long." Joyce looked from Natt to Brad, but Brad had already put his cane down to take a step toward the nook.

"Take what time you need, Gramma Joyce. I'm sure Grandad'll even have a second cup if there's time. We'll see you later."

Natt turned his grandad toward 'the nook' and Joyce rushed out the door. When the door was closed, Brad let out a long sigh. "Natt, my boy, that woman's about to drive me to drink somethin' I've never had in my life! Believe me, it's a lot stronger than any coffee you've ever made! But let's get on up there and have us a cup. I think havin' a cuppa your good stuff is just what the doc ordered for this here fella."

"Okay, Grandad, we're on our way."

"So how's your wife?"

"Um, she's doing pretty good."

"Good, good. Didn't I hear tell you got your cousin here with ya?"

"Yes, Grandad, he needed to do some banking, so he's off in Blairsville this morning."

"Oh, I don't wanna hear that word again for a very long time. Jes' get me that coffee!"

Natt chuckled. "Sure, Grandad, coming right up!"

Emi was anxious for the evening to be over so she could talk with Naomi. She didn't want to admit it, but she was getting a little excited about leaving Barney's. However, something that made the evening go a bit faster, she'd had to dodge the wayward hands of Harry who came in, ordered the house special, then gave her a bill to cover his meal and told her to 'keep the change' as her tip. She rang up the amount of the meal as Harry walked out the door and sighed as she pocketed the few coins that made up the difference. She smiled at the man's back. Soon she wouldn't have to put up with him. Every day she worked brought her that much closer to leaving Barney's for the new place in Vansville. She definitely had no intention of telling Harry she was leaving! Let him find out from Minnie or whoever Barney got to replace her – she didn't care.

Emi stood in the kitchen after she'd washed down the coffee island in the dining room. When Naomi walked in a few minutes before her shift started, Emi motioned her to the breakroom. Naomi nodded, but looked at the clock and did her routine first, making sure she clocked in before she went to the breakroom. At midnight there was no one who would squeal that patrons were being neglected.

When they were in the room and the door was shut, Emi said, "Naomi, I got a text from my friend Allison. She and her husband, Jack, want to meet you some day this week, because they're moving up to Vansville this weekend."

Naomi scowled. "I work every night. How could that happen?"

"Alli wondered if they could meet you at some other restaurant besides Barney's some morning after you get off."

"Well, sure, any morning would be fine. Do you have a phone number? I could call them first thing in the morning and see what we can come up with." Naomi acted unsure of herself, as she asked, "Are you sure they'll want to have me, Emi?"

"Naomi!" Emi said fiercely, slamming her hands on her hips, "Don't you even think like that! Of course they'll want you! I told them how good you are."

Naomi smiled. "Thanks, girl, for your vote of confidence."

"Of course!"

Mrs. Beecham left the dining area after setting down the plate of still hot sweet buns and filling two mugs with coffee. The construction men were driving up and parking their pickups along the edges of the huge driveway and the two people who lived in the main part of the house rushed into the large dining room and sat at the massive oak table. It was another work day, Derek and Carolyn must eat and run, because both of them had a half hour drive to Blairsville. They couldn't go together, neither of them knew if they could get off on time or they must stay to iron out some crisis, Derek, because he was president of the bank and Carolyn, because she was a department head at the medical complex in town. But tomorrow was Saturday!

Derek had just raised his head from saying a short grace over their breakfast when Carolyn said, "Dad, Eric and I want to get married in the back yard."

Derek couldn't help the grin that enveloped his whole face. He placed his hand over Carolyn's and said, "My dear, you do whatever you want! This entire house is available and so's the back yard. Sweetheart, just having you here is balm to my soul! If you want Sandy to play, we'll bring in a piano. You name it, it's there." He sobered and said, "There was a time when I didn't think I'd ever be back in yours or Lance's good will, but God is gracious."

Carolyn picked up a still steaming sweet bun and took a bite. After savoring it for a while she said, "Thanks, Dad. We really don't want anything too extravagant, but we have our heart set on a few things and having it here and having Sandy play are two of the things."

"When are you thinking about?"

Carolyn made a face. "That's the only problem. We're thinking about the weekend before Thanksgiving and that's getting on close to cold, nasty weather."

"Yes, that's true, but you could always have the great room as a backup. You know the men aren't including that as part of the renovation."

"Yes, maybe we'd better go with that. We can always have those doors open and it'll be easier for Sandy not to have to go on the ground. Eric's coming for dinner; we'll look around and figure it out tonight."

"Sweetheart, whatever you do is fine with me. You'll have Lance and Linda come?"

"Oh, yes, Dad! We were very close all those years, but you'll be the one to give me away, there is no question about that."

Tears glistened in Derek's eyes. He squeezed Carolyn's hand, but he could hardly speak, but he whispered, "Thank you. Thank you so much for that honor. Carolyn, you have no idea how that brings me joy!"

She squeezed his hand and smiled. "I'm glad, Dad. Do you think the renovations will be finished by the time we get back from our honeymoon? That'll only be a week later, you know we can't get much time off, since we've only started our jobs."

"Sweetheart, don't worry about that! I'm sure they'll be finished, but if they're not, there's still room for a husband to take his wife to bed in this part of the house."

Carolyn chuckled. "Yes, I guess that's true. Thanks, Dad."

His emotions so close to the surface, Derek whispered, "It's I should thank you!"

Carolyn usually arrived home earlier than Derek. That afternoon when she pulled up on the driveway, she couldn't park in the garage because a car she didn't recognize blocked the door. Fortunately, she hadn't pushed the garage door opener before she saw the car. However, the engine was running and the driver sat in the driver's seat. Carolyn didn't know the car or the occupant, so she left her car to go enquire. Perhaps the woman was lost.

The woman saw the movement, so she had her window down as Carolyn came up. "Could I help you, Ma'am?" Carolyn asked kindly.

With a nasty look on her face, the woman demanded, "Where's that jerk who lives here?"

Carolyn was so taken back, she stepped back from the car and asked, "Who? What?"

The woman began screaming, "You know who! What are you doing here? Who are you? What right have you here?"

"I'm Carolyn Casbah, I live here. This is my dad's house…"

The woman interrupted, "What! You…"

The BMW raced up the driveway and seconds later the driver's door burst open. "Then it's true! I couldn't believe it when Sid called me!" Derek stormed over beside Carolyn and demanded, "Millie, what do you think you're doing here! Get off my property before I call the sheriff to remove you!"

"I… I… Ah, this is my…"

Derek, shaking his head emphatically, interrupted Millie, "This is **not** your home! You gave up that right months ago! Put that car in reverse and get out of here! NOW!!"

While Derek was still speaking the sheriff's car wheeled onto the last piece of driveway still available close to the house. However, Millie was now hemmed in and as was her habit, her eyes turned glassy and her nose turned red, but no tears spilled down her cheeks. "You… you really called the sheriff? Oh, my! I'll leave…" She turned to look behind her, but she was blocked in. Beseechingly, she looked at Derek, "I… I can't leave!"

Eric was coming for dinner, of course, but when he saw the strange car on the driveway and both Carolyn and Derek standing beside it, he pulled up behind the car, blocking it in. He immediately slapped his sheriff's hat on his head, grabbed his citation pad from its ready holder and proceeded from the car looking very professional with the usual sheriff paraphernalia, including his revolver, around his waist. Acting totally in his role as sheriff deputy, Eric walked across the driveway toward Derek.

"Mr. Casbah, is there a problem?" he asked even before he reached the car.

It had been some time since Eric had seen Millie, she had changed many things about herself, but he recognized her. Even the car was different, a much older car, rather dilapidated compared to the car she used to drive when she was Derek's wife. Before Derek could answer, Millie wailed, "Oh, please, please, I'll leave. I'll leave right away. Please, let me out!"

Eric didn't so much as look at Millie, he turned his complete attention to Derek and said again, "Mr. Casbah, you have someone trespassing on your property?"

Catching on immediately, Derek said, "Yes, Deputy, this woman came here, drove up on my driveway and made several demands and accusations, none of them are valid."

"Shall I have her removed and her vehicle impounded?"

"Oh, please, please, **no!** I'll leave right away! Please let me go!" Millie seemed genuinely distressed. A tear actually slid through her eye make-up.

"Mr. Casbah?"

Derek looked at his former wife, then up at Eric, as if he was contemplating what he would do. Finally, he said, "Deputy, I think perhaps if you will escort her back to the highway and see that she doesn't enter town that will be sufficient." Of course, in saying that, it meant Millie couldn't see her son or her grandson.

"Very well. Ma'am, prepare yourself to be escorted back to the highway."

By this time, Millie's heavy eye make-up was washing down her cheeks. She looked up at the deputy, whom she didn't recognize, then at Derek, then at Carolyn. She looked back at Derek and whispered, "I'm sorry, I'm so sorry."

Derek shrugged, he wasn't sure what Millie was sorry for, but after several months it didn't matter. Not letting her distress bother him, he said, "Nothing you say makes any difference, Millie. As soon as the deputy gets his car backed around, get yourself off my property and don't expect to be welcomed on this property ever again."

Eric returned to his car, which was still running and backed around the circle, giving Millie plenty of room to back up and turn around. Millie's car was still running. She pulled the stick into reverse and as she often did when she was upset, gunned the car backwards. Tears were clouding her eyes, so that she didn't watch closely or judge her distance well, her speed took her much too far. Before she had even placed her foot on the brake, the back of her car slammed into a large tree, it rocked her forward with such force that her head hit and shattered the windshield. She slumped against the steering wheel, unconscious.

Of course, Eric immediately opened his emergency line and called for assistance, while Derek and Carolyn ran across the driveway to the car. Derek groaned. "Oh, my!"

The very next weekend was Labor Day weekend, which meant Thomas's store would be closed for two days. For some time Natt had planned to take Marcy away from town. He had no intention of visiting either his parents or hers, although Colleen wanted very much for her youngest child to come home, but that was to stay, with or without a husband. Neither Natt nor Marcy was interested in that option; especially since only days before a certain little test had confirmed that Marcy was expecting their first child and both of them were ecstatic. Of course, at this early stage they had told no one.

Ever since Matt had learned that Natt was leaving town, he wondered what to do with his two days off. As soon as he'd found out from Mr. Messmerson that he had inherited his aunt's CD he decided to make a trip to the southern part of Georgia and make an all-important visit to one lovely blond young woman, who once had the same last name as his. They had been Emailing for some time, but that was hardly good enough.

Signs were posted in the front windows of the store and the Laundromat that the complex would be closed for the holiday. The only people who would be unhappy about that would be travelers who would find they couldn't get gas at the unlighted pumps. The townspeople expected the complex to be closed.

All day Saturday both Matt and Natt watched the clock on the wall. The store was busy all day, mostly with townspeople who knew things would be closed up and wanted a full tank of gas or had to wash clothes that couldn't wait until Tuesday. Several people also bought things in the hardware store intent on doing some job they didn't have time for on a workday.

The coffee urn emptied about four thirty and Natt took it to the back to wash out. Anyone else who came in could be satisfied with the smell that still lingered in the store. As Natt walked the urn to the back he said to Matt, "Start shutting down the register and hit the switch for the pumps. No one's in the store, laundry or at the pumps, we are out of here!"

Matt grinned at his cousin. "You don't have to tell me twice! I'm on it!" Quickly, he stepped up to the counter and opened the register, then hit a few keys to start the machine into sleep mode that would take them through until Tuesday!

Matt had driven to work today intent on leaving from the store. Marcy had packed their suitcases last evening and Natt had loaded his car this morning and driven Marcy to work before coming to the store. Both Natt and Matt planned to be on the road as close to five o'clock as they could be. Matt emptied the cash register into the safe and twirled the dial at the same time as Natt turned off the water and dumped out the urn. Natt flipped the lock on the back door, Matt turned off the gas pumps and the lights except the security lights and they both made a beeline for the front door. It was minutes before five as the front door clicked behind them and they dashed to their cars. Matt would be out of town before Natt who had to stop at the clinic for Marcy. Neither man was upset to see the outside of the locked store door.

"Bring her back with you, Cousin!" Natt said over the roof of his car.

Matt grinned. "I'll do my best!"

They both started their cars at the same time, but Natt reached the road first. They both blasted their horns as Matt sped past the clinic out of town.

Barney's Diner employees were not so fortunate. Barney had decided that people needed to eat no matter that Monday was a holiday. He had nowhere to go, so his regular wait staff could find themselves at work, just as he would. As far as he was concerned, Sunday and Monday were business as usual, even down to the night cook and waitress.

Emilyn didn't know that Matt was coming. She also didn't know he had inherited a large CD. As far as she knew, the man she loved was nearly as poor as she was and he would be spending his holiday weekend in Vansville, just as she would spend her weekend in uniform, waiting tables in the 24/7 diner. She hadn't asked for any special time off since her four day weekend in July. She didn't plan to ask for any special time off before she gave Barney her two weeks' notice near the end of October. She and

Naomi were planning to leave at the same time, but Barney didn't know, at least Emi and Naomi hadn't told him or given any hints.

Sunday morning, quite early, Emi woke up to knocking on her door. It was such a foreign sound that she was totally confused. Usually what woke her was her alarm clock, the chime for a text message or the other sound that her phone made when an Email was coming in. She opened her eyes, pushed her hair from her eyes, checked the clock and then her phone. Both the clock and her phone told her that it wasn't even time to get up for church. However, the knocking came again. Barefoot, she staggered out of bed to the door.

However, she wasn't groggy enough not to check the peephole in the door and nearly fainted when she saw who was standing on the other side. She slid the chain off and yanked the door open, exclaiming, "Matt! What are you doing here? When did you get here? Why are you here, did you get tomorrow off?" She knew she had to be babbling, but she was so shocked the words kept coming out of her mouth.

He opened his arms and took a step toward her. She fell into his arms and he stepped into her tiny apartment. After a kiss, he said, "I got to town around one this morning. I've booked a room in a motel two blocks away, but I just had to see you! Doing anything special?" He decided that the woman he held in his arms, still tussled and spike-haired from sleep, was the most beautiful young woman he'd ever seen.

"In two and a half hours I'm to meet Naomi at her church for Sunday school."

"Great, I'll come with you."

"You came for the weekend?"

"Yup, and to convince you to come to Vansville with me."

"I… I… What?"

By now, they were far enough inside that the door would close, but as Emi closed the door, Matt reached in his pocket for something and when Emi turned back, Matt was down on one knee looking up at her. He smiled as she gasped, her eyes, as big as saucers, glued to him. "What?" she murmured.

"Emilyn used-to-be-Thomas, would you give me the highest joy to become my wife? I promise to love, honor and cherish you as long as we both shall live."

She covered her wide open mouth with her right hand, but Matt snagged her left and held a sparkling diamond just in front of her ring finger. In a whisper, Matt said, "Will you, please?"

"Oh, my! Oh, my! Yes, yes, Matt, I'll marry you."

He slid the ring on her finger, came to his feet and pulled her to his chest. "Darling, you have made my day perfect, this trip completely worthwhile and my heart overflowing with happiness. How soon can you move to Vansville?"

After a kiss, she said, "I guess I could give Barney two weeks' notice today."

"Do it, my love! Emails just don't cut it."

Several emotions zipped across her face, as she said, "But… but… I don't have any money saved up! I don't have enough to pay rent for a cabin or… or for anything, Matt. And I just rented this place for a new month."

Matt still didn't want to influence her just because he was well off, so he said, "Darling, leave that to me. Isabel and I are good friends. We'll get things all worked out, you just put in your two weeks' notice and head on up to Vansville."

"Umm, what about Naomi? We'd planned to come together and live together. Neither of us can afford to rent a place until we start working for Jack and Alli. Honey, that's two months!"

"When are they moving to town?"

"I guess real soon. Maybe even this weekend. They wanted to meet with Naomi last week because she said they'd be leaving town last weekend. So maybe they've already gone."

Hugging Emi again, Matt grinned at her and said, "I'm a great one for solving problems, my love, leave all that to me, just put in your notice, please?"

Emi looked at her clock and asked, "Did you eat breakfast yet?"

"No, Love, just came right from the motel here."

Emi took his hand and grinned. "I have this great coffee maker that turns on by itself when it's time. Come have breakfast with me, I'll make an omelet. I'm going to have to dress for church soon after that."

"Count me in! I'm all for a good cup of coffee with breakfast. Is what I have on good for your church?"

Emilyn sighed, "Matt, you look great. I'll be honored to sit with you in church."

"Thanks, Love," he said, simply. "I will be so honored to sit with you."

Tears glistened in Emilyn's eyes, but she dashed them away. A thought came to her mind that Matt would never have said something like that to her when they were married before and certainly not in that loving tone of voice. Yes, he'd held her, kissed her back then, but he'd been a teen aged boy and it was his hormones talking and acting. Now he was a man, well past that teen aged era and he treated her like she was his treasure. She loved this man. She'd thought at one time he was her soul mate, now she knew he was.

The week after Labor Day Isabel had two more long term renters. Jack Albertson had called her and asked to rent her number one cabin for two months or until the apartment over the restaurant was finished enough they could move in. They had stored their furniture for that long and Jack felt he needed to be in Vansville. Isabel was never shy about accepting renters, especially ones she could count on for some time. However, she was a bit reluctant to rent out her handicapped cabin to people who weren't handicapped for that length of time. She did, however, so now the restaurant owner and his wife were in town and he often joined Jason and his construction crew for morning coffee break on DeLord's parking lot.

As his mama handed out cups of steaming coffee to the workers, Jon toddled beside Jason, holding tightly to his hand as they crossed the street and made a toddler-sized inspection. Now it was mostly inside work, the building itself looked like it was finished. Of course, anyone knew that the inside of a building took much longer to finish than the outside.

Being in the restaurant business as long as he had been, Jack had ordered things for his kitchen that made the project very unique and he was overseeing the installation quite closely. He was on hand every time there was a delivery and because this restaurant was being done exactly as he wanted, he would make sure there were no mistakes. By this time, Jack was used to seeing the lady in the wheelchair and her little boy across the street. Usually, he waved to Jon and welcomed him when Jason brought him across the street for that 'inspection.' Jon even allowed 'Mizzer Jack' to pick him up and nuzzle his neck.

Not long after the Albertson's had moved to Vansville, Emilyn got another Email from Matt. She had been totally shocked when he came for the Sunday and Monday of Labor Day weekend and also had given her a beautiful diamond. Even Barney had commented about it. That was his first clue that she was leaving.

Sweetheart, Matt wrote, *how soon can you come to live here?*

Matt, Honey it'll be soon. Naomi didn't feel comfortable putting in her resignation the same time I did, so she's waited a few days. We'll be there long before Jack opens the restaurant for Thanksgiving, don't worry.

I'll need to rent another of Isabel's cabins so you can live there until... until you don't need to live in a cabin any more.

How's Saturday, Honey?

Perfect! I love you, Sweetheart. See you then, Love.

Oh, Yes! I love you, too!

Matt hadn't told Emi about his inheritance, in fact, he hadn't told many people at all. Being who he was, he decided that this was one thing that Vansville's grapevine didn't need to spread around town. With what he had in mind to use some of that money for, people might figure it out soon enough. However, he continued to open up Thomas's store each morning and work along side his cousin each day. Natt and Eric both knew he had inherited a CD from his great aunt, but only Derek knew for how much, that was because of his position at the bank.

Once Joyce brought Brad to the store that one morning, he surprised everyone, including Natt and most of all, Joyce, by taking his cane in hand each morning and making his way slowly across the street to the back door of the store. He arrived at around nine o'clock and stayed two hours, then made his way back home. After his lunch and long nap, he came back and spent several more hours at the store. He totally shocked everyone in his family, now that he was at home from the hospital and rehab center, he seemed like a changed man. Of course, it didn't happen overnight, but it was a radical change.

Natt and Matt both looked forward to having him come. In fact, now that he was in the store, sales increased and there was always someone sitting in the 'coffee drinker's nook' having coffee with Brad. Neither of the store managers could remember Brad being so friendly. He didn't try to do any of the business, only was a friendly person, always in the 'coffee drinker's nook'. Of course, he had a cup of coffee in his hand and usually a smile on his face.

True to her word, Emi and Naomi arrived Saturday afternoon. Isabel had the cabin next to Matt's ready for them. Surprising both women she had found two single beds and had them in the bedroom for the women. Naomi fell in love with the little house. She was sure she could live in Isabel's cabin the rest of her life. However, she was anxious for Sunday to come; she wanted to see Sandy to know if she was the lady that had been the baby she had cared for so many years before in Philadelphia.

Sunday morning, when the church bell rang, there were two new people coming up the walk for Sunday school. Of course, Roger stood in his usual place and greeted them. "Let's see, I believe I met you one time before. You came to town the weekend before that restaurant started up, is that right?"

Emi smiled shyly, "Yes, I'm Emi and this is my friend, Naomi. We're both going to work in the restaurant when it's open." Emi saw the look on Roger's face, so she added, "I know it won't open for a while, but, umm, Matt Thomas asked…"

"Ah," Roger interrupted, "I get the picture! Naomi, we're so glad to have you. Would you go in our young adult class or feel more comfortable in with the older folks?"

Feeling a bit intimidated, Naomi said, "Ahmmm, I think I'll go with Emi." Her voice loosing even more sound, she asked, "Does Sandy go to one of those?"

"No, Sandy teachers our little kids, but her husband teaches Emi's class, but Sandy plays for our morning service."

Naomi nodded, "Thank you, sir. That's good to know."

However, while Naomi still spoke a light blue van pulled into the handicapped spot right in front of the church. Of course, Roger saw the van and said, "There they are now! It'll be a minute, but Sandy, Ramon and Jon will be coming up in a minute."

Emi turned and a smile burst across her face. "Yes! I recognize that van. Naomi, Sandy was still on her lift when she helped me know Jesus!"

Of course, everything about the van worked in slow motion. The ladies stepped out of the way to let another person walk up and speak to Roger, but finally Sandy, Ramon and Jon all appeared on the lift and Ramon pushed the button in the handle to bring them to the ground. Jon, of course, saw his friends Heidi and Lennie, so as soon as they hit the ground, he was off to play. Sandy didn't know she was under scrutiny, but with her usual smile, she headed for the ramp while Ramon closed up the van and followed her.

Sandy was still on the ramp when she saw the new lady standing next to Emi. Sandy's grin stretched the muscles in her face. "Emi! You're here! Already? Who's your friend?"

Emi gasped. "You remember me?"

"Of course! Who is this lovely lady with you?"

"My friend, Naomi. We've worked together in my hometown for several years."

Sandy finally reached the top of the ramp and held out her hand to Naomi. After looking at her for several minutes, she said, "When I was a tiny girl I remember a lady coming to our house whose name was Naomi. I loved that lady!"

Tears immediately came to her eyes and streamed down Naomi's cheeks. She grabbed her hand back from shaking Sandy's and threw her arms around the younger woman. Through her tears, she choked out, "You are my baby Sandy! You are! Oh, my! God is so good!"

Of course, Sandy hugged her back. "Ms. Naomi! I can't believe it! God is wonderful! After all these years… and you're here! You'll be living here?"

Nodding enthusiastically, Naomi exclaimed, "YES!! I'm to work in the new restaurant! Oh, my! Thank You, God! I can't believe this!"

"Wow! We'll be eating there a lot."

Naomi pulled back. "Don't be silly, child! Why, you have your mama's recipes; that is very silly! But may I come see you?" Self-conscious because of the tear tracks on her cheeks, Naomi pulled her wrist across her eyes.

Scowling at the older lady, Sandy shook her finger in Naomi's face and said, "Ms. Naomi, you had better come see me! Come meet my husband, Ramon and that little guy with the brown hair running around is our son, Jon."

Naomi straightened and held out her hand to Ramon. "I am so happy to meet you. I was one of the first people to know your wife. It was a long time ago, but she was very, very precious. I see one thing about her that hasn't changed – her smile."

Ramon shook her hand and nodded. "Yes, she does that all the time."

The very next Monday another construction company brought in some heavy equipment. Jon didn't know about this work, it wasn't where he could see it. The first anyone knew was when the bulldozer started excavating a spot on the new street behind Isabel's house. Since it wasn't on the front side of her house, she didn't know about it until she and Ruth ate lunch in the kitchen. The area that the bulldozer cleared and dug the hole for was the size of a house and was across the street from Natt and Marcy's place. The contractor that had been employed hoped that bad weather would hold off in Vansville at least until he could get the house under roof and he hoped, enclosed. The man who authorized the work expected that the house would be finished around Christmas. That's when he planned to bring his bride to her new home. At least he had the contractor's word that that would happen.

That evening, after Emi and Naomi visited with Allison and spent some time watching the work on the restaurant; Emi went to Matt's cabin and cooked supper for both of them. His eyes twinkled as he came in from the store and said, "Mmm, I think by the aroma that someone's cooking has improved one hundred percent since I tasted it last!"

Emi nearly snorted. "Humph! You think in ten years, working most of that time in a restaurant I haven't learned some things? Get a grip, Mr. Thomas!"

Emi stood at the stove, but Matt came up behind her and put his arms around her waist. He kissed her ear before he said, "Darling, I'm sure that's true. Even so, there will be no comparisons." Then he spoiled it by saying, "Anything's better than those frozen dinners I've been buying at Alex's." He straightened up and looked out the window. "Ah, look, there's some more construction on the street back there."

"Well! Mr. Thomas, you know how to build up a girl, then in the next breath tare her down! I mean, a TV dinner? Well!"

Matt kissed her neck and chuckled. "Darling, I'm teasing. I know there is no comparison. I'm just so happy to finally have you here. If all you did was pull out two TV dinners I'd eat it with you gladly."

It had been a rather warm day, so after the dinner that Emi had created from scratch, Matt took his gallon jug of tea and their mugs onto the porch. When he knew Emi was coming to Vansville, he'd ordered a porch swing through the store. He had set it up on Saturday and moved Isabel's wicker chairs out of the way, but left the little table beside the swing. He set the tea and mugs on the table, but gathered Emi close and sat on the swing with her.

Matt kept her in the circle of his arms and kissed her neck, but that was not enough for Emi, she made sure her lips were in the right place for the next kiss. They enjoyed a lingering kiss for several minutes. When they finally came up for air, Matt said, in a husky voice, "Love, will you do me the honor to be my date for Eric's wedding?"

"But, Honey, I was going to that big house to help Naomi! I don't know hardly anyone who'll be there for the wedding. I don't know the bride at all."

"Oh, Darling, please?"

"But I already told Naomi I'd help."

"Tell you what – you can help her before, but I want you sitting on Eric's side so I can look at you any time I want! You know he's asked me to be his best man, so I'll have to do that, but when I'm not doing stuff for him, I want you right beside me."

"I don't know, Honey."

"Is anyone else helping her?"

"Well, Alli said she'd help."

After another kiss, Matt grinned and said, "There you have it, Love. Naomi won't be alone. I'm sure she'll have all the help she'll need with you before hand and Allison and Derek's housekeeper. Besides, he's told me they aren't having a big wedding, so the reception shouldn't be too hard."

"Yes, you're right. Are you sure I should be your date?"

"Sweetheart, of course! You are my heart's desire, it'd be a bit rushed, but I wouldn't mind if it was our wedding day too."

Jon watched every day as the construction workers came to work on the building across the street from his home. By now, the outside of the restaurant was finished, but many days different trucks came and of course, Jon was there to watch. He was always excited to go out to see what 'mizzer Ja-son' was doing and Jason was very willing to provide a toddler-sized tour at least once a week for the little boy. The workers always took their breaks whenever they saw Sandy's wheelchair come out of her house. Now she usually brought coffee to the men, but sometimes she had cookies or brownies for their breaks.

On the last Friday of October, Jon stood at the window in the office as he usually did, but this time as he watched two semi-trucks with several large pieces of equipment pulled passed the gravel driveway across the street. When the first one stopped, Jon ran back to his mama and exclaimed, "Mama! Mama! Wuk!" He waved his one arm at the window, while slapping Sandy's armrest with the other. He was intent on getting her attention.

"What is it, Sweetheart?"

"Donno, Mama! Donno!" Only minutes later, he exclaimed, "Mama, more, wuk, more! Lozza tar-ucks!"

Before Jon finished exclaiming, several dump trucks collected on the road and two machines with big rollers turned onto DeLord's parking lot. Jon was beside himself with excitement, wanting his mama to take them outside even before coffee break time so they could see what was going on. Of course by now, it was cool enough that Sandy had to make sure Jon had on a warm sweater before he could go outside.

"Sweetheart, Mama's going to finish in here first. Why don't you get your sweater so you'll be all ready when it's time?"

"'K, Mama!" Sandy was sure Jon would be back with his sweater long before she had finished her office work. Even though today would close down the hikes, there was still much she had to do in the office. She was glad they'd survived another hiking season without any mishaps or accidents and their guides would all be returning.

Sandy finished her office work and before she could say anything, Jon pulled his sweater from the chair and as he pushed his arms into the sleeves, he said, "Mama, hurry, ge' coffee. We go ouside now! BIG tar-uck! Wha they do?"

Sandy went to the window, from the desk she hadn't been sure what was happening. At the window, she said, "I think they're putting tar on the parking lot today!"

Jon scowled. "Tar?"

"Yes, Sweetheart, they'll put black stuff on top of the stones on the parking lot like we have on ours. It makes it easier for cars and trucks to go on it then."

"Mama go?"

"Yes, mama can go on the tar after it's finished."

"Yea, Mama go!"

After the morning coffee break time on DeLord's parking lot, Jon stayed in the office all day, except for his lunch and a very short nap, watching the machines do their work covering the stones with tar. There was lots of activity, the semi's unloaded their machines, the dump trucks emptied their loads into an asphalt spreader and the machines with rollers smoothed out the asphalt. Some of the machines used DeLord's parking lot to turn around in. Jon was most excited because they started laying the tar at the road and he could watch the whole process.

By the time his daddy came home from his last hike of the season later that afternoon the job was finished and all the trucks and equipment had left. Jon found it very hard to go to sleep after supper, he thought of many things he needed to tell Daddy about everything that happened all day across the street. Even through several yawns and a drink he kept on. Ramon skipped the Bible story that evening and Jon fell asleep while he said his bedtime prayer.

In the little town of Vansville, life became complicated, there was so much going on. Of course, in the south people didn't move as fast as those in the north. The residents of Vansville were sure someone should come to town and put a stop to all this frenzied activity. The restaurant across from DeLord's was nearing completion, the house on the new street had a dozen busy beavers putting on a roof and nailing on insulated outdoor sheeting and renovations were being completed on the mansion out of town.

As if that wasn't enough going on, there were plans in the works for the wedding to take place in only weeks at the huge house just out of town right before Thanksgiving. Even as those plans were in the works, people heard that another wedding was being planned for a month later, except that one would happen at the church in town. They nodded when that word became common knowledge in town, didn't twins always do things together? The fact didn't matter that it was the men who were the twins and usually it was the brides who did most of the planning and these two brides hardly knew each other.

Carolyn's sister-in-law, Linda, would be her matron of honor, but she had taken Carolyn's measurements and was fashioning a most beautiful, semi-old-fashioned winter wedding gown. Linda was well qualified for the job, since she was part owner of a very exclusive boutique in the town where she and Lance lived. Lance, Linda and little Brenda planned to spend the week before the wedding with grampa Derek, so that grampa would have plenty of time to spoil his precious grand-daughter. As any doting grampa, as soon as he knew their plans, he insisted that his adopted grandson would also be spending time at the mansion. Jon was so excited that Ramon and Sandy could hardly refuse. They also spent several mornings at Derek's house getting better acquainted with Lance and Linda.

Since weather could be rather unpredictable in the foothills of the Appalachians in November, Carolyn and Eric had decided to have the wedding in the great room of Derek's house. Because that was their desire, Derek made sure the renovations were finished. They would use both the great room and the patio just beyond. Sandy had agreed to play for the wedding and of course, Matt would be his brother's best man. However, Mrs. Beecham would have help with the reception. Now that Naomi was in town, the Albertson's had spread the word quickly that the lady was a master chef and would do her best for the bride and groom.

When Emilyn learned that Naomi was a master chef it made her wonder why she'd been stuck in Barney's Diner as the over-night waitress for at least nine years. However, she didn't ponder that too much; she was happily planning her own wedding and watching the house on the next street over take shape that would be her new home. She rarely thought about Murphy's Law these days. It seemed things were exciting and many of her dreams were becoming reality right before her eyes. Matt was her loving and attentive fiancé.

The day had finally come. It was the Saturday before Thanksgiving. Lights came on in cabin number four early, earlier than usual, especially for a Saturday. Now that it was past the middle of November, daylight didn't come very early, but preparations had to begin. Emi and Naomi were up very early. Emi planned to take clothes to change into and ride with Naomi to start those preparations for the lovely reception. Derek Casbah had told Naomi that the sky was the limit and not to worry about any expense. His darling daughter deserved anything her heart desired for her wedding.

The cabin had smelled very inviting for several days. Naomi had worked on many things for the reception, including the large wedding cake. When it was time to leave for the mansion Saturday morning, Emi and Naomi made many trips from the cabin to Naomi's car with platters and dishes with many fabulous things on and in them. Naomi had felt intimidated to work on her creations in Derek's kitchen, but she was excited to be able to use her skills for the reception.

Just in case the weather wasn't perfect at six o'clock in the morning, Derek had told Naomi she should park in the garage. Of course, Mrs. Beecham was expecting them, so when the garage door went up, she greeted them at the door into the kitchen. With three of them carrying all the platters and dishes inside, the job was finished quickly. Naomi started in assembling the cake, while Emi and Mrs. Beecham started on other things. They worked well together and soon the aromas spreading out from the kitchen into other areas of the house brought both Carolyn and Derek to the doorway to watch.

Carolyn's face could hardly contain her smile. "Ladies! This is super, terrific! Oh, my! Dad, look at that cake! Naomi, wow!"

"Sweetheart, it's fantastic! When it's finished we must take a picture."

Mrs. Beecham left her work on the reception long enough to take coffee and some sweet buns into the dining room for the Casbah clan's breakfast. Carolyn knew she was very excited and wasn't sure she could put anything into her stomach, however, she managed a cup of doctored coffee and one sweet bun. After the last mouthful she declared she was stuffed.

Because Carolyn and Eric were so well loved in town, the guest list had grown from 'a few friends' and 'nothing extravagant' to nearly the whole town. Of course, Derek's place could easily accommodate all who planned to come. Because Eric had booked plane tickets to Maui for a week's honeymoon, the wedding would start at eleven and be followed by a light lunch and the wedding cake. The bride and groom must be on their way to Atlanta airport by two o'clock.

Being the man that he was, Derek made sure all the renovations were complete at the mansion in plenty of time for a cleaning service to come. They had finished deep cleaning, not only the part of the house that had been renovated, but also the entire house, so that everything sparkled, including the marble floor and the exquisite chandelier in the entryway. Nothing was too good for Derek's delightful daughter. Of course, the part that had been renovated was the wing that the newlyweds would have as their private quarters.

On Friday, a rental truck had brought in a small grand piano for Sandy's use in the great room. Derek's friend, Mr. Christopher Jehling, had come only moments after the rental truck had left to tune the piano. The Casbah's were content to stay upstairs, with doors closed tightly while Mr. Jehling was downstairs making sure the piano was tuned to perfection. The only shame was that the rental company would be back for the piano on Monday, but that made no difference to Mr. Jehling. Any piano he tuned must sound absolutely perfect.

Eric and Matt were scheduled to arrive close to ten o'clock, but by that time only a few last minute things needed to be done for the reception. Emi had left the kitchen only a few minutes before the men arrived, but Matt didn't have to go far to find his own fiancée. When she left the small bathroom, Matt could hardly take his eyes off the lovely creature he loved with all his heart. She was not the bride or even a member of the wedding party, but Matt was convinced that she would out-shine the bride.

He opened his arms the instant he saw her and as she stepped into his embrace he said, "Darling, oh, my! What a lovely creation you're wearing!"

Emi gave him a shy smile and said, "When Naomi and I went shopping for supplies the other day she insisted we also find a dress for me. This is what we found." She looked up at him, her eyes shining. "I was sure you'd like it."

"It is perfectly lovely, Sweetheart. I only wish you could be standing up there with me."

"Just wait," she whispered, "Not too long from now I'll be in white for you."

"Oh, Love, I can hardly wait!"

"Well, it's less than a month."

He kissed her again and whispered, "Yes, but it's passing much too slowly. I never thought I was an impatient man, but then, maybe I am."

Emilyn giggled, "Ah, yeah, I think you may be."

Matt sighed and nodded. "Yes, probably I am at that."

Carolyn, Linda, Nancy and Marcy were all in Carolyn's bedroom suite getting ready for the trip down the aisle. When the door was shut, Linda opened a large garment bag and pulled out her wedding gown creation. Even Carolyn hadn't seen the finished product, even though her sister-in-law had been there all week. The gown was a masterpiece and all the ladies exclaimed at the lovely gown. The three ladies were eager to help Carolyn dress and fix her hair. Raylyn had declined being a bridesmaid, she had a month to go before her baby was due. She had agreed to tend the guest register. Sandy, of course was playing lovely music at the piano in the great room. Her playing was like a mini-concert.

Eric, Matt, Ramon and Natt were also dressing in another area of the house. Carolyn had requested that Eric dress in his Marine uniform, while the others dressed in the tuxes that had been rented for them. Duncan had reluctantly agreed again to shave his beard since he was the only one of the groom's friends who wore one. He had already left the dressing room to act as the usher for the guests. Roger, of course, would be the officiating pastor. Derek's two grand-children would be flower girl and ring bearer. Jon, of course, took his responsibility very seriously. His mama had made the little pillow that would hold the rings. He never let the little pillow out of his sight. However, he claimed a very prominent place in the men's dressing room.

Isabel, the proud stand-in grandmother, had found her own seat on the second row on Eric's side of chairs. Since she had supplied Eric with his home for all these months she claimed the role of grandmother without any qualms. She sat enjoying Sandy concert, knowing of course, that she always played like an angel. Ruth was much more retiring and stayed at the back until Duncan was ready to escort her to her seat next to Isabel. Eric's family had arrived from south Georgia on Thursday and had rented Isabel's other cabins for several nights.

Guests started parking on the driveway and beside the road. Of course, the driveway was very long and could accommodate lots of cars, but even so, there were many who parked on the side of the road and had to walk to the mansion, but with nice weather, that wasn't a problem. The hour approached and the great room filled up. Of course, townspeople came, but many more from Blairsville came to be part of Carolyn and Eric's wedding. Even though the room was huge, Derek stood at the back hoping that the aisle would be wide enough for him to walk Carolyn to the front. As the time grew short for the ceremony to begin, he and Duncan had to put an extra chair beside every row in the aisle. They had already placed chairs on the outside on both sides, leaving no room for an aisle on either side. Derek was glad the fire chief hadn't been invited to the wedding.

The weather had cooperated. For six days before Thanksgiving the temperature was a mild sixty-five degrees, the sky was blue with only a few scattered white clouds and none of them spent much time covering the brilliant sun. Much to Carolyn's delight, the reception would be held upstairs on the deck. As people entered the great room they couldn't help but inhale the wonderful aromas coming from Derek's kitchen. The wedding cake was finished and waited in Derek's cool dining room until time to take it to the special table on the deck.

Just before Duncan ushered Eric's family to their seats, he brought a lovely Emilyn to her seat on the front row where Matt had told Duncan to seat her. As he had told her, she was on the front seat, only a few steps from the spot where Matt would stand in the wedding party line up. Her heart was in her throat, she knew her fiancé would be devastating in his fine tux. As she sat and waited her heart beat so loudly she was sure anyone around could hear it. Only four weeks from today she'd be walking down the aisle at their church on her dad's arm. Their wedding would be much different from this one, but she would marry the man she loved.

Just before eleven Sandy paused in her playing and glanced at the back of the room. Duncan was there with Eric's mom on his arm and his dad close behind. Sandy started playing the piece designated as 'The Mother's March' and Duncan brought the couple to their designated seats. They sat beside Emilyn who hadn't seen them since her own wedding to Matt a dozen years before. She smiled at them, unsure how they would feel sitting beside their son's ex-wife. However, Eric's mom instantly saw the difference in the young woman and gave her a bright, happy smile. The lady had never held anything against Emilyn. She had been opposed to the wedding but had nothing but love for the girl who'd married her second son. Matt had quickly told her that Emi was now a believer and had consented to be Matt's wife again. That information made his mom and his dad very happy. Now their two older sons would both have Christian homes. They were ecstatic!

When the couple was seated and Duncan had pulled the white aisle-liner to the back, Sandy started the wedding march and the men came in from the patio while Linda moved Jon and Brenda into the doorway. Sandy knew the children would be first and to everyone's surprise she played a few bars of her *Melodies on the Nursery Rhymes* for them to walk in. They had rehearsed their parts well. When the children reached the front, Sandy changed back to the wedding march and the first lovely lady started down the aisle. The three ladies seemed to float down the aisle in their lovely dresses, smiling at all the guests as they came. Finally, everyone was in place except for the bride and her dad.

Again Sandy paused. The proud dad stepped into the doorway and Carolyn moved to the spot beside him. Duncan had been given instructions to smooth her train, but he'd asked Raylyn to help him. He was sure he'd be all thumbs when he had to arrange something so delicate. After the pause Sandy pounded the first note and everyone stood up and turned to watch the lovely bride come down the aisle. Sandy made a grand production of playing the wedding march especially for Carolyn and Derek to walk in.

Sandy and Roger had a secret surprise. Of course, Ramon knew, but he'd been sworn to secrecy too. Sandy had written a song especially for this bride and groom. Derek brought Carolyn to the front and had taken Eric's hand and drawn him beside Carolyn. As he linked their hands, Sandy stopped playing the wedding march, hit one note very softly and began to sing.

"'Don't urge me to leave you or to turn back from you.
Where you go I will go, and where you stay I will stay.
Your people will be my people and your God my God.
Where you die I will die, and there I will be buried.
May the Lord deal with me, be it ever so severely,
If anything but death separates you and me.'"
(Ruth 1: 16,17)

Dear Readers,

Thank you for reading my series based in the fictitious town of Vansville, Georgia. I hope you have enjoyed meeting all of those young people who have brought new life to the little hamlet. I certainly have enjoyed writing about, first Sandy and Ramon, then Roger, Raylyn and Heidi, Duncan and Nancy, Marcy and Natt, Carolyn and Eric and last of all, Matt and Emilyn. Of course, we can't forget Sandy and Ramon's little son, Jon.

Friends, if Jesus Christ isn't your Lord and Savior, as Sandy told Emilyn, "For God so loved the world that he gave his one and only Son, that whoever believes in him shall not perish but have eternal life. For God did not send his Son into the world to condemn the world, but to save the world through him." (John 3: 16,17)

That's what you need to know. God loves you so much that He sent His beloved Son, the Lord Jesus, to die on a cruel cross to take away all your sin and make you a new person who can go to heaven when you die to live with Him forever.

May He be your Savior today!

Bette Pratt

All Scripture in this series was quoted from the New International Version of the Holy Bible.

www.ingramcontent.com/pod-product-compliance
Lightning Source LLC
Chambersburg PA
CBHW061605190726
48288CB00007B/2182